CATCHING SERENITY

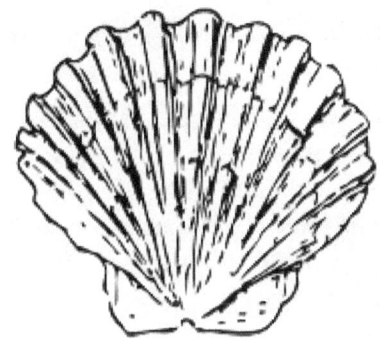

CATCHING SERENITY

JoAnn Durgin

SonShine Books
New Albany, IN

ISBN 978-1-940727-02-8

Scripture quotations are taken from the NEW AMERICAN STANDARD BIBLE®, Copyright © 1960,1962,1963,1968,1971,1972,1973,1975,1977, 1995 by The Lockman Foundation. Used by permission. All rights reserved.

Interior Book Design by **EBookListingServices.com** (a subsidiary of Taegais Publishing LLC).
Cover Design and Cover Image by Dino Piccinini (**dinopiccinini@gmail.com**; WEBSITE **brandslamcreative.com**)

Visit JoAnn Durgin's Web site at www.joanndurgin.com

1 3 5 7 9 10 8 6 4 2
Printed in the United States of America

Dedication

For my precious Seashell.

Love always,

Mom

Catching Serenity

~ The Legend of the Starfish ~

A vacationing businessman was walking along a beach when he saw a young boy.

Along the shore were many starfish that had been washed up by the tide and were sure to die before the tide returned.

The boy walked slowly along the shore and occasionally reached down and tossed the beached starfish back into the ocean.

The businessman, hoping to teach the boy a little lesson in common sense, walked up to the boy and said, "I have been watching what you are doing, son. You have a good heart, and I know you mean well, but do you realize how many beaches there are around here and how many starfish are dying on every beach every day? Surely such an industrious and kindhearted boy such as yourself could find something better to do with your time. Do you really think that what you are doing is going to make a difference?"

The boy looked up at the man, and then he looked down at the starfish by his feet. He picked up the starfish, and as he gently tossed it back into the ocean, he said, "It makes a difference to that one."

~Author Unknown

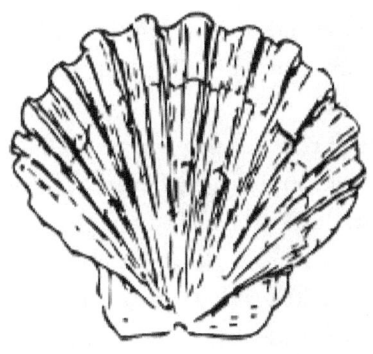

~CHAPTER 1~

Come home, Serenity. Things aren't as they seem. Time to find your answers.

Ever since she'd received that unsigned, cryptic note in Atlanta six weeks ago—scrawled in loopy, cursive letters with no clue as to its sender except the postmark from Croisette Shores—the words lingered in Serenity's mind, never far from her conscious thought. Lifting her face to the early May sun, she dug her toes in the sand, luxuriating in the sensation as the warm grains filtered between her toes. How she'd missed her lovely little South Carolina town.

The slight breeze lifted strands of her hair in an airy dance and a happy squeal caught her attention. A pregnant woman held the hand of a toddler girl who skipped beside her, giggling when the gentle waves kissed her toes. Uninhibited and joyful, the sound of the child's laughter transported Serenity back in time to the carefree days when she'd played alongside her parents on this same stretch of beach. Days when it seemed the world was ripe with possibility and opportunity. Days when making a sand castle and discovering a beautiful seashell, simple yet intricate in its complexity, thrilled her like nothing else.

"Freud!"

Shielding her eyes with one hand, Serenity scanned the beach. *Freud?* A gorgeous gray and white Siberian husky skirted the shoreline, dodging the seaweed and marine life deposited by the receding waves. A magnificent creature, grace in motion, but who would name a dog Freud? In its own way, though, it was rather cute. She couldn't remember ever seeing this particular breed of dog in Croisette Shores before. His coat was well-groomed and short, and thank goodness she sat far enough removed to avoid the sand he sprayed in his wake.

"Come here, boy!" The man jogging behind the dog captured her attention as he slowed to a walk, a red Frisbee tucked under one arm. The last time she'd given any man more than a passing glance seemed like a lifetime ago. In some ways, it was. This one definitely stood out in the small crowd of beachgoers. Tall, broad-shouldered and muscular, his wavy dark hair was long enough in back to curl over the collar of his light blue polo. She guessed he must be late twenties or early thirties. Barefoot with the bottom of his khakis rolled on his calves, he looked the part of a well-to-do tourist renting a luxury cottage on one of the private beaches. Cheeks flushed with color, he hadn't yet developed the sun-kissed tan of the locals.

Stopping, he tossed the Frisbee and laughed as the dog darted after it, venturing into the tide. Amazing a dog that size could jump so high. Serenity sat up straighter, fascinated, as the two repeated their game. The man moved a bit slower, appearing to favor one leg, and a slight grimace creased his attractive features. Was he in pain? She startled a few seconds later when the Frisbee skidded to a stop at her feet, showering her with sand. Freud lunged in her direction—quickening her heart rate tenfold—and scooped the plastic disc in his mouth before bounding off again. Willing her pulse to slow, Serenity brushed sand from her shorts and tugged down on her pink cotton tee.

"Sorry!" the man called to her with a friendly wave. "He's harmless. Hope he didn't scare you. Are you okay?"

She waved back. "I'm fine, thanks." She wasn't worried about the canine so much as her reaction to Freud's companion, but how nice of him to consider her feelings. The guy had a killer smile and strands of dark hair whipped over his forehead. Couldn't he at least have a high-pitched or nasal voice? No, it had to be deep, smooth and rich as melting chocolate. Good thing she generally avoided chocolate.

He lingered about twenty yards away as though debating whether to come closer. Well, she'd make the decision easier for him. *Have a nice life, handsome stranger.* Lowering onto the towel, flat on her back, Serenity closed her eyes, mentally dismissing him. She had enough on her mind with the command visit to her dad in an hour before heading to Martha's Cup & Such for her three o'clock meeting.

My very first client. Dr. Jackson Ross. She'd studied hard, spent a lot of sleepless nights and lived like a miser to earn the right to even *have* a client. Thanks to Charlie Mathias, her lifelong family friend, the initial meeting had been arranged a couple of days ago. Dr. Ross was a psychologist newly transplanted from Chicago who needed help decorating his new office. That thought triggered a nervous—but good—flutter in Serenity's stomach. She envisioned Dr. Ross to be a bit younger than Doc Rasmussen, the town's retiring psychologist. More likely than not, the new shrink was a middle-aged man or older, married with a child or two and maybe grandkids, wire-rimmed glasses and some type of facial hair. Not many young people moved to their beach community these days. Even with the tourist trade, there simply wasn't enough year-round commerce or opportunity. On the other end of the longevity scale, those on the short path to retirement adored the slower pace in Croisette Shores.

Wait a minute.

Sitting upright and clasping her arms around her knees, Serenity scanned the wide expanse of beach. The Siberian husky and his owner played further down the beach.

Now it made perfect sense. The flutter in her stomach resurged with a vengeance.

What kind of man might name a dog Freud? *A psychologist.*

*R*eaching the outside top step of her childhood home, Serenity opened the creaky front door and found it unlocked, as usual. She wouldn't make an issue of it. Given normal circumstances, Croisette Shores was a safe enough community. Making a mental note to oil the door's hinges, she'd focus first on the easy fixes and then tackle the larger ones. For now, she'd get through life day-by-day, the same as she'd done for almost five years on her own. She'd gotten pretty good at it. The first order of business was to get her father out of this stale house and his self-imposed exile from life. Then she'd work on reviving and updating both the house *and* the man.

"Dad? You here?" No answer. Of course, he'd be here. From what she knew, he didn't venture out much these days. A quick glance at the sofa confirmed the sage-colored chintz throw pillows were positioned the same way Mama always preferred. As a test—subconscious or not, she wasn't quite sure—she'd changed them around when she'd dusted during her last visit. Ditto the arrangement of periodicals on the coffee table. Ten to one those magazines dated back to the spring of five years ago, as if time within the walls of the small house had been suspended. Closing the front door, Serenity moved through the living room on her way to the narrow, cracker box kitchen.

She suppressed a sigh and dropped her purse on the table. Unwashed dishes were stacked in the sink and crumbs littered the table and linoleum floor. The broom propped against the back corner, neglected, disgruntled her. Opening the refrigerator door, she wrinkled her nose at the stench of cooked broccoli from last night's dinner. How could such a healthy vegetable smell so foul? She pushed aside a jar of olives and a tub of margarine and placed the box of Chinese takeout on the shelf. Cashew chicken had always been one of his favorites, and she doubted his food preferences had changed much. Although it might not be the healthiest choice, the key to changing his bad habits was to slowly introduce healthier foods into his diet. She made another mental note for the growing list: make a few well-balanced meals and put them in the freezer.

As she rounded the corner of the family room, Serenity spied her father in his usual position—stretched out in the recliner, remote balanced on his undershirt-covered stomach, eyes half-closed. She carefully extracted the remote from his loose grip. After turning off the television, she carried his empty plate and glass into the kitchen. Digging out a clean dishtowel from the drawer, she dropped the stopper into the sink and glanced at the ancient wall clock. Shaped like a pear, another one of her mother's eccentricities. She'd once counted all the things with a pear motif in the kitchen but finally stopped at thirty. Any more seemed a ridiculous excess. When Mama loved something, she went above and beyond.

Dad used to say he was surprised they hadn't named her Pearl since at least it'd have the word "pear" in it. She'd been teased about her unique moniker by a few kids early on in school. When she was six, she'd looked up the word "serenity" in the dictionary and found synonyms like *tranquility, peace* and *calm*. At thirteen, Danny told her he loved her for the first time. The way he'd whispered her name—and followed it with their first "grown-up" kiss—made her rethink a few things. From that point on, she'd embraced her name and learned to appreciate it.

Then everything in her life suddenly crumbled like the sand castles on her beloved beach. Much like the crushed chips—the "dregs" as she called them— left in the bottom of the bag of potato chips on the kitchen table. With a frown, she tossed the bag in the garbage can under the sink. Time to clean up this mess.

Airy, translucent bubbles danced around her head when she squeezed the liquid soap—environmentally safe, nontoxic and pear-scented—into the warm dishwater. Blowing a bubble toward the ceiling, Serenity followed its bouncy path, higher and higher. A wistful smile tipped her lips. When the bubble landed on the clock and popped, she snapped to attention. If she kept moving, she'd have enough time to clean up the kitchen and throw in a load of laundry before her client appointment.

As she scrubbed a plate with crusted-on food—processed cheese from the looks of it— Serenity darted a glance at the end of the counter. Sure enough, the green glass bowl sat in its usual spot, filled with fresh pears. Dad never ate them but kept that bowl filled in case Mama ever decided to return. Like she'd just waltz in the door one day as though nothing had ever happened and pick up the shattered pieces of their lives. This was starting to get borderline creepy, like a shrine to the...well, that was the problem. According to the police, Mama's case was "cold." She hated the term and everything it implied, and the thought made her shudder as it always did. Of all the available options—kidnapped, missing, in hiding or deceased—the one option she refused to contemplate was that Mama *voluntarily* left them.

"Leave the dishes, Serenity," her father called from the other room. "Come on out here. I need to talk to you."

Twisting the knob to stop the water, she dried her hands and swallowed her apprehension. When he'd called earlier that morning and asked her to stop by the house, she could tell something important was on his mind. Squaring her shoulders, she prepared for what might become another battle of wills. As he lowered the footrest on his chair, Clinton McClaren narrowed his eyes and beckoned to her as she lingered in the doorway. Based on the deep lines etched around his eyes, and the faint circles beneath them, he hadn't been sleeping well.

"I knew the answer to that last question, you know." He waved his hand toward the television. "It tickles me when they mention Newport." Newport, Rhode Island, playground of the rich and famous, and her father's hometown. The city where a young senator from Massachusetts named John Kennedy married elegant Jacqueline Bouvier in 1953. The birthplace of America's Cup racing and home to the International Tennis Hall of Fame.

To anyone who'd listen, he loved telling stories of growing up on the *other* end of the street from grandiose homes such as The Breakers built by the socially-prominent Vanderbilt family, mansions to most but mere summer residences for those her father termed "wealthier than God." As a teenager, he'd delivered groceries to a millionaire twice acquitted for attempting to poison his wife and maintained a first-name relationship with butlers and servants, including those for an eccentric spinster heiress who willed her substantial fortune to two pampered dogs.

Newport was also where he'd met her mother at the world-renowned Newport Jazz Festival. Serenity's free-spirited parents volunteered at the festival one sweltering August day nearly twenty-six years ago. They'd shared a blanket on the lawn and apparently a whole lot more considering she'd been born nine months later, almost to the day.

Humoring her father now seemed the best option. "What was the clue?"

"Name the summer White House during the Kennedy administration," he said. "Two of the contestants guessed the family compound in Hyannis. Figures. But the third one," he said, shaking his finger, "*she* was smart and knew it was Hammersmith Farm. Speaking of smart, sit yourself down, girl. We need to talk about this big plan of yours." He nodded to the threadbare chair across from his recliner. No matter how many times she'd offered, her father refused to have it reupholstered, as if preserving Mama's favorite chair might somehow bring her back home. She was surprised he'd even allow her to sit in that chair, holy as it was.

A grunt preceded a loud clearing of his raspy throat as Clinton reached for the unopened box of cigarettes on the table.

"Dad." She hoped her tone would stop that hand mid-air.

"Save the lecture, Serenity. This is about you, not me."

She met his eyes, holding them steady. He always thought he could stare her down, but no more. "Make you a deal. I don't lecture you, and you don't lecture me."

He pulled off the cellophane wrapper and unwound the tab from the pack of cancer sticks. "You're still my daughter, and from the sound of it, you're not too old to sass your dad."

For a man in his mid-fifties, he looked ten years older and she hated how his once robust shoulders slumped. For most of his working life, he'd proudly served the public as a member of the Croisette Shores Fire Department and been active in community events. He'd lived healthy, ate right, exercised regularly. After Mama's disappearance, he retired and nicotine became his poison of choice, rendering him a shriveled shell of the man he'd once been. Now, he couldn't understand why his only child preferred to live in a small rental a half-mile away instead of staying with him in the old family homestead. The concept of secondhand smoke hadn't yet infiltrated his clogged mind.

The solace was the love written in his weary, dark eyes. Beneath the gruff exterior, her dad's heart was one of the most tender she'd ever known. One glance could melt her strongest resolve, ease away the years, the heartache and loneliness. In his eyes, she was still the scrawny, awkward ten-year-old with long blonde pigtails who snuck out of the house to pay visits to her best friend Deidre's puppy. Then she'd morphed into a seventeen-year-old who thought she knew more than her parents and snuck out with Danny almost every night.

The constant sadness in Clinton's expression made her furious at her mother all over again for leaving him. Leaving *them*. For reasons she couldn't understand, without fail, he always defended her. She no longer believed Mama would return, but he'd held onto the hope. Serenity had run away from home, but he'd stayed. She'd fought the past and made strides toward her future, yet he couldn't seem to move on. If nothing else, her life was filled with irony.

Resisting the urge to cross her arms, Serenity frowned at the onset of another round of coughing spasms. He wouldn't accept help, turned away from sympathy and pity made him angrier than anything. Feeling helpless, she darted into the kitchen, grabbed a glass from the overhead cabinet and shoved it under the water dispenser on the refrigerator door. By the time she placed the glass on the end table beside him, his latest spell had finally subsided.

"Drink up," she said. "You need to stay hydrated."

His face twisted as he drained the glass. Smacking his lips, he handed it to her. "You're a good daughter for watching over me."

"Well, someone's got to do it. Need some more?"

"Nah. That'll do me. Sit down again and tell me about this business plan of yours." The skepticism in his tone irritated her. "Seems a little risky in this town."

Inhaling a quick breath, Serenity dropped into the chair. Would he rather she hadn't come home? "Maybe it is, but I have to try." Sure, she might fail, but she'd be able to look in the mirror with some semblance of self-respect. "What do you expect me to do, Dad? I've worked hard the past few years to earn the right. I suppose I could waitress at The Happy Crab or cashier at McHenry's Market. Better yet, I could set the pins at Bowl-A-Rama." Try as she might, she couldn't squelch the defensiveness and sarcasm in her tone. Instead of being supportive, he wanted to fight her at every turn. She swallowed a sigh of exasperation.

"Can't do that last one." A spark of humor surfaced in Clinton's voice, surprising her. "Sid at the bowling alley got one of them automated machines last year. Can't you hang a shingle and work from that little house of yours instead of spending big money on an office?"

"An office projects a more professional image," she said. "It's in a prime location in the center of town, and it'll be a good place to meet potential clients on neutral ground. Deidre and Wes own the building and they're giving me a ridiculously low rental rate in exchange for client referrals."

He nodded. "Your friend's done real well for herself. She checks on me once a week, you know." Clinton shifted in his recliner. "I know I'm not the easiest person to be around, girl, but I figured you might come around more."

Serenity bit back her quick rebuttal. "Deidre came to visit me in Atlanta a few times, too." She didn't know her friend regularly visited her dad, but it was another reason to love the woman. She'd been one of her strongest lifelines to sanity. "I promise I'll be around more once I get settled. You have to give me a little time, okay?"

Ending that spiel with a question made her sound a little desperate, as if she was imploring him for reassurance. Like a pat on the head for earning a good grade in school. Or the thumbs-up when she slid into home and won the softball game for her team when she was twelve. What did she have to prove, anyway?

That she was an independent adult and could do this on her own? That she knew what she was doing? *That I don't need my daddy to hold my hand?* If nothing else, the events of the last few years taught her to work for what she wanted in life. No one—not even God—would hand her a free pass with a "Here you go. Have a great life."

Her dad had to know his words heaped more guilt on her already burdened conscience. Unleashing her anger would only drive the wedge deeper between them, and she needed to rein in the growing resentment. If only he knew how many times she'd started toward the house only to change her mind and turn in the opposite direction. How could she tell him it was almost too sad to visit her own father? The memories overwhelmed her the minute she stepped inside the house.

"I've been here a few times, Dad, but you're usually asleep." She raised a brow and attempted a half-smile. "I suppose you believe the laundry fairy's washed your clothes and the catering elf's left food in the fridge?"

"Yeah, and I appreciate it, girl. Right charitable."

A small concession, but she'd take it. "I'm sorry I haven't been around much, but starting a new business takes a lot of time. I've furnished the office space, hired a part-time assistant and filed all the paperwork with the state and the town. There's a budget to be made, advertising revenues to consider..." Justifiable or not, they were feeble excuses and they both knew it.

Faint whimpering and scratching from the side door caught her attention. Telling him she'd be right back, Serenity hurried through the kitchen, thankful for the brief reprieve. Warm sunshine filled the room with light as she opened the door, inhaling the sweet headiness of rose shrubs—her mother's beloved Vi's Violet roses—planted along the back of the house. She was surprised they'd survived without her mother's loving cultivation, but seeing the miniature lavender blooms always made her smile.

At least something comes back every year.

Serenity clapped her hands. "Ginseng! Come here, girl." Sinking to her knees as the aging golden retriever padded through the door, tail wagging, she buried her face in the dog's luxurious fur. "You're my anchor. I love my girl, yes I do." She rubbed behind Ginseng's ears and planted a kiss on the dog's ten-year-old head. "If only you could talk, you'd have some mighty big secrets to spill, wouldn't you? Oh, how I wish you could."

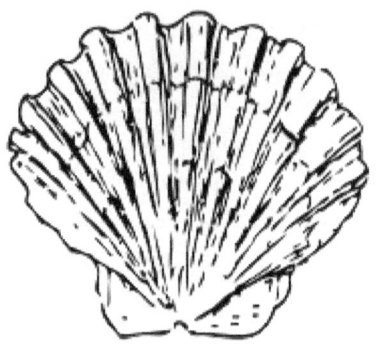

~CHAPTER 2~

*J*ackson startled as the buzzer on the phone interrupted his concentration. "Yes, Mrs. Lange?"

"Your two o'clock appointment is here, Dr. Ross."

"Thanks. I'll be right out." After a final glance at the computer screen, he closed out the file and said a quick prayer. Although it was the two-minute version, he knew God listened and figured He'd appreciate the brevity. Strolling toward the outer lobby, prepared to greet his first patient in Croisette Shores, Jackson paused in the doorway when he heard a woman speaking with a young boy. They sat together on the sofa as he read a book aloud. This must be Justin and his guardian, Mrs. Johnson. With painstaking care, she encouraged him after he stumbled over a word. Justin couldn't be any older than five, but he handled the words with aplomb. Bright kid. Cute, too, with handsome features and a mop of dark, curly hair. When he laughed, his smile revealed straight baby teeth framed by two deep dimples.

Content to observe, Jackson admired the woman's dedication and patience. Lost in the world of Dr. Seuss, neither one noticed him. They'd recently come to South Carolina from New York, but whether the stop in Croisette Shores was temporary or permanent he had no idea. It didn't help that Mrs. Johnson refused to fill out the requisite paperwork—claiming she didn't want to involve an insurance company—and insisted on paying cash.

His initial inclination had been to refuse the appointment, but the Lord sent every child to him for a reason, and he accepted the responsibility as a higher calling. At the very least, he needed to meet with Justin, form his conclusions and help him if he could. So, with an underlying reserve of caution, he'd booked the appointment. He resolved to garner as much information as he could during their initial session and record his notes immediately afterward. Without really knowing why, he suspected Mrs. Johnson wouldn't make his job easier.

"That's right, Justin. Good job." The woman patted the boy's arm and looked up as Jackson approached. She wore sunglasses, making it difficult to guess her age, but he estimated early fifties or a few years older. Could be she had a sensitivity to light, but Jackson hoped it wasn't anything more. Domestic abuse cases were difficult and he hated them, no more so than when they involved one of his patients.

He'd heard celebrities sometimes camped out in this little coastal town, so perhaps Mrs. "Johnson" was an actress or socialite going incognito. Could be she'd recently undergone a "cosmetic procedure" or whatever they called plastic surgery these days. No matter the woman's identity, other than "Smith" or "Jones," she couldn't have picked a more generic last name.

Closing the book on her lap, she placed it on a nearby table and took the boy's hand. "Let's meet the doctor."

Big brown eyes stared up at him with all the innocence of a seemingly happy, healthy child. "Justin?" He nodded as Jackson crouched in front of him. "I'm Dr. Ross, but you can call me Doc Jack if you want. Thanks for coming to see me today. Want to come in the office and talk for a few minutes?" When the boy hesitated, looking at the woman for reassurance, Jackson sweetened the offer. "I have gummi worms. Mrs. Lange makes them, and they're a whole lot better than the ones you buy in the store." As expected, that did the trick when the boy's eyes lit and he dropped his guardian's hand.

"You said the magic words," the woman said, her lips twisting with the hint of a smile. "I lose to gummies all the time. I'm Violet Johnson."

"Nice to meet you." Jackson rose to his feet and grabbed the arm of the sofa for support, grimacing with the effort. When would he learn to be kinder to his knee? Probably never since he preferred talking to kids at their own level and was willing to pay the price. After jogging on the beach earlier, he thought he'd loosened up his joints, but obviously he was operating under a misconception.

"Are you okay?" Mrs. Johnson placed one hand beneath his elbow as though it was second nature, steadying him. "Old football injury?"

"Something like that. Thanks," he said, hating the admission of weakness but appreciating her compassion. "Why don't we move into the office?" He motioned toward the doorway. Justin led the way, smiling as he plopped into the kid-sized armchair across from the desk.

The woman followed. Tall and thin in a toned, athletic way, her deep auburn hair was stylishly cut. Well-dressed in a khaki skirt, sleeveless blouse and sandals, her movements were graceful and fluid, making him wonder if she'd been a professional dancer. He should stop overthinking and concentrate on his *patient*, not the boy's guardian, but it was all part of the big picture. After closing the door to the office, Jackson seated himself in the adult-sized chair beside Justin, opposite his desk, while Mrs. Johnson took the armchair by a side wall lined with bookshelves. Trying not to be too obvious, he lightly massaged his right knee.

Squirming in the chair, the boy's eyes widened when his feet reached the floor. Most kids had the same reaction, and he scored extra points for having that kid-sized chair, the one piece of furniture he'd brought with him while he met with patients in Dr. Rasmussen's office.

Justin darted a quick glance around. "Is this your room?"

Jackson's lips curled. "This is another doctor's room. I'm borrowing it until mine's ready in a few more weeks. I recently moved here from Chicago."

"That's the Windy City, right?" Justin said, smiling. "I like the Sears Tower, but it's called something else now." He glanced at Mrs. Johnson. "What's it called?"

"The Willis Tower," she said, crossing one long leg over the other.

"Have you been to Chicago?" Jackson asked.

"Yup. I like riding the El train." The boy nodded and swung his feet back and forth before sweeping his gaze over Jackson. "You don't look like a doctor."

"Justin, honey, be nice."

"I *am* being nice," he said. "Dr. Morgan always wears a white coat and that stetho thing around his neck."

"I don't have a white coat and I never wear a stetho thing around my neck. I'm not that kind of doctor." His answer seemed to satisfy the boy. "Now, for those promised gummi worms. Tell you what," Jackson said, walking around the desk and pulling out a plastic bag from a drawer, "I'll ask you a question, and when you answer, you can choose whichever worm you want."

"What if I get it wrong?" He didn't appear nervous or scared, only curious.

"There are no right or wrong answers. Just tell me whatever comes into your mind first."

Justin looked to the woman for confirmation. She nodded, still wearing the glasses.

"Why don't we start with you telling me something you like to do?"

The boy gave him an impish smile. "I like to eat red gummi worms."

Clever child. Settling into the chair again, Jackson chuckled. "What else?"

"I like the zoo."

"Me, too. Which animal's your favorite?"

"Giraffes. I like their spots and their really long necks"—Justin made a stretching motion with his hands—"and they have big google eyes."

"Yes, I guess they do have google eyes," Jackson said, watching the boy fish out a couple of red gummi worms and then withdraw his hand when Mrs. Johnson cleared her throat.

"I'll tell you something else," Jackson said. "I'm planning on having some animals in my new office. So, when you come see me again, I might even have a giraffe." Perhaps he was foolish to promise something like that, but he'd make his best effort. He'd mention it to the decorator he was meeting almost immediately after this session. If she had kids, she'd probably know where to find one.

The boy gulped. "A *real* giraffe?"

Mrs. Johnson cracked a small smile. Jackson chewed the inside of his cheek, determined he wouldn't laugh. If he did, he'd risk losing his little patient's trust in which case he'd clam up tighter than a lockbox with no key. They were off to a good start, but he didn't want to risk or jeopardize their early, tenuous bond.

"I don't think a giraffe would fit, do you?" Jackson said. "He'd be too tall and probably wouldn't like being cooped up in an office." Unwittingly, this conversation served as the perfect segue to his next question. He figured he might as well take a chance but dared not look at Mrs. Johnson now. "Have you ever felt like you were cooped up, Justin? Like you were someplace you didn't like and couldn't leave, even if you wanted to?"

The woman coughed but remained silent. Appearing to consider the question, the boy shrugged. "Guess not."

His answer shot relief through Jackson. From his experience, the answer to that question could prove significant and telling. From all indications, he was a well-adjusted child. He'd looked him straight in the eye and wasn't overly nervous or shy. Question was, why *was* he here?

The rest of the short session, Jackson concentrated on establishing a solid rapport. With an easy give-and-take, he discovered Justin was four and turning five in June. Instead of toys, he wanted books and a trip to the beach, confirming this kid wasn't average in any sense of the word. Sure, he swung his legs back and forth in the chair and crossed them every now and then, fidgeted a bit, leaned his chin on his hands and appeared distracted at times. But in many ways, he'd demonstrated he was far beyond his chronological age. He'd been taught well. Evidenced by his easy wit, he'd spent time in the company of adults and intelligent conversation. He gave the impression of being well-traveled or, at a minimum, he'd visited museums and been exposed to cultural events, music and the arts. He'd been encouraged to form and articulate his opinions. This child had been *loved.* Justin was unique from any other patient he'd encountered in his previous practice, and as such, fascinated him.

As far as his guardian, Jackson didn't know whether it was her quiet demeanor—not aloofness, exactly, but more a reserved quality—or the sunglasses she hadn't removed, but something niggled at his brain. It might drive him crazy until he figured it out. *If* he figured it out. Nothing sinister, by any means, but something out-of-the-ordinary. He only hoped they'd return so he could dig a little deeper. If Mrs. Johnson decided to bring Justin again, she'd need to complete some of the new patient forms. It had nothing to do with money and everything to do with state and federal compliance, often the bane of his existence.

Bringing the session to a close, Jackson rose to his feet, smiling at the child. "Would you mind reading a book in the lobby for a few minutes while I talk with Mrs. Johnson?"

The boy tilted his head and gave him a curious stare. "She's not—"

"Honey, do as he asks, please." Quickly crossing the room, she ruffled Justin's dark curls. "We'll leave the door open, and I'll be right here if you need me. We won't be long."

"I think there's several Dr. Seuss books," Jackson said, walking him to the doorway. "Mrs. Lange, could you please find *Green Eggs and Ham* for Justin?"

"Sure thing." The good-natured woman smiled and motioned for him to follow as she led the way toward the rack of books. "Let's see what we can find. We have *Horton Hears a Who* if we can't find the other one."

When he was settled with a book, Jackson gestured for Mrs. Johnson to take a seat again as he moved behind the desk. "Justin seems to be a very healthy and well-adjusted child. Why exactly have you brought him to see me?"

The glasses stayed in place, but Mrs. Johnson bowed her head and twisted her fingers in her lap. "He's been sheltered his entire life. It's time to get him out in the world, meet kids his own age, have fun and go to school. He's also a sensitive child, and he might need help to make the adjustment."

Fair enough. "May I ask where he's been?"

Mrs. Johnson sighed. "Living in a mostly adult world and I've homeschooled him."

"I take it he lives with you?"

"Yes."

"You've raised him?" Her nod was almost imperceptible. "How long?" When she didn't answer, he persisted. "Since he was a baby?"

She hesitated and finally nodded, offering nothing more. Where were the child's parents? He'd let it go and hope it'd be revealed in a later session. "Why do you think now's the time for a change?"

"The environment in New York was getting somewhat...oppressive, and I thought it was in Justin's best interests to leave. I love it here in Croisette Shores and always have." As if afraid she'd let something slip unaware, Mrs. Johnson lowered her head again. "I think this town might be a good place for him."

"A *safe* place?"

She jerked up her head, and Jackson wished he could whip the glasses from her face so he could look her in the eye. He'd struck a nerve. Good. He'd no doubt strike a few more before he was done. Not being able to look someone in the eye when he spoke with them drove him nuts. Combined with evasive answers, this conversation was like his worst-case nightmare when it came to dealing with a patient's guardian.

"Why do you say that?" The muscles in her jaws tensed and she stilled her fingers.

Jackson leaned across the desk, purposely keeping his voice low. Time to play hardball. "For starters, the name Johnson isn't exactly original. You won't remove your sunglasses, a pretty good indicator you're hiding something, but whether physical or otherwise, I have no idea. You can't sit in the chair for more than a few seconds without fidgeting and you're measuring your words carefully so you won't reveal what you *don't* want me to know." He sat back in the chair. "Look, it's not my job to figure out your motivation. It *is* my responsibility to help Justin. But in order to do that, you're going to have to work with me. I hope you're willing to do that."

Instead of slamming him—and admittedly, she had every right—Mrs. Johnson remained in the chair. The lines around her mouth were drawn, the lines on her forehead more evident, but she hadn't bolted, a promising sign. She had her charge's best interests in mind, and that was key. Was it a subconscious test? Perhaps, but unfair or not, she'd passed and that pleased him.

Her deep sigh was audible. "He has close relatives in Croisette Shores he's never met. It's time."

"What's your relationship to Justin?"

She lifted her chin and squared her slender shoulders. "I love him. Isn't that enough?"

That much was obvious, but it'd do. For now. "Is Johnson your *real* last name?"

"No." It was barely more than a whisper. He was surprised she'd allowed that much.

"Are you in the Witness Protection Program? Be honest. Whatever you tell me won't go beyond these walls."

The corners of her mouth lifted. "Heavens, no."

"Good. Then why all the secrecy?" Lightening up and taking it easy on the woman would be advisable, but as long as she seemed willing to answer, he'd keep asking.

"All will be revealed in due time." Looking down at her lap, she smoothed a hand over her skirt. "I don't mean to sound mysterious, Dr. Ross, but I'm asking you to trust me." She visibly swallowed. "I assure you I have that child's best interests at heart."

"Can you tell me his last name?"

When she gave him a startled look, he sighed. "Fine. I'll list it as Johnson for now. Are you planning on settling permanently in Croisette Shores?"

"I want to make sure he likes it here before making any definite decisions."

"Have you made contact with his relatives, arranged a meeting?"

"Not yet." She half-rose from the chair. "I have another appointment now, but I appreciate your time and trust I've answered your questions sufficiently to warrant another visit."

Jackson nodded and that odd sense of relief filled him once more. "Please make an appointment with Mrs. Lange. She'll give you some paperwork to fill out." That might intimidate her. "Give me what information you can, the basics, and I'll take it from there."

"Very well. Thank you, Dr. Ross."

He nodded. "Thanks for coming and bringing Justin. He's a great kid and I'll try to help him in whatever way I can."

She paused by the door. "Yes, he is. I'll see you again."

After saying goodbye and recording his observations, Jackson glanced at his watch. Fifteen minutes. That'd give him plenty of time to walk the four blocks to the coffee shop and meet his decorator with the intriguing name. Serenity something-or-other. She came highly recommended by their mutual friend Charlie Mathias. In actuality, he'd only met Charlie since he'd been in town, but he'd known instinctively the man's word was as good as gold.

Heading out into the sunshine a few minutes later, in the direction of Martha's Cup & Such, Jackson's thoughts wandered to the beautiful blonde woman he'd spied when he'd gone back to the cottage for lunch and taken Freud for a quick run on the beach. Purposely tossing the Frisbee in her direction hadn't been the brightest idea, but it'd caught her attention. She'd seemed friendly enough but then promptly cut him off from further discussion. To be fair, she'd appeared deep in thought and Freud had startled her.

Hopefully, he'd have another opportunity to meet her. For whatever reason, he suspected she was a local of the area and not a short-term visitor. That thought encouraged him. Tomorrow, he'd jog on the beach again with Freud.

He'd go every day, both for his own health and so Freud could expend all that excess, pent-up energy. Next time, he'd find the opportunity to meet her and share a conversation. After all, Croisette Shores wasn't *that* big.

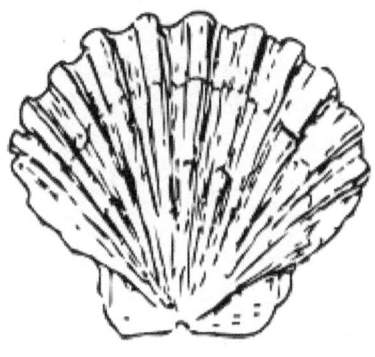

~CHAPTER 3~

Serenity filled Ginseng's water dish and carefully lowered it to the kitchen floor.

"Thanks for letting her back in," Clinton said when she returned to the family room. Ginseng plopped down beside the recliner, watching her with big, sad eyes and resting her head on crossed paws.

"Are you getting out every day and walking Ginseng?" Serenity sat again in her mother's chair, marveling how it smelled faintly of her honeysuckle-scented lotion, even now. A glance at the fraying threads on the edge of the seat brought unexpected tears. Funny how mundane or seemingly insignificant things could trigger memories of Mama in any given moment. Perhaps her tears were more a concession to the idea she might really be gone. *Gone.*

Her dad pulled a cigarette from the pack. Probably for effect, he'd waited for her to come back inside. Clamping it between his lips, he curled his fingers around a lighter with a scene of Croisette Shores, the kind sold in the tourist shops down by the waterfront. The years of firefighting had left his palms callused and his hands were gnarled from encroaching arthritis. "So, where'd you get the start-up capital for this business of yours?" he said. "I don't think I've heard the answer to that one yet. Did you get a small business loan?"

Serenity turned her head as he inhaled a long drag before blowing out a smoke ring. Insinuation wound its way into his words and she struggled to keep her voice calm. "No loans. I've lived frugally and worked part-time while I went to school. I used public transportation and lived with three roommates in student housing to save on rent. Money I didn't need to survive went straight into my savings." She'd anticipated her dad's questions and rehearsed that speech to where she could spout it in her sleep.

"Good girl."

"It's called doing what I needed to survive and hang onto what shreds of sanity I had left." Biting her lower lip, she avoided the intensity of his gaze.

He grunted, one of his longtime aversion tactics. "This is an old town, Serenity. You know that. They don't call it 'historic' for nothing. Don't know how many people will want the services of some fancy decorator."

She tried not to smirk. "Businesses and homeowners still need to update sometimes, Dad. This house is a classic example. Unlike some people, I can't sit around and dwell on the past." She closed her mouth. Best not to alienate him and that last statement sounded a lot more sarcastic than she'd intended. She'd given him enough to chew on for one afternoon and hoped she hadn't already pushed him too far.

Thirty minutes later, armed with a lecture about the likelihood her business would fail in an uncertain economy—especially in a town the size of Croisette Shores—Serenity gave her father a kiss on his temple. Dutiful yes, but she appreciated the fact he cared enough to voice his concerns. His skin felt a little warm and clammy and she pressed the back of her hand across his forehead.

In a surprise move, Clinton clasped his thin, wiry hand around hers and held on tight. Touched by the unexpected show of tenderness, she glanced down at their joined hands. The blue veins in his hands were prominent and the misshapen knuckles had to be painful.

"I should have stopped you from running off before." Tired eyes met hers and softened.

"You couldn't have stopped me, Dad."

Clinton released her hand from its vise-like grip, something else left over from his firefighting days. "You always were stubborn, like your mama, but you've got a strong backbone, and that's stood you well. Pretty as a picture like Elise, too, with all that long blonde hair and big blue eyes. Sure to break a good man's heart." Another raspy cough escaped, and he turned his head, bringing a fist over his mouth. Thankfully, this one didn't last long, only a few seconds. "I'm glad you got her looks, not mine."

"Admit it, Dad. You miss her." She stopped short of tacking on the word, "too." As mad as she was at Mama, she'd been a good mother until the day she simply...disappeared. The not knowing was the worst thing of all. Like sensing you have cancer but not having a diagnosis. All over again, she silently promised herself and her father she'd find answers so they could have some kind of closure and move on with their lives.

The horizontal creases marching across Clinton's brow deepened. Leaning his head against the chair, he squeezed his eyes tight and pinched the bridge of his nose. The cigarette was still clenched between his fingers. "God help me, I do." Opening his eyes, he lowered his head to meet her gaze straight-on. "There's days when I don't want to go on without her."

What possessed her to bring up the subject of her mother when she had an appointment to keep in less than twenty minutes? Getting all emotional wouldn't be the best thing before meeting a potential client. "I inherited things more important than looks from you, Dad."

"Yeah? Like what?" How she'd missed his smile, the one that hinted of the handsome man he'd once been. Then he spoiled the image by taking another deep drag from his cigarette.

"For starters, how to save money for what's most important," she said. "Not to judge someone based on the color of their skin, their bank account or what they do for a living. How not to take anything or anyone for granted."

"Don't you forget those lessons either, girl." Clinton shifted in his chair. "Why are you *really* back in Croisette Shores, Serenity? Are you finally here to stay?" Her dad's voice caught. Coughing again, he thumped his chest a few times. While she waited, she grabbed the water glass and refilled it and then retrieved the remains of scattered newspapers and stacked them in a neat pile on the brick hearth. From the corner of her eye, she saw him take a long drink and empty the glass.

"I hope you know I didn't run away from *you*." She hesitated. "I just couldn't—"

"I know." His eyes met hers again. "We'll get through it together."

She swallowed the lump in her throat and nodded. "I brought your dinner. Cashew chicken from Mr. Wong's. It's in the fridge." She checked her watch.

"Listen, I've got an appointment soon and should scoot. Do you need anything else before I go?"

"I'm good. Thanks for spoiling me, girl. Don't know what made you finally decide to come back, but I'm glad you did."

His statement confirmed what she already knew. No way he'd mailed that note urging her to come home. The scrawl was nothing like Clinton's small, squeezed-together letters. Her trip to the post office last week had proved pointless. The postmistress—a girl from her graduating class named Tina—could tell her nothing other than confirm what she already knew: the Croisette Shores postmark was authentic, but without a return address, there was nothing to go on. Even if Tina *did* know anything, privacy rules trumped personal relationships. Until someone stepped forward or she figured it out, the sender's identity would remain a mystery.

"Croisette Shores is my home, Dad. Always has been."

Clinton shook his head. "You'll have to do better than that. You should have found a rich man in Atlanta to take care of you and give you lots of beautiful babies. You deserve better after all you've been through."

"People in big cities aren't immune from heartache, Dad," she said. "God has nothing personal against us or this town. You could have left, too, you know. Other than memories and a few buddies, you haven't had much to keep you here."

Deep-set eyes met hers again. "I do now."

Blinking hard, she stemmed the tears. How could he be so gruff one minute and steal her breath with unexpected sentimentality the next? "God's been teaching me I can't run away from my problems. Besides," she said, patting his arm and sniffling, "you gave me this name for a reason. It's about time I lived up to it, don't you think?"

"Elise named you. I wanted to name you Prudence." His lips upturned. "Your mama always had a way of convincing me to come around to her way of thinking. But since when did you start thinking about God? Find yourself some religion in Atlanta, did you?"

"No, not religion, Dad. I discovered *faith* and a relationship with Jesus. It's all pretty new, but it's precious and...special, so please don't spoil it for me."

Instead of scoffing—or calling it a crutch, as she suspected—he cocked a brow and stared at her for several long seconds. "I'm real happy for you,

Serenity, but if the Almighty's really watching out for you, He wouldn't have brought you back to this God-forsaken town."

Serenity knelt on the floor beside his recliner. "I'm not sure about a lot of things, Dad, but in my heart, I *know* this is where I belong. I learned that I'm never alone and that gives me an unbelievable comfort. I promise you I'll find answers so we'll both know what happened. Once and for all."

She hated what he was doing to himself, sitting in that chair hour after hour. Either loneliness or lung cancer would eventually kill him. The saddest thing of all? It's probably what he wanted, but it wouldn't happen if she had anything to say about it.

Cupping the side of his face with one palm, her heart swelled with emotion when he leaned his leathered cheek against it. Rough stubble prickled her fingers and the contours of his face felt familiar—although painfully thin—beneath her hand. As a little girl, she'd put her hands on his puffed cheeks and squeezed until he released the trapped air. Then he'd cover her face with kisses and tickle her as she giggled. As a teenager, she'd teased him about the roughness of his beard and ducked to avoid his kiss. A tear slipped down her cheek, but she let it go.

"Aw, don't go and get all female on me," Clinton said, tugging a handkerchief from the pocket of his shorts and offering it to her.

Serenity waved it away with a small smile. "No, thanks." She wiped her damp cheek with the back of one hand. "I didn't know men under eighty used those disgusting things."

He shoved it back in his pocket. "Sure we do. We keep them handy to offer crying women." She was afraid that wry comment would prompt another cough, but surprisingly, no warning rattle surfaced. "I understand you've got yourself a date. You'd better get moving along, girl. You don't want this guy to think you're always late. Wouldn't make the best impression."

"It's an initial meeting with a potential client, not a date, but how..." Rising to her feet, the beginnings of a grin tipped the corners of her mouth. "I never could keep anything secret from you, could I?"

"Word gets around. I get out every now and then, and believe you me, people talk plenty."

"Dad, tell you what. We have a date on Sunday afternoon. Just you and me."

He eyed her. "You gonna treat me like an invalid?"

"If you act like one."

"Where do you suggest we go?"

"How about the beach? It'll put color in your cheeks. You're too pale. No more excuses."

"Can I smoke?" Even though he scowled, Serenity glimpsed the spark in his eye. The small victories could be so sweet.

Serenity blew out a deep sigh. "I don't even know if it's legal there anymore. I certainly hope not."

"Okay, okay," he said, holding up one hand. "Lots of kids at the shore, anyway." He shot her a look. "Don't need a bunch of angry people glaring at me if I'm blowing smoke. Getting that glare from my daughter is bad enough."

She ignored his comment but found it surprising how quickly he'd conceded. "Is Hermann's still down by the shore? You used to like going there. We could have an early dinner together." The familiar sadness surfaced in his eyes, and self-congratulations were premature. How could she have forgotten it was a favorite place to go with her mother? Great. She was trying to cheer him up, infuse some life into him, and she'd reminded him of Mama all over again.

Clinton slapped one hand on his knee and stubbed out his cigarette. "You're right. My back end's fallen asleep in this chair one time too many. The beach sounds like a good idea."

"Do you have any swim trunks?"

He half-laughed. "I said I'd go to the beach, but don't think I'm exposing this lily white chest to anyone much less the sun. Bad enough I'll be showing these peg legs of mine, but I have *some* pride left. I'll get my exercise walking up and down by the water." He paused and his eyes softened. "We could build a sand castle like we used to, and I can twirl you under my arm, and say, 'Dance, Princess Serenity, dance...' Remember that?"

She'd never forget their special little sing-song. "You must be thinking of Prudence. That settles it then. Sunday afternoon, we have a date to go to the beach and supper. Be ready at two-thirty."

When Clinton reached for the cigarettes, he caught the look on her face and dropped his hand. "Hope your meeting goes well, and you get your first paying client."

Serenity swallowed the lump lodged in her throat. "Thanks. I'll see you soon."

"Come back again tomorrow." Although muffled, his words floated to her as she retrieved her purse and walked through the living room.

"I'll try," she murmured, closing the front door behind her.

*T*he day was beautiful with the salty ocean breeze wafting in from the Atlantic as Serenity walked on a quiet side street near the waterfront, drinking it in like a visit with an old, dear friend. How she'd missed the sound of ocean waves lapping on the beach, the sight of palm trees swaying in the breeze and the caws of the seagulls.

The bright pink coffee cup hand-painted on the front window of Martha's Cup & Such beckoned to her and the bell on the door jingled as she stepped inside, announcing her arrival. Glasses clinked, silverware clattered and the low, steady hum of the kitchen staff and customers' conversations filled the popular coffee shop. She breathed in the familiar smells.

Yes, she was *home.*

"Serenity McClaren?"

She turned back toward the cashier's counter located just inside the front door. Two men stood to one side, but which one had called her by name? One was short, balding, middle-aged and rotund. The other was tall, broad-shouldered, chestnut-haired and impossibly attractive. And played Frisbee on the beach with a dog named Freud.

Pasting on a tentative smile, she moved toward them.

This should be interesting.

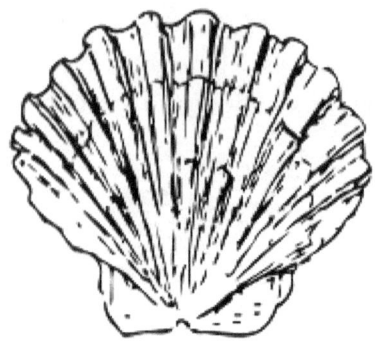

~CHAPTER 4~

*T*he shorter man stepped forward. "Serenity? I thought that was you."

Serenity smiled as he pumped her hand a couple of times. "Yes, and you..."

"Art Masmer. Your dad and I used to play trombone together in the Salvation Army Band. I'd heard you'd moved back to town. Sure is good to see you. Too many young folks move away and never come back. Your dad must be tickled to death to have you home again."

Glancing over Art's shoulder, Serenity caught the amusement in the younger man's expression. No doubt this was her first client. For his part, Dr. Ross appeared to be enjoying this scenario. She gave him a slight nod—one she hoped appeared polite and professional—and returned her attention to Art.

"I hope your family's doing well," she said. Try as she might, she couldn't place him. She didn't know what else to say and prayed Art had a family or she'd be backpedaling fast. Judging by his wide smile, she'd made an appropriate comment.

"They sure are. Our oldest, Susie, married Mark Blanchard a couple of years ago, and they just gave Nell and me our first grandson. Wyatt's five months old already. Here, let me show you a photo." Pulling out his wallet, Art flipped it open and pointed to a photo of a chubby-cheeked, bright-eyed baby. He beamed when Serenity expressed her congratulations. "Tell Clinton I hope he's planning on playing in the Fourth of July band this year. We could use another trombone." Saying goodbye, he waved to someone in the back of the restaurant and departed.

Stepping forward, her client offered his hand. "I couldn't interrupt a proud grandfather moment. I'm Jackson Ross. It's nice to meet you, Serenity."

"Likewise." Eyes the color of rich brown velvet met hers and his grip was firm. Dressed in the same light blue polo he'd worn at the shore—khakis rumpled a bit below the knees, no socks and deck shoes, basic Croisette Shores casual chic—this man would fit in perfectly fine with the locals. His hair looked slightly windblown, which only added to his rugged appeal.

"Our friend Charlie left out a few important things when he told me about you."

Even though it sounded like a questionable pickup line, the sincerity in Jackson's tone suggested flattery and nothing more. This man was the polar opposite of what she'd envisioned. Stereotyping never led to anything good, after all.

"I could say the same. For one thing, you have a furry companion named Freud."

He smiled. "Freud belongs to Doc Rasmussen. I'm staying in Doc's cottage while he's on an extended European vacation. And Freud takes *me* for a daily run, not the other way around."

"I could see that, but you seem to be getting along famously." She returned his smile.

"Yeah, we're buds. He's a fun companion, but he's a real sofa hog."

Clearing a nearby table, Lucinda Miller called over her shoulder for them to seat themselves at any available table. Open from early morning until late afternoon seven days a week, Martha's Cup & Such was the daily hub for gossip among the locals. Tourists occupied tables and packages from local shops rested on the floor beside them. A young couple with two small children looked tuckered out and sunburned, and four older ladies shared an animated discussion.

"Shall we?" Jackson gestured for her to go first, and Serenity led the way toward a small corner table. The heels of her sandals clacked on the black and white tile floor, but thankfully the sound was absorbed by the bustle of activity. A group of men hushed their conversation as she passed by their table. Many of the same waitresses from when her dad used to bring her to Martha's on Sunday mornings moved around the coffee shop wearing black and pink uniforms with white aprons tied around their waists. The outfits hadn't changed much, and the women moved a bit slower, many of them now grandmothers.

When Jackson pulled out her chair and waited until she was settled, the entire patronage seemed as if in slow motion. Serenity could almost hear the whispered approval floating about the shop, but perhaps it was her overactive imagination. Since she'd come back to town, she'd glimpsed expressions ranging from pity to borderline suspicious. Hanging her purse on the back of her chair, she overheard old Earl Watkins mumble something about how nice it was to see her in the company of a real gentleman. She tucked a strand of hair behind one ear, as if that simple gesture might dismiss her sudden case of nerves.

Jackson took the seat across the table. "Tell me about the name Serenity. There's bound to be an interesting story behind it."

Those warm eyes, heightened by the blue of his shirt, would make her crave chocolate something fierce even though she rarely indulged. At least his question was an easy one and seemed a safe topic. Getting to know her client would be a good thing before they discussed business. She'd prayed about this first meeting ever since Charlie arranged it a few days ago, asking the Lord to help her say the right things, act appropriately and not scare off the good doctor with her lack of experience.

"My mom and Dad were quasi-hippies and loved anything promoting peace and unity," she said. "He grew up in Newport, Rhode Island and she was raised in Connecticut. They shared a blanket on the lawn of the Newport Jazz Festival when they were both in their mid-twenties. To hear them tell it, they found a kindred spirit in each other and fell in love between sets by Grover Washington, Jr. and Thelonious Monk."

He grinned. "I was right. Interesting story and romantic for quasi-hippies. Care to guess how I got *my* name? It might not be as interesting as yours, but it's kind of fun."

"Then, by all means," she said, relaxing a little more. His raised brow invited her to play along. "Okay...your parents are fans of artist Jackson Pollock?" He shook his head. "Andrew Jackson?" Another shake. "Reggie Jackson?"

"All very good guesses," he said. "According to urban legend, Mom and Dad couldn't agree on my first name. My dad was a golf buddy with one of the surgeons at the hospital where I was born. Dad had stepped out of the room for a couple of minutes. Mom was holding me and she hadn't met the doctor before. He introduced himself and said, 'So, this is Jack's son?' Mom misunderstood and thought he said 'Jackson,' liked it, and the name stuck."

Serenity smiled. "I never would have guessed. Cute story." With his personable manner, Jackson would relate well to children. To anyone, really, although that anecdote was more telling than he probably realized. Words like *golf buddy* paired with *surgeon* implied his family was one of means. No big surprise there since she'd thought that very thing when she'd first spied him on the beach.

"So, did you grow up here or in New England?" he asked. "Your accent sounds southern."

"My dad took a job with the fire department here three months after my parents met. Croisette Shores reminds him a lot of Newport and Mama was always fascinated with the ocean." Her gaze traveled upward to meet Jackson's again. "She said the waves always comforted her and made her feel at one with the earth, at peace with herself and her world. She was a lover of economic awareness and environmental causes. It was her passion, and she poured her heart and soul into it."

He smiled. "Trust me, I know all about that. My mom was heavy into Green Peace, the Sierra Club and worked with the Peace Corps for a few years before she married Dad." Jackson chuckled low in his throat, and it was deep and slightly husky. "In other words, if an organization had the name 'peace' in it, Mom was right there on the front lines."

Jackson's features were strong and well-defined, his cheekbones sculpted to perfection. The blue polo barely contained those impressive muscles. This was one psychologist who took his workouts seriously. Trying not to be obvious, Serenity's gaze strayed to his left hand. No ring, but he must have left behind a string of broken hearts in Chicago or wherever his life's path had taken him. A man like this would attract female attention without even trying. He exuded self-confidence and an innate charm without cockiness, an anomaly in itself. Surely all the single women and their mothers in Croisette Shores must be on high alert of Jackson's arrival in town. He'd be busy enough dodging all the passes being tossed his way. Another reason to steer clear of the man. She hadn't been interested in dating while she lived in Atlanta and she wasn't about to start now.

Dr. Ross was her client, first and foremost. She might need to repeat that to herself a few hundred times to keep from getting distracted by his gorgeous smile and those muscles, but no way would she jeopardize her professional reputation by dating her client.

"Serenity?"

She prayed she hadn't ogled the man in full view of the entire patronage of the coffee shop. Hopefully, mind reading wasn't one of Jackson's talents. Warmth flooded her cheeks as she slowly crossed and then uncrossed her legs under the table, one of the tricks she'd learned to control nervous mannerisms in subtle ways. In a well-timed moment, Nancy Higdon arrived to take their order.

Nancy's eyes met hers above the order pad poised in one hand. "Serenity McClaren, as I live and breathe!" Pocketing the pad, she gathered her in a bear hug. "Why, honey, don't you look prettier than ever! I heard you were back in town. Bet your dad's pleased as punch to have you home." She turned her attention to Jackson. "And I understand *you're* the man they're calling Doc Jack. Welcome to Croisette Shores. I heard you were coming to take over Doc Rasmussen's practice. Nice to meet you." She looked from one to the other of them. "Imagine you two sitting here together, making nice." Nancy had a hearing problem, and she'd raised her voice at least ten decibels. Evidenced by the prevalent hush in the diner, her words must have carried across Martha's Cup & Such. Wonderful.

Thankfully, the handsome psychologist and the friendly waitress kept the conversation flowing as if Nancy hadn't just fired up the old gossip train. "To be fair, Nancy, I'm not exactly taking over Doc's practice," Jackson said. "Phil's been a mentor for me, and we both felt it best if I moved here now and got my practice established before he officially retires." Listening to their conversation, Serenity envied the kind of instant camaraderie where two people—those who'd never met or even talked before—formed an automatic bond and chatted away like fast friends who'd seen each other the day before. How was that possible? It didn't take a genius to see Jackson was the type of guy to make friends easily. She'd always admired that quality.

Hearing her name hollered from the kitchen, Nancy frowned and called over her shoulder. "I'm coming, Harold! Hold on to your britches. So,"—she turned back to them—"what can I get you two?"

"I'll have regular coffee, please," Serenity said. Coffee was her one vice, and she'd missed her morning cup. "With two creamers."

"I'll have the same, but no creamer. Want to share a slice of cherry cheese-cake?" Jackson asked her. "I have it on reputable authority it's very good here."

Nancy grinned. "Oh, it's better than good, Doc. You two enjoy yourselves and get acquainted. I'll get your coffee and the cheesecake's my treat."

Thanking Nancy, Serenity straightened in the chair and smoothed her hand over the shiny, black tabletop. "So, are your parents still card-carrying Green Peace devotees?"

"No, but I'm sure they support it one way or another. Are yours still jazz-loving, quasi-hippies?"

Focusing on the antique neon wall clock, Serenity wondered why she'd continued the same conversation when they needed to discuss business matters. "Dad's a retired fireman and slowly killing himself with cigarettes, and Mama hasn't been seen or heard from in almost five years." She almost gasped. What on earth possessed her to say so much to a man she'd known only a few minutes? Jackson straightened in his chair, but—to his credit—he didn't look the other way, grunt or appear shocked. Of course, he probably heard all sorts of things in his practice and was experienced at hiding his gut reaction.

"I'm sorry," she said, warmth invading her cheeks again. "I don't know where that came from. I apparently inherited my bluntness from my father, and some of his cynicism." She couldn't blame Jackson if he bolted and avoided her the rest of his days, although it might be difficult in a town the size of Croisette Shores if he intended to stick around.

"It's an honest and real response," he said. The compassion lacing Jackson's words surprised her, doctor or not. It seemed to come from somewhere deep inside, more than mere words meant to placate her. "I'm sorry about your mom, Serenity. I can't imagine how tough that must be. I noticed you talked about her in past tense. If you ever feel like talking about it, I'm a decent listener, or so I've been told."

"I imagine you are." She hadn't meant to sound flippant. "I mean, being a psychologist, I'm sure you spend a good deal of time listening to people...talk." That might sound inane, but if only he knew her mother's disappearance was only the tip of the iceberg. Should she ever start spilling the whole story, she feared she'd never stop. Best not to go down that road.

"That's true, although I specialize in working with children."

Nancy brought their coffee, placing their cups on the table without a word, but her smile was broad as she winked at Serenity.

"That must be a unique challenge." Charlie hadn't told her Dr. Ross worked with kids. Could be because most people familiar with her background avoided any mention of children.

"It can be, yes, but it's my specialty and what I feel called to do. It's hard to accept what so-called adults thrust on kids too young to handle it—the forgotten innocents—when they're not emotionally or mentally equipped to process the hurt, the guilt or the pain. I wonder if anyone's ever ready for the twists and turns of life. No amount of training can prepare me for what I hear sometimes. Then again, life's often not fair, no matter how old we are." He raised his eyes to meet hers. "Sounds like you might know a little something about that."

Serenity took a long sip of her coffee. "Yes, but I've been learning lately that God doesn't give us more than we can handle, if you'll excuse the cliché. I think it's more the idea He equips us with what we need to cope. As far as children, I think they have an uncanny ability to see things grown-ups are too jaded to see. Their approach to faith and their perspective is fresh and open." She raised her chin. "Is that how you see it?"

A light of interest flickered in his eyes. "Exactly. I want my patients to understand there's hope. There's an inherent trust children have. The way I look at it, it's a sacred thing. But, unfortunately, it's also that same innocence that makes them easy targets for exploitation." Jackson's eyes were moist as he cleared his throat. "My role is to be a facilitator and help them understand things that have happened in their life and help them cope, as you said." Lowering his gaze, he fiddled with the handle of his coffee cup.

This man's personal scorecard shot through the roof. Overwhelmed with emotion, she remained silent even though she felt the somewhat irrational impulse to reach across the table and smooth the lines on his brow. Instead, she kept her hands on her lap.

"Did I say something wrong?" Jackson asked after a full minute passed, although the time lapse hadn't felt awkward. Strangely enough, she felt entirely comfortable with him.

"Not at all," she said, swallowing hard. "I was just wondering where you were when I could have used you a few years ago. I mean..." This conversation was much too heavy, especially considering they'd just met. Other than Deidre, she'd shared more with Jackson than anyone—man or woman—since she'd left Croisette Shores. In Atlanta, she'd kept to herself for the most part and focused on her studies, rarely going out for social events although she'd had plenty of invitations.

Nancy brought the slice of cherry cheesecake with a plate and two forks. "Eat up. Holler if you need anything." Good old Nancy. Forcing intimacy by bringing only one plate. At least she'd brought two forks. *Stop overanalyzing. It's what the concept of sharing is all about.* Still, there were a lot worse things in life than sharing germs with a healthy-looking doctor.

"Thanks. We'll do that." Jackson handed her a fork. "Do you mind if I ask a blessing?"

Embarrassed, Serenity lowered her fork from where she'd poised it above the plate. "Not at all. Please. Go right ahead." Feeling silly and inarticulate, she bowed her head and listened as Jackson prayed for the food and asked God to bless their working relationship. Never in her life had she been with a man her own age who prayed outside the doors of the church. *Wow.* When he ended the prayer and she raised her head, she felt the stares focused on her. Well, to be fair, none of the regulars had ever witnessed her in prayer before. More than likely, it'd start a whole new thread of speculation and gossip. At least it'd be about something positive.

"We should probably discuss decorating your office," she said. That *was* the purpose of their meeting, after all. "Why don't you tell me some of your ideas?"

Jackson was even more attractive when a slow smile spread across his face, revealing a small but deep dimple on the left side. A similar smile framed by two dimples had been her undoing, so she should tread with extreme caution. This man jumpstarted her pulse unlike any man since Danny, and she needed to stick to business.

Pulling her notepad from her purse, Serenity listened as Jackson began to share his vision for a kid-friendly but functional office. "I brought most of the furniture I had in my Chicago office, but I need to update it. Throw some pillows on the chairs, a rug or two on the floor, liven it up. It's all pretty plain and boring, and that's why I need your help. The goal isn't to put my patients to sleep, but to stimulate their imagination so they'll be at ease and comfortable." He grinned. "I have animals, though. That's what saved me before."

Serenity raised a brow. "Animals? Are we talking live or inanimate?"

"Let's save that for when you visit the office."

"Okay. What are the floors made from?"

"They're hardwood. Oak, I think. Maybe maple. Sorry, I'm not sure."

She made a notation. "I'll take a look. Northern red oak was used in a lot of the buildings near where your office is located. Are the floors in good condition?"

"Seem to be," Jackson said. "It's not my intent to cover them up, but to enhance them or whatever."

In-between bites of cheesecake and sipping coffee, she posed her prepared list of questions. Jackson seemed at ease with himself and his world, as much as anyone she'd ever met. If he'd experienced heartache in his life, he'd buried it deep inside where no one could see it on the surface. He intrigued her. *Dr. Ross is a client. Don't start speculating on his personal life.*

Jackson lowered his fork and crossed his arms on the table. "After listening to me babble for the last ten minutes, I'd like to hear your thoughts for decorating my home-away-from home."

"If it's a second home, then maybe we should start with a portable cot?"

He ran a hand over his chin. She'd meant it to be amusing, but he appeared to take the question seriously. "Using my practice in Chicago as a guideline, it might come in handy. Sometimes I lose track of time and spend hours researching case histories, that kind of thing."

"Workaholic tendencies or an abundance of clients?" Serenity swallowed, hoping he hadn't taken offense. Should have stuck with her prearranged questions, her "script."

The muscles in Jackson's jaw twitched. "I prefer to call it attention to detail." Leaning back in the chair, he crossed his arms. "Your turn."

She glanced at the notes she'd taken. "I'm envisioning light, bright, fun and colorful." As she shared her ideas, Jackson nodded on occasion and made a comment here and there. From his remarks, he seemed pleased with the majority of her suggestions. The vertical line that surfaced between his brows clued her in to the ones he didn't particularly like, and she scratched them off her list.

"Sounds good," he said when she finished, "but I have a make-or-break question."

Her pulse escalated. "What's that?"

"Do you think you can find a giraffe for my office?" When her eyes widened, he laughed. "Strictly a cute stuffed animal. My first patient in Croisette Shores tells me it's a personal favorite, and I aim to please."

Serenity slowly eased out her sigh. If nothing else, this man would keep her attention. "I love them, too, and I'll get on it this afternoon." Wasn't a giraffe the mascot for a chain of toy stores? Later in the day, if she had time, she'd find the nearest location and get a giraffe. Going into a toy store might be a little difficult, but she'd manage somehow. Maybe she could convince Deidre to go with her.

"Great. I think we'll make a good team." Finishing his last bite of cheesecake, Jackson drained his coffee and those dark eyes met hers above the rim of his cup. "The coffee here is strong, but good. So was the cheesecake." Glancing around, he nodded at a few of the older men. "Seems there's a lot of local flavor in this coffee shop. If you're game and have time, I'd like you to take a walk with me."

She wiped the corners of her mouth with her napkin, wondering what was in his mind. "Now?" Where could he take her that she hadn't already been, didn't already know? She knew this town inside and out. From all appearances, it hadn't changed much since she'd been away. Croisette Shores hadn't changed much since she'd been *born*.

"I have a flexible schedule, and where I'd like to take you actually involves the project with you. Well, sort of. If you're not free…"

"It's not that."

"I assure you, I'm completely honest, above-board, and have no criminal record. Or no ulterior motive."

What prompted *that* speech? No way could Jackson know her personal history. Charlie knew plenty, but he was her friend and even orchestrated this meeting, so no, he wouldn't sabotage her. She liked Dr. Ross but didn't wish to diffuse any bombs so soon after meeting him. She imagined most women would jump at the opportunity to go anywhere with this man. The expectant expression on his face was rather endearing.

"All right, but only because you've made me curious. Can we get something settled first?"

He held her gaze steady. "Sure. Name it."

"Are you definitely contracting my services for the decorating job?" Standing, Serenity ran a quick hand over a wrinkle in her pale pink cotton top, not wanting to seem too eager. Her question probably gave her anxiousness away, as it was. If he was pleased with her work, he might be amenable to giving her a recommendation and referring her services to other professionals in Croisette Shores and the surrounding towns.

Jackson rose to his feet, a good three or four inches taller and—at almost five foot nine—she was no slouch in the height department. "Yes, you're *definitely* hired," he said. "Do you have the contract with you now? I'll sign it, shake your hand, whatever you want. I look forward to working with you, Serenity. After all, any woman who can appreciate my affinity for animals and not veto it on principle is my kind of decorator."

"I'll have my assistant deliver the contract to you tomorrow morning if you'll be in your office." How she loved saying that...*my assistant.*

"Great. I'm working out of Dr. Rasmussen's office while he's on holiday or until my office is ready. Do you think we can get it put together in the next couple of weeks, or is that pushing it? I don't want to rush you."

"Since you're keeping most of your furniture from your previous office, I don't see why not. And," she gave him a small smile, "you're not rushing me." Other things, yes, but no rushing was involved.

Jackson tossed a few bills on the table, more than enough for their coffee and the cheesecake, although Nancy told them she'd cover the cost of the dessert. If Sophia in the deli at McHenry's Market was to be believed, Nancy had gone through some tough times lately. Maybe Jackson somehow knew *that,* too, and wanted to repay her.

"Where are we going next, Doc Jack?"

His smile disarmed her. "Somewhere that might change your life."

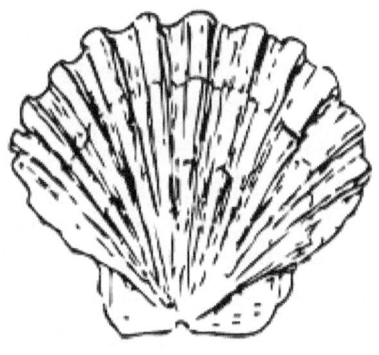

~CHAPTER 5~

Where is Jackson taking me?

Serenity appreciated how Jackson waited beside her chair as she stepped around the table and made her way toward the front door. She nodded at a few of the townspeople and exchanged a quick hug with a couple of the ladies. As she introduced Jackson, she tried to ignore the knowing smiles and once-overs from all directions. Jackson seemed to take it all in stride, but she wondered what he was thinking as they continued on their way to the cashier. Without a doubt, they'd be the subject of speculation by day's end. Aretha Simmons—*Old Persimmonhead*—sitting by the picture window, would make sure of that. An unkind nickname, yes, but the woman's head *was* irregularly-shaped, her lips puckered in a permanent state of displeasure.

She offered to pay her portion of the bill, but Jackson waved his hand in dismissal. "Thanks, but I'm a paying client, and that includes the initial meeting." The girl behind the counter was young, pretty and gave Jackson a flirty glance while handing over his change. Joining her a few seconds later, he opened the glass door and sent that bell jingling. If the patrons inside hadn't yet noticed their departure, the bell sounded the alarm. Through the years, many customers had tried to yank that bell away, but the owner insisted it stay.

"Nothing like being the subject of town gossip," Jackson said under his breath as they stepped outside in the bright sunlight.

"Welcome to small town living." Pulling her sunglasses out of her purse, Serenity positioned them. "It's not so bad once you get used to it. Which way?"

"Would you prefer to drive or walk?"

"Depends on how far we're going." Her new leather sandals were comfortable, but not for an extended walk.

"Only a few blocks. It'd be a shame to waste such a gorgeous day." He motioned to the right and fell into step beside her.

"How long have you lived in Croisette Shores?" she asked.

"All of four days. Didn't you see the headline in the *Croisette Shores Daily News* when I hit the town limits?"

That made her laugh. "Sounds like you've already got us pegged. Rest assured, someone's already digging into your background to find out if you're a long-lost descendant of Croisette Shores royalty."

Stepping ahead and pulling a low-hanging branch out of her way, Jackson arched a brow. "Royalty?"

Thanking him for his gallantry, she nodded. "Legend has it French royals discovered and settled our fair village in the mid-1800s. Somewhere along the way—no one seems to know when—the bloodline petered out. It doesn't stop people from speculating about a royal surfacing here again someday."

Jackson chuckled. "Sounds fun, but if I *was* descended from royalty—which I'm not—I'd prefer to keep my life private. The life of a royal would be too burdensome, don't you think? Now, if you'll excuse me, I'll go bring around my yacht." He might not be royalty, but the man had a devastating smile.

She laughed. "Right. I think you'll discover soon enough the people here are loyal to their own."

A small gust of wind whipped hair across his forehead as they walked. She liked how the sun brought out highlights in his hair and it curled on the ends. Danny had curls like that, and she'd always loved them. Even though Jackson possessed a casual, friendly air, he also projected an air of easy sophistication. This man would probably be equally at home in a tuxedo—brushing elbows with the elite at one of town's charity galas—or casual on the beach.

"Tell me."

Serenity snapped to attention, but she tried not to be obvious about how distracting she found him. "We might annoy each other to the point of nausea sometimes," she said, choosing her words carefully, "but deep down, the people are here for each other in a heartbeat. Loyalty means something."

Jackson slid his hands into the pockets of his khakis. "I have to ask, are you speaking from personal experience?"

She slowed her steps, as measured as her thoughts. "The answer to that one could take a while." No way could she tell him she'd run away because she'd felt claustrophobic in Croisette Shores. Pity and too many stares could do that to a person, no matter how well-meaning the intent.

"You're a puzzle, Serenity McClaren."

If only you knew. Because he was a psychologist, he'd probably embrace the opportunity to unravel the mysteries in her life and try to fit the pieces back together. But no, finding the answers was something she needed to figure out for herself. What would be the point of bringing someone else into the tragedies of her life? It served no worthwhile purpose and she wouldn't—she *couldn't*—impose that burden on anyone else.

The image of the note popped into her mind. Well, at least *one* other person knew the truth or wanted to help her find it. It's not like she could post a want ad in the paper or make the rounds, asking what anyone might know.

Averting her eyes from the intensity of his gaze, Serenity forced a lightness into her tone. "What exactly did Charlie tell you about me?" Surely Charlie wouldn't have blabbed her secrets.

"Confession time. He told me you love cherry cheesecake."

"And I thought it was a lucky guess."

"He also told me you beat the boys in kickball in first grade. Outran them all. You're also uncommonly smart and won the South Carolina statewide spelling bee when you were in the eighth grade."

"Sixth grade, but I don't know how smart I am."

"Something Charlie didn't tell me was how humble you are," Jackson said. "Tell me something else he *wouldn't* know."

Clever man, he'd turned the conversation around to suit his purposes. "I don't spill my deepest secrets to anyone I've only known an hour, even if you *are* a psychologist and a paying client." Her *first* paying client, but who was counting?

"I'm not asking for deep secrets. I figure if we're going to work together, Serenity, we might as well be friends. I'll tell you one about me."

"I'm listening." He'd stated his case well, although they didn't technically *have* to work together. Basically, he'd tell her what he envisioned for his office and she'd take care of seeing those needs realized. But no, her first client wanted more.

"I play the piano," he said, breaking into her thoughts. "I'm spectacularly terrible, but I try. That's got to count for something, right? Your turn."

Sticking with musical instruments should be a safe enough topic. "I play the saxophone. Or I did in middle school."

"Really? I would have pegged you more for a flute or clarinet player."

"How so?"

"Most of the saxophone players I've known are big guys who blow a lot of hot air on a regular basis. You seem more...delicate, for lack of a better term."

I'm not as delicate as you might think. "Here's one," she said. "I stink at navigation. Even with a map, I can't find my way out of a paper bag."

"Do you have a GPS?"

"Yes, but we have a love-hate relationship." She darted around an overgrown tree encroaching the sidewalk. "Another reason to love Croisette Shores. Not much changes around here, and I know where everything is. I was a mess in Atlanta, but it didn't help that every street downtown was named Peach something-or-other. Don't city planners know that confuses people?" Engrossed in their conversation, she hadn't noticed they were nearing the fringes of her old neighborhood. Stopping, she looked around in dismay. "This is the area of town where I grew up. My dad still lives in the old homestead a few streets over. Why are we here?"

Stopping beside her, Jackson nodded to the left. "The playground."

Immediate sadness engulfed Serenity when she followed the nod of his head. "It's so rundown," she said, removing her sunglasses. How could the disrepair of one of her favorite childhood places change her life? Taking a steadying breath, she dropped her purse on the ground and lowered into one of the swings. She pulled on the chain and bounced a couple of times, testing it. Thankfully, it seemed sturdy and strong enough to hold her weight.

"I'd like to rebuild this playground." Jackson dropped down into the swing beside her, grimacing at the rusty iron chains. "Meaning this is a two-project offer, if you're willing."

This is a surprise. "I've never heard of decorating a playground before."

"In this case, it's helping with the selection and placement of the equipment, colors to use, that sort of thing."

"So, you want me to take care of the esthetics while you take care of the logistics?"

"Right. I'll take care of getting the permits, licenses and other legalities if you'll help me with the rest."

She hesitated. "Need I remind you, I'm an interior decorator, not an...exterior one. I'm not sure what a project like this would involve. Have you talked to the town engineer and planner?"

"We've been in preliminary talks and there's an initial planning meeting set up in Town Hall at the end of next week."

"Then I'm sure they'll be able to give you all the direction you need."

"Okay, I'll tell you another thing about me." Jackson blew out a sigh. "I stink at fundraising, and I was hoping you'd be willing to help."

Ah, there it was. The bottom-line reason he needed her for this project. The thing Jackson couldn't know was it intimidated her. "I'll tell you another thing about *me*," she said. "I'm not the best with people." She hesitated. "Interior decorating allows me to work one-on-one for the most part. I like that." Pushing off from the ground, Serenity started to swing and Jackson followed suit.

"I saw the way the locals in the coffee shop watched you today," he said. "They admire you, and I'd venture to say they're protective of you. Kind of brings that fierce loyalty you mentioned into play."

She pondered his comment as they passed each other on the swings. "I think rebuilding the playground is a very worthwhile project, Jackson, but the obvious question is, *why* are you doing this? Isn't it enough to move to a new town and set up your practice? That'll take a huge chunk of your time, as it is." He kept pace beside her on the swing, but Serenity slowed, not putting much effort into it as her mind worked overtime.

Surprising her, he chuckled. "I like to get involved and plug into projects as I see the need. Obviously, the need is here. If I find I'm getting in over my head, one thing I do very well is recruit."

"I can see that. But where did you come up with the idea for renovating the playground? Surely you weren't walking around this neighborhood and stumbled upon it?" Stopping her swing, she lightly kicked a piece of broken pavement with her foot to reinforce her point.

"Actually, Charlie mentioned it to me." Jackson stopped beside her.

"I see." Charlie had been busy. "I've known Charlie as long as I can remember," she said. "When did you meet him?"

"A couple of days ago. He stopped by the office to leave something for Doc Rasmussen. We got to talking and ended up having lunch together. He's a great guy with a wealth of wisdom." He made a "V" with two fingers and positioned them between his brows. "It's all in the eyes, you know."

"Good assessment, and I completely agree. Charlie retired from his accounting practice a few years ago. I'm sure you could recruit him for the playground renovation, too."

Jackson's grin was slow and easy. "Already done. He's the one who suggested I ask *you*."

"Let's look at this objectively." Serenity caught his curious glance as he passed by on the swing. "You hardly know me and vice versa. Why would you invest such an important job in a stranger?"

"First of all, we're not strangers since we've shared cherry cheesecake and conversation. Secondly, I've already hired you to decorate my office, an equally important job. The way I look at it? It's *trust*. You've proven yourself intelligent, articulate and you come highly recommended from a trustworthy source. What more could I want?"

"Thanks, I think." She frowned.

"Sorry. That might sound clinical, but what I'm trying to say is, I think you'd do a great job, and I'd rather get started sooner than later."

"In a town like Croisette Shores, with its galas and charity events, there's plenty of people far more qualified to help in your fundraising quest." Plenty of *women* would trip all over themselves to help this man raise just about anything.

"That might be true, but I'm asking you *first*. It's your job to turn down, Serenity. Because you grew up in this neighborhood, I thought you might want to help and you'd certainly have more of a vested interest. Listen, I know you're busy getting your own business going, and I don't want this to be a burden to you. I'll pay you a consulting fee for your time. We'll get a group of town citizens together to form a committee, and you'll more or less help me coordinate the effort. Plus, it'll be spread over a period of almost a year before the playground is operational. If you turn me down, I'll understand. Disappointed, but I'll understand."

She held up one hand. "You're pretty good at heaping on guilt, too, it seems." First Dad and now some guy she barely knew. "I'm not saying no. I'd love to help out my old neighborhood, but this is...unexpected. All I ask is that you give me a couple of days to think about it."

"Fair enough. You're hired to decorate my office and you promise to consider the playground project. Whatever you decide, I'll pay you well for your expertise and your time. Deal?" He offered his hand.

Hesitating only a moment, Serenity put her hand in his. As she suspected, it was warm. Strong and manly, like his voice, his laugh and seemingly everything about him. "Deal."

When she started to withdraw her hand, Jackson held on tighter. From the spark in his eyes, it's like he could see inside her soul, as crazy as it seemed. Danny could never "read" her the way this relative stranger could. What a scary thought. Was she an open book? No, more like Dr. Ross could see past the façade and delved straight into her deepest insecurities and vulnerabilities. For years, she'd kept so busy that she'd fallen into bed from exhaustion every night. In large part, doing that very thing became her manner of survival. This man was her client and she needed him, but it'd be much easier all the way around if they kept any relationship between them strictly business.

"Serenity, I sense—"

Withdrawing her hand, unease swept through her. She didn't want him making conclusions about her personal life. Better to cut him off now. Aware he watched, Serenity pushed her foot on the ground to start the swing. "Do you make a habit of sharing personal conversations with women you've just met? Or is it the psychology thing kicking into high gear?" That sounded harsher than she'd intended, but it was too late to retract.

Jackson stopped his swing and reached to stop hers. She didn't protest and he waited until her swing stabilized and slowed. "I was going to say I'd be honored to pray for you."

"Oh." She shot him a sheepish glance. "I've never shared cheesecake, deep conversation and swings with a practicing, praying psychologist. Bet you can't swing as high and fast as me," she said, digging her foot into the ground to gain a solid push, feeling childish.

Beside her, Jackson mirrored her actions. "The one minute challenge has begun. This I can do, but don't challenge me in a spelling bee. That's another thing I don't do so well."

"Only if you can spell l-o-s-e-r," she said, laughing, as she passed him. Silly, yes, but he seemed to like it. He was also gaining on her, but being lighter and a few inches shorter, she had the distinct advantage. She'd always loved the swings as a kid. It freed her, and her inner child emerged as she giggled. Leaning back in the swing, she soared higher and closed her eyes.

Not long after, Jackson whistled to gain her attention. "You win."

Serenity felt the seat beneath her shift precariously to one side, and she cried out as she lost her grip. Her fingers slipped down the chain, and she was powerless to stop her fall, landing in a heap in a rather unladylike sprawl in the dirt a few seconds later. With dust swirling around her, she struggled to pull down the hem of her skirt, thankful it wasn't twisted around her waist. Of all days to wear a skirt and sandals, it had to be today. Still, it could have been so much worse. Small consolation.

Jumping off his swing, Jackson rushed to her side, kneeling on the ground beside her. "Don't move. Does anything hurt?" When she burst into laughter, his expression registered surprise.

"Only my pride. If you don't mind, please help me sit up and recover what's left of my dignity."

"I'll do you one better." He plopped down in the dirt beside her, flat on his back, waiting while she recovered her breath and shaky composure. "Let me know when you're ready to get up so I can keep you steady and make sure everything's...intact."

Serenity deep-breathed a few more times. "Ready."

Sitting up, Jackson held out one hand and she allowed him to pull her to her feet beside him. She took a tiny step backward when he put both hands on her elbows, steadying her. His presence, his nearness and all that masculinity radiating from him was unnerving. Why did her first Croisette Shores client have to be this incredibly mannerly, caring man? And why was he looking at her cheek? She brought a hand to her face. "May I ask why you're staring at me? Do I have dirt smudged on my face?"

"A little...right here." Jackson brushed the pad of his thumb over her left cheek. "Better." He dropped his hand. She dusted off her skirt and righted her blouse while he did the same with his khakis and polo. "I'm glad you weren't hurt."

"I'm hardier than I look, but I'm not sure if it was better or worse that I was on the uphill climb. Not bad for a girl whose middle name is Grace, huh?"

Jackson's gaze fell on her and the admiration she glimpsed shot up more red warning flags. Oh, he was handsome. This couldn't be good.

"Only one thing better than a beautiful woman." When she didn't take the bait, he smiled. "A woman who knows how to laugh and find the joy in life. Remember, the offer's on the table if you ever need someone to listen, Serenity Grace."

She raised her chin. "In spite of appearances, I don't need a hero, Dr. Ross."

"Ah," he said, "now we're back to the formality. Come with me, please."

She groaned. "Client or not, you're exhausting me. I think I've seen—and done—enough for one afternoon." She was still trying to recover from his compliment.

"All I want is to escort you to your office or wherever you're going next, if that's allowed."

"If you answer one question." She started walking and he fell into step beside her.

"Ask away."

"Exactly how will renovating this playground change my life?"

Her mistake was glancing over at him to see his quirked brow and that dimple surface. "Well, for starters, it got you here, didn't it?"

Oh yes, this man was *dangerous*.

~CHAPTER 6~

*T*aking a deep breath, Serenity climbed out of her car, locked it and approached the outside stairs of the old stone church in the center of town. Why was she so nervous? The words of her friend, Andrea, in Atlanta came to mind. "The church isn't a scary place, Serenity. It's bricks, concrete, wood and mortar. The people inside? Well, they're supposed to encourage and build you up, but sometimes they won't. It's sad, but it's a fact, so tune them out if they have their own agenda. Keep your focus on Him and you can't go wrong. *He's* the reason you're there. Worship Him. Sit and breathe. Allow His peace to fill your soul and let all that blessed grace and mercy flow over you."

You can do this. Placing one hand over her stomach, Serenity deep-breathed a few more times as she slowly started up the stairs. Growing up, she'd only visited this church—one of three in Croisette Shores and the one with the biggest congregation—on occasional holidays. Neither of her parents were church-goers, although Mama was raised in one. Somewhere along the way, she'd rebelled, but she'd never shared the details with her.

Dad always called Grandma and Grandpa Wells Bible-thumpers and holier-than-thou. She didn't see them much, but she'd liked them and they'd seemed perfectly normal to her. It's not like they tried to shove Jesus at her or spouted Bible verses at the dinner table or during random moments. Now they were gone—thankfully before her mother's disappearance or that alone might have killed them—and her dad's parents passed away when she was very young. Serenity couldn't help but wonder what Grandma and Grandpa Wells would think if they could see her now as she climbed another step, bringing her closer to the opened front doors of the church. Maybe her grandparents *could* see her now. The Almighty Himself must be smiling. She hoped it wasn't wrong to think that way.

"You know I'm new at this, but I'm trying, Lord," she said under her breath.

"Serenity?" The voice was a bit gravelly and vaguely familiar.

She turned on the top step outside the church doors as a brawny, well-dressed man bounded up the concrete stairs, two at a time. *Spencer Walton.* Danny's nemesis in high school. The guy who'd played her for a fool and asked her out to make Kendall Robinson jealous. All it accomplished was to make Danny crazy out-of-his-mind, especially when she'd admitted to harboring a big crush on Spencer. What girl hadn't? Silly high school stuff that seemed so life-and-death important when she was sixteen.

Like most of their classmates, Spencer had moved away after graduation. Most couldn't get away fast enough. The same age as Danny, he'd been a year ahead of her in school. From all outward appearances—the shiny leather shoes, well-tailored suit and expensive-looking watch—Spencer had done quite well for himself. He obviously kept in great physical shape as he reached the top step beside her, appearing not at all winded.

"Hi, Spencer. It's nice to see you again." She didn't know which one of them was more surprised to see the other on the steps of the church, of all places.

"Same here. You look incredible, Serenity. My dad mentioned you'd moved back to town." Spencer's appraisal was none-too-subtle before the megawatt, high school quarterback grin emerged. Some things never change, but gone were the dark curls the girls used to drool over, replaced by a stylish, shorter cut. Tall and confident, Spencer was more attractive than ever. Considering a lot of women found the scruffy, unshaven look sexy, Serenity surmised his day-old stubble must be a concession to the lopped-off curls.

"Are you visiting your dad and stepmom?" she asked as they moved into the front vestibule and accepted bulletins from the greeters. Seeing Spencer reminded her that his mom, Doreen, had succumbed to cancer while she'd lived in Atlanta. A sweet woman, she'd always had a kind word for everyone and volunteered to help with a lot of school functions. His dad, a retired cop, was a quiet man. The cops and firefighters shared a longstanding rivalry, and while her dad and Ed appeared friendly, an underlying tension always existed between them. But unlike *her* dad who preferred living in the past, Ed Walton had chosen to move on with his life. Not that remarrying was necessarily the answer, but at least he'd taken a step forward.

"Listen, I'm really sorry about Danny, your mom and…everything you went through." Appearing awkward, Spencer shoved his hands into the pockets of his fitted dress slacks and the muscles in his jaw tightened. "To be honest, I'm surprised to see you back here again." Five years must have brought about this new-and-improved, more sensitive, grown-up version of the former high school jock.

"Thanks. I'm doing okay. Croisette Shores is my home, so here I am."

The beginning chords of the organ wafted through the half-closed doors, inviting them into the sanctuary. Spencer offered his arm. "Care to share a pew?"

"Sure." She looped her arm through his and gave him a smile.

Halfway down the aisle, Spencer stepped aside, waiting for her to be seated. As she sank onto the soft cushions, Serenity tried to ignore the whispers. She should be used to tongues wagging by now, even in church, but it bothered her. Spencer glanced at the bulletin and pointed out names of former classmates. They sang the opening praise choruses and shared a hymnal for "Blessed Redeemer." Bowing her head during the morning prayer, Serenity prayed for her mother if she still had life and breath in her, her father's health, her decorating business, Deidre and Wes and their kids, Danny's family who'd moved away before his untimely death…

The pastor's voice broke into her thoughts as he began the morning message. As she listened to his words and the passages of scripture, Serenity's thoughts wandered, making it difficult to focus. Pastor Tom broke into her thoughts with a question, "What are *you* doing with God? Are you pushing Him away, like Peter and so many others, effectively denying you even know Him, much less have any kind of personal relationship with Him?"

Serenity closed her eyes as she pondered those words. *Dear Lord, I pray others in the town, and especially Dad, will see a difference in my life.* She didn't know much scripture, didn't know much about the Bible, didn't know the "right" God-speak or whatever people in the church called it, but she'd given her heart to Him when she'd lived in Atlanta. Accepting Andrea's invitation to church was one of the best things she'd ever done. The way she looked at it, He'd chosen *her.* He'd found her among the ruins of her life and lifted her from the ashes. Even as she cherished that thought, she feared if she talked too much about it, she'd prove herself ignorant and somehow that new, fragile faith would slip away like most everything she'd considered precious in her life.

She snapped to attention with the pastor's challenge near the end of the service. "I want to encourage you to share the love of the Savior by *showing* others that love. It's amazing what a well-placed, kind word can do. Share fellowship with others who share the love of the Lord, but if someone doesn't know the saving grace you've experienced through Christ, then invite them to breakfast or share a slice of pie and a cup of coffee and tell them about the hope you have of walking with Jesus in eternity one day."

Her thoughts strayed to Jackson at the mention of sharing a slice of pie. The doctor was obviously a man of faith. For all she knew, he might be sitting in this very congregation. *Not the time. Focus.* She concentrated on the pastor's message.

"It could be a store clerk here in town or a visitor you meet on the beach. Take a walk with them and really listen, offer biblical counsel if needed, give them a book, even a Bible." He waited while a soft ripple of laughter floated through the congregation. "Get to know them better and try to do one thing toward furthering the Kingdom. After all," Pastor Tom said, "it's what our Lord commands us to do. Sometimes it takes baby steps. Brow-beating people over the head will turn them away from the truth, but being their friend and meeting them where they're at in life is often the best way to demonstrate Christ's love in action. Now, it's *your* turn."

After the closing hymn and benediction, Spencer leaned close, his voice low. "All in the spirit of furthering the Kingdom, how about I take you to lunch at Rosario's? We can relax over some good Italian food and get reacquainted."

Without a doubt, it was an interesting but self-serving interpretation of the pastor's message. Karen Gorham chose that moment to swoop her into a hug, immersing Serenity in the overwhelming scent of pungent roses. "Serenity, honey, it's great to see you here today! Please give Clinton my best, and tell him we'd love to have him visit us some Sunday morning." Before she could react, the woman moved on to greet someone else.

From what Deidre told her, the widow Karen had made it known around town she harbored romantic inclinations toward her father, but Serenity knew he'd never look at another woman in a romantic way. No, he preferred to pine away for her mother. It was a toss-up whether to be proud of Dad for his faithfulness to Mama or be irritated he couldn't move on with life in general. Moving on with his life would entail admitting Mama was gone and having her declared legally dead, something he'd never do. Several others greeted them on the way out the door as they shook hands and shared a few words with Pastor Tom.

"I don't believe I heard your answer." As he reached the bottom step, Spencer turned, waiting. She imagined he wasn't the type of man to be turned down by many women. Since she needed to eat, what could be the harm?

Glancing at her watch, Serenity noted she should have enough time for lunch before picking up her dad for their promised trip to the beach. "Sounds good, but I need to be somewhere in a couple of hours. I'll take my car and follow you." Climbing into her silver Toyota Prius, she pulled her seat belt over her lap and clicked it in place. As she started the car, she glimpsed Jackson talking with Hayley Foster on the church steps. She bit her lower lip and tried not to stare. The man apparently worked fast. Or else Hayley did. Maybe it was a spontaneous, mutual attraction thing. If Dr. Ross wanted to talk with one of the prettiest and available single women in town, why should it bother her?

Problem was, it did.

Drumming her fingers on the steering wheel, Serenity startled when a black Mercedes pulled alongside her and the driver tapped on the horn. Although she couldn't see the person behind the wheel through the dark-tinted windows, she knew it was Spencer. Motioning for him to lead the way, she pulled her car out behind him, all the while resisting the overwhelming urge to peek in her rearview mirror.

"*I* hope you'll agree to dinner with me on Wednesday night. I'm thinking The Black Oyster." Spencer pulled a cloth from his pants pocket and wiped a smudge from the door of the sleek Mercedes.

Serenity leaned against her car, opposite his, in the parking lot outside Rosario's. "How long are you staying in town?"

"Long enough, if you'll go out with me. I'd like to get to know you again." Using the cloth, he buffed the smudge to a high shine. Did the man carry a car-buffing cloth at all times? She tried not to smirk.

In the past, Spencer hadn't known her as anything more than a momentary distraction. Spencer was direct and to-the-point and—as far as she knew— wasn't trying to make another woman jealous this time. But The Black Oyster? Located by the waterfront, it was one of the swankiest restaurants in town.

Pocketing the cloth, Spencer tilted his head and light gray eyes bore into hers. "Are you already seeing someone? I heard something about a new shrink in town. Talk around town is you two were getting cozy at Martha's the other day."

Serenity turned her head and blew out a sigh. "You should know not to believe everything you hear, Spencer, especially in Croisette Shores. 'Getting cozy' was nothing more than sharing cheesecake and coffee. Dr. Ross is a child psychologist and my client." For a woman who prided herself on keeping her personal life private, it seemed she'd freely offer information to any attractive man who asked these days.

"Dinner sounds wonderful," she said. As soon as the words were out of her mouth, she regretted accepting his invitation. Even if it wasn't a date, she hadn't been out with a man in so long, she wouldn't know what to wear, how to act, what to say. Other than a few random outings to the beach or to the movies in high school, Danny was the only man she'd ever dated. All at the ripe old age of twenty-five.

Running a hand over her hair, Serenity glanced away, trying to push the image from her mind of Jackson sharing food with Hayley the former prom queen at this very moment, those brown eyes probing the depths of the pretty brunette's soul. A very single and available soul. But neither was she going to dinner with a former school acquaintance because she wanted the news to get back to Jackson. Heavens, if she did that, how would it be any different than

Spencer using her to make another girl jealous in high school? They weren't in high school anymore.

"Excellent," Spencer said with a wide grin on his way-too-handsome face. "Wear something fabulous."

That comment struck her as territorial. Warning flag. "Spencer, if we have dinner, it's nothing more than a trip down memory lane." She flinched. "Sorry if that sounds rude, but I don't want you to harbor illusions of anything more. It can't happen."

Something flickered in his eyes, but he nodded. "Understood."

Serenity started to climb in the Prius, but she hesitated. "I'm not living at the old house with Dad. My house is over on—"

Spencer's smile grew broader and he winked. "I know where you live. I'll see you at seven on Wednesday."

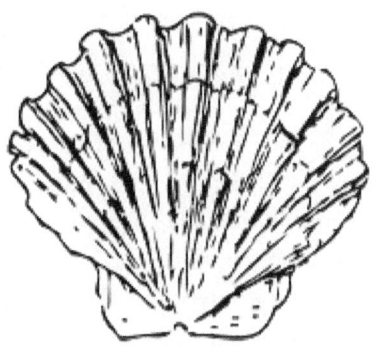

~CHAPTER 7~

*F*orty minutes later, Serenity and her dad made their way across the beach. As usual, tourists and locals alike wandered up and down the shoreline while others sunned themselves or flirted with the gently lapping waves in the low tide. Although they hadn't quite reached their familiar section of the beach, she wasn't sure her dad could walk much further without exhausting himself. She stopped. "How about we set up camp here?"

Clinton nodded. "Seems as good a place as any." As she suspected, he sounded a bit winded.

"Serenity!"

Her heart skipped a beat as she and her father both turned. Sure enough, Jackson waved and gave her that blinding smile as he approached.

Beside her, Clinton chuckled as she waved to Jackson. "In town a few weeks and you've already got a man?" Raising one hand, he shielded his eyes and squinted. "Wait a doggone second. Is that the doctor?"

"Yes, it's the doctor, but he's certainly not my man," she said, making a big show of putting down her oversized tote bag and cooler, staking their claim on the small area of the beach. "At least not in the way you mean. He's my client. Big distinction."

"Yeah, right. Be a good girl and put that pretty smile on your face," her dad said under his breath. "Don't want you to be a hermit like your old man. One in the family's enough."

She resisted moving her hand to her hip. "That's exactly why I got you out of the house. But matchmaking? I didn't know you had it in you." Patronizing yes, but she didn't expect him to push her at a man.

"I'm not dead yet, and I can tell when a man's interested in my daughter."

"You can tell all that by the way he's walking over here? Besides, he was with Hayley Foster this morning in church."

"He was probably just chatting with that Foster girl. She's attractive enough, but she can't hold a candle to my girl. And, from what you told me, you were chatting up that Walton boy. Doc Jack looks harmless enough and there's nothing wrong with a little friendly conversation."

Reaching them, Jackson smiled, the ends of his hair curling in the ocean breeze as it'd done during their walk to the playground. She'd liked it then, and she liked it even more now. His hint of a dimple winked at her and flecks of warm golden honey danced in those incredible eyes. With bare feet, swim trunks and his shirt unbuttoned halfway down his chest, Jackson must have every woman on the beach drooling. *Lord, have a little mercy.* Serenity averted her eyes when all she wanted was to stare. Her thoughts unsettled her but served as a reminder why she'd stayed away from men in recent years, especially unbelievably attractive ones.

Her dad grunted, and Serenity snapped to attention. "Dr. Dad, this is my Clinton Ross." *Oh joy.* "I mean..." She opened her mouth, but what more could she say? The damage was done.

"Mr. McClaren." Having the good sense not to look at her, Jackson stepped forward and extended his hand. "It's an honor to meet you, sir."

Clinton gave Jackson the once-over. "So, you're the new guy in town." He darted a quick glance at her as he shook Jackson's hand. "Doctor, huh?"

"I'm a psychologist, yes."

"Which means you're pretty smart." Clinton jerked a thumb in her direction. "Figure this one out yet?"

Shifting from one foot to the other, Serenity's cheeks burned as she sank further into the sand. If she was blessed, it'd be quicksand. The end would be quick and she wouldn't suffer. Raising her face to the sun, she closed her eyes and willed her father not to spill all her secrets or make her humiliation worse than it already was.

"Serenity decided I needed some fresh air and color in my cheeks," Clinton said. "She treats me like an invalid. Her mama's a nurse, so I guess she comes by the nurturing honestly."

Opening her eyes, Serenity caught Jackson's curious glance. She surprised her father by planting a quick kiss on his cheek. "Be good," she whispered.

"Seems to me your daughter has your best interests in mind, sir."

Clinton laughed. "Now you sound like a politician. Diplomatic. Well played, Doc. You and I should get along fine."

The two men talked while Serenity pulled the portable beach umbrella from the tote. All over again, Jackson's ability to make friends easily impressed her. When he offered to put the umbrella together, she willingly handed it over and watched as he assembled it in a matter of seconds, securing it in the sand while she prepared the folding chair for her father. "I'll get you a can of iced tea, Dad. Would you like one, Jackson?"

"Well, sure he would," Clinton said. "The way he's looking at you, girl, he's not going anywhere soon. Where's that other chair, Doc? Pull up a seat and let's get acquainted."

What was *with* everyone and their comments? Turning aside, Serenity tried to hide her embarrassment as she dug two cans of iced tea from the cooler. From the corner of her eye, she saw Jackson pull the other chair from the tote and put it together. She popped the tab on her dad's can of tea and handed it to him. Perhaps he was right about her treating him like an invalid. But he had no one else, and he certainly wasn't taking good care of himself. When she handed a can to Jackson, the warmth in his voice with a simple thank you was enough to get her heart pumping.

Pulling her dad's hat from the tote, Serenity tugged it down over his head, making sure to cover the tips of his ears. "Don't want to forget this." His once thick, naturally blond hair was thinning on top and she didn't want his scalp to get sunburned.

"I have the umbrella, girl. That's enough shade." Yanking the hat from his head, Clinton tossed it across the sand.

"You stay put and I'll go get it," Jackson said, handing back his can of tea before jogging across the sand. Retrieving the hat, he stopped to chat when someone called out a greeting.

"That man runs like an athlete," her dad said. "Firm handshake, too."

"I suppose," Serenity said, her thoughts scattered as she dropped into the chair beside him. She'd also noticed a faded scar running horizontally across the length of Jackson's right knee. Whatever caused it must have been very painful. Snapping her gaze away from Jackson, she refocused on her father. "Dad, when Jackson comes back, please don't embarrass me."

"Don't you worry about that," Clinton said, lowering his voice as she settled in the chair beside him. "I tossed that hat to give us a second or two. I've got a plan. Give me a few minutes with the guy and then I'll conveniently pretend to fall asleep. Ten-to-one he'll ask if you want to take a walk." He ignored her quirked brow. "You look very fetching today, girl, and he's a blame fool if he doesn't ask."

"All this and an actual compliment, too? Thanks." His words warmed her more than he could know. Ever since she was a little girl, she'd sought her father's approval. Her mother's, too, but that was probably a moot point now.

Spying Charlie further down the stretch of beach with his granddaughter, Serenity scrambled out of the chair low to the sand. Jackson jogged back toward them and she motioned for him to sit down beside her father. "I'm going to say hi to Charlie and Maya. I'll be back in a few minutes," she said, handing him the tea.

"Give them my best," Jackson called after her, and Clinton murmured his agreement.

"Sure thing." Serenity adjusted her oversized, floppy hat and strolled toward her friends.

When she spied her, Maya waved and squealed a greeting she couldn't quite make out, carried away by the sound of the surf. Dropping her grandfather's hand, the child flew across the beach toward her, arms opened wide. Serenity's heart swelled with love tinged with the familiar aching sadness as she dropped to her knees. Maya flew into her embrace, wrapping her small hands around her neck and burrowing into her.

This child had no idea what a soothing balm she was for her weary soul. Sharp twinges pinched her heart as she hugged Maya closer. What would it be like to hug her son like this? Born only a month after Maya, Liam would be a playmate and good friends with this adorable child. It's what she'd always hoped.

Serenity tightened her hold for a few seconds before releasing Maya. "How's my favorite girl in the whole world?" Pulling out of the hug, she laughed as the youngster planted a sloppy, wet kiss on her cheek. "I need to catch up on my Maya love. Let me get a good look at you. You've gotten so tall!" She smoothed her unruly spiral curls with one hand.

"You look pretty, Miss Serenity. Like a real princess." Maya appraised her with sparkling eyes and a dazzling smile minus a front tooth. She'd inherited the height and light brown skin of Charlie's son, Ray, and the mesmerizing green eyes and lighter hair from her mother, a devastating combination.

"Thanks, sweetie, but *you're* the prettiest princess in Croisette Shores by far." Serenity tilted the child's chin with one hand. "Someone's lost a tooth."

"Yep." Maya grinned at her grandfather. "I put it under my pillow and got a whole dollar."

Serenity smiled. "The tooth fairy sure is a lot more generous than when I was your age. Did you buy something with it?"

"Nah. Mom says to save it since a dollar won't buy much these days. I need to put it in the bank."

"Your mom's right. Tell you what. Have her bring you by my office tomorrow morning, if she can." She tweaked Maya's nose. "I have a birthday surprise for someone very special." She made a mental note to buy some paper to wrap the sundress and hat she'd found at a local consignment shop, brand new with tags from an expensive designer still attached.

"For me?" Maya's eyes sparked with excitement. "Oh look, it's Carly!" Waving to another girl making a sand castle a few hundred yards away, Maya looked up at her grandfather. When Charlie nodded, she took off with a quick wave. Her long curls trailed behind her as she ran, the picture of a happy, carefree child.

"Maya's such a beautiful child," Serenity said before glancing back at Charlie. "She's put the sparkle back in your eyes."

"That she has. Maya inherited Marcela's spirit and sense of adventure. She fills my soul." His wife had been gone almost a decade, she of the flowing, colorful caftans, gold bangle earrings and exotic beauty. More than that, she'd radiated a joy from within. Serenity heard the deep emotion in Charlie's voice and squeezed his hand before releasing it. He angled his head to where Jackson and her father were engaged in a lively discussion. "From the looks of it, they're getting along well. I understand my favorite decorator's working with the good doctor." The corners of Charlie's lips upturned.

She appreciated his attempt to lighten the mood, but gave him a mock-pout. "I'm not looking for male companionship, Charlie."

His laugh was rich and hearty, another thing she'd missed. "I'm talking about helping you get started with your business, child. You can't tell me you're going to turn down a paying client."

"No, and thank you. I'm most obliged."

Charlie's broad smile sobered. "Have I told you how glad I am you're finally back home, Serenity? Back where you belong?"

For a half-second, Serenity considered asking her dear friend if he'd written the note, but something held her back. "Yes, a few times."

Charlie darted another glance Clinton's way. "He's missed you more than you know."

Kicking up sand, she nodded. "I know, although sometimes he has an odd way of showing it." Following Charlie's gaze, she couldn't stop her grin. "At the moment, I'm hoping it wasn't a major mistake leaving Jackson alone with him. That could spell trouble."

"You know your dad. Clinton's not always big on showing his emotions, but it doesn't mean they're not there. Just means they're below the surface." He smiled as Clinton gestured with his hands and Jackson's laugh carried on the wind. "He held out hope you'd come home sooner or later, and I can see you're already doing him a world of good. If I know him like I think I do, he's singing your praises to the doctor."

"Perhaps," she murmured. "I'm worried about him. He won't let anyone else take care of him. Either that or he runs them all off with his ill manners and sour attitude."

Charlie's dark eyes met hers. "I think he did that on purpose, too, as a way to get you back here. And here you are."

"We both need closure, Charlie. Until we know once and for all what happened, neither one of us will be completely free." She lifted her shoulders. "Problem is, I don't have the first idea where or how to look for answers."

"Free in what way?" Charlie tilted his head, watching her closely.

She had a feeling he already knew but wanted to hear it from her. "I need to find that peace that passes all understanding the Lord promises."

Charlie's face brightened and a grin stretched his mouth wide. "You've finally met Jesus, have you, child?" When she nodded, he opened his arms and gathered her close in a bear hug, dislodging her hat and knocking it to the sand. She felt the low rumble of his rich chuckle. "Praise God. I've been praying a long time. And my Marcela's surely rejoicing in Heaven with this news." He kissed the top of her head and smoothed her hair. "And God bless that angel out there somewhere who led you to our precious Savior."

How she loved this man. "I've missed you so much, Charlie." Leaning her head on his massive chest, Serenity blew out a long breath. "Thanks for praying for me even when I didn't know I needed it."

"That's one of the best things about praying for your loved ones, honey." Charlie lifted her chin with a gentle hand. "It's a privilege and an honor. We have a great and merciful Father who graces us with exactly what we need, including bringing special people in our lives. When I lost my Marcela, the Lord knows I wanted to die in her place, but God showed me how blessed I was to have her in my life, no matter for how long. Now, your dad? Well, he's stuck between the knowing and the not knowing, and that's a mighty tough place to live." Charlie's dark, expressive eyes were full. "Mark my words, the Almighty's working miracles in your life, and you need to be open to embracing them."

"The Lord's working miracles in *my* life, Charlie? That's really what you believe?"

"Sure as I know you're standing here with me on this beach. Joy follows suffering, and I want to be here when you find your joy, your peace." Lifting his face to the sky, Charlie raised his arms. "And, oh, what a day of rejoicing that will be!"

He'd loved and lost...and survived, just as she had. She knew Charlie thought of Liam, the same as she did. In his all-too-brief day of life, Liam had settled in her soul. In their well-meaning way, people told her she'd marry again one day and have more children. But "more" was only a number, a word that couldn't mean the same thing. Although precious, no child could take the place of, or replace, her son.

Swallowing her tears, Serenity nodded. "I hope you're right, Charlie." Looking out over the distant horizon, she pushed aside long strands of her hair from her cheeks and her long, white cotton skirt swirled around her ankles. "I need to find out if Mama's still breathing somewhere on this planet. I want to know more about how and why Danny was murdered." Retrieving her hat, she turned back to him. "I need to find out what really happened the day Liam died. You're right about the not knowing part. It's what makes it so difficult to sleep and truly rest, you know?"

Love for her was etched into Charlie's weathered but still handsome face, nearly stealing her breath. A face filled with incredible hope and steadfast faith. "I'm here to help, if you need me, child, and I'll keep on praying." His gaze strayed over her shoulder and he chuckled. "I think there might be another reason you were meant to come home now, too."

Serenity shook her head with a small smile. "Did you not hear what I said before?"

Taking her by the elbow, Charlie walked beside her. "I did, but the Lord also knows what you need. Look to Him and you'll find your answers, child. *All* of them." Putting his arm around her, Charlie squeezed her shoulder. "And cliché or not, I'm gonna pray they'll finally set you free."

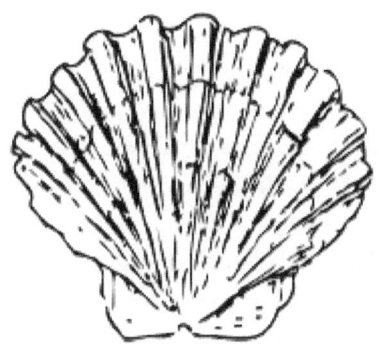

~CHAPTER 8~

*L*ate on Tuesday morning, Serenity sensed movement outside the picture window of her outer office. She smiled when she spied Jackson, half-hidden behind a tall, robust potted plant. Returning her attention to the message she was writing to her assistant, Kelsie, she tried to focus.

Jackson opened the glass front door a minute later and strolled inside. "Greetings, my lovely decorator. Where should I put my office-warming gift for Inner Serenity? Great name for your business, by the way. Clever." Surveying the small office, he nodded as if in approval. The sleeves of his pale yellow cotton shirt were rolled to his elbows, and he wore it open and loose over a white T-shirt. Well-worn jeans, no socks and tennis shoes completed today's version of dressed-down casual. No man wore it better.

"Thanks." Scribbling the rest of the message to Kelsie, Serenity stuck the bright pink note on the computer screen. "What a beautiful plant. It'll definitely liven up the place. How about putting it next to the chair and table?" She pointed to the side wall. "I think it'd look great over there."

"Sounds like a plan." Following her suggestion, Jackson lowered it to the floor.

She could tell he hadn't bought the plant in the anemic floral department at McHenry's. Sure enough, a glance at the familiar logo on the tag told her it came from Lefevre's Nursery the next town over, known across the region for their award-winning arrangements.

"Why didn't you tell me you might need some help unpacking boxes?"

"What little Croisette Shores seagull told you I might need help?" No doubt Charlie had something to do with it.

"Oh, I don't know. I thought I saw a notice in the *Croisette Shores Daily News*." Amusement surfaced in Jackson's dark eyes.

"I certainly hope not, but I'm pretty sure I can't afford your rates. If you insist on sticking around, fair warning, I *will* put you to work."

"I'm sure we can come to terms," Jackson said as a smile lifted the corners of his mouth. "Oh, wait a sec." He dug into the pocket of his jeans and pulled out a folded piece of paper. "Sorry it's not in pristine condition, but here's your signed contract. You'll notice I added an addendum at the bottom since you've agreed to help with the playground. By the way, have I told you how happy I am about that?"

"I think you just did." Unfolding the paper, Serenity glanced at the bottom where he'd handwritten—scrawled, really—but she could still read the words, "Secondary project: Beacham Street Playground." He'd listed more than generous terms of payment and signed it.

"Thank you," she said, putting it on Kelsie's desk. "I'll sign it before you leave and give you a copy. I feel silly asking you to sign a contract, but..." She'd probably negate the bottom portion of the contract at some point, anyway. In good conscience, how could she accept payment for help with a project meant to benefit her old neighborhood?

"No need to feel silly," he said. "I completely understand. Business is business." He cocked his head to one side and peeked around the corner into her office. "Is that Mozart coming from what I assume is your office?"

"Why, yes, it is. Name the symphony and I'll give you a gift."

"Haven't a clue, but come on, you've got to give me *some* credit for the recognition factor."

"You're right. Let me go get your gift."

"Seriously? I thought you were joking. Should I close my eyes?"

"If you want. And, for the record, it's Mozart's Symphony Number Five in G Minor, a must for all Mozart lovers."

"I like it," Jackson called after her when she walked into her office. "This part's light and fun. Makes me feel like we should be in a ballroom and dancing the pirouette or whatever they danced back then."

Smiling, Serenity grabbed the bag Deidre had dropped off earlier that morning. Jackson stood in the middle of the outer office, eyes closed, a goofy grin on his face. Pulling out the stuffed giraffe, she held it up. "Okay. You can open your eyes now."

He laughed as he took the giraffe from her. "This is great! Thanks. My patients will love this little guy. What shall we call him?"

"Why don't you let your patient who likes giraffes name him? And you can thank my friend, Deidre. She ran to the toy store yesterday and picked him up."

"I'll do that," he said. "You want to go with me sometime to get more animals to populate my small zoo? After all, we can't leave...the giraffe-with-no-name all by his lonesome for long."

"As long as you're not like Noah and need two of every kind," she teased.

"I'll be sure to keep that in mind." Jackson's smile was irresistible, and she needed to be strong and not surrender to her inclination to spend a lot of time with him even though he was her client. Especially because he *was* her client. Then again, if Jackson needed her help, who was she to resist?

"Let me check my schedule," she said. "I'm sure we can work something out."

"Great. Now, time to put me to work. Where shall I start?" Jackson rubbed his hands together. He motioned to the boxes lined up in front of Kelsie's desk and arched a brow. "Want me to open some of those?"

"It's not like I have a U-Haul to unload," she said. "It's only a few boxes of things Dad's kept at the house. He figured whatever's in these boxes will give my office character and infuse it with my personality...or something like that." She stopped when she realized she was rambling. "I'll start on this one." She motioned for him to open another one. Sliding scissors down the middle seam and opening the flaps of a cardboard box, Serenity pulled out bubble wrap and newspaper filler and tossed them to the floor.

Turning a smaller box around to read the label, Jackson raised a brow. "Princess Serenity Keepsakes?"

Her gaze dropped to the box. "Dad used to call me that."

"Have you been holding out on me?" Jackson's eyes widened. "You're one of those long-lost French royals, aren't you?"

She waved her hand as if in dismissal. "Thou shalt not mock Her Royal Highness lest thou risk being separated from one's head." Rolling her eyes, she smirked. "Wow. I make a terrible royal."

Jackson laughed. "Don't most dads call their little girl princess?"

Serenity tried not to stare as he removed his shirt. The T-shirt beneath it was form fitting and showed off his muscles to full advantage. *Why am I thinking such things?* "I wouldn't know, but sand castles are involved in my story. Might as well go ahead and open it." She averted her gaze and nodded to the box at his feet.

"I have no idea what's in them," she said. "Dad made me promise not to look until I brought them here." She blew out a breath, wondering if she should open the boxes in private. "It could be fun, but it could also prove a nightmare of untold proportions. Anything you open is at your own risk, and *you* might be the one needing a shrink."

Jackson chuckled and tugged a pocket knife from his jeans, hesitating with it poised in mid-air. "I'll take my chances. If it's too personal, I won't intrude. Say the word."

"No, it's okay," she said, motioning for him to continue. As she unpacked desk supplies from her box, she kept one eye on him as he split the small box down the middle in one swift motion. That one contained knick-knacks but she paused a couple of minutes later when she saw him open a wide, flat box marked *Fragile. Handle with care.*

When Jackson removed the bubble wrap, unearthing the treasure beneath it, her breath caught in her throat. She remembered the day that photograph was taken. A framed, medium-sized black and white photograph, it depicted her mother blowing a dandelion toward the five-year-old version of herself. Elise's long, blonde hair fell in soft waves over her shoulders. Joy was written in every nuance of her face, mirrored by Serenity's expression as she reached toward the sky. She loved the crispness of the image. The eye was drawn to the subject without the distraction of color. The photographer had captured a spontaneous, whimsical and tender mother-daughter moment. She remembered the day like it was yesterday.

Oh, Mama, where are you?

Taking the photo from him, Serenity moved one hand over her heart. The reality of how much she'd missed her mother was as sharp as a physical pain. "I haven't seen this in a long time. It used to hang in my parents' bedroom and I always loved it." Her father did, too, but it must have been too much for him to face it on a daily basis.

"You look a lot like her." Jackson glanced up at her. "She's beautiful."

"Thank you. She is—was." She caught his compliment but ignored it, not sure how to respond. "Mama won a few beauty pageants when she was a teenager before she decided it was more cool to be anti-establishment."

Jackson turned the frame over, inspecting the back. "Elise and Serenity. No year listed, but I'd guess you were about six or seven?"

"Five, actually." She ran one finger across the glass. "She always spoke in a firm voice, but beneath it all, she was very loving. Her skin was soft and smooth and smelled like honeysuckle. Sorry, you probably don't care about things like that."

"Sure I do. *You* care about them, so that makes it important. Where do you want to hang it?"

Shaking her head, a pervasive sadness settled inside her. "I don't. I know it's not the mature thing, but I can't, Jackson. Seeing this only reminds me how much I miss her. My memories can't bring Mama back from...wherever she is, and I'm not sure I could face this every day. It'd probably be counterproductive." It was the first time she'd admitted to anyone else the very real possibility that her mother might be dead.

"If you want to share more about her, I'm willing to listen," Jackson said.

"You don't always have to play the psychologist role, you know."

It was his turn to ignore her comment. "I'll put it over here for now." He propped the framed photograph against the wall. Picking up the pocket knife, he opened another box as she sorted through small containers of more miscellaneous desk supplies. When he asked her where to put certain items, she pointed to her office or Kelsie's desk.

They worked in silence for a few minutes. Finally, she blew out a breath. "Okay, here's something for you. Mama loved pears." She hated using past tense, but it was becoming more natural. Pushing the thought aside, she focused on Jackson.

His lips twisted in a grin. "Pears? You mean like the fruit?"

That made her smile. "No, like the basketball team. Yes, like the fruit. They were on her apron, bordering our dishes, painted on the drinking glasses, the clock... Everywhere you looked, there they were. Happy little pears with smiley faces, dancing pears, you name it." Raising her hands, Serenity danced her fingers through the air. "They were ridiculous but still kind of cute. She limited them to the kitchen, thank goodness. I think Mama knew Dad would overrule them anywhere else in the house. Even though he'd never admit it, I think Dad found them sort of endearing, too."

"Well, everyone needs a...hobby." Jackson's grin deepened, and the hint of his charming dimple made its appearance. "Tell me now, do you share a similar fruit obsession?"

"No," she said with a return grin, "believe it or not, that's one area of my psyche that's remained remarkably sane."

"Now see? You've got to stop saying things like that." Jackson surprised her with the sudden firmness in his tone. "You're more well-adjusted than most people I know, Serenity. Trust me on that one."

Dropping to the floor, he patted the carpet beside him. "Come and sit with me. If you have time, I'd like to hear more."

She eyed him for a long moment. Revealing more of her life would strengthen the bond already developing between them. Surely Jackson must know that. It's the way it always worked. Problem was, could she tell him about Mama without everything spilling over?

"I don't bite. Promise."

"Jackson, I..."

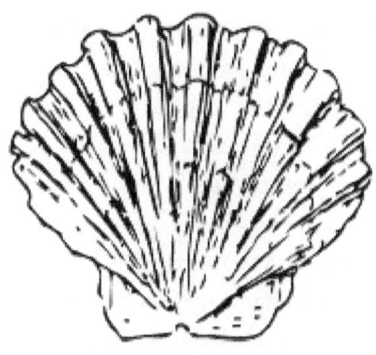

~CHAPTER 9~

I have no willpower whatsoever.

Serenity sat facing Jackson, both cross-legged on the floor of Inner Serenity. "Mama was eccentric, but that was part of her innate charm."

"Exhibit A, a predilection for anything pear-related," he said, chuckling when he caught her glance. "Sorry. Zipping my lips. I'm all ears. Speak to me."

"When all the other moms showed up at school in their normal mom clothes, Mama breezed in with her long, flowing broomstick skirt, halter top, flip flops and long, dangly earrings. She didn't wear much makeup, but she liked to wear lipstick so shiny you could see your reflection in it. Mama refused to wear a jacket in the colder months. The thing is, she rarely got sick or caught a cold. Said it had something to do with the immunity she'd built up working in the hospital."

"What else?" Jackson leaned his chin on his hand, elbow resting on one knee. He appeared genuinely interested in hearing her memories. Serenity hoped he'd return the favor sometime and tell her about *his* family. Other than that he was from the Chicago area and raised in a privileged family, she didn't know much.

"Mama taught me to crochet and how to cook some of our family's favorite dishes. She taught me to say please and thank you. We went on fun trips every summer. My parents wanted to make sure I understood the history of my country, so we toured Philly and visited the Liberty Bell and the Betsy Ross House, exhausted all the museums in Washington, D.C., rode to the top of the Empire State Building, visited the Gateway Arch in St. Louis, walked the Freedom Trail in Boston..."

"They sound terrific," Jackson said.

"They were," she said. "They never missed a parent-teacher meeting, and were right beside me making school projects—active volcano, Indian pueblo and the Alamo included—and helping with Girl Scout field trips. They were very hands-on and involved, not overbearing in any way. Dad used to tell me firefighters don't always follow the rules, and he seemed proud of that fact." The corners of her mouth upturned. "He was daring and a risk taker, my brave, strong daddy willing to take on the world for me or my mom." Her eyes misted and she glanced down at her lap, overcome with emotion.

"Mama always took me to the beach on Friday mornings during my summer breaks. The only time she missed was when there was a bad wreck on the outskirts of town and she got called to the hospital to help in the ER. She never told me about it, but I found out later there was a six-year-old girl killed by a drunk driver. Things like that affected her deeply, when she saw firsthand the devastation of the family left behind. She got very involved with MADD after that and was the president of the local chapter. I always admired her passion and regret not telling her. At the time she disappeared, they were planning a big MADD event, and that's one reason I think she might really be gone."

She ran a hand across her brow. "She wouldn't have left them in the lurch, and she'd never willingly devastate her family. I can't imagine anyone wanting to hurt her, and she and Dad were happy. They had a good marriage, a lot of good friends. That's what makes what happened so hard to accept. She didn't seem unhappy or depressed. We were very close, and I think I would have suspected something wasn't right. Even more than me, I'm sure Dad would have known."

For two seconds, she thought about showing him the note tucked in her purse. But what would be the point? No sense in dragging Jackson into the quagmire of her life. She needed to do this on her own and she'd already said more than she'd intended. "Maybe there's something to this psychology thing," she said. "I managed to get through all that without shedding a tear."

"Thanks for sharing," Jackson said, rising to his feet. Holding out his hand, he helped her do the same. "I promise you, it gets easier."

"I guess it does. Time can be a gift from God sometimes. So can the people He brings into our lives. Thanks for listening, Jackson."

His smile was as gentle as his voice. "Agreed." In that moment, something changed between them, something so vivid it was almost tangible. By sharing about her mother, she'd allowed him more access to her life. Perhaps more surprising, she'd *wanted* to share her memories with Jackson. Was it possible she'd only known him a few days?

As they continued their work, Jackson told her he'd toured the local historical society museum, enjoyed a cup of Sally's Famous Lemonade from the cart set up by Queen Victoria's Park and sampled seafood down by the waterfront. She appreciated his lighthearted approach to their task.

"Who do we have here?"

Serenity turned. A wide grin creased her lips when she spied the ceramic giraffe resting on Jackson's palm. "Arnie! I've missed you, my old friend." She reached for the yellow and brown animal with its ridiculously long neck, misshapen legs and irregular spots.

Jackson chuckled. "Arnie was wrapped in enough bubble wrap to preserve a mummy. Someone highly valued this little guy."

Running her hand over his smooth, shiny back, Serenity smiled. "No matter how hard I tried, I couldn't get his legs right and finally sculpted Arnie sitting down, as you can see. I made him in Mrs. Jutz's third grade art class, and I gave him to Mama for Mother's Day. I labored over this project and wanted him to be perfect. Obviously, I didn't achieve perfection."

"Probably because perfection's not possible," Jackson said. "I'm sure your mother loved it because you made it and she knew you tried your best." Taking it from her, he turned it upside down and studied the inscription. "I love you, Mama."

"Funny how we automatically look to the back or the bottom of things, isn't it?" she said. "It's like seeing the date somehow validates it." After he handed Arnie back to her, Serenity perched him on Kelsie's desk.

"It helps keep things in perspective, I suppose. You're right although I never thought about it that way before." Jackson's expression was thoughtful.

"Would you consider loaning Arnie to me? I'd like to take him to my office for a couple of weeks."

"Let me guess. You want to show him to your patient who likes giraffes?"

"Exactly. This particular patient isn't your typical kid. I think he'll appreciate Arnie."

She handed him over. "Sure, you can borrow him, but you have to promise to take excellent care of him and return Arnie in his original, imperfect condition. He's getting quite old, after all." She grabbed some of the discarded bubble paper from the floor and gave it to Jackson, observing as he wrapped it around the giraffe.

"Promise. You know, that's another thing about kids that I love."

Serenity shook her head. Keeping up with this man's thoughts would be a challenge. "You lost me. What do you mean?"

"Most kids don't see things as imperfect. That's a fault reserved for adults. Kids see them as they are, at face value. For instance, I guarantee you my patients will look at Arnie and they'll see a really cool, sitting giraffe, not an animal that's misshapen."

"That's because kids are much better about accepting people with physical deformities or issues," Serenity said. "A good example of that happened yesterday, as a matter of fact."

"Yeah?"

"I went to lunch with Charlie's granddaughter, Maya, and her mother. There was a girl in a wheelchair in the restaurant. She had a prosthetic leg. Maya slid out of her chair at one point and talked to her. When she got back, Charlotte—her mom—asked what she'd said. The first thing Maya asked the girl? 'Does it hurt?' How many adults would think to even *ask* something like that?" Serenity shook her head. "We're too wrapped up in our own lives"—she paused to consider the irony as she glanced at Arnie entombed in the bubble wrap—"and we don't ask the simple but most important questions."

"A lot of people have compassion, but they've been sensitized through the years and don't feel comfortable discussing someone else's pain. Ever consider psychology as a career?"

"No," she said, wiping away a stray tear, embarrassed. "If anything, I belong on the other end of the spectrum."

Jackson tilted his head and stepped closer, making her pulse erratic. His eyes searched hers. "Does it hurt, Serenity?"

She managed a small smile, marveling how this man seemed to *know* her already. How was that possible? "Let's save that discussion for another day."

"Fair enough. How about I empty a couple more boxes and then take you to lunch?" he said. "Jackson, not that I don't appreciate your help, but I'm afraid I won't get much work done with you around."

"I'm helping a friend and I disagree. We're getting a lot done here. Only two more boxes left, by my count." Crouching beside another box, he glanced her way as he opened it. "You artfully evaded my question, you know. Seems you have an uncanny knack for doing that. It's quite a talent."

An involuntary shiver ran through her. "What question? I'm sure I don't remember."

"Cold?"

Jackson's powers of observation were equal parts unnerving and wonderful. She crossed her arms over her mid-section.

"Give me one good reason," he said.

"You're being obtuse again. A reason why I'm cold?" With Jackson in the same room—pretty much the same town, hemisphere or planet—no way she'd be cold. What she didn't want to do was explore the reasons why.

"A reason why you can't, or won't, have lunch with me. And the words 'paying client' aren't allowed. Wait a minute." He raked his hand through his hair and gave her a sheepish grin. "That sounded a whole lot better in my head." The look on his face was so little-boy cute she melted a little more inside. "Bottom line? If I have to, I'll fire you."

She gasped. "You wouldn't!"

"I might." He didn't flinch.

"Just to get me to go to lunch with you? That's extreme, don't you think? Coercion isn't seemly, Dr. Ross. Neither is pushiness."

He chuckled. "I haven't heard the word 'seemly' used by anyone younger than eighty, but what do you say we discuss it together over a meal?"

Picking up a ball he'd fashioned from used strapping tape, Serenity tossed it at him. Jackson laughed and dodged it. "You're as bad as Deidre in being relentless until you get what you want, aren't you? Remind me never to get you two in cahoots."

He laughed outright at that one. "Cahoots? Serenity, you're absolutely priceless."

"You're making fun of me now? Maybe I'll quit and then you can fend for yourself with decorating that office of yours. Better yet, I'll withdraw the offer to loan Arnie to you."

"You didn't offer, I asked. Big difference."

Oh my goodness, you're flirting. Stop that!

Seeing the look on his face, she raised one hand. "If you care anything about me, you'd know firing me could destroy my professional reputation in this town. Don't forget we have the playground project, too. I can't believe you'd even suggest such a thing." She blew out a mock sigh. "You're impossible."

"Well, you're right about one thing, Ms. McClaren. We couldn't have that. The professional reputation destroying part." He rubbed a hand over his chin as if contemplating all the available options. The gleam in his eye should stop her but only served to encourage her.

"I don't need you to humiliate me, Dr. Ross. I've already done that fine on my own. I'm trying to get a fresh start here. Have a heart." This conversation was absurd but wonderful.

"Oh, I definitely have a heart," Jackson said. "It's making itself known right now, as a matter of fact."

Serenity's heart pounded as he moved closer. *What's he doing?* She took a step backward.

Kelsie breezed through the door, bringing sunlight into the small office as well as some kind of light, fruity scent. "Howdy hey! Don't let me interrupt." She tossed her purse on the floor beside the desk. "You two are having way too much fun. This is a place of business and I need to get back to work. I have a boss who depends on me, you know?" Giving them an impish grin, she eyed the items from the boxes they'd stacked on her desk. "Guess you've been busy, but if you two kids want to get friendly, you'll have to take yourselves elsewhere."

Serenity glared at Jackson who appeared much too smug for her liking. "Now, see what you've done? Have you no shame?"

"Don't forget Old Persimmonhead standing on the outside looking in," Kelsie said with a grin as she angled her head toward the window.

Serenity groaned while Kelsie and Jackson exchanged amused glances.

"I guess that's what you get for having windows in your office," Jackson said.

"Not helping," Serenity said under her breath. "Who doesn't have windows? Without them, it'd be positively claustrophobic in this small of a space."

"We couldn't have that," Kelsie added.

This was weird considering Jackson said the exact same thing although the subject was different. Serenity looked from Jackson to Kelsie. "I take it you two have met?"

"Yeah, at Cup & Such," Kelsie said. "It's the happening place between seven and nine in the morning. You should come by and bring your dad sometime, Serenity. Jackson's starting a study group on Wednesdays with some of the high school boys, right Doc?"

"Right." For whatever reason, Jackson seemed a bit embarrassed.

"A *Bible* study?" Serenity said.

"That, too," he said. "Whatever subject they need help with, academic or otherwise. It's kind of an all-inclusive study group."

"Don't be surprised if the guys ask you a ton of questions and try to pick your brain," Kelsie said, settling in her chair. "They think it might help them understand girls with you being a psychiatrist and all."

"Psychologist." They'd simultaneously corrected Kelsie.

"Yeah, well, good luck with that," Jackson said, shooting her a grin. She felt like throwing something at him again.

"The good doctor brought in his signed contract, Kelsie." Grabbing a pen from the holder on the desk, she signed it. "I need you to copy it, give Dr. Ross a copy and start a new file, please. Then I need you to call Thompson Lighting about the lamps for his office. Oh, and we need to also contact Lewis Manufacturing for that ridiculously overpriced chair he wants."

Kelsie saluted. "Sure thing, boss. Give me a minute to warm up the copier."

Serenity turned to Jackson. "I can take it from here, but I appreciate your stopping by and your help with...Arnie and everything."

"Always happy to help you, Serenity." Stepping close, he lowered his voice. "Don't be too hard on Kelsie. She's a good kid and has your best interests at heart."

That stymied her. "Am I being hard on her? Kelsie's my employee and I need to keep her busy. She *was* a little impertinent, after all." She frowned. "Don't you dare make fun of that word. It's valid." She lowered her voice. "Did I really come across like a taskmaster?"

Jackson tweaked her chin. "A beautiful one."

She blew out a breath. "Must you keep saying things like that?"

"Yes, but if it makes you too uncomfortable, I'll try to stop." The sudden seriousness in his eyes told her he meant his words.

"You don't—"

"Here you go," Kelsie said as she came back into the room and handed Jackson an envelope. "I gave you two copies for good measure."

"Thanks," he said. "I'll see you later, Kelsie." Swooping the stuffed giraffe under one arm, Jackson headed for the door. "Maybe you should follow the tradition at Martha's Cup & Such and install a bell on your office door. You never know what riff raff might decide to drop by."

"Bye, Doc Jack!" Catching Serenity's stare, Kelsie buried her head in a spreadsheet.

Halfway out the door, Jackson gave her his easy and all-too-familiar grin. "So, I take it lunch is out for today?" A light flickered in those gorgeous dark eyes as she walked toward him.

"Maybe another time. I'll call you this afternoon once I find out the availability of the lamps and armchair."

"I see. Back to business. Fine. I'll look forward to hearing from you again soon." With a salute, Jackson departed.

Remembering Arnie, Serenity grabbed him from the chair and yanked open the door. "Wait a minute!" Jackson turned, brows raised, his expression one of pleased surprise. "Here." She hurried down the sidewalk. Catching up to him, she offered bubble-wrapped Arnie on her outstretched palm. "I can't think of a better home than your office. Keep him. The kids might like him." Thinking better of it, she pulled back her hand. "Forget it. I guess that's a dumb idea. Arnie's not very pretty..." Her voice trailed as Jackson slowly closed his fingers around hers.

"Thank you." He waited until she met his eyes. "Arnie was made with loving hands by a little girl for her mother, and kids can relate to that. I'll highly value him and I'm sure he'll become a favorite."

"Thank you," she said. "I'd really like that."

"I'll talk to you soon." With Arnie clasped in his hand, Jackson turned to go. She watched as he headed down the street, stuffed giraffe under his arm and whistling as though he hadn't a care in the world.

Going back into her office, Serenity paused. A woman stood on the street corner the next block over. That wouldn't be unusual except for the fact she was looking straight at her instead of watching Jackson like most women in their right mind would do. With dark, wraparound sunglasses and a white floppy hat pulled low on her head, it was impossible to see her hair color or guess her age. Tall and thin, she wore casual, white workout clothing—pants and a stretchy T-shirt and tennis shoes, also white. Perhaps sensing Serenity's attention, the woman turned and strolled in the opposite direction a few paces behind Jackson. She carried no purse or shopping bag. Although it could mean nothing, Serenity couldn't shake the feeling of unease.

"Well, that was fun," Kelsie said when she came back in the office.

"That's because Doc Jack makes anything fun. Don't you have some work to do?" Her mind spinning, Serenity headed toward her office.

Kelsie laughed. "I'm on it, boss. Thompson Lighting...looking it up now."

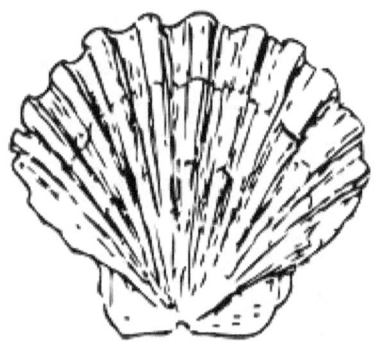

~CHAPTER 10~

*O*n Wednesday morning, Justin shifted in his chair. From the way he stared at the bookcase, Jackson could tell he'd spied Arnie. Scrambling down from his chair, the boy walked over to the bookcase and reached for the ceramic giraffe. Jackson expected Mrs. Johnson to stop him. Darting a glance in her direction, he noted her pinched lips and the set of her jaw although she remained silent.

The child stopped with one hand poised in front of the shelf and shot him a sheepish grin over one shoulder. "Doc Jack, can I please see your giraffe?"

"Sure thing. That's Arnie. Hold on a second and I'll get him down for you." Pulling Arnie from the shelf, Jackson handed him over.

"Be careful, Justin," Mrs. Johnson said. "That's breakable and it might be valuable to the doctor. He's got the bigger giraffe if you want to hold him instead."

"I promise I'll be careful. I like Arnie." The boy ran his hand over the smooth, shiny contours of the giraffe and circled his finger over one of the irregular brown spots. When he turned it over to inspect the bottom, Jackson smiled. "I love you, Mama," Justin read before handing him back. "Did you make this for your mommy?"

"No, but a very special lady made it for her mommy and she loaned it to me." Jackson wasn't sure why he used that term since Serenity more or less gave it to him. Still, she might change her mind and want Arnie back eventually since he obviously meant a lot to her. Several of his other patients had also noticed the giraffe. As Serenity had predicted, Arnie was a great conversation starter.

Justin tilted his head to one side. "What does *loaned* mean?"

Mrs. Johnson spoke up again. "It means his friend gave Arnie to Jackson to keep for a little while, but she wants him back sometime." Her voice sounded tight, bothered somehow.

Justin looked over at her as he returned to his chair and plopped into it. On this, their second visit, Mrs. Johnson again wore the oversized sunglasses that swallowed half her face. In her sleeveless dress, her thin, tanned arms revealed no external bruising or marks of any kind. The lift of her chin, the squared shoulders and proper posture spoke volumes. She didn't speak much, but when she did, she made intelligent comments occasionally laced with dry humor. When they'd arrived a few minutes earlier, Mrs. Johnson had handed the paperwork he requested to Mrs. Lange. He suspected the forms would be incomplete, but he'd deal with it. He was too intrigued by Justin and wanted to learn more.

"You always tell me I can keep what you give me," Justin said, frowning. He eyed the open bag of gummi worms on the desk.

"Help yourself." As usual, he fished out the cherry ones. Leaning his head against the chair, Justin tilted his chin to the ceiling and lowered one into his mouth. Chomping on the treat, he grinned at Jackson, his dimples deepening.

"So, what do you think of Croisette Shores?" Jackson said. "Do you like it here?"

The boy nodded with enthusiasm. "I like the beach. Nana got me a sand pail and we made a sand castle."

"That sounds like fun." Jackson's gaze slanted to Mrs. Johnson, but her chair was empty. "Excuse me a minute. Here, have another gummi worm. Or two." Strolling to the outer office, he glanced around the reception area. Mrs. Lange sat reading a book at her desk. Startled, she closed it with a guilty look. "It's okay," Jackson said to reassure her. "Mrs. Johnson disappeared. Have you seen her?"

Mrs. Lange pointed to the bathroom. "She darted in there a couple of minutes ago."

"Thanks." Deep in thought, Jackson grabbed one of the children's books from the small bookcase in the lobby. Returning to the inner office, he dropped the book in Justin's hands. "Why don't you show me how well you can read until Mrs. Johnson gets back?" Settling in the chair beside Justin, his thoughts were miles away.

The glance Justin gave him was equal parts confusion and smirk. "Why do you keep calling her that?"

Jackson leaned forward, elbows on his thighs. His pulse raced. "Because that's her name."

"No, it's not." The child buried his head in the book, but he peeked at Jackson with an impish grin.

This session was getting more interesting by the minute. Jackson swallowed hard, knowing he should stop and not take this conversation further. Mrs. Johnson made it clear from the outset she was to be in the room at all times during their sessions. No way could Justin know or understand it, but he'd thrown down the gauntlet and Jackson wasn't about to stop him now.

"She's my Nana, but her name's..."

"Justin, why don't you wait for me outside with Mrs. Lange?" Standing in the doorway, one hand on the door, Mrs. Johnson's face was drawn. Reminded Jackson of the time he'd been sent to the principal's office in grade school. But he'd done nothing wrong this time, unlike his childish prank in fifth grade. He met her gaze head-on, refusing to feel or act guilty.

"Our visit with Dr. Ross is over, but I need to talk with him in private for a minute."

Justin pouted. "But we've—"

"Now, young man." Her voice, although calm, was unyielding as Justin scrambled down from the chair.

Jackson watched in silence as she closed the door behind the boy. Walking around the desk, he motioned for her to be seated in the chair he'd vacated.

"No thanks, I'll stand," she said. "I'll get straight to the point. What gives you the right to question Justin when I'm not present?"

"With all due respect, I didn't ask. Justin freely offered the information." Since he probably wouldn't see them again, Jackson figured he might as well speak his mind. "Why did you leave the room? You set the rules and specified you were always to be present during our sessions."

Frowning, she crossed her arms and turned her head. "I should think that would be obvious."

"The session's only thirty minutes. Couldn't you wait?" That comment only made him sound like a jerk. "Sorry. I didn't realize you'd left the room and mentioned your name. Now that it's come up, we might as well discuss it. Are you denying you're Justin's grandmother?"

Mrs. Johnson released an exasperated sigh and uncrossed her arms. Walking over to the bookcase, she picked up Arnie and turned him in her hands, examining the bottom for a prolonged moment. "If I'm going to continue bringing him to see you, I want your word you won't try to pry information out of him. I don't want him upset."

Jackson bit back a sharp comment. "Of course, I'll give you my word. As long as *you* understand in my profession there's a fine line between prying and the inherent right to know. He wasn't upset in the least. Remember, you came to me and *he's* my patient, not you. If you don't want him upset, you might consider telling your grandson why you use a fake name."

She gasped. "That's none of your business!"

Jackson narrowed his eyes. This woman—with all her secrets and mystery—was his most unique yet difficult challenge. "I beg to differ since you've come to me for guidance. Dishonesty is annoying enough for adults but incredibly disingenuous when dealing with a child. Kids expect honesty and can slice through insincerity and lies faster than anything. It's not fair to them and they deserve better, especially from the people they trust."

The muscles in her jaws twitched. "Justin understands the reasons and they in no way affect what I've asked you to do for him."

"They definitely affect his past and it impacts our sessions as a direct result."

She seemed startled. "But it's your responsibility to help me deal with Justin's future, not his past. Isn't that correct?"

Jackson tried to contain his aggravation, not sure he succeeded. "We're going in circles here. Do me a favor, please. Would you please remove your sunglasses?"

In a sharp movement, she turned her head toward him again. "I hardly see how that matters."

"If you won't comply, then I want your word neither you nor Justin have been abused in some way."

She scoffed. "The answer to that is a definitive no. As you said, *I'm* not your patient, Dr. Ross. I'm equally sure I could bring you up on charges for harassment to whatever board oversees the professional ethics of South Carolina psychologists or mental health professionals."

"For simply asking you to remove your sunglasses and asking for reassurance you haven't been abused?" Jackson kept his eyes trained on her and crossed his arms over his chest. "I hardly believe that's a crime." To her credit, she didn't turn away, but a sudden urge seized him to yank those ridiculous sunglasses from her head. The desire to get a good look at her eyes was at the top of the list. Not to mention it'd also put her facial features into perspective.

"I don't think you'll file charges against me, and I'll tell you why," he said. "It's clear you're hiding your true identity for reasons known only to you at this point." Pushing out of the chair, he walked across the room. "For one thing, if you *do* file charges, your identity will be revealed and I'm pretty sure—based on your behavior—you'd like to avoid that. So, it's your call. Take your pick."

"All right." With a deep sigh, she replaced Arnie on the shelf. He wondered why she'd picked it up, what ran through her mind when she looked at the inscription on the bottom. "Justin likes you, so I'll continue to bring him here. You've earned his trust. I'd like you to start preparing him—mentally and emotionally—to reconnect with his...family."

"What can you tell me about them?" he asked.

"Why do you need to know?"

Again, Jackson tried not to show his aggravation with the guessing games she put him through, making his job that much more challenging. "I won't ask for actual names, but I'd like to know if they're aunts, uncles, grandparents or whatever. Can you tell me that much?"

After a moment's hesitation, she nodded. "Very well. Next visit."

"Fine. Does Justin know about these relatives?"

"Yes." The word was barely more than a whisper, so soft he had to lean closer to hear it.

"I have one more question for you," he said. "Why me? If you're in no hurry, Dr. Rasmussen will be back soon enough and he'll be practicing for another year before he retires."

"I should think that would also be obvious." Retrieving her handbag from the floor by her chair, she slung it over her shoulder and appeared prepared to bolt.

"It's not or I wouldn't have asked." He couldn't begin to second guess this woman.

"Let's just say I'd rather not involve Phil Rasmussen. And, with all due respect, why *not* you? You're not doubting your ability to help us, are you, Dr. Ross?"

Was she teasing him? Hard to tell.

"Fair enough. Just do me a favor and don't leave the office during our sessions. Save yourself some trouble and visit the ladies room before coming into the office, Mrs. *John*son." She was an intelligent woman, and he suspected the meaning of his thinly-disguised—albeit bad—pun hadn't escaped her understanding.

"We'll see you next week," she said, ducking her head and departing, but not before Jackson heard what sounded suspiciously like soft laughter. *Laughter?* He hadn't thought it possible.

Perhaps he was getting somewhere, after all.

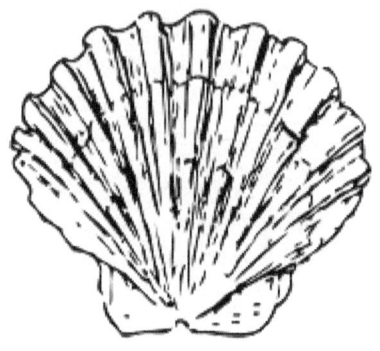

~CHAPTER 11~

"What's up with you and the most gorgeous child psychologist in the land?"

Serenity looked up from her paperwork as Deidre waved at Kelsie and sashayed through her half-open office door on Wednesday afternoon. "Don't you ever knock?"

"Why would I do that?" Deidre's deep southern accent dripped with affection as she sat down in the chair in front of her desk. "As your oldest and dearest friend, not to mention I'm now your landlord, I've earned certain rights and privileges. It works both ways, you know. Feel free to drop in at my office any old time you please. Knocking's not a requirement."

"Want some coffee or a cup of water? I got my new water cooler today." Serenity laughed. "Funny the things that make me happy these days. I must be getting old."

"Never. Fill me in, please. I need details about you and Dr. Ross-a-licious." She leaned closer, putting one well-manicured hand on the desk.

Serenity couldn't hide her grin. "Don't get your hopes up, Deidre. There's nothing to tell."

Deidre sat back in her chair, skepticism written all over her pretty face as her pink-rouged lips upturned. "Nothing, you say? That's not what I hear around town, girlfriend. The good old boys' club down at Martha's is laying odds on how long until your big wedding." Dressed in what must be the latest designer label, Deidre's hair and makeup were always perfect without looking overdone. In spite of appearances, she was one of the most down-to-earth, approachable women Serenity had ever known.

"Even if we *were* a couple, what are the odds on how long it'll take to get to matrimony? Oh wait, I should get pregnant first." Serenity cringed. *Ouch*. It was bad enough to think it, but she really should think before speaking her mind. "Sorry," she mumbled, embarrassed. "I'm trying to work on my sarcasm." Being around her crotchety father hadn't helped her disposition.

"Get over yourself, honey. You're not the only girl in the history of Croisette Shores to get pregnant before you were married and you won't be the last. It happens in the best of families. If you want me to start naming names, I will, and I'm sure some of them will shock you. *Shock* you! You loved Danny and you married him." Deidre's cheeks colored and she twirled a short dark curl around her finger. "I'm sorry. I shouldn't be bringing up the past."

"It's okay," Serenity said. "No sense in burying it. It's time to face what happened five years ago and try to make sense of it all."

"No luck in finding out who wrote that note, huh?"

Serenity shook her head. "You, me and the person who wrote it are the only ones who know. Since I started working, I haven't had time to think much about it."

"How many clients do you have now?"

"Four, including Jackson."

"Great! Now we're getting somewhere. Glad to hear you're on a first-name basis with the psychologist. That's a good start."

She ignored Deidre's raised brow. "Back to the note, please. You saw it, and it wasn't threatening in any way. Still, I can't help but wonder why the sender hasn't stepped forward to tell me what he—or she—knows."

A frown creased Deidre's brow. "Could be their motive was to get you back home and, if that's the case, their plan certainly worked. You're positive your dad didn't write it?"

"I'm sure as I can be. You should have seen him when I was at the house the other day. He was as sentimental as I've seen him since Mama disappeared. In-between all his raspy coughs and blowing out smoke, he was actually very sweet and told me he was glad I was back home even though he didn't know why."

"Didn't know why he was glad?"

"No," Serenity said with a small laugh. "Didn't know what brought me back home. That's how I know he couldn't have written the note."

Deidre brightened. "How about Charlie?"

"That's a possibility. I saw him at the beach Sunday afternoon and almost asked him then. I can't explain it, but something stopped me."

"What? God?" Deidre's question sounded so spontaneous and innocent, it almost made her laugh.

"I don't really know. Charlie and I had a nice talk and he told me he's praying for me to find my answers. Told me he's been praying for me a long time."

"Well, you know I'm generally not a praying kind of gal, but you can count on me to put in a good word." Scooting closer to the desk, Deidre's grin widened. "Not to change the subject, but it's time to tell me more about you and the handsome doctor." Deidre used to compare every guy to the men in her mother's romance novels, the ones she'd been forbidden to read but snuck under the covers and devoured anyway. She'd enlightened a number of the girls in their class, including Serenity, about the ways of the world and the facts of life. Only problem was, most of the guys they knew paled in comparison to the tall, chiseled and passionate yet sensitive men in those books. Deidre had always liked Danny, though. Likewise, Serenity adored Wes and she'd been Deidre's maid of honor in her wedding the year after they graduated from high school.

"Jackson's wonderful, and he's becoming a good friend. I thought about showing him the note, but I'm not sure if I should."

Deidre leaned her chin on one hand. "I'm listening."

"You sound like that radio personality with the saccharine, velvety-smooth voice that drives me crazy. Jackson's been nothing but kind. He's a complete gentleman, polite to senior citizens and kids and perfect—"

"Yeah, he's a real saint," Deidre interrupted, waving her hand. "I'm sure he's a friend to all mankind and animals, to boot. Not to discount those fine qualities, but is there any heat between you two? You know, the sizzling stuff that curls your hair and fogs your imaginary glasses?"

Serenity smiled. "I'll admit there's an attraction, but more than that, I like the way he looks at me, Deidre. It's like he wants to know everything about me. Jackson's sensitive, caring and has a great sense of humor. He makes me laugh and he really listens, you know? Like a friend and not just because he's a psychologist. Even though my history's not pretty, somehow I don't think it'd change his opinion or the way he treats me. For all I know, he *does* know my history since a lot of people in this town seem to have loose lips. Present company excluded, of course."

"Well, he's quite the man," Deidre said. "All that, gorgeous eyes, a head of hair most men only dream of, and muscles that won't quit. What's not to love?" Shifting in her chair, Deidre gave her a sly grin. "I haven't had the pleasure of meeting Dr. Ross yet, but I've seen him from a distance. I swear the man's like a magnet. Not to mention half the women in town are chattering about him."

"I'll be happy to arrange an introduction. Do your kids need a psychologist to help them cope with their mother?"

"Very funny. You know I believe my Wes hung the moon, but Jackson's got even old, blind-as-a-bat Mrs. Alston primping before church on Sundays. Cheryl Jenkins at the bank puts out extra mints at her station hoping he'll come over to her window. I heard Marcy Watkins actually shoved another cashier out of the way at McHenry's so she'd check out the doctor, in more ways than one. And then there's—"

"I get your point," Serenity said. "Jackson's the best thing to hit Croisette Shores since the last royal graced our shores. Whenever that was. For all I know, it's a fabricated legend, anyway."

"It's a fact and you know it or else all our teachers in grade school were seriously delusional. Don't get off topic, girlfriend." Crossing her arms on the desk, Deidre leaned closer. "Has Jackson asked you out yet?"

Serenity met her friend's intense blue eyes. "I need this job and Jackson's my boss, more or less. By the way, I'm working on another project with him, too. He's renovating the playground in my old neighborhood."

Deidre's brows rose. "The one over by Beacham Elementary?"

"The same."

"Well, that's quite admirable, isn't it? I've been expecting them to bulldoze that whole block. How are you going to help with the renovation? Are you going to play in the sandbox together? Now, *that'd* be fun."

Shaking her head, Serenity smirked. "You don't give up, do you?"

"No, but you should know that by now. Still, have I taught you nothing? It's really black or white. Either a man's interested or he's not. Either he asks you on a date or he doesn't." As always, Deidre used her hands, moving them up and down on an invisible scale, weighing the options. "When a gorgeous male specimen like Dr. Ross asks, you need to allow your basic instincts to guide you. I was thinking about a double date. You and Jackson, me and Wes. Dinner and dancing next Saturday night sounds about right. How about it?"

"Like I said, I work with the man, so I can't date him," Serenity said. "And I'm not about to ask him, either."

"So what? I'll ask him for you. Where does he live? Is he in the market for a house?"

Serenity gasped. "You wouldn't dare! Ask him on my behalf, that is. Even for you, that's bold. You'd actually pick up the phone and call someone you don't know and ask him to come to dinner?"

"Why not? I'm a realtor. We're not exactly known for being shy. I'm also on the Welcome Wagon committee in town. Which reminds me, I owe you a plant. Welcome home."

"They still have Welcome Wagon?"

The smile crossing Deidre's face was infectious. "Here in Croisette Shores we do."

"Thanks for the welcome, but I already have a lovely plant out front." Deidre didn't need to know Jackson gave it to her.

"I noticed, and it's lovely, but it needs a companion. So do you. Honey, consider going to dinner. Guaranteed you'll enjoy yourself. Who knows? If you wear a pretty dress and heels and smile at the man every now and then, you might even get a slow dance out of it."

"I couldn't dance before, so I doubt my talents have improved the last five years."

"So what?" This conversation was beginning to sound repetitive. "Half the male population can't dance. All Jackson needs to do is wrap his strong, manly arms around you, hold you close and shuffle his feet. Bottom line? We're talking about *dating*, Serenity, not finding a cure for cancer. Look, if you two were in lab coats, working side-by-side, where every teensy weensy little thing mattered and you could change the world—or possibly blow it up—by what you concocted in a test tube, you might consider holding off on romance. But this is an entirely different kind of chemistry, my friend."

Deidre moved one hand over her heart and deep-breathed in an exaggerated, dramatic way, a reminder why her friend had been the female lead in most of their school plays from the time they were in fourth grade. A dying Juliet had been her finest hour on the stage. "Give up the protests. For one thing, I know you like Jackson because your eyes light up every time I mention his name. I wish you'd admit it already."

Serenity fixed her with a hard stare. "Fine. I like him. A lot. Satisfied? But no dates. Final answer."

"Okay, fine. No dates, but promise me one thing. Please stop overthinking everything. Allow yourself to relax a little and *enjoy* life. You can't punish yourself forever."

Serenity shook her head. "It's kind of hard for me to do that. You, of all people, know that." The only blow-up they'd ever experienced in their long friendship was when Deidre accused her of "dumbing down" in order to make Danny look good. She had, but it'd been worth it. Sometimes you need to sacrifice for the ones you love.

Deidre's eyes softened. Reaching across the desk, she took her hand and squeezed. "I don't mean to be insensitive or disregard what happened, but you need to get on with your life. The way I see it, maybe Jackson can help you find out what happened to your mom. I guess all I'm saying is, try to be open to the opportunities that come your way and the people that come into your life. It's all for a higher purpose. Trust me on that one."

Serenity blinked back tears. "If I didn't know better, I'd say you've found Jesus, too."

"No, but keep working on me," Deidre said. "I have a feeling I'll come around. The kids have been asking some tough questions lately and I've found myself calling out to God a lot more these days. And I don't mean that in a flippant way, either."

Serenity tried not to stare at her friend. She'd been praying for her but also knew she couldn't push Deidre. Her parents had divorced when she was ten, and it was a bitter, drawn-out custody fight with her mom irrationally blaming God for her dad's infidelity. Some of that anger had spilled over into Deidre. Serenity's best hope was to be a good example of how God had worked in *her* life, just as she'd prayed in church. Sure, she didn't have all the answers, but did anyone? Jesus found *her*, so He could reach anyone. The key? Being willing to meet Him halfway. That's what she'd pray for Deidre.

"Here's the thing," Deidre said. "You can't do anything about your past. It's done. Over. Change what you can and make your future what you want. You started down that path by getting away from this town and moving to Atlanta. I missed you like crazy, but I think it's the best thing you could have done. You earned two degrees and, from all appearances, you managed to wrap your head around and survive circumstances that would have decimated most people. And somehow you kept your sanity and emerged stronger than ever. After what you'd been through, that's nothing short of a miracle. Look at you! How many women would have had the strength, moxie or whatever you want to call it, to even *do* something like that? Not many, my friend, mark my words. Call it God or call it whatever you want, but I happen to think it's pretty incredible. In some ways, you're like my...well, you're my hero—heroine."

Serenity wiped away a tear. "Thanks, but that's just it. I've spent so much time taking care of me that I think my heart needs time to catch up." She smoothed her hand over the rich dark wood of her new executive desk, the most expensive piece of furniture she'd ever owned. "I don't want to mess up Jackson's life." In spite of her best resolve, her eyes filled with more tears that threatened to overflow. "I have a way of somehow tainting or harming everyone precious in my life and I can't do that to Jackson. I just...can't."

Her words broke as Serenity surrendered to the emotion and burst into tears. So much for keeping it together. But even Jesus wept, so she was in good company. Still, what a mess.

"Oh, honey." As the waterworks started, Deidre grabbed the tissue box on top of the file cabinet. Tossing it on the desk, she ran around behind her, squeezing her shoulders. The cloying scent of expensive Chanel cologne enveloped Serenity. She'd always hated it but didn't have the heart to tell her best friend.

"Let it out." Pivoting the chair in a half-circle to face her, Deidre lifted Serenity from the chair and drew her into a warm, much-needed hug.

Through her tears, Serenity glimpsed Kelsie peeking around the corner. "Is, um, everything okay?"

Couldn't it be enough that Deidre had witnessed her mini-breakdown? Having Kelsie see her made her more miserable. Taking the tissue Deidre shoved in her hand, Serenity dabbed at her eyes. Her shoulders heaved with the force of deep, gulping breaths.

"She'll be fine, Kels," Deidre said. "Having a long overdue cry. I'll take care of her."

Serenity started to ask Kelsie to close her door, but what would be the point?

"Sweetie, listen to me." Plucking another tissue from the box, Deidre pressed it lightly beneath her eyes. "First order of business is to get you a tube of waterproof mascara. Look, I've been your best friend since forever and no harm's come to me because of my association with you. You didn't taint anyone or anything, but life happens. What I *know* is you're scared to open yourself to a possible new relationship, but—like it or not—you're a beautiful woman, and men notice you. And, I hesitate to mention this, but I heard from Spencer Walton's stepmom you're going to dinner with him tonight."

"This town's too small." Balling the tissue, Serenity tossed it in the trash can. "I also made it clear it's not a date. No expectations. A chance to catch up with an old friend. Well," she said, blowing out a sigh, "not even that. He caught me in a moment of weakness, I guess."

Deidre glanced at her expensive watch and moved back around the desk to grab her handbag. "I hate to leave, but I have a showing in thirty minutes. Will you be okay? I can reschedule my appointment if you want."

"Go. I'll be fine," Serenity said with a half-hearted wave. "Really," she said when Deidre hesitated.

"One last piece of advice? Jackson won't be your client forever. It's not like he'll need the ongoing services of an on-call interior decorator the rest of his natural born days. And *you* need to let someone love you."

"I love *you.*" The beginnings of a smile curled her lips.

Deidre paused at the door. "Not the same thing and you know it, girlfriend, but I love you, too. Always. I'll call you tonight."

Serenity sank back into her chair as Deidre blew her a kiss and departed. Staring into space, she pondered her friend's words. Fall in love again? No, thank you. What a scary concept. Sure, she liked Jackson. Liked him a *lot*. He was her client and friend, first and foremost, but Jackson belonged with a woman who could come to him freely without a sullied reputation and a dark past. Her heart heavy, Serenity attempted to get back to work, knowing it would be difficult to concentrate.

Just you and me, Lord.

*R*eading at home while eating leftovers, Jackson startled when his phone buzzed on the kitchen table beside him. He glanced at the screen and smiled before picking up the phone. "Hey there, Mr. Mathias. How are you this fine evening?"

Charlie chuckled. "Probably not as good as you. I hear you and Serenity hit it off well."

Jackson frowned. "If you're talking about our working relationship, yes. She has some great ideas and I hired her. Thanks for the referral." He didn't expect the defensiveness that crept into his tone. "Stop by the office again sometime and I'll take you to lunch."

"I'll do that, but I'm sure you know I'm talking about more than a professional relationship with Serenity."

In the short time he'd known Charlie, the man hadn't said anything without specific purpose or intent. "She told me a little about her mother. Pretty unbelievable story. I feel sorry for her although she'd hate it if she ever heard me say that."

Silence on the other end of the phone ensued for a few seconds before Charlie spoke again. "What exactly did Serenity tell you?"

Interesting. The old *tell me what you know before I slip up and tell you something you shouldn't know* technique. He'd employed it often enough in his practice to recognize it in others. Or his analytical mind was working overtime like it usually did.

"Jackson? You still there?"

"Yeah. Sorry." Moving into the living room, he collapsed on the sofa. He extended and flexed his leg, grimacing at the moderate pain. His knee was tightening up again, and he needed to find a physical therapist soon. "She told me what you might expect." If Charlie could be cagey, then so could he. "I encouraged her to share memories of her mother. I sensed Serenity needed a friend to listen, and I'm glad I could be there for her."

"Meaning what?"

Good old pragmatic Charlie. Perhaps *he* should be the psychologist. "She's obviously floundering in terms of her mother's vanishing act and needs closure." A sharp pain stabbed him in the knee, and he bit his lower lip hard not to groan as sweat beads broke out on his forehead. Shrugging out of his shirt, he tossed it on the carpet and sat back, allowing the air circulated by the ceiling fan to cool him down. He willed Charlie to speak again so he'd be spared a few precious seconds while he regained his breath.

"Be her friend, Jackson. She needs that more than anything else."

"I know. Besides, we've both got too much going on right now to complicate it."

"She sure is pretty, though, isn't she?" He heard Charlie's chuckle.

Not making it easier. "Serenity's beautiful, Charlie. Distractingly so." Serenity was every man's dream. He knew it, and Charlie knew it. The entire male population of Croisette Shores could see it or else they were blind. Serenity had no clue how gorgeous she was, and that made her even more appealing. She also came with a ton of baggage. Sure, it was his job to figure out what made people "tick," but everything about her intrigued him. He wouldn't be honest if he couldn't admit—even to himself—that he wanted to get to know Serenity better. A *lot* better. Nothing about her shadowed past or her present could scare him away. In spite of all that had transpired in the past, she seemed relatively well-adjusted. He suspected a reservoir of strength was hidden deep beneath her outward, fragile beauty. To be able to help her, he'd need to strip away the layers of hurt, resentment, sadness…guilt.

"You two will be spending some quality time together," Charlie said, breaking into his thoughts. "If Serenity wants to share more, she will, but let her call the shots."

"Right. Thanks for the advice." Leaning his head against the sofa, Jackson debated the merits of getting up to retrieve the bottle of ibuprofen. At the moment, he'd stay camped out until the worst of the pain passed.

"You need a friend, too."

"I've got you and the crew down at Martha's Cup & Such every morning. What more could a man need? Listen, I have to sign off now, Charlie, but I'll talk to you again soon." His breathing was labored again. Tomorrow morning, he'd make an appointment.

He heard Charlie's sigh through the phone line.

"Do yourself a big favor, son, and go get that knee checked out."

Jackson ran a hand through his hair. Even through the phone lines, the man knew.

"Thanks. I'll do that, my friend."

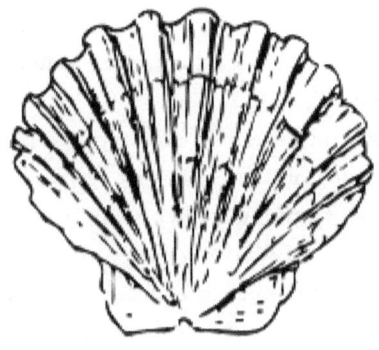

~CHAPTER 12~

Serenity surveyed her reflection in the full-length mirror. She'd swept up her hair in a loose chignon, leaving a few loose strands to frame her face and fall on her neck. The pale pink dress and off-white sandals—the best things she owned—should be elegant enough for The Black Oyster. After fastening the clasp of her dainty silver necklace around her neck and putting on the matching earrings, she closed the bedroom door. Would Spencer apologize for the way he'd treated her in high school? Everyone did foolish things when they were kids. Whether or not he asked forgiveness, the "new" Serenity could give him that much, even if she couldn't forget.

The doorbell rang loud in the quiet of her small, one-story house as she retrieved her lightweight wrap from the hall closet. The ringing of the doorbell a second time startled her into action. Swinging the front door wide a few seconds later, she welcomed him with a bright smile. "Hi, Spencer."

"Hello, gorgeous. These are for you." He held out a bouquet of exquisite, deep red roses—two dozen, from the looks of it—wrapped with a matching red ribbon. "To the fairest of them all. Beauty becomes you." Handsome in his dark suit and royal blue silk tie, Spencer's hair was slicked back, the facial stubble expertly groomed.

Serenity tried to ignore the way his eyes roamed from her head to her feet in an invasive manner that made her feel exposed and vulnerable. Not sure whether to be affronted by his boldness or touched by his sentiment, she murmured her thanks and walked into the kitchen, catching a whiff of the heady fragrance from the flowers.

"You shouldn't have, but these smell heavenly." He followed her into the kitchen. Locating a vase beneath the sink—a crystal heirloom Waterford her grandmother brought back from one of her many trips to Ireland—Serenity set about arranging the blooms. "Are you enjoying your visit?"

Spencer leaned against the kitchen counter, watching her, arms crossed. "I always like coming home to Croisette Shores. You never know what interesting people from the past you'll run into."

She lowered her gaze. "How's Kendall these days?"

The question seemed to make him uncomfortable and the corner of one eye twitched. "She moved to Charleston from what I heard. Or Savannah. I can't remember. We lost touch after high school. I've got an entirely different life now. I'll be honest, Serenity. It's nice coming back knowing I've made something of myself. People don't exactly hold high expectations for the high school quarterback. It's not like I was the high scorer on the SAT in my graduating class, like someone else I know in this kitchen."

Surprised by the honesty of his admission, she added water to the vase and finished arranging the roses. "Being a good test taker didn't mean I made the best choices in my life."

"You did the best you could and you seem fine considering everything you've been through." Spencer squared his broad shoulders and pushed away from the counter.

She placed the vase in the middle of the kitchen table and nodded her approval. "Thanks again."

"My pleasure. Are you ready to go?"

"Sure. Let me grab my purse." As she stood on the top step and locked her door a minute later, her elderly neighbor, Mrs. Marciano, waved from her front yard.

"Evening, Serenity." She tossed Spencer a wary smile. "You look familiar, young man. Grow up around here?"

"Yes," Spencer said, but it came out a low grumble. It was doubtful Mrs. Marciano could hear him, and he didn't appear inclined to engage her neighbor in polite conversation as he steered her in the direction of the Mercedes.

"Serenity? A word?" Serenity hesitated beside the passenger door as Spencer held it open, waiting. Mrs. Marciano signaled to meet her on the front walkway.

"We have reservations in twenty minutes," he said under his breath.

"This will only take a minute, promise. I'll be right back."

Mrs. Marciano met her halfway and tugged her close. "I remember that guy now. He's that Shores football player who owns some big sports store in Hilton Head and wouldn't give a dime to the school when they needed new uniforms last year." Shaking her head, she clicked her tongue. "Blame fool."

Serenity's brows rose. "Are you calling *me* a blame fool?"

Her neighbor pumped the rubber heel of her shoe up and down. "Well, of course not. You're a darling girl, but I don't want to see you with this man. He's not the right one for you. Didn't I hear something about a handsome doctor who's new in town? Now *he's* the one who should be bringing you roses and squiring you to dinner, not some full-of-himself hotshot in a fancy suit who thinks he's too good for the town where he grew up."

"Spencer might have had a valid reason for not donating money, and I'd like to give him the benefit of the doubt," Serenity said. Everyone knew way too much about her private life. Hearing a loud commotion, they both looked up to see Spencer by the car. Gyrating like a man gone wild, he shook his leg with Mrs. Marciano's cat, Mr. Darcy, latched onto his pant leg. His cheeks were beet red as he glared at Mrs. Marciano. *What on earth?*

"Is this your stupid cat?"

"See, even Mr. Darcy knows a rat when he sees one. I wouldn't trust that one further than I could throw him." Her neighbor stomped toward the car, clapping her hands and calling to her cat. Releasing his prey, the feline bounded into the arms of his mistress, leaving behind his flustered victim. After mumbling a few words of apology to Spencer, Mrs. Marciano passed her on the sidewalk with a wink. "Mr. Darcy's a good judge of character. Don't let that guy try anything tonight."

Serenity swallowed her grin. "I appreciate your concern, but Spencer's passing through town, and he's only taking me for a friendly dinner."

Mrs. Marciano huffed and snuggled Mr. Darcy close. "Chances are that's not all he wants. Tell what's-his-name to go amuse himself and stay home with me tonight, Serenity. I'll fix you one of those peanut butter and banana sandwiches you love. Then we can make popcorn and watch *Who's the Boss*. It'll be fun. Just you and me. The only man allowed is Mr. Darcy."

"It's tempting, but Tony and Angela will have to wait." Serenity gathered the woman's bony shoulders in a quick embrace. "Another night soon. I promise." Spencer chose that moment to lean inside his car and tap the horn, and both women startled.

Serenity closed her eyes. "Please tell me he didn't just do that."

"Well, I could, but I'd be lying." Mrs. Marciano quirked a brow. "My offer still stands."

"It's more tempting by the moment, but maybe it won't be so bad. Say a prayer for me."

"You got it, honey, but I'll have my eye out when he brings you home tonight." That statement brought more comfort than it should.

Seeing her approach the car, Spencer scurried around by the passenger door, still open. "I'll never understand old people," he groused, watching as she settled in the leather seat and buckled her seat belt. When he slid behind the wheel, he continued his spiel. "Don't they have anything better to do than meddle in everybody else's lives? Guess it makes their own lives more interesting." Before starting the car, he gestured to his pant leg. "That crazy cat put teeth marks on the bottom of my pants. I doubt my tailor can fix them."

"I'm sorry about that, Spencer." Time to distract him. "Tell me more about your business." That seemed to soothe him somewhat and the lines on his forehead relaxed. Leaning back against the seat, Serenity glanced out the window and spied her neighbor still standing on the front walkway, shaking her head, as he pulled away from the curb. She listened as he told her about his life in Hilton Head, grateful he didn't seem to expect much of a response. His voice was rather husky, but nice. As he drove, he asked her a few questions about her business, but he managed to bring the conversation full-circle soon enough.

During dinner, they reminisced about growing up in Croisette Shores and the places they used to go as teenagers. They'd run in different groups in school, so they didn't share many memories. Still, she enjoyed their conversation about some of the more quirky teachers. As she suspected, he perked up when she told him she'd always liked watching him play football. Thinking better of it, she stopped herself from telling him she'd harbored a secret crush on him. When the subject turned back to the wonder that was Spencer, Serenity focused on the delicious dinner. In the end, listening to the inflections and nuances in his accent was more entertaining. She'd never met a man more impressed with himself.

After returning to her small rental home a couple of hours later, Spencer shifted in the seat to face her. "Why don't we stop tiptoeing around the real issue here?" He ran a finger up her arm in a too-familiar manner. The first genuine question he'd asked her all evening, and it had to be *that* one?

Removing her arm from his reach, Serenity frowned. "We had a nice dinner, but please don't spoil the evening, Spencer. I thought I made it clear this isn't a date."

He sighed and leaned his head against the seat. "Look, Serenity, I'm sorry for that stupid stunt back in high school. I know I acted like a real jerk, but I say it's time to get over it. We're grown-ups now, not silly kids."

She nodded, somewhat appeased. "Apology accepted. Thanks for a lovely dinner, but if you'll excuse me, I should go inside now."

"Not so fast." He exerted gentle pressure on her arm with his fingers, warm but again too familiar. Seeing her deepening frown, he released his hold. "Why didn't you ever return my calls or emails? I was in Atlanta on business several times, and I know my grandparents told you." While not accusatory in tone, he sounded pouty, a quality she found neither appealing nor attractive in a man. Slowly running one finger down the curve of her jaw, he kept his eyes on her face, moving from her eyes down to her lips. "I'm sure you appreciated the benefits their generosity offered."

When he brushed his thumb over her bottom lip, she recoiled from his touch. Never would she give into this man's intimidation or anything else. "Yes, your grandparents invited me over for meals and helped me get on my feet when I first moved to Atlanta, but I worked my way through college completely on my own." Why was she bothering to justify herself? This man deserved no explanations. Her anger almost overtook her as Serenity ground her teeth and stared out the front window of the car. "I'm only going to tell you this once, so please listen."

"Anything you want to tell me, babe." His fingertips caressed the top of her shoulder.

Enough is enough. Throwing open the door, Serenity scooted across the leather seat and out of the car. She marched toward the house, not bothering to close the car door. Only a few steps behind her, Spencer was so close that by the time she reached the top step, she could feel his warm breath on her neck. Fear didn't enter the equation, only irritation and annoyance that she'd fallen for his old tricks.

Whirling around, her lips almost collided with Spencer's chin as he leaned close. She should have slammed his luxury car door when she had the chance. "I'm not your *babe*, I owe you nothing, and the only thing I owe your grandparents is a debt of gratitude. I paid them back in full for every monetary thing they ever gave me." She should send them condolences they had to suffer Spencer for a grandson. "You played me for the fool and used me to make Kendall jealous back in high school, and it seems you haven't changed your spots." Inhaling a quick breath, she glared at him. "If you think my friendship with your grandparents gives you inherent rights or liberties, then you're sadly mistaken. Please leave. This evening is over."

A small smile played about his lips, a smile she no longer considered the least bit attractive. "You're a gorgeous woman, and I'm extremely attracted to you. Come on. We're consenting adults. Give me a chance to make up for my past transgressions. You don't want to spend the rest of your life alone, do you?"

How dare *he?* "There are worse things in life, trust me." *Like spending it with the likes of you.* Her words dripped with barely-concealed loathing. To think he implied she'd be alone the rest of her life if she didn't give into his selfish desires. How colossal an ego must this man have? One hand on the front door, Serenity hesitated, not willing to turn the key in the lock until Spencer was gone. Her hand trembled and she pulled it out-of-sight, not wanting him to see how much he'd affected her. If he dared to touch her again, she'd slap his face hard and not look back.

"The lady asked you to leave, Quarterback. You'd best do as she says, you yellow-bellied, no good varmint." Mrs. Marciano stood on the ground below the front steps, iron skillet at-the-ready. How in the world could such a seemingly frail, older woman handle a heavy cast iron skillet like it was featherweight? Dressed in her housecoat and fluffy pink slippers, the elderly woman pressed her lips together and her dark eyes flashed.

Serenity suppressed the urge to run and throw her arms around the dear woman. Poised behind his mistress, Mr. Darcy kept up a steady stream of hisses at Spencer. From all indications, the cat was a better judge of character than she'd been. Gullible. That's what she was. Why had she ever agreed to go out with him? How foolish she'd been to give Spencer the benefit of the doubt and fall for his sweet-talking ways. Never again.

"Mind your own business and shove it, Granny." Spencer's words came out a rude snarl. "Go back in your little house and leave us alone. This is between me and Serenity."

He turned back to her. "You'd better watch it, Serenity, or you'll end up all by yourself like Granny, a lonely old woman with a crazy cat to keep you company. That'd be a real shame." Those words stung as much for her neighbor as herself. One thing her mother and father taught her was to never let anyone see you flinch.

"Say whatever you want about me, but I can't tolerate anyone who insults my friends."

"Look," he said, raking a hand over his short hair. "Truce, okay? I thought...well, after what you'd been through—"

"What, Spencer? That I might be a little lonely? That I might need a big, strong man to take care of me? Let me tell you something." Another thing she couldn't abide was arrogance from someone who thought they knew what she— or anyone else—needed. With one finger, she beckoned him closer. He complied, moving so close they were almost nose-to-nose. Serenity bit her tongue not to say what a year ago she *would* have said.

"Sure. Tell me, babe." Leaning one hand against the outside of the house, he gave her a salacious smile.

Raising her chin, she met his eyes. *You are a new creation in Christ. Let your words be seasoned with grace.* "I'll...pray for you."

He snorted. Instead of turning away in disgust as she suspected, he surprised her by putting his hand around her waist and drawing her closer. "Religion's a crutch. You can pray for me all you want as long as you let me—"

With a disgusted grunt, Serenity pushed him away. He flailed his arms to catch himself as he teetered on the edge of the top step. "I'll pray the Lord will teach you a few lessons, Spencer. I should have let Mrs. Marciano beat you over the head with that skillet when she had the chance. But I doubt even cast iron would penetrate your thick skull. I'll take loneliness over being with a man like you any old day of the week, *babe.*"

"Serenity! I saw Sheriff Harris patrolling the next street over. Want me to flag him down?" Mrs. Marciano sat on her front stoop, the skillet beside her.

Bless her heart, she'd probably sit there all night, if needed. As foolish and embarrassed as she felt, Serenity adored her neighbor's watch care over her.

Spencer scowled. "I swear, that old snoop's worse than a bloodsucking leech. Like I said, we could be real good together. Call me if you ever come to your senses." Muttering under his breath, he stalked down the sidewalk. After closing the passenger door, he hurried around the front of the car and climbed into the Mercedes. The tires squealed as the car sped away from the curb and tore down the street.

Mrs. Marciano scrambled to her feet and walked across the short expanse of yard that separated their homes. "You okay, honey? That overgrown hormone didn't hurt you, did he?"

Serenity blew out a breath and tried to shake off the lingering repulsion. She shivered and crossed her arms over her middle. "No, he didn't hurt me. Thanks, Mrs. Marciano. You did me a huge favor tonight. I appreciate how you always watch out for me. I feel pretty stupid."

"That's what neighbors are for, and no reason to beat yourself up about it. You learned your lesson and it's time to move on." She smiled. "Tony and Angela are on every night, you know. Back-to-back episodes." The older woman eyed her. "You sure you're okay? I could keep you company, or you can come over if you want. Mr. Darcy and I are good listeners."

"I'm tired, and I'm sure I'll be better once I get inside and shake it off. I'm sorry Spencer was so rude to you. No one deserves that kind of treatment."

She shrugged. "That guy'll get his due one of these days and then maybe he'll understand you get back what you give in this life. Seems to me he's doing his share of taking."

Sad fact, but also true. She'd pray for Spencer. Wasn't that the right thing to do as a Christian? "How about I come over tomorrow night?"

Mrs. Marciano brightened. "Sure thing. Seven o'clock. You bring the popcorn."

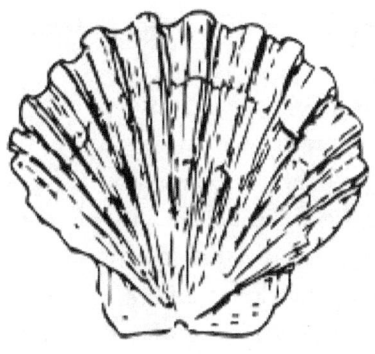

~CHAPTER 13~

On Thursday afternoon, Jackson sat beside Serenity on the floor of his office. Oversized paint and wallpaper sample books were scattered around them. They'd been making selections—some permanent, some tentative—for well over an hour. Stretching her arms over her head, she stifled a yawn and shot him an apologetic grin. "Sorry." She crossed her legs and balanced one of the books on her lap.

"Late date last night?" Jackson adjusted his position so he'd carry the burden of the book's weight as he casually thumbed through wallpaper samples. Although he moved his eyes across the page, he saw nothing.

"I don't date. Not really." Reaching across his lap, Serenity's silky hair brushed against his arm as she flipped a few pages. Long and straight, her hair reached halfway down her back. Smelled great, too. So many women wore their hair short these days, but he'd always preferred long hair. The color of spun gold, it was enough to drive a man to distraction. While surprised she didn't swoop it off her neck like most women in town—probably because of the humidity—he was glad she didn't. He'd lost some serious sleep thinking about her. For the last twenty minutes, he'd tried not to think about how great Serenity looked in her fitted jeans and pretty blue top. He liked how she didn't wear much makeup, and her skin actually seemed to glow from the inside out, as ridiculous as that seemed. She was like a walking advertisement for healthy eating and clean living.

Matter of fact, he hadn't been able to stop thinking about her since Sunday afternoon. The woman was incredible, and not just physically. He liked the way she fussed over her crusty father, the close relationship she shared with Charlie and Maya, the carefree spirit she exhibited when playing in the waves with Maya later in the day, how she escorted her dad to supper at Hermann's. They'd invited him to come along, but he'd declined, wanting her to have time alone with Clinton. Somehow he sensed that's what they both needed. Then, as now, he'd tried to be discreet in how attracted he was to her, but he figured she'd noticed his frequent glances although he tried to avoid outright staring.

Her nearness now had him conjuring up ways he could spend time with her without her accusing him of trying to date her. Serenity was right about one thing. Starting his new practice and renovating the playground should absorb most of his energies. He'd known his share of beautiful women, but the one sitting next to him now was different in more ways than he could count. Odds were, she'd laugh in his face if he told her he hadn't dated anyone seriously the last four years. Sure, a few outings here and there, some kisses, but nothing he cared to take to the next level. His decorator would be more than annoyed if she suspected he wondered how soft her hair would feel sifting through his fingers. Wondered what it'd be like to take her hand in his, draw her close and kiss her...

He needed to stop this trail of thinking. Time to focus. He'd gone too long without female companionship. That's all he needed. Good old friendship. Right. More like the psychologist needed *his* head examined. Seeing Serenity with that slimy guy at church had bothered him. Sure, he'd been good looking, but Jackson could spot overconfidence and a wolf in sheep's clothing a mile away. Not one to jump to judgment as a general rule, he'd irrationally disliked the man on sight. He was too smooth and impressed with himself.

Serenity flipped over a few more pages before pointing to a pale yellow wallpaper with a small palm tree design. "This one would look great on the bottom portion of the walls if you want to do a chair rail."

Jackson snapped to attention. "What's a chair rail? And why don't you date...not really?" He tried to keep his voice even. Call him selfish, but if *he* couldn't date Serenity, he didn't want anyone else keeping her company.

"That's a two-fold question."

"I've got time. Remember, I like two-fold things."

"How can I forget?" With a small smile, she angled her head toward the long, empty wall behind his desk. "A chair rail is a dividing strip of molding lining a wall horizontally. It's a good way to break up a wall and make it more visually appealing. A chair rail usually runs anywhere from two to four feet from the floor. There's wallpaper below the wood strip and a solid color painted above it, so it's a backdrop for paintings, photos or whatever you want to hang on the wall."

She stopped, her brow furrowed as she absently curled a long strand of blonde hair around one finger. It'd been a long time since he'd seen a fully-grown woman do it. The action was playful, almost wistful. "Did that sound as cut-and-dried boring as I think it did?" When he didn't answer, she smiled. "Earth to Jackson. You're staring at me."

"Am I? Sorry. And no, it wasn't boring. Not at all. A chair rail sounds like the perfect solution to break up the monotony of the walls." The way he felt right now, Serenity could tell him he needed a snake with ten heads mounted on the long wall behind his desk and he'd think it was the mark of genius. She was the decorator and knew best, after all. Stretching out his legs, Jackson chewed the inside of his cheek not to reveal the sharp pain in his bum knee when he lowered the book to the floor beside him. The bulk of its weight was too heavy and he shouldn't have left it there so long. "What colors do you suggest for above the chair rail?"

"Probably a solid but pale yellow, unless that's too cheery or nauseating for you. It's like sunshine. It's happy, light, and a great color for kids. What's the average age of your clients?"

"Generally seven to ten." Justin came into his mind. "Sometimes younger. Any older than ten and you get into a whole different dynamic with raging hormones and even more emotional upheaval. I leave it to the heavy hitters to handle the older clients."

"They might look at *you* as the heavy hitter since they're perhaps more vulnerable when they're so young," she said. Interesting observation and he appreciated her perspective. "Why do you prefer working with the younger kids?"

Jackson considered her question. "They're perhaps more open to change, more likely to take what I say to heart. And, as a general rule, they're more in tune to the ways the Lord can work in their lives."

Tilting her head, watching him, Serenity's blonde hair tumbled to one side and an entrancing smile played about her lips. *Beautiful.* "So, are you saying when they're younger, they're more pliable—for lack of a better word—but when they're older, they can be more jaded and resistant to change?"

"It depends, but that's usually the case, yes. Another thing I find interesting? For whatever reason, the majority of my patients are boys." Serenity shot him a curious glance, and he raised a hand in the air. "I don't personally ascribe to the theory that girls are more vulnerable or in any way the weaker sex. Not at all. If anything, what I just said proves it." He paused, waiting until she met his eyes. "Even young girls can be uncommonly strong. Women never cease to amaze me with their resourcefulness and resilience. I'm looking at one right now, as a matter of fact."

She surprised him when she laughed, warm and genuine with a hint of huskiness. "Right. You're only saying that to get on my good side." Serenity nodded her head in the direction of a terrarium in one corner of his office. "So, who's the creature over there?"

Jackson chuckled. "That, my friend, is Señor Igor the iguana. Having animals in the office brings out nurturing qualities, helps form a bond and makes kids more inclined to talk. If this partnership is going to work, please tell me you can appreciate the aesthetic and esoteric qualities of Igor." He gave her what he hoped was his most winning smile.

"Oh, I can," she said, "but cute as Igor is, he'll forever be a *reptile.* Not all youngsters are fond of them, especially little girls. It could work against what you're trying to accomplish. That, and using words like aesthetic and esoteric. Please don't tell me you say things like that to your patients. They'd probably run away screaming."

He liked her sense of humor. Her sass. Her intelligence. Liked the slight curl of her lips. "I'll keep that in mind. Besides," he said with a shrug, "I only tossed those in there to impress you since they seemed like words you'd use, being a decorator and all." He returned his attention to the sample book on the floor beside him.

Leaning forward, Serenity captured his eye contact. "Okay, here's what you do. Get a fluffy white cat and a cute puppy dog—not real, of course—with big, irresistible eyes and give them cute names. That'll counteract the reptile effect."

"I'll concede on that point, and I'd like a few animals to keep the giraffe company. Some of the stuffed persuasion, yes, but I'd also like to add some more of the breathing but non-threatening variety," Jackson said. "At the very least, some exotic fish. But no piranhas since no self-respecting insurance company would carry my practice, and rightly so. And definitely no parrot." He laughed at her raised brow. "Parrots repeat everything. Trust me, it's not a good idea, especially when I'm often in the company of impressionable young minds."

"Is this a confession?"

"No."

"Make you a deal," she said. "I'll pick out some cute, furry friends as long as you realize you're responsible for the general care and feeding of these living, breathing animals. And, please, nothing that'll make your office smell bad." She wrinkled her nose.

"Are you saying Igor stinks?" He fought to keep a straight face. "Come on, these kids live near the ocean. They're used to ocean smells, good and bad."

"We're getting off topic here."

"Ah, and just when I was going to offer to let you hold Igor."

"Going to have to pass on that dubious honor, but there's one other important thing we need to discuss." Rising to her feet, she walked across the room and retrieved some kind of weird ruler from her tote bag.

"What's that thing?"

She tossed him a look. "Don't get excited. I need to take some measurements for the chair rail."

"Oh, right. When you're done, you can tell me about your not-really-a-date with the quarterback."

Serenity's eyes lit. She shook her head, but continued measuring. "Spying on me, are you?"

"Hardly."

"Then how'd you know?"

"Welcome to small town living, my friend."

"Right," she said. "Nothing like throwing my words back in my face." She didn't bat an eyelash as she continued her work. "I suppose I could ask you the same thing."

"How so?"

"How was your date with the prom queen?"

"Excuse me?"

The corners of her mouth quirked. "Word on the street is you've been keeping company with Hayley Foster." Why did spending time with a woman—whether five minutes or five hours—start the rumor mill? Jealousy didn't seem to be on Serenity's radar, but he liked that she cared enough to pay attention. That was a start.

"Hayley's a nice woman and we're friends," he said. "She's a social worker and we met through work. So we're clear, Hayley's not my girlfriend. Matter of fact, she's not even my type." Now that he thought of it, he'd noticed Hayley's tendency to touch his arm, lean into him, laugh at something dumb he'd said like it was the most profound thing she'd ever heard. Yeah, no wonder people had gotten the wrong idea. He needed to be more careful.

"Oh." The tiniest frown creased her forehead.

"Go ahead. Ask."

"Judging by recent behavior, I'd have to say the borderline neurotic, micro-organizer type might be right up your alley."

He laughed. "Sorry, but with you standing there holding that ruler thing, that statement strikes me as highly ironic. For the record, I prefer blondes. So, my turn. Are you going to tell me about your date with the stud?"

Serenity stared, appearing unsure whether to throw something at him or give in to her laughter. "Spencer's not a stud. He just thinks he is. And it wasn't a date. Spencer played me for a fool in high school and thought he'd make it up to me now, but he's ten years too late," she said. "As far as I'm concerned, he can't go back to Hilton Head and his fascination with himself fast enough."

That was the best news he'd heard since he'd moved to Croisette Shores. "Not to change the subject, but I haven't been to The Summer Palace yet," he said. "I understand it's the residence of one of the royals who founded our fair village."

Her eyes widened. "Well, it's definitely something worth seeing," she said, clearing her throat. "Especially if you plan on sticking around." Tossing her hair over one shoulder, she avoided looking at him and finished her task while he watched.

"I think I will. Stick around that is," he said slowly, hoping that might be Serenity's way of asking-without-really-asking a question. "Need any help over there?"

"No, I'm fine, thanks. You could find something to do. All your staring is...well, it's distracting me."

"Good."

"*Not* good," she said as she continued with her work. The way she twisted her lips sure looked like she was trying not to grin. He'd thrown her off-kilter as evidenced by the pretty pink flush in her cheeks. If he wasn't mistaken, she liked his dimple, so he wanted her to catch a glimpse of it as often as possible. "What I meant is, I need to know the focal point of your office."

"Okay, tell me something." Stretching his arms behind him, he leaned on his hands. "Why exactly does my office *need* a focal point?"

"Because all spaces should have one. It's not mandatory, of course, but again, it makes them more interesting." He couldn't miss the relief in her voice as they got back to business. "It's something you build around. Like a conversation starter. In your case, it'd be good if it's something connected with the specifics of what you do and tie it in with kids. Igor could be one, but it'd be good if you had something behind your desk, mounted on the wall." Her eyes darted to the terrarium. "Hey, you could—"

He sat up straighter and held up one hand. "Don't even think of suggesting anything to do with taxidermy, but I get your point. A dentist has a chair and the rinse-and-spit thing, a pediatrician has an examining table. That sort of thing. For the record, I don't have a miniature shrink couch for little people. I prefer to shrink my patients with them sitting upright, but I have a kid-sized chair. But, always, gummi worms are included as enticement." The corners of his mouth twitched in spite of his best efforts. "They're indigenous to my practice."

"Cherry's the best flavor, of course, but gummi worms aren't a focal point."

"Right," he said. "Let me think on it a few days. How about you meet me—and Charlie—at The Summer Palace—tomorrow morning, and I'll have the answer for a focal point." He already knew the perfect focal point for his office, but why not parlay it into another opportunity to see her? He could almost read her indecision. "If it entices you to come, I'll bring along a personal supply of cherry gummis."

"Tell you what," she said, "I haven't been to The Summer Palace in years. It might be fun, and we can discuss more decorating ideas while we're there. As I recall, there's a huge library and home office there. You can tell me what you like and don't like amidst all the opulence."

"Serenity, you *do* realize I'm not inviting you to actually discuss wallpaper or room design?" What possessed him to say that? Because it was the truth, screaming to be said.

"I know, and as long as you understand it's not a date." She shrugged. "Take it or leave it."

Jackson couldn't help his wry grin. "I heard you the first time. You don't date. Not really. If it's better for you, we can consider Charlie our chaperone."

"Why are you inviting me, Jackson? Be honest." She pushed her hair behind her shoulder with an annoyed frown. "Do you have a rubber band?"

Shooting her a curious glance, he moved over to his desk and fished around in the middle drawer. Locating a medium-sized band, he tossed it to her. "Will this work?" He couldn't wait to see how she'd use it to measure a wall. Putting the ruler on the floor, she quickly secured her hair in a high ponytail. He liked her hair down but this look was...cute and playful and showed off her long neck and enticing curve of her jaw to full advantage.

"You're staring at me again."

"Hazard of being around you." That comment brought the lovely flush to her cheeks again. "I want you to come along because you're my friend who happens to be my decorator. I'll give you my opinion of the moldings and the layout of the sitting room or something. They might even have a chair rail or two, so we can call it an educational tour. Oh, and don't forget the playground renovation meeting is at Town Hall at three tomorrow. If you want, we can tour The Summer Palace and then go to lunch before the meeting. Make a day of it."

There was a lot more he'd like to say to her, but if he voiced his thoughts aloud, he knew she'd run screaming. As it was, he wondered about his growing feelings for Serenity. He couldn't stop thinking about her and wanted to know more about her story. He'd picked up on all the little hints the townspeople had dropped. Then they'd bring up another subject, and for that, he was thankful. Sure, he wanted to know everything about Serenity, but he wanted to hear it from her and no one else. The irony? She was the first woman he'd wanted to date in a long time, but she kept herself so far off-limits he might as well forget hoping for anything more. This was a woman who had deep issues from her past to resolve before she could move forward in any kind of relationship. The way she kept him at a safe distance, he suspected she wouldn't let *anyone* close.

"Okay," she said. "As you would say, it sounds like a plan. What time shall I meet you at The Summer Palace?"

"You won't because I'm picking you up at your office."

At first, she looked as though she might resist, but then the slightest hint of a smile emerged. As he watched, her lips curved even more. Patience was reward enough as Serenity's smile found a whole new place inside him.

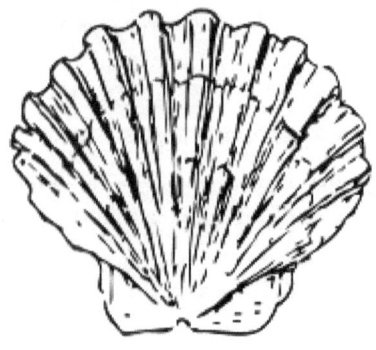

~CHAPTER 14~

*A*fter meeting with another new client late in the afternoon, Serenity dropped by the realty office in the hope she'd find Deidre there. "Is she in?" she asked the receptionist. The young woman was on the phone but nodded and motioned down the hall. Swinging around the corner, Serenity breezed into Deidre's office. As recently as six months ago, she couldn't have done it, and she'd have waited to be announced. Far be it from her to know where this new confidence was coming from, but she liked it. She'd ponder the possible reasons why another time.

"Don't you ever knock?" Deidre said, glancing up at her from beneath the tortoiseshell rim of her glasses. The woman even made wearing eyeglasses the height of sophistication.

"As your best friend, I have inherent liberties. I didn't know you wore glasses."

"They're readers and my concession to getting older. I don't allow many to see them, you know, so you should feel special." She removed them and placed them on the desk.

"You're like fine wine, Deidre. I was in the area and thought I'd stop by and say hi."

"Glad you did. Tell me about your non-date with Spencer last night. Subconsciously, I'm sure that's probably why you're here." Deidre inspected a nail and reached into her desk drawer, pulling out a scary-looking metal file. "Did the big man on campus behave himself? For starters, I'm sure he told you all about his incredibly successful business empire."

"Yes, I heard all about the sporting goods store in Hilton Head," Serenity said, taking the seat across from her friend's desk. "He talked about it incessantly during dinner, but I tuned out the drone after a while. I think he's expanding into other cities, but don't quote me on that."

Straightening in her chair, Deidre pointed the nail file at her and looked ready to dispense more advice.

"Please don't point that thing at me. People have done time for less," Serenity said.

"Sorry." Opening the drawer again, Deidre dropped it inside. "Tell me what Spencer asked about *you*. Surely he didn't talk about himself the entire evening?" When Serenity didn't answer, her friend slapped one hand on the desk. "Are you kidding me? That guy must be an even bigger jerk than before!"

"Spencer tries too hard to earn friends the wrong way. From what I remember, he's always been that way. It's nothing new."

"You're being too generous, and don't be naïve. At least you got a decent meal out of it, but did he try to weasel his way into your house under the guise of a cup of coffee?" Deidre's blue eyes widened. "Don't even tell me you offered him one?"

"I'm not completely clueless. Of course not. I didn't even get to that point."

"I take it Spencer got a little too friendly?"

Deidre knew her as well as anyone. She blew out the breath she'd been holding. "He thinks because his grandparents helped me financially when I first moved to Atlanta, it'd give him an advantage and I might be inclined to grant him...special favors."

"Listen to me," Deidre said. "Since I'm feeling a little generous, I'll give him the benefit of the doubt and believe he might have a tiny sliver of sensitivity running through that quarterback body of his, but his brain's clearly stuck in neutral. In high school, he was impressed with himself because of his athletic ability, but now he's impressed with his success in the business world. Let me tell you something. His little brother Brody's the brains behind those stores.

Spencer's only the pretty front man." She shrugged. "They should call it Brawn & Brains—Athletic Goods for the Thinking Man."

"I always liked Brody," Serenity said. "I didn't know he was part of the business, but it makes perfect sense now that I think about it." She'd always been impressed by Brody's self-confidence. Physically smaller and less self-aggrandizing than his older brother, he'd been the quiet, studious one who'd shocked them all with his sharp debating skills in high school. She'd heard he'd won a full scholarship to the prestigious Wharton School. Well, good for him.

The corners of Deidre's mouth upturned. "Brody also married a gorgeous girl a few years ago. Some heiress from a Jersey manufacturing company or something. If you ask me, Spencer's jealous as all get out and that's a real thorn in his side. At the rate he's going, he'll be driving into the twilight with no one in the passenger seat of that Mercedes."

Spencer's pointed comment about spending the rest of her life alone—his last parting gift—nagged at her, and Serenity couldn't shake it. "In a way, I feel sorry for Spencer," she said. "I guess the best thing we can do is pray for him. He was in church, after all, so perhaps there's hope."

"Don't think too hard about that one."

"What do you mean?"

"Let's say he had an ulterior motive, and I'm not talking about drawing closer to the Almighty." When she gave her friend a blank stare, Deidre sighed. "Come on, honey. Spencer only showed up because he thought you might be there."

Serenity narrowed her eyes. "Tell me what you know."

"Okay, don't get mad, but my hubby ran into Spencer at McHenry's last Saturday and they got to reminiscing. Your name came up. At some point, I'd told Wes about your...faith, and I might have said something about you going to church. My husband apparently passed on that little tidbit to Spencer. Sorry if Wes sent the octopus your way, but you know Spencer always took advantage of every opportunity. How'd you manage to get rid of him, anyway? I hope you didn't have to call the authorities."

The corners of Serenity's mouth twitched. "Mrs. Marciano, my self-proclaimed bodyguard, stomped across the yard wielding a cast iron skillet. I don't know how she even lifts that thing, and I hope she doesn't hurt herself. She threatened Spencer and he took off like a scared rabbit. It did the trick. I don't think I have to worry about him coming around again."

"Good thing," Deidre said. "By the way, I heard Jackson was at that new Asian place Wes's cousin opened the other night." She raised a perfectly-arched brow. "With Hayley Foster. Word is they're working together on some project, but she wants it to be more."

Serenity tried to ignore the sudden pang of jealousy. She stared out the window at the gathering dark, low-hanging clouds, ripe with the promise of rain. Jackson had explained his working relationship with Hayley, and she had no reason to doubt him.

"Isn't that what Jackson's doing with you, working on a...project?"

"Deidre, you know very well we're working together." Serenity didn't bother masking her annoyance. "Not to sound like a whiner, but I'm tired of everyone in this town knowing what I'm doing, where I am at any given moment, who I'm with, what I order for dinner, what time I get home. The looks, the insinuations I get at the bank, the store, and pretty much everywhere. If Jackson wants to work on a project with a different woman every night of the week, that's his prerogative and none of my business."

Deidre gave her a penetrating look, the corners of her exquisitely-painted red lips threatening another impending smile, this one much too smug. "I didn't say that to make you jealous, but somehow I think I hit my mark. Look, here's the thing. I know you're scared, but you can't let one bad date"—she raised her hand—"okay, technically *not* a date, but don't let it spoil the chance for a relationship with anyone else. So, you went out with Spencer hoping to clear up some old baggage from high school. Bad move, girlfriend, but you learned your lesson and now it's time to move on. All I'm saying is, you might want to play nice with yummy Dr. Ross and see what happens."

"Deidre, this insatiable desire to know everything about my personal life is starting to border on harassment. I have to tell you, it's a little scary sometimes."

"Oh, it's not harassment." Deidre sat back in her chair and crossed her arms, appearing pleased.

Serenity met Deidre's gaze. "What would you call it then?"

A smile creased her friend's face. "Love."

*E*ver since Jackson had pulled out that old black and white photo from the box he unpacked in her office, Serenity couldn't stop thinking about her mother. She sat at the kitchen table with her dad as they shared a simple meal of chicken salad sandwiches and fresh fruit salad later that evening. After bowing her head for a quick prayer, she began eating and observed how his appetite seemed improved. The color in his cheeks was better and he'd been getting out for some fresh air every day.

He asked about her business and seemed pleased to hear she'd gained a few more clients. When she told him their names, he nodded. "Watch out for old Bing Warren," he said with a chuckle. "That guy tried to date your mama when she first moved here to Croisette Shores. He spurred me on to put a ring on Elise's finger to let him know she was taken."

"I'm sure Mama made it perfectly clear. And I don't think he'll be coming after me. At least I hope not." She cringed at the thought. He was her father's age.

Clinton shook his head. "The old codger's still single. If he'd clean himself up a bit and mind his manners, he might have half a chance."

"Karen Gorham might be interested," she said, giving him a sly glance.

Chewing a bite of apple from the fruit salad, he grinned. "You might be right. She keeps trying, bless her heart."

They ate in silence for a couple of minutes as she tried to formulate questions in her mind. Questions she needed to ask even though she risked upsetting him. "Dad, why do you think Mama left?" she said. "Or do you even believe that's what she did?" She pushed aside her empty plate. "I guess what I'm trying to say is...do you think Mama even had a choice whether to leave?"

Clinton fiddled with his spoon and tapped it against the ceramic bowl. Finally, he put it down and ran a hand over his grizzled chin. He needed a good shave and a haircut. "Too much sadness, I think."

"So, you're saying you think she left voluntarily?" She let out a low groan. Thinking such a thing was bad enough, but hearing it from her father somehow made it worse. More like a reality she hadn't wanted to face. Still, it was the first time she'd been able to broach the subject with him since moving back home. "She was my mom, and I *needed* her. Running away was the easy thing, the selfish thing. Leaving didn't solve anything." Tears stung the back of her eyes.

Clinton snapped up his head and curled his fist on the table. "Your mama's not selfish, Serenity. You don't know what you're talking about. She gave up everything for you."

"How can you defend her, even now? After all she's done?" She could see the muscles in his jaws flexing. Good. If he unleashed his anger, yelled, stomped, screamed or whatever, at least it'd be raw, honest emotion. Then they could deal with it and try to move past it.

"She hated like anything to see you hurt. When Danny was murdered, your mother wished she could have traded places with him." His eyes flashed. "Don't think she wouldn't have done it in a heartbeat if she could. Me, too."

Tears slipped down her cheeks. When he dug the ever-present hanky from his pants, she took it from him without hesitation. "I'm sorry," she said, wiping her face. "I know I sound selfish to you, but especially when Liam died, I needed Mama more than ever before in my life." A sob escaped. "I still do."

Reaching across the table, Clinton grabbed her hand and held on tight. "One of these days, you'll have your answers. These things always have a way of working themselves out one way or the other."

Serenity withdrew her hand, her eyes wide. "What do you mean? What about *your* answers? You lost your wife. Don't you want to know what happened?" She stared at him, wide-eyed and dabbed beneath her eyes. He seemed too calm, too accepting. "Dad, do you think Mama's alive?"

Slumping back in his chair, he remained silent. He also avoided her eyes. She waited him out. A couple of times he seemed ready to say something, opening his mouth but then closing it again. "I'm not sure what to think anymore, girl."

For now, she'd accept those words. But something still didn't ring quite right. "Do you know anything about the note someone from Croisette Shores mailed to me in Atlanta?"

"What note?" The obvious surprise in his expression told her he knew nothing.

"Hang on. I'll show you." Opening her purse, she retrieved the paper, unfolded it and handed it to him as she sat in her chair again. The letters were starting to fade, but it was still legible. "Do you recognize the handwriting?"

Clinton shook his head. "Can't say as I do. When did you get this?"

"A few months ago."

His eyes met hers. "This note is why you came back?"

"No, but it was the catalyst. Getting it confirmed in my mind it was time to finally come back home. I'd been thinking about it, anyway."

"What do you make of it?" Letting the note fall to the table, he stared at it.

"I don't know any more now than I did when I first got it. At first, I thought you'd sent it, but then I figured out pretty quickly you didn't. Then I thought Charlie sent it. As you can see, it's plain paper without a watermark or anything distinguishing to go on other than the handwriting. I even smelled it, thinking it might hold the scent of its sender, but nothing. Based on the timing, I can't help but wonder if the person who sent it might have known I'd just finished my studies and might be contemplating coming back home. Truthfully? Other than gossiping about me, there's only a handful of people who might know or care where I was in the world or what I was doing."

"You really believe that, girl?" He snorted and shook his head.

"More or less...yes."

Returning his gaze to her, her father stared her down. "You broke hearts when you left town. And I'm not just talking about mine." His eyes grew moist, and it surprised her. "When you left, you took away the sunshine. *My* sunshine. And now, I can't help thinking you might pick up and leave again." He glanced away again and sniffed.

She sat stunned, staring at her father. "Dad, look at me." Crossing both arms on the table, Serenity waited until he moved his gaze back to hers. The vulnerability in his dark eyes could have blown her over. "I told you this is my home," she said, lowering her voice. "I'm not planning on going anywhere. No matter what happened here in the past, I don't hold it against this town. I don't belong anywhere else. Croisette Shores is part of me, and it's in my blood. I needed to get away for a while. It was a good move for me personally, and I'll never regret coming back. But I can't help but wonder—if Mama's still out there somewhere—if *she* feels the same way. Do you think she'll ever come back?"

Serenity couldn't stand it when her father avoided her questions, and she liked it less when he wouldn't look her in the eye, like now. Avoidance in general seemed second nature with him since she'd moved back home. Somehow she'd break through the fortress he'd built around his emotions if she had to drag him to see Jackson for counseling sessions.

Finally, he grunted. "Elise loves you more than anything, Serenity. If nothing else, believe *that.*"

Why *did* he always speak about her in present tense? Not to mention he hadn't answered her direct question. "If that's true, then how could she leave us? Answer that one, please."

Shaking his head, Clinton pushed his chair away from the table and rose to his feet. He carried the coffee cup and plate to the sink. Planting both hands on the counter, he lowered his head.

"Fine," she said, following suit. "If you won't answer, then I'll leave. After all, it's the thing to do in this family." She put her plate on the counter beside him and grabbed her purse. Pausing at the door, she turned and walked back to where he still stood by the sink, staring out the window. "I'll be back to check on you tomorrow. Do me a favor, though."

"What's that?"

Serenity placed her hand on his arm. It lacked the muscle definition he used to have, and he was much too thin. "Do you ever pray? Prayer and belief in God isn't a crutch, and it's helped me get through the not knowing whether Mama's alive or dead."

"Is that a fact? Has God given you any answers, girl?" He shook his head. "You sound like Elise with all your talk of God." His voice held more resignation than scorn.

"I don't have any answers yet, Dad, but I've learned one truth. He's *your* God every bit as He's mine. You just have to believe that and reach out to Him. Meet Him halfway. My faith in His mercy and grace has given me the strength to face every single day the last few years. Days when I didn't want to get out of bed and go on any more. He's helped me face my fears and stare them down." Planting a soft kiss on his cheek, she whispered against his weathered cheek, "I came home for you, too, you know. We *need* each other. Now more than ever, Dad."

Grabbing her hand, he held on tight. "Yeah, we do, girl. We do."

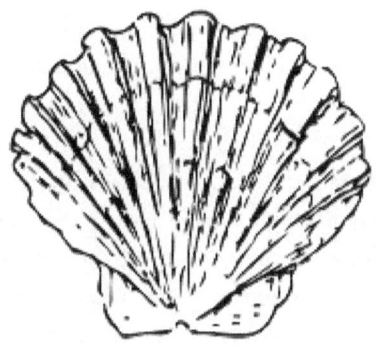

~CHAPTER 15~

*T*wenty minutes into their tour of The Summer Palace on Friday morning, Serenity heard a phone ringing. Pulling his cell phone from his pocket, Charlie mouthed to her that it was Maya's school. He covered his ear with his hand and walked to a quiet corner and listened, nodding his head every few seconds and speaking in low tones. Coming back a few minutes later, he spoke with Jackson. With a small wave and a nod, he departed.

Jackson stared at the ceiling and crossed his arms over his chest. "Would you look at those moldings?"

Her laughter prompted several tourists in the immediate vicinity to glance their way. "Now, see what you've done, troublemaker? Where'd Charlie go?"

"Hey, you're the one causing the disruption," Jackson said under his breath, steering her toward a large painting. "I'm your client, so be nice to me, please. In case you're thinking this morning was a set-up and this was some elaborate scheme to get you here under false pretenses, that really *was* a call from Maya's school." He slanted his gaze to hers as if issuing a nonverbal challenge to prove him wrong.

Her smile sobered. "In that case, I hope everything's okay."

"Charlie said Maya has a stomach ache. Since her mom and dad both work, he's the emergency contact." Sounded like he knew the family pretty well already. They lagged behind the others, a tour group sporting Swiss Air tote bags strapped across their chests. Jackson faced her with an indefinable expression. "Did Charlie ever tell you what your dad did for his son?"

Serenity turned from her study of the layout of the sitting room. "My dad? For Ray?"

"Ray used to work part-time at a local elementary school as a janitor after hours to help pay his way through college and to make extra money so his wife could stay home with Maya. I don't know all the details, but the school fired him for allegedly stealing a computer. From what Charlie said, Clinton found out who the real culprit was and hauled him into the police."

That revelation stopped her in her tracks. She tucked a strand of hair behind one ear and shook her head. "When did this happen? I wonder why no one told me."

"About three years ago, I think. From what I know of your dad, he didn't think it was anything extraordinary. He made such a stink about the firing that it ended up going all the way to the school board. They offered Ray his job back, but he said no. He'd won the victory. My point being your dad is a hero to Charlie and his family."

"Mama and Dad always believed in fighting for equality, racial and otherwise," she said. "I guess I shouldn't be surprised. Do you know how Dad found out who the true culprit was?"

"Charlie said Clinton overheard some guys talking at McHenry's right after Ray was fired. They were joking around and one of the kids was bragging about what he'd gotten away with. Not to change the subject, but I'm growing rather fond of that light fixture," Jackson said, pointing to a hurricane-style lamp. "Do you think we can find one?"

"I'm sure we can find a reproduction. It's a fairly popular design." Taking out her phone, Serenity snapped a photo, hoping it wasn't against the rules. They talked about a few more fixtures in the room and she made notes about Jackson's preferences for rugs. If all her clients were as forthcoming as Jackson about what they liked and didn't like, it'd make her job much easier. Trying to second guess or not having much to go on could make for a difficult assignment. She'd already found that with a couple more new clients, but each and every client was a blessing, and no doubt they'd all teach her something valuable.

"What made you decide to go into interior decorating?" Jackson asked as she tucked her phone back in her purse.

"I've always been fascinated by colors, textures and designs. How they work solo or blended." She smiled. "When you think about it, I'm sort of a salesperson, but in the nicest sense of the word. I make recommendations and tell people what I believe works or doesn't. Based on my study of design techniques and applications, of course. Then it's up to them to make their own decision and either accept or reject my ideas."

"You're selling me on it all right now," he said, returning her smile.

"Stop flirting."

"Can't help it," he said. "Seriously, you do a great job. I guess we'd better go rejoin Swiss Air. Thanks for all the good suggestions, though. Next field trip, we'll go to one of the art galleries down by the shore to look at some of the watercolors. See if we can't find some nice scenes of Croisette Shores for the walls."

A young, attractive woman who looked to be of Spanish descent stood on the peripheral of the tour group as they rejoined them in a hallway leading to the bedroom wing. "You two, um, how do you say...make a...beautiful couple." Her eyes lingered on Jackson a bit too long.

"Oh, we're not a couple," Jackson said, his offhand manner irritating her. "She's just my interior decorator and we're here to look at chair rails and moldings." He nodded in approval at the ornate ceiling. "Those French royals had the right idea. Overstated opulence. Write that down," he said to Serenity, waving his hand at her in a dismissive way. If he hadn't winked when he said it, she might have swatted him. *Just my interior decorator?* She bristled.

Danny had been handsome in a charming, bad boy way, yet a part of her always wondered if she could trust him. But Jackson? Well, he was solid and good with that hint of naughtiness she found irresistible. Like the little boy you couldn't stay mad at for long because you knew beneath the mischievousness was a decent and honorable soul.

The woman gave them a curious look before moving on. Serenity exchanged amused glances with Jackson as he ushered her into the adjoining room where the tour group gathered around the guide. "You realize you played right into that woman's hands," she whispered, leaning close. My, he smelled great. Danny never would wear cologne, even when she hinted she liked it.

"How so?"

"Tell me something. How long have you been oblivious of your effect on women?"

He cleared his throat. "You don't think she caught my wink, for *you?*"

"Even if she did, you told her we're not a couple. It's called mixed signals. Look, Jackson, I don't want to cramp your style. If you want to ask out a woman, then please go right ahead—"

Catching the chastising glance from the tour guide, Jackson placed a light hand on her elbow and steered her back out into the hallway. "I think it's time to get something straight."

"Okay." She swallowed the lump in her throat.

"I'm not interested in dating that woman or anyone else."

"Oh."

With one finger, he tipped her chin. "Want to know why?"

"I'm not sure."

With a low chuckle deep in his throat, he released his hold on her. "If anything, I want a solid, lasting relationship, and not just a date here and there. I've done enough of it, and I'm over it."

"Good to know."

"I thought you'd be happy about that."

She glanced up at him. "Why would you think that?" *Silly girl, asking him a leading question when you know the answer.* Her only excuse was she wanted to hear Jackson say the words. From his lips straight to her heart.

He stopped and turned to face her. "All right. Since you apparently want me to spell it out for you... If I have a relationship with *anyone*, hopefully it will be with the woman standing in front of me now." Stepping closer, he lowered his voice. "But I know she's not ready. And, for the record, I can be a patient man when I need to be, believe it or not."

Not giving her time to respond, Jackson nodded to the back patio and garden area. "Want to go check out the gardens? It might give us some landscaping ideas for the playground."

Unable to speak, she motioned for him to lead the way.

After they'd walked through the gardens for a full twenty minutes, trading occasional comments, Serenity knew it was time to show Jackson the note. He was right. She couldn't think about a dating relationship. If nothing else, by sharing it with him, he'd know she trusted him. She sensed it'd be important to him. Reaching into her purse, Serenity pulled out the note.

"I need to show you something. It's a note I received in Atlanta six weeks before moving back home. It was postmarked from here and mailed two days before I got it." Unfolding the slip of paper, she handed it to him. "It's getting sort of faded, but you can still read it."

Taking it from her, he appeared puzzled. He read it out loud, slowly, as though digesting the message before refolding it and handing it back to her. His brow creased and he sat on a huge rock along the pathway. "Interesting. Any theories on who sent it?"

Her pulse skipped a beat. What if no one had told Jackson about Danny and Liam? She felt the blood rush to her head. What had she done? *Calm down.* Nothing in the note indicated there was anything other than her mother's disappearance to solve. For all she knew, someone might have already spilled her secrets. Still, she didn't think so. Knowing Jackson, he would have asked her about them. Wanted to discuss her feelings about it.

Walking to the end of the walkway, she looked out over the ocean. Perhaps it was fitting that a cool breeze had kicked in and the clouds had darkened in the last few minutes alone. Any minute, there'd be the rumble of thunder.

"At first, I thought Dad sent it even though it's not his handwriting. Based on something he said, I realized he wasn't the one. Then I wondered if Mama could actually have sent it. Of course, the big 'if' in that statement would be if she's still alive. For one thing, it's not Mama's handwriting. If she *did* send it, then someone else wrote it."

"How about Deidre?" he asked.

That made her smile. "Impossible. Besides, she wouldn't bother with a note. She'd just call and order me to come home." A smile curved her lips. "As it was, she'd been begging me to come back as soon as I finished my degrees."

"Degrees plural?" Jackson's tone conveyed a mixture of surprise and admiration.

"I figured business administration might be a nice complement for decorating."

"You're as smart as you are beautiful. Then again, I already knew that." He gave her a crooked grin. "Anyone else you can think of who might have sent the note?"

Serenity discussed her ideas with Jackson, same as she'd done with Deidre.

"Playing devil's advocate for a minute," he said, "have you ever seen Charlie's handwriting?"

"I don't think so. If I did, I wouldn't recognize it now, anyway."

Jackson pushed away from the rock and pulled out his wallet. "As a matter of fact, I might have a sample. Charlie's doing the painting and wallpapering." He smiled. "Even the chair rail. He picked up the wood at the lumber yard early this morning and signed for it." Tugging out a small receipt, he held it out to her. "Take a look. Compare it to your note."

Glancing at the paper in her hands, Serenity held the two side-by-side. Jackson leaned over her shoulder, so close his cheek was millimeters away from hers. So close she could breathe in his woodsy scent. "Must you lean so close?"

He moved away. "Sorry. Am I offensive?"

"Not at all, but you're...distracting."

"Best news I've heard all day." A loud clap of thunder made her jump, and she burrowed into Jackson's chest. The wonderfully weird part was how natural it was. "Now *this* is fun," he said with a chuckle low in his throat.

She shook her head and pushed away from him. "The letters don't look the same to me. The ones in the note are big and loopy. Charlie's letters are small and precise." She held them both up for Jackson to see. "What do you think?"

"I agree," he said. "Based on this, Charlie didn't write your note." Another ear-splitting boom of thunder startled them both as Jackson pushed the invoice back in the front pocket of his jeans. "We'd better make a run for the car." He grabbed her hand. "Come on."

Note in hand, Serenity jogged beside him the few hundred yards to where he'd parked his car. As large drops started to pelt them, she shooed him away. "Don't worry about me. Get in before you're soaked and drip water all over this beautiful car."

"Water doesn't bother me, but hail's a killer," Jackson said. They both jumped into the car and pulled the doors closed mere seconds before the heavens opened and torrents of rain hammered down on them.

When he'd pulled the sleek, pale blue metallic car—some kind of classic British import, and no doubt worth a lot of money—to the curb outside her office earlier that morning, she'd been surprised. In a way, the car suited him perfectly—unique, powerful and distinctive. The citizens of Croisette Shores drove "normal" cars, but they were used to seeing the wealthy zipping in and around town in cars like this one. Still, she was surprised she hadn't heard about it until now. Could be because Jackson walked almost everywhere, like she did.

Serenity ran a hand over her hair and smoothed it down the front of her top and jeans, more from nerves than anything else. She'd never been so close—in a confined space—with Jackson. "Where'd you get the car?" she asked, trying to calm her breathing.

"It's an Aston Martin from the early 2000s. I found it through a dealer in Chicago, but he imported it from London. Get this. The dealer actually said, *This car draws admiration from any living, breathing man with red blood running through his veins.*"

Serenity laughed. *Boys will be boys.* "As opposed to a man with *blue* blood running through his veins? I really *do* think you're a royal incognito or whatever. And you sure won't be inconspicuous carting around town in *this* baby."

"I didn't buy it to impress anyone. I just happen to think it's really cool."

"Well, you don't need a car to accomplish that." She gave him a coy smile. "You've already got that covered."

Jackson shifted in the seat and turned toward her, making her more aware of him than ever. "Is that a compliment?"

"Yes, but don't get too excited. They're few and far between."

They talked for another few minutes, waiting for the rain to let up. Serenity talked about this and that and nothing in particular. Not normally a chatty person, she hadn't *chattered* so much in years. Sensing Jackson's amusement, she kept going, passing the time until he could start the car. "I'm sorry," she said at length. "I don't know what possessed me to go on and on like that."

"Notice I'm not complaining," he said, slanting her a grin. "I've learned more about you the last five minutes than I would have otherwise in a year. So, I'm actually praising the Lord for this rain."

Serenity watched as Jackson doodled on his notepad during their meeting in Town Hall. The group of four men and three women listened, asked questions, and answered questions they posed to them. Serenity thought they made good headway with the plans for the renovation of the playground. She and Jackson sat behind a long, narrow table facing a U-shaped grouping of tables where the others sat. All the talk about permits and licenses made her head spin, but Jackson took charge and impressed her with his research and how he took command of the discussion. She usually saw the fun, relaxed Jackson, but in this environment, he was articulate, forthright and downright admirable.

After nudging her arm with his elbow, Jackson tapped his pencil on the notepad. *Are you as bored as I am?*

Picking up the pencil, she scribbled, *More.* Still full from their lunch at The Happy Crab and a nice, quiet walk on the beach where they'd primarily discussed the playground plans, she fought overwhelming sleepiness and brought a quick hand to her mouth in an attempt to disguise her yawn. Embarrassed, she attempted to focus.

When she put down the pencil, Jackson took it and jotted notes, chiming in the active discussion every now and then. He cleared his throat at one point, prompting her to glance at the notepad. *Do you think these guys were ever kids?* When he drew a caricature of one of the men with oversized ears, a wide mouth and big teeth, she turned her head and stifled the urge to laugh. Picking up the pencil, she scribbled, *You're a very bad man.*

"Miss McClaren, what do you think of that idea?"

Warmth flooded her cheeks. Great. Jackson had a knack for getting her in trouble. All she'd heard was something about monkey bars. She'd never liked them. The indoor monkey bars in her school were too big for her small hands. Nerves always made her hands clammy and she'd fall... *Focus.*

"I think..." she said, searching for a diplomatic and halfway intelligent response when she had no idea of the specific issue. "I think it's a valid suggestion and one we should take under consideration. Why don't we discuss it at the next meeting?" She held her breath, hoping they didn't look at her like she had two heads. Jackson nudged her leg under the table.

Before the meeting ended, she'd played three games of tic-tac-toe with Jackson and won two. Taking the pencil, Jackson scrawled *XOXOXO* along the bottom of the page.

Smiling through tense lips, Serenity murmured her goodbyes while Jackson shook hands and talked with a couple of the men. How did he do it? Most likely, the man could charm anyone into doing his bidding. "Please tell me I didn't make a huge fool of myself," she said under her breath as they filed out of the meeting room.

"You didn't," he said, walking beside her as they descended the front steps of Town Hall. The rain ended long ago but a few dark clouds remained. "You were politically correct. Well-played, as your dad would say."

She smiled. "So, do *you* know what they were talking about?"

"Nope. Haven't a clue. May I have the honor of walking you back to your office?"

"No," she said. "It's late on a Friday afternoon, and I already told Kelsie to take off for the weekend." Looking around, she breathed in. "You'd never know it rained buckets earlier."

"Don't change the subject, please. Have a hot date tonight?"

"Sure do." She almost laughed at the expression on his face. "With Mr. Darcy."

"Fan of Jane Austen?"

"That, too, but it's the name of my neighbor's cat. A total misnomer. Trust me, this Mr. Darcy is no gentleman. I take popcorn, Mrs. Marciano makes peanut butter and banana sandwiches and we watch back-to-back episodes of *Who's the Boss.*"

"Sounds like fun. I might have to crash the party sometime. I can bring the snacks and some cat treats to get on Mr. Darcy's good side."

Serenity laughed. "You do, and you're golden." *Not that you're not already.* Her cell phone rang. "I'd better get it," she said, pulling it from her purse, not recognizing the number. "It might be a client. Or Dad."

"Is this Serenity McClaren?" The voice was female.

"Yes."

"This is Kendra Lawson. I used to work with your mother at Croisette Shores Hospital."

"Yes, of course. Hi, Mrs. Lawson. How are you?"

"I'm at the hospital, Serenity. They've just admitted your father. He came in by ambulance."

"My dad?" *Oh, no.* Serenity moved her hand over her chest. "What happened?"

"We're not sure, but we think he might have had a heart attack."

"Is he okay? How bad is it?" Her heart pounded so hard her ears throbbed. Jackson put a supportive hand on her arm.

"They're running tests now. Just come as soon as you can. Hopefully, we'll have some answers by then."

As soon as she thanked Kendra and disconnected the call, Jackson grabbed her hand.

"Let's go."

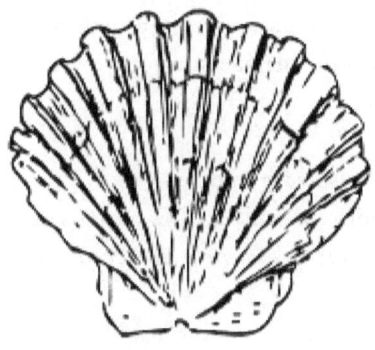

~CHAPTER 16~

When Jackson cut the engine in the Croisette Shores Hospital parking lot ten minutes later, Serenity darted out and sprinted toward the revolving front door. That odd sensation came over her again, as though she moved in slow motion. Or like she was someone else and watching from a distant place. Although her dad could be gruff and infuriate her, he was all she had left.

Hold on, Dad. Don't leave me now.

She squinted as her eyes adjusted to the lights inside the hospital lobby. With Jackson right beside her, she hurried to the information desk, thankful a volunteer manned the station.

"My dad was brought here by ambulance. Can you tell me where we need to go?"

The volunteer asked her a few cursory questions. When she couldn't choke out her dad's name, Jackson answered for her. Faltering a few times, she managed to provide the needed information. The woman checked her computer and told them Clinton was being prepped for surgery and instructed her to go to the family waiting room on the fourth floor.

Thanking the woman, Jackson put a light hand on her elbow and headed for the elevators. After shifting from one foot to the other while they waited, Serenity finally stalked toward the stairwell and ran up all four flights without stopping.

Another woman sat behind a reception desk near the elevator doors. She seemed sympathetic and told her the surgeon would be out to speak with her momentarily. "There's water and coffee in the waiting room. Help yourself."

"Serenity McClaren?"

"Yes." Turning, she spied a middle-aged surgeon in green scrubs walking toward them from an adjacent hallway. His expression was impossible to read, worrying her even more. *God, please help me accept whatever he has to say.*

"I'm Dr. Saunders."

She swallowed hard as she shook his hand. "How's my dad?"

"We're prepping him for a procedure now. Your dad noticed a weakness and tingling in his arms. He had a bad headache and felt dizzy. When he called 9-1-1, his words were slightly slurred and he was having trouble with his motor coordination. I've conducted an angiogram and discussed Clinton's case with his physician. Combined with what he experienced today, everything points to a significant carotid artery blockage."

"So, it wasn't a heart attack?"

"No," the doctor said, "but the symptoms very closely mimic a heart attack. The carotid arteries are the two large blood vessels on either side of the neck that supply blood and oxygen to the brain. The blockage is caused by a buildup of plaque on the arterial walls called atherosclerosis, a progressive vascular disease that's an accumulation of fatty substances inside the walls of the arteries. That condition leads to narrowing of the arterial walls and causes the carotid blockage."

"What procedure do you need to do?" she asked. When Jackson covered her hand with his, Serenity gripped it tight.

"Traditionally, the surgical procedure is to perform an endarterectomy. That's where we open up the neck, expose the artery and physically remove the plaque. But there's a newer procedure that's been highly successful—and minimally invasive—called a carotid angioplasty. We pass a catheter from the blood vessels in the groin to the carotid artery. Then we'll inflate a balloon to open the artery and put in a stent to hold the artery open. That's what I'd like to do for your father unless we see we need to do the endarterectomy once we get him in the OR." Dr. Saunders focused on her again. "I'll need your consent for the surgery, Miss McClaren. The nurse has the form at the desk."

"Of course. I'll sign it right away."

Dr. Saunders nodded. "This type of blockage is one of the major contributing factors for a stroke. If the plaque hardens and narrows the arteries completely, the blood supply and oxygen to the brain is restricted. That causes the brain cells to begin dying, leading to a loss of brain function, permanent damage or even death. It's a good thing your father called for help as soon as he recognized the warning signs."

The surgeon's words were factual and to-the-point, but Serenity admired the compassion in his eyes and expression. She trusted her dad would be in capable hands for the surgery. If he thought her dad was in imminent danger, he wouldn't be explaining it all now.

"Thanks, Dr. Saunders," she said. "I appreciate all you're doing for him." Her mind was spinning as she returned to the desk to sign the consent form.

"Do you have any idea how long the surgery might last?" Serenity asked the nurse.

"Depends on what they find, if there's any complications and how much repair work they have to do. I'm sure he'll be fine, dear," the nurse told her with a sympathetic smile.

"Repair work?" Serenity grumbled. "That makes Dad sound like an old, broken down car."

"Try to relax," Jackson said, his voice soothing. "I'll go get you some water. Unless you'd rather have coffee?"

She shook her head. "I've heard about rancid hospital coffee. Water's fine. Thanks."

Nearly an hour and several cups of water later, Serenity bit her lip to control its trembling. Although it sounded like it was a fairly routine procedure, she couldn't stop worrying. Jackson remained seated beside her, a solid, quiet presence. From the way he bowed his head often and clasped his hands together, she understood he'd been praying off and on. That alone touched something deep inside her. She hadn't been able to pray. With her stomach twisted in knots, she felt like she might be sick. After visiting the ladies room and gulping down more water from the fountain, she returned to her seat.

"Thanks for being here," she whispered.

"I'm honored."

Her eyes filled with tears and she lowered her gaze. *Is this man for real?* She wasn't worthy of this man, didn't deserve him. Jackson was so strong in his faith. God's grace was one thing, but what had she ever done so right to deserve his friendship?

After another twenty minutes, Dr. Saunders returned to the waiting room. Not waiting for him to call her name, Serenity jumped to her feet and rushed over to him.

Removing his surgical cap, the doctor rubbed one hand over his brow. "He's fine. We performed the angioplasty and put in the stent. He'll need to stay overnight in the cardio rehab unit for observation, and I might be able to send him home as early as tomorrow. I'll make that determination when I check on him in the morning. We'll give you literature and instructions for an extended treatment plan," he said. "The recovery time can take as little as a few days or weeks, depending on how your father reacts to the procedure and how well he follows the directions." The slight irony in his tone suggested the surgeon might be acquainted with her father.

"Clinton needs to quit smoking and eat foods low in saturated and trans fats. His weight isn't an issue, but he needs his blood pressure checked regularly and daily exercise." The doctor's expression was kind. "If he adheres to a healthier routine, the prognosis is good for a longer and more productive life than he would have had without the procedure. I'd take this as a warning, Miss McClaren. If there's a next time, your father might not be as lucky."

Tears flooded her eyes and relief filled her soul. "Thank you again, Dr. Saunders. I'm grateful for everything you've done. I'll make sure my dad follows your orders."

"Good." The doctor nodded. "I'll be around to check on him later tonight and again in the morning. If you have any questions at any time, feel free to call my office."

"When can I see him?"

"He's resting in the post-op recovery room and needs to lie still for a period of time. Then we'll check his vitals before moving him to a room. Give him about an hour."

Jackson reiterated his thanks before turning to her. "Want to get something to eat while we wait?"

She shook her head. "I can't possibly eat, but I'll go with you. It'll be good to stretch our legs and get a change of scenery." After speaking with the woman behind the desk and being told to go to the sixth floor—the cardiac wing—

upon their return, they headed into the elevator and then down to the cafeteria on the ground floor.

A few minutes later, Serenity watched with faint amusement as Jackson attacked his turkey sandwich. Even when life was in turmoil, men could always eat. Then again, it wasn't *his* dad who could have died. Her lemonade was tart, and when she winked, Jackson returned it. "You goof," she said. "The lemonade's really sour."

"My mistake. I thought you were trying to relieve the tension." He swallowed a huge bite of his sandwich and wiped his mouth before offering his bag of chips to her.

"No, thanks. I have half a mind to snatch that bag out of your hands. My dad eats too many of those and look where it got him."

"Point taken, but come on. Sometimes you have to bend the rules a little. I don't scarf them down all the time. Who knows? I might find one that looks like Jesus."

She almost spit out her lemonade. Unfortunate timing. "What?"

Jackson examined a chip before popping it in his mouth. "Haven't you heard how people are always finding food oddities that resemble deity?"

"If nothing else, I appreciate your blatant attempt to make me smile." Lowering her empty glass, Serenity ran her finger slowly around the rim, lost in thought. "Why does Dr. Saunders seem so familiar?"

"Maybe he played the tuba in the Salvation Army band with Art what's-his-name and your dad. Or he's a big supporter of the fire department. Does it matter?"

She glanced at Jackson across the table as he chomped on another chip. "No, I guess not. And it's trombone, not tuba. My mind tends to wander to trivial things when I'm under stress. Surely you've seen it in your profession. Must be some kind of coping mechanism."

A woman eating alone at a nearby table caught her attention. She wore dark-rimmed glasses and her hair was completely hidden beneath a black scarf. Her shoulders were narrow and she wore plain clothing—jeans and a nondescript, plain, dark T-shirt. Deep red fingernails. Like with Dr. Saunders, something about this woman seemed familiar. Was it possible this was the same woman she'd seen on the street when Jackson left her office? For one thing, why would she keep her features hidden or disguised in a hospital cafeteria, of all places? Was she finally going crazy and exhaustion combined with worry was making her loopy?

"I guess I should have known something like this would eventually happen," she said.

"Oh no, you don't." Pushing his plate aside, Jackson grabbed her hand and held on tight. "Don't you even think about blaming yourself for your father's condition."

Serenity blew out a breath and focused on a group of people at a nearby table. They barely touched their food. She wondered which of their relatives or friends was in the hospital. Although her mother always wanted to be a nurse, it was the one thing she'd *never* wanted to be. She hated hospitals. They reeked of antiseptic and death.

"I should have come home sooner, Jackson. Should have gone through every cabinet, every drawer. I should have checked everything in the pantry and his bathroom medicine cabinet. Thrown out every single thing that's unhealthy or contributed to him being here now." She pushed her curled fist against her lips, steeling herself not to shed any tears when all she wanted was to break down and sob. "I knew he wasn't well. Knew he'd probably end up here and yet what'd I do? I ran away. Dad could have died here all alone while I was ignoring him in Atlanta. I'm a horrible daughter." Full of self-loathing, she couldn't even look at him.

Jackson squeezed her hand. "Listen to me, Serenity." He waited until she raised her eyes to his. "You weren't ignoring him and you're a terrific daughter, but you can't take on the weight of the world. I know you've been doing everything you can to get your dad to eat better. You're getting him out for fresh air and exercise. His sedentary lifestyle and bad habits landed him here, and it's in no way your fault. If anything, you *saved* his life."

She tilted her head to one side, taking comfort from his words. "How do you figure that?"

"By coming home. *That* was the best gift you could have given him." His gentle smile filled her heart. "Let's go see how he's doing."

*T*hree hours later, crawling into bed, Serenity eyed her Bible. If neglect formed cobwebs, that holy book would be full of them. But she couldn't focus on God's Word until she cleared the cobwebs from her mind. The ones crowding her in, threatening to suffocate her. Questions, so many questions. Tonight she could barely keep her eyes open. Tomorrow she'd blow off the dust and crack open that Bible. And then she'd pray. She didn't really know what she was doing, but one of the best things about the Lord was that He'd meet her wherever she was in life. After turning off the bedside lamp, she closed her eyes and crossed her arms behind her head.

She'd wanted to stay overnight at the hospital, but the doctors assured her Clinton was stabilized, medicated and would sleep through the night. Jackson convinced her she'd be more help and comfort to Clinton if she got some decent rest and returned in the morning. When she called Jackson to thank him for being so wonderful and staying with her at the hospital, she heard suspicious noises in the background.

"Jackson, where are you? Don't make me feel like the guilty daughter all over again. You're still at the hospital, aren't you?" She tried to keep her tone from sounding accusatory. The man was a saint. Someone would likely find *his* likeness in a potato chip someday. Irreverent as it was, she smiled at the thought.

"No reason to feel guilty, so get over it. I knew you really didn't want to leave, but I could tell you're exhausted. I'll take the overnight shift and stay until you come back in the morning. I can help you get your dad settled at the house, if you want."

I want. How did he manage it? With his ready smile and kind gestures, Jackson was working his way into her life to the point where she couldn't imagine not having him around. "Anyone ever tell you you're a prince among men?"

"Not anyone who counted. Coming from Princess Serenity, that's high praise."

"And you're such a big flirt." She stifled her yawn.

"Only with you."

"Take care of my dad, will you, please?"

"I'll be here. With prayers. The doctors will do the rest. Get some sleep and bring me some stiff coffee in the morning, if you please. One creamer."

"Will do. Goodnight."

"Night night."

"Thanks, Jackson," she added. "For everything."

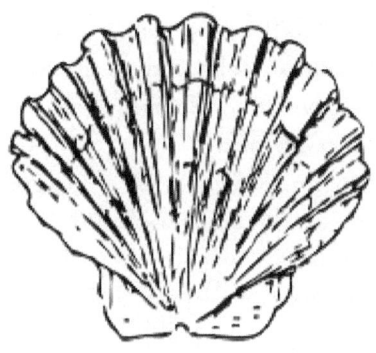

~CHAPTER 17~

*D*riving to the hospital the next morning, Serenity started a mental checklist of things that needed to change. Should she move back in the house with her dad so she could keep a better eye on him? Alternatively, she could move him into her small rental at least until she was assured he was recovered. Bad idea. They'd probably be at each other's throats in less than a day. Still, she hated to think he could have an emergency and she wouldn't be there to help. Not that she could possibly be with him every waking hour. He'd accuse her of smothering him and treating him like an invalid again. He didn't know the half of it. The thing was, she'd already lost two men in her life and she wasn't about to lose her father on her watch.

The most likely scenario? She'd air out the house and do exactly what she'd told Jackson. Go through the entire place, scrub and disinfect every surface. Get rid of every pack of cigarettes and toss out all the unhealthy food in the refrigerator and freezer. Restock it with nutritious, natural foods. To her knowledge, her dad didn't drink alcohol except an occasional beer, but nothing was beyond the scope of possibility. When she couldn't be with him—at least for the next couple of weeks—she'd hire a part-time nurse to make sure he ate regular meals and walked around the block if nothing else. She couldn't afford to take much time away from work, but maybe she could work more from home and Kelsie could forward her calls.

The ring tone on her cell phone sounded as Serenity approached the information desk in the hospital lobby. Setting the coffee cups on the counter and a bag with her dad's clothes on the floor, she retrieved her phone.

"Good morning, Princess Serenity."

She smiled. "Good morning to you, too." Catching the knowing grin from the woman behind the desk, she turned aside and lowered her voice. "How's Dad? Is he awake?"

"He's groggy, but he managed to say a few words. By the way, who's Prudence?"

Good thing she wasn't sipping coffee. As it was, she sputtered and almost choked. Jackson was dangerous to have around when she had a beverage nearby. "My alter ego. Never mind. That's actually very encouraging. He's his old ornery self, so he must already be on the road to recovery."

"I think so. Dr. Saunders is checking him over now. Hang on a sec." She waited, feeling silly that Jackson was a few floors above her and she was down in the lobby, getting the play-by-play on her cell phone. "Dr. Saunders signed the release papers, so your dad's free to go as soon as he's dressed. Come on up. I'll meet you at the elevator."

Five minutes later, she glimpsed Jackson as soon as the elevator doors parted. "Are you my personal welcoming committee?"

"I hope that's not a complaint," he said.

"Never. Here's your coffee. One creamer, as requested."

He accepted the cup with a tired smile. Lifting the lid, he inhaled the brew and took a quick sip. "Thanks. Ah, honey, that's great coffee. Perfect." Even with his hair tousled, shirt rumpled and faint circles beneath his eyes, Jackson was easily the most appealing man on the planet. Her heart increased its pace and Serenity cleared her throat, hoping none of the nurses on duty were single and gorgeous. This man was a keeper, and any female with eyes and a functioning brain could see it.

"You'd better lead the way. I hope it's okay to take coffee in his room," she said, almost as an afterthought as Jackson fell into place beside her.

"He's down this way." Jackson angled his head further down the ward. "I think it's fine to take coffee in his room. I'll warn you, though. He doesn't look much better than he did last night."

"But he's *here*."

"Yes, he is." Jackson guided her toward a room near the back corner. "Let's go get your dad ready to check out." He raked his fingers through his hair, messing it up a little more. Could the man be any more adorable? When he was tired and a little off-his-game, he seemed rather vulnerable and that appealed to her on many levels. None of which she cared to contemplate now. "Okay, you know what I meant, right?" he said. "I'm tired and need some serious sleep. It's my only excuse."

"You're very cute when you're sleepy and unkempt," she said, smoothing the hair on the top of his head. "There, that's better. Do you have any patients today?"

"Nope." He shook his head. "No patients on Saturday. Cardinal rule. Well, unless there's an emergency."

"Right," she said, running a hand over her hair. "Good rule. I forgot it's Saturday."

He gave her another tired smile and she took a deep breath. "Okay. Time to face the ornery one. I'm sure he's even worse since he's been cooped up in a hospital bed."

"You might be surprised."

When they entered the room, a nurse was helping him sit up on the bed. "I'll take it from here," Clinton said. His eyes rested on her and he made an effort to smile. "Here's my beautiful Serenity."

"How are you, Dad?" Putting her cup on a table, she walked to the side of the bed and put her hand over his. It felt dry to her touch and he looked so small, swallowed by the hospital bed and the starkness of the white sheets. Jackson was right. He looked terrible. Dark circles rimmed his eyes and his face held an unnatural pallor. Dr. Saunders wouldn't release him if he didn't believe he was ready to leave the hospital.

She hated seeing him like this but coached herself to stay strong for his sake as well as her own.

"How's it look like I'm doing?"

She darted a glance to where Jackson stood by the window. Catching her look, he motioned to the door. She hoped her pointed glance answered his silent question. In truth, she needed him here with her even though she knew how tired he was. "Well, you're in good humor this morning," she said to her father. "I'm here to take you home, so be nice, please." She glanced at the other bed in the room, grateful it was unoccupied.

"I have your mother to thank for being here, you know." Clinton's tone held no animosity and not a trace of irony.

She stared at him, trying not to gape. "What are you talking about?"

"Elise taught me the signs to watch for when you're having an attack, heart or otherwise—the numbness, the sharp pains, the tightness in the chest. Soon as I started feeling weird, I picked up the phone and called."

"I'm glad you did, but I'm sorry I wasn't there for you."

He waved his hand and winced when he shifted on the bed.

"Are you okay? What can I do? Call the nurse?"

"Just felt a pinch. I think I'll live. Can you grab my clothes over there in the closet?"

"You'd better. Live that is," she said. "I stopped by the house and brought you some fresh clothes." Opening the bag, she pulled out a pair of his shorts and a nice shirt.

"Thanks. The good doctor's taking very good care of me, you know."

"I'm glad to hear it. That's why they're here, after all."

Clinton snorted and angled his head toward Jackson. "*That* doctor over there. He's got a real nice bedside manner."

Serenity felt her cheeks flush. Her dad's wry sense of humor never failed to give her an anchor for her unsteady emotions, as embarrassing as it could be at times.

"I'm much obliged for you sticking around last night, Doc," Clinton said. "Right kind of you."

Leaning close, Serenity kissed his cheek and her hold on his hand tightened. Her gaze fell on a simple, clear glass jar overflowing with Vi's Violet roses sitting on the window sill. "Dad, where did those roses come from?"

Clinton shrugged. "One of the nurses brought them in. Don't rightly know where she got them." He scratched his head. "She said, 'Someone's thinking of you, Mr. McClaren,' and put them over there by the window. I was kinda out of it and didn't think much about it."

"I guess someone else besides Mama knows about them," she said, half under her breath. She couldn't take the time to puzzle over it now. "I'll let you change while I go fill out the release forms or whatever I need to do. Try not to annoy the nurses too much. Or Jackson."

"Can't promise that." When he chuckled, Serenity was afraid he'd start coughing and dislodge something. She was grateful when nothing happened.

"I'll stay and help him get dressed," Jackson said. "If he plays his cards right, I might even do some wheelies with his wheelchair."

Shaking her head, she hoped Jackson was teasing. "Listen, I talked to Charlie this morning, and he's planning on coming by the house this afternoon for a visit, if you're up to it."

"Did you tell him to bring his checkers?"

"I did, and he already had them by the door, ready to go. Don't be surprised if you get a visit from Deidre tomorrow, too."

"Guess I'd better put on my designer duds for that girl. She's a real fashion setter, that one. You met Deidre Payne yet, Jackson?"

"Haven't had the pleasure," he said, crumpling his coffee cup and tossing it in the trash can from several feet away.

"Good aim," her father said. "You should take Serenity and have one of them double dates or whatever with Deidre and her husband. You'd like Wes. He's a landscaper and developer here in town. Got a solid reputation."

"Is that a fact?" Jackson moved his gaze to hers, a question in his eyes. "I might have a project for him if he's game."

An hour later, Serenity's eyes misted as she watched Jackson with her father. The two men in her life. That stopped her thoughts cold, but Jackson was undeniably part of her life now.

"Park me in my recliner and I'll be fine," Clinton said as Jackson opened the front door. Finding it unlocked, he arched a brow. Feigning innocence, she shrugged and darted off to check the mailbox.

"Are you hungry, Dad?" She set a glass of ice water on the table beside his chair a few minutes later.

"A little. Wanna stay for lunch, Doc?"

Jackson glanced at her. "Sure, if it's okay with Serenity." She could tell he was pleased by the offer. "Can I help?"

"Keep Dad company while I get it ready. I guarantee it won't be anything fancy."

"The simpler the better."

Another five minutes later, she'd pulled everything out of the refrigerator. Ginseng scratched at the side door. "Hang on, Ginseng. I'm coming," she called. Hearing a chuckle from behind her, Serenity whirled around to face Jackson.

"Great name for quasi-hippie canine parents. Where's the leash? Your dad's resting, so I can take Ginseng for a walk if you want."

She smiled her thanks. "That'd be great." Grabbing the leash from its hook, she handed it to him. "How's Freud these days?"

Jackson's grin grew broader. "Still a sofa hog, but a lovable one. How much time before we eat?"

"Well, I'm heating the soup now and then I need to make the sandwiches. Maybe ten minutes?"

"Sure thing." By the time Jackson returned, she'd refilled Ginseng's water and food dishes and put them outside the door.

"We're ready to eat if you can call Dad to the table." She eyed the arrangement of Vi's Violet roses in another Waterford vase inherited from her maternal grandmother. Hopefully, her father wouldn't turn up his nose at their lunch of lean turkey breast on whole wheat sandwiches and homemade, low-sodium vegetable soup.

Serenity smiled as she heard Clinton insisting he was fine to walk into the kitchen on his own. As they gathered around the small table, Jackson took her hand to ask grace. Her heart sputtered when he reached for her father's hand. To her surprise, Clinton accepted the gesture without comment or protest. She couldn't remember the last time she'd seen him bow his head in prayer. Probably at their neighbor's funeral, but never—*ever*—in a church. Closing her eyes, Serenity concentrated on Jackson's prayer.

After fussing over Clinton during the meal, he finally cut her off. "I'm not dead yet. Take it easy on me, girl. It's not like the surgeon cut me open. I had a little medical procedure, that's all. Charlie's had something like it and so have half the men over fifty down at Martha's Cup & Such on any given morning." He glanced at Jackson and chuckled. "Not that it's a reflection of the food at Martha's since I hear you're there almost every morning, Doc. Glad you've taken to the locals around here and vice versa."

Serenity paused her spoon halfway to her mouth and lowered it back to her bowl. "I didn't know Charlie had any trouble."

Clinton waved his hand. "Not anything major. It was a couple of years ago. He's fit as a fiddle now."

"Well, he looks good. I'm sure he wants to be around for Maya," Serenity said. "Just like I want to keep *you* around."

"Glad to hear it." Her father gave her a rare wink. When he inclined his head toward Jackson and waggled his brows, she continued eating her soup and ignored him.

They enjoyed small talk and Jackson filled them in on the latest developments with the playground renovation while they ate. Her father brightened and laughed a few times. She hadn't seen him act this relaxed and at ease with someone new in a long time.

"Great soup," Jackson said when he finished. "I insist on helping you with the dishes."

"That'll take all of five minutes, but anything to be close to my pretty daughter, huh, Jackson?"

"You bet. You found me out." Jackson and her dad shared a look she couldn't begin to comprehend, like they were members of a private, two-man boys' club. "Nothing I'd like better."

She had to admit, working with Jackson beside her in the kitchen was fun. Danny always plopped in front of the television and watched dumb, mindless shows instead of engaging in conversation or showing much interest in her day.

"Jackson, what are your hobbies?" She handed him the last plate to dry. "Assuming you have some."

"Sure I have hobbies," he said. "I like to read thrillers and medical mysteries, that type of thing. I stick with Christian fiction now since the mainstream ones have too much...stuff. It really started to bother me." Unfolding the dish towel after drying the last plate, he laughed. "Ah, the happy, dancing pears."

The amusement in his voice made Serenity smile. "Don't start counting pears or you'll be here the rest of the day."

With her father dozing comfortably in his bed an hour later, Serenity walked Jackson to the front door. Stepping outside, Jackson raised his face to the sky. "I think we're going to get a storm soon. You can smell it."

She smiled. "I don't know if it's the ocean air or what, but you're right. Very astute for a city boy."

"City boys know about rain," he said. "Here's another observation: we need a landscaper for the playground project. I was getting ready to start gathering bids, but I have it on good authority your friend Deidre's husband has a solid reputation. Why not give him first dibs on the job?"

"Dibs? I haven't heard that word in ages, but somehow I think you have a plan."

"Always." He turned to her. "Your dad had another great suggestion. Let's have dinner, the four of us—Deidre and Wes, you and me. Call it a working dinner or whatever works for you. We'll discuss landscaping ideas for the playground. Just so you know it's not a date. Not really."

"Let me talk to Deidre and we'll set something up."

He appeared mildly surprised. "Don't forget."

"I won't. You have my word."

"Sit with me in church tomorrow morning?" Jackson's smile was enough reason to say yes.

"Sure," she said, "as long as Dad doesn't need me."

"I already asked him, and he gave his blessing. Said he'd be fine and Deidre's coming over and bringing lunch. Said she could stay for however long."

"I can't tell you how much I appreciate all your help. I don't know many guys who'd be so nice as to stay all night with a crotchety old man in the hospital."

He chuckled. "I don't mean to sound irreverent, but he *was* asleep most of that time."

"He likes you."

"I like *him*. Listen, there's a church picnic tomorrow, right after the service," he said. "Want to go together?"

"As long as my dad's okay and Deidre can stay, I suppose it's okay. Would it be all right if I invite my neighbor, Mrs. Marciano, to go with us?"

With a smile she felt to her toes, Jackson tweaked her chin. "More than all right, but there's one little problem. My car's only a two-seater."

"I'll drive separately then," she said. "Besides, it'll make it easier to come back and check on Dad and then go pick her up. I think she'd have fun. Mrs. Marciano spends too much time alone in her house, but from what I can see, she gets around fine. Should I bring a covered dish?"

"Not this time. You have enough to do with your dad, and I'm sure there'll be more than enough food."

"If it rains, will they cancel the picnic?" she asked, glancing up at the sky.

"Not sure. I guess we'll have to wait and see what happens."

Serenity nodded and walked him to his car parked in the driveway. She leaned back against it, her hands behind her. Jackson mirrored her actions. Thinking better of it, recalling how protective men could be about their cars, she moved away. "Sorry. I shouldn't lean against such an expensive sports car."

With a gentle hand on her arm, Jackson guided her back to her original position. "Lean away. I don't mind. Notice I'm doing it, too. But, I don't give free leaning rights to just anyone, you know."

"Thanks." The fragrance of her mother's roses wafted to her in the warm afternoon air. "Mama's roses. Can you smell them?"

Jackson lifted his head and nodded. "Very nice."

"My mom loved them. They're called Vi's Violet. They're pretty rare. I helped her plant them along the back wall of the house when I was six. They've come back every year since then. You can always catch their scent when the breeze blows a certain way. Of course, I can't help but see the irony of how those rare roses come back even without Mama here to tend to them."

Jackson appeared momentarily startled.

"Something wrong?"

He shook his head. "No. Sorry. What kind of roses are they?"

"Vi's Violet. I know, I'd never heard of them either. It's another thing that makes my mother unique. Cultivating those roses was one of her favorite things."

Jackson nodded, but he still looked stunned for reasons known only to him. "I imagine your father tends to them or else he hires a gardener."

She considered his words. "I hadn't thought about it, but you're probably right. Dad can be cheap when it comes to certain things, but when it comes to something of Mama's, he doesn't want to change anything—from the pillows arranged a certain way on the living room sofa, the bowl full of pears on the kitchen counter or the frayed chair in the family room. If it takes a gardener to keep those roses alive, you're right. That's exactly what Dad would do."

"That's kind of sweet in its own way, don't you think?" Jackson said.

"I suppose." She turned to face him directly. "The flowers in the jar in Dad's hospital room were Vi's Violet roses. I can't imagine who brought them. I've never seen them anywhere but at the back of our house." They'd left them on the nurse's station.

"Jackson, I wanted to tell you about something Dad said when I was here at the house on Thursday night." In some ways, it felt like much longer. "At first, I was upset and not thinking clearly. But now, I think it might be pretty significant."

"Tell me."

Serenity inhaled another deep breath. "I think Mama's alive."

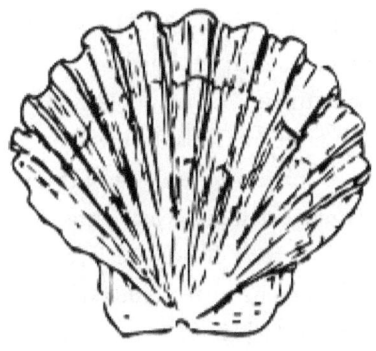

~CHAPTER 18~

"Dad always talks about Mama in present tense," Serenity said. "I mean, that's nothing new. He's done it since she disappeared. At first, I thought it was because he's still unbearably lonely without her and it's his subconscious way of keeping her memory alive."

Jackson nodded. "Could be. It's a common response to grief, especially in cases of missing persons." He didn't seem unduly shocked by her statement. *Does he share my belief Mama's alive?*

"I was pretty horrible to him." She dug her toe into a loose section of pavement on the driveway. Something else to have repaired.

"You couldn't be horrible if you tried. Please don't tell me you think that triggered his attack."

"No, not really. You're right about that. Dad brought it on himself. But I blasted Mama, and in his eyes, that's like the cardinal sin. I asked him why he thought she'd left and then accused her of being selfish and leaving when I needed her most."

"What was his response?"

"He said the sadness was too much handle." She ran a hand over her brow and smoothed long strands of her hair away from her face. "I don't know. Something like that. I was impatient and didn't want to accept that answer. It wasn't good enough, I guess. Not that he can give me one I'll accept." She shrugged and darted a helpless glance at him. "I asked him if he thought she was alive, but he said he didn't know what to think."

"Then what makes you think your mom's alive?"

"I told him how my faith in Christ helped me get through the last few years. I half-expected him to make a joke about faith or organized 'religion' like he's done in the past. I remember him saying Christianity is something for the weak to hang onto when they can't handle their own lives. Ever since I came back to Croisette Shores, though, he's been remarkably...non-combative."

Serenity raised her eyes to Jackson's. "This is the thing: even though Mama was raised in a church, I can count on one hand the number of times I ever heard her mention God when I was growing up. Before I left the house, Dad made a comment about how I sounded like Mama in always talking about God."

A new light came into Jackson's eyes. "I'd say that's a pretty good indicator he knows something all right. What's your heart telling you?"

"That she's alive. And..."

"And...what?"

She swallowed hard. "Maybe Dad *knows* she's alive. It makes me absolutely furious to think he might be holding back on me. And sad. And overjoyed to think she might really be out there. She *rejected* us. Do you know how that feels?"

"Yes, I do," he said, his voice quiet. "Not in the same way, of course, but pushed out of someone's life? Yeah, I've been there. When you get to be my age, it's inevitable someone along the way's stomped on your heart."

"I'm sorry. How selfish you must think me." She glanced up at him. "If somebody stomped on your heart, they were sadly misguided." The tears she'd tried to hold back stung her eyes. "I wonder why—if Mama *is* alive—where is she and why won't she come home again?"

When she collapsed against him, Jackson stroked one hand over her hair and whispered words of comfort. What he said, she didn't know. He was there, and that's all she needed. "I'm sorry," she sobbed against his shoulder. "I don't know what to think, how to feel, anything right now." Gazing up at him, she bit back another sob. "I'm tired of crying but it seems all I'm capable of doing. Tell me what I'm supposed to feel, what I'm supposed to do, Jackson."

"I wish I could, but I promise we'll find your answers. We'll find your mother."

Pulling away, Serenity wiped a hand across her damp cheek. "Should I confront Dad? Demand answers?"

"Not yet. If he *does* know something, it could be he's afraid to tell you. Could be he's afraid of how you'll react. On the other hand, it's possible he 'slipped' on purpose, hoping you'd pick up on it."

"Do *you* think she's still alive? Tell me your honest opinion, professional or not. Please." Bunching his T-shirt in both hands, Serenity felt the steady vibration of Jackson's heartbeat beneath her hands. Life-affirming and strong. The connection between them was intense and she couldn't let go of him. She looked into his eyes, seeking answers she knew he couldn't give but reassurance he *could* give. "You 'read' people all the time, so tell me what you believe. I need to know."

"Yes, baby, I think your mother is alive."

Releasing her hold on him, Serenity smoothed her hand over the front of his shirt. "You'll need to change. Sorry I messed you up." She sniffled and turned the other way. "*I'm* kind of messed up, but at least you still have a good reputation in this town."

"No, Serenity, you're not messed up. If you are, then you're the best messed up person I know." Shaking his head, he chuckled. "That didn't come out right, but believe me, you have it more together than most people I know. There's a lot of dysfunction in the world, and from people who've been through a whole lot less than you." He tipped her chin and gazed into her eyes. "I think you're one of the strongest people—man or woman—I know. You've also got the love of the Lord in your heart, and, although I didn't know you before, I sense you're even stronger now."

This man sensed so much it scared her. In a weird way, it also comforted her. The deep affection in his eyes awakened parts of her she thought had died right along with Danny. "I think the best thing to do is to see if your dad says anything else that might clue us in that your mom might be alive. Even more important, clues that he might be in touch with her."

She frowned. "It'll be hard, but I'll try. How can someone disappear into thin air?" With a snap of her fingers, she gave him a quizzical look. "Poof! No trace of a life. Just...gone."

"Have you or your dad tried to find her, either on your own or hired anyone?"

"I haven't, no, but Dad hired a private detective and kept him on retainer for a couple of years. Nothing ever turned up, obviously. Considering the guy's currently in jail for fraud, I'm wondering if he ever tried. Probably took the money and made a couple of dead-end phone calls. I've done a little research on the Internet, but I haven't been able to find anything and haven't had the money to do more." Serenity wiped under her eyes with the back of her hand, absorbing the last of her tears. "If Mama's alive, she either doesn't want to be found, or—"

"If you want, I can make a few phone calls, but I don't want to overstep my boundaries."

She glanced up in surprise. "Do you know a private detective?"

"I've hired one in the past. My brother Kyle is a lawyer and has access to a program that tracks down people. It might be the place to start. I guarantee they could at least find your mom's last known address and then we can go from there."

"What if it's Croisette Shores?"

"Is that what you're most afraid of?"

She held his gaze. "Maybe. I don't know."

"I won't do anything until you say the word, but as soon as you do, I'll make some calls."

"Okay. Thanks. I appreciate your willingness to help me." Reaching for his hand, she ran her thumb back and forth across it. "If you're hoping to be my knight on the big white horse, riding in to save me, there's really no need."

"I'd like to pray with you, Serenity."

She nodded, unable to speak. An unexpected warmth filled her, similar to what she experienced the night she'd invited Jesus into her life. That moment changed her life. This moment was changing her *heart*, especially with this wonderful man beside her. Bowing her head, Serenity focused on Jackson's words and liked the feel of his hand, warm and protective, around hers.

"*Father God, I ask You to give Serenity the kind of comfort only You can and that peace that passes all understanding, Let it fill her with a renewed sense of who You are. Draw her close so she might rediscover how much You love her and have always loved her. If it's in Your will, please help her find the answers about the past and her mother so she can move forward. And if I may help her, please guide me as Your servant. I ask these things in the precious name of Your Son, Jesus. Amen.*"

Jackson waited a few moments, not squeezing her hand, not nudging her to say anything. But the words wouldn't come. At some point during his prayer, she'd leaned against his shoulder and he moved his arm to circle her shoulders.

"The words are stuck somewhere inside me," she whispered. *Wow. I'm a failure at saying a simple prayer.*

"It's okay," he whispered back. "I'd rather you not say anything than say something because you think it's what I want or expect. It'll come in time, but it needs to come from the deepest part of you. God understands. Some people jump onto the Christianity bandwagon with feet first but then they falter after a while and revert back to their old ways. Slow and steady is always the best way to go, in a lot of things in life."

Serenity sensed Jackson also meant in terms of their growing relationship, and again, it gave her comfort. If he pushed her too far, too fast, he knew she'd run away emotionally. By being her friend and confidant, Jackson was working his way into her heart. He'd proven himself an incredibly compassionate and loyal friend. Snuggling further into the curve of his arm, she released a deep sigh. It seemed as natural as breathing. They fit together so well. Much more than she ever had with Danny. *Whoa.*

"Jackson? Go ahead and ask your brother to see if he can find out anything."

"I'll make the call tonight."

"If Mama's alive," she whispered against his shirt, closing her eyes, "I have an idea who might have sent that note to me."

"Your mother?"

She nodded. "Exactly."

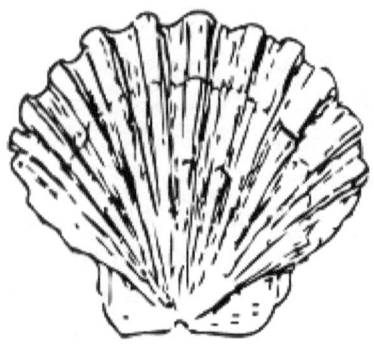

~CHAPTER 19~

Serenity breathed in deeply of the ocean air and surveyed the same stretch of beach where Mama and Dad used to bring her. Dad would carry the picnic basket her mother had filled to the top with homemade sandwiches, fruit and juice. Never prepackaged stuff. Never potato chips or sodas. The thought made her smile. Closing her eyes, she lifted her face to the evening breeze.

She sensed Jackson's presence before she opened her eyes. He sat beside her, arms clasped around his knees, quiet. His shoes were parked nearby and he'd changed into swim trunks and a tank. Even though he was subtle, she felt his admiring gaze on her one-piece, aqua-colored bathing suit and matching, colorful sarong. "Make it a habit to sneak up on women on the beach on a lazy Saturday evening, do you? I didn't expect to see you until tomorrow morning."

"Sorry, but I hope you'll forgive the intrusion since I brought food."

"No intrusion. I'm glad you're here. How'd you find me?"

"Your dad, of course. Charlie's with him, and he said I might find you here."

"More like he ordered me to get some fresh air, but he also knows my habits pretty well. I should think you'd have something better to do on a Saturday night."

"Look, if you're talking about Hayley again—"

"I'm not," she said. "I guess I thought you might be...reading a book or something."

The breeze whipped his hair across his forehead and he smiled. "The truth? Your dad asked me to make sure you're okay. The food was strictly my idea."

"You've already gone above and beyond the call of duty the last couple of days." She absently traced a circle in the sand with one finger. When she finished, Jackson drew a heart inside her circle. Serenity momentarily lost the ability to breathe. She avoided his gaze and focused on the surf. Inhaling a deep breath, she drew the ocean air into her lungs and released it before speaking.

"I used to come here a lot when I was a kid. It was always my refuge, my escape. When I'm not around the ocean, I miss it. It's part of me." She shot him a sheepish glance. "I even bought one of those ocean CDs when I lived in Atlanta. Hearing the sound of the waves soothed me and helped me sleep better."

"Tell me more about when you came here as a child."

"Yes, doctor," she said, tossing him an amused glance. "We'd bring a picnic basket. Mama would read while Daddy and I made a sand castle." She angled her head to where a young family played in the sand. "I had a pink plastic sand pail like the one the little girl over there is using. It had this bright yellow shovel and a lime green sand sifter. Dad was so healthy back then and carefree. We all were. He'd take my hand, help me over the wall of the sand castle and then twirl me around inside, beneath his arm. Then he'd say, 'Dance, Princess Serenity, dance. This is your kingdom, and may all of God's riches be added unto you.' It was..."—she blew out a breath—"magical." She closed her eyes again, blocking out the sadness. "There were times when I almost believed I *was* a princess."

"Because he made you feel like one. You were his world." Jackson couldn't know how precious it was to have him beside her. "Speaking of food on the beach," he said, "are you ready to eat?" When she nodded, he dragged the small cooler across the sand. Opening the lid, he handed her a bag of sandwiches. "Hope you don't mind simple."

"Best way to go." They shared a grin as she selected a ham and Swiss on rye and he took a roast beef. "Did you make these?" Unwrapping one, she lifted a brow. "Brown mustard? Pretty fancy. Looks great. I'm impressed."

"Welcome, and yes, I made them. I eat a lot of sandwiches, so I had all this stuff on hand." He handed her an apple and pulled out a bag of chips for himself. "So, tell me more about the French royals who founded our town," he said after he'd asked a blessing.

She was surprised how quickly it all came back to her considering she'd been in third grade when she'd learned the history. Maybe because it was important, it'd all stuck in her brain during the ensuing years. The stories *were* fun, and Jackson seemed to enjoy hearing them. He laughed often and asked a question here and there.

"This is nice," he said after he finished his second sandwich while she finished her apple. "Okay, time to get a little more serious. I have a question I'm hoping you'll want to answer."

Her pulse tripled. "After that statement, I'm not quite sure."

"Will you tell me about Danny?"

Serenity's heart thudded to a stop. Clearing her throat, she twisted her fingers on her lap. She'd been careful not to ever mention Danny to Jackson. Or Liam. So far, the tragedies of her life had only concerned her mother. "What exactly do you want to know?"

"I was hoping you'd feel comfortable enough to tell me about him." When she met his gaze briefly, Jackson's expression revealed compassion yet something deeper. Intimate almost. Falling for her would be one of the worst things Jackson could ever do.

"It seems you've done pretty well getting information about me," she said, her tone brusque as she dusted crumbs from her lap. "Ask your sources. I'm sure there are several people in this town who'd be more than happy to fill you in on the details of my life." Serenity hated the sarcasm that snuck into her tone but couldn't seem to stop it.

"Your dad mentioned Danny sometime during the night at the hospital, but he *was* a little incoherent at the time, so don't blame him. I suspected you'd been married before, but I'd much rather hear about Danny from you. Just so you'll know, I haven't asked anyone, and no one's volunteered any information. I care about you. I think you know that." His voice was low, soothing, gentle. "However, if you're not ready to talk about him, that's okay. Whatever you want. I'm not going anywhere."

Serenity stared straight ahead at the gentle waves lapping on the beach. "It's not something I freely tell people, Jackson. Don't feel special."

"I know one thing. You're hurting. It's in your eyes and the tautness around your mouth sometimes."

"Thanks for the roundup," she said, realizing how snippy she sounded. "I must look like I'm fifty years old."

"Not at all. I love it when you're relaxed, though. I've seen that side of you, and it makes me happy to see you laugh like you don't have a care in the world even though I know you do." Leaning close, he nudged her shoulder. "Hands down, without a doubt, you're the most beautiful woman I've ever known, inside and out."

How was that even possible? A man like Jackson must have known a number of women in his life. Good women. Women without an unsavory past. As much as she wanted to believe he truly meant his words, she couldn't. "You're a very special man," she said. "While I appreciate your compliment, any woman would be blessed to have you in her life. You should go find one of them instead of trying to make nice with me."

"Stop making disparaging comments about yourself." His voice was forceful, stronger than she'd ever heard it. "It's self-defeating." She moved her eyes back to his. "I'll tell you something else."

"What's that?" She swallowed hard.

"You're not only beautiful, but you're kind and generous. A loving daughter and a terrific friend. Everyone has stuff in their past—skeletons in their closet—they regret. It's part of being human. That's why the only Man who was ever perfect was Jesus."

She nodded, but couldn't speak.

"Repeat after me, 'I will not disparage.'"

Clearing her throat, Serenity dug deep and found her voice. "I will not disparage."

"Promise?"

"Yes, I promise, Doc Jack."

"Want to know what I see when I look at you, Serenity?"

The man would not be easily deterred. She blew out a breath but it didn't slow her heart rate any, not that she thought it would. "Go ahead. Tell me."

"I see a woman who's much stronger than she knows. Sure, I've seen how sweet and caring you can be, but whatever's hurt you in the past has made you vulnerable. You cover it up with sarcasm to keep others at a safe distance. You've built this invisible shield around you, not allowing anyone too close for fear they'll actually penetrate that wall. Heaven forbid you might actually start to care about someone else."

Tears stung her eyes, but she refused to give into the overwhelming emotion. "You don't know anything about it."

"That's why I'm here. I want to help, if you'll let me."

"I'm not one of your patients, so please don't treat me like one."

"I know that," he said. "But you're my friend, first and foremost. And friends help their friends. It's pretty obvious you've got an iceberg on your shoulder large enough to sink the Titanic."

"Not very original, Jackson."

"Sorry," he said with a shrug. "It's the best I've got right now." He rubbed his fingers across his chin in what was becoming a familiar gesture when his thinking mode kicked into high gear. In spite of her resolve, it endeared him to her even more. "When that iceberg thaws, it's a beautiful thing. Look, I'll take whatever you're willing to give me, but it's difficult when you shut me out. Whether or not you mean to do it, you do. I hope knowing I'm here gives you some kind of comfort. And, for the record, it has nothing to do with my profession." Was it possible he really didn't know her story? Surely someone would have told him. *Warn* him was more like it.

Serenity's lips formed a firm line and neither one said a word for at least a minute. "What do you want to know?" Those deep pools of chocolate brown in Jackson's eyes probed deep, finding a cavern buried so deep beneath the surface she thought no one would ever find it again. Psychologist or not, he saw the person inside her and not merely the often flippant exterior. And yet he still chose to sit beside her and be her friend.

"I'm asking you to tell me what you don't want me to know," he said. "No sarcasm, no avoidance. Get it out and then we'll deal with it. Together."

She averted her gaze, staring straight ahead again but seeing nothing. "Danny could have been so much," she said finally. "He was handsome and athletic, but he had a bad boy streak. Every girl wanted him, but for some reason, he chose me."

When Jackson reached for her hand, lacing his fingers through hers, she didn't resist. His touch was warm and she welcomed it.

"Did you love him?"

"Yes, of course, I did." She dared to meet his gaze. "But how many of us know what we want at nineteen? Danny was my first love, my first and only...everything." She cleared her throat. Might as well tell him and then this wonderful Christian man could run for the hills when he learned the truth. "I was pregnant, and Danny did the honorable thing. As it was, we waited until after high school. He was twenty-one and I was twenty. We were married, and five months later, our son, Liam, was born. You know what they say about the apple not falling far from the tree? In some ways, we were like Mama and Dad all over again although I'd known Danny since we were kids. Not that I'm blaming my parents for anything." She shrugged. "It's just what it was."

Talking about Danny wasn't as difficult as she'd imagined, a surprising relief in some ways and a soothing balm for the weariness she felt in her bones. Sometimes she couldn't believe how old she felt, emotionally and physically. She hadn't told anyone about Danny in a long time and certainly no one to whom she felt as drawn to as she did to Jackson.

Keeping his hand in hers, Jackson shifted position, turning toward her. "You have a son?" No condemnation, no judgment surfaced in his voice, only curiosity. By his tone, Serenity could tell he was surprised by that revelation. Why no one had told him any of this information, she couldn't begin to comprehend. But Jackson was right. It was best *she* was the one to tell him so he could hear the truth straight from her.

"I did." A tear escaped and coursed down her cheek. Easing her hand away from his, she wiped away the tear. "He died not long after his birth." When Jackson opened his arms, Serenity didn't hesitate to move into his chest. He held her as she cried, burying into him, taking comfort in his warmth and the shelter of his embrace. She'd never told anyone outside of Croisette Shores about Liam. And it'd been a long time, even in private, since she'd cried like her heart was being ripped from her chest all over again.

"I'm so sorry, baby," he murmured, stroking her hair. "I had no idea." She felt the increased rhythm of his heart. Sure and so strong.

Serenity didn't know how long they sat together, wrapped in one another's arms. When the tears finally subsided, she turned aside and fumbled in her purse for a tissue before accepting the paper napkin Jackson handed her. "Thanks." Taking in a big gulp of air, she almost choked. "That's not all."

Jackson waited as she gathered her thoughts and tried to regain her composure. "Before Liam was born, Danny was killed." Hearing his sharp intake of breath and murmur of sympathy, she continued, afraid to stop, afraid *not* to stop. "He was working alone at a convenience store and some guys came in, probably wanting money. And they, um..." Her voice trailed and she squeezed her eyes tight, willing the tears to stop. "I got concerned because it was almost midnight and he wasn't home yet. I called my dad, and he went to the store."

"Your dad was the one who found him?"

"Right, and then when Liam died a few months later, it was only a couple of days later that my mom...well, she was gone. Never to be heard from again."

Jackson gathered her close again and leaned his chin on the top of her head. She clung to him, moving her hands around his waist. He couldn't take away the hurt and pain of the past, but he was here, cared about her and wanted to help her. The man must be a glutton for punishment.

"Serenity, it's hard to know what to say," Jackson said, pulling away and tipping her chin so she'd look at him. "Losing people you care about is never easy, but you've had more than enough to handle. And then some. Wow. Words are woefully inadequate in a situation like this."

"I know," she said, shaking her head. "There's not a whole lot anyone can say. I've learned to accept it and get on with my life as best I can, but I still need to find some answers."

She wiped beneath her eyes and grimaced when she glimpsed the black streaks on her fingers. "My baby was perfect. Beautiful and healthy, with good color and all this thick, dark hair, but he developed some kind of weird lung infection and..." When she cried a little more, Jackson held her again, running his hands over her hair and rocking with her, back and forth. In his arms, she was protected. She should push him away, but she couldn't. She never wanted to leave.

"In your heart, why do you think your mom left?"

"That's the other mystery," she said, resting her cheek on his chest, exhausted and emotionally spent. "Of my parents, Mama was the stronger one, the disciplinarian. I needed her after Danny died, and she helped me get through everything until Liam was born. If anything, I needed her even more. I was this young kid with a dead husband who didn't have a clue how to raise a child, much less on my own. And then when Liam died, she disappeared. That's when Dad withdrew into himself and simply shut down." She shook her head. "It was wrong of me to leave him, but I had to get away to survive. Maybe it was selfish, but I couldn't stay here." Her eyes met his. "If I *had* stayed, I probably wouldn't be here with you now."

Jackson held her gaze a long moment and nodded. "From what I've seen, your dad doesn't fault you for leaving."

"No, he doesn't, but he was so...terribly sad." Her throat tightened. "It broke my heart all over again. Dad withdrew from the world. We were hurting each other more than helping, lashing out at each other in anger and pain. He couldn't face his own grief, much less deal with mine. So, I left. Only difference was, I called Dad and told him where I was and how to reach me. I wanted him to know I wasn't too far away, and I hope he knew I'd be back in a heartbeat if he ever said the word." She heaved a deep, shuddering sigh. "But he never did."

"Your dad probably felt like his life was ripped apart," Jackson said. "And I'm sure knowing how you suffered made it even worse for him. Trust me, Serenity, I know how guys can close up and not let anyone in, even those we love most. It's not in our nature to share our feelings. When we're hit with tragedy, we turn into ourselves and think we can handle things on our own without help from anyone else. You're right, though. In your case, getting away from Croisette Shores was probably the best possible option. As hard as it was, it was incredibly brave."

Serenity sniffled, unable to speak.

Lifting the corner of his tank, Jackson offered it to her, but she shook her head and managed a small smile. "Dad's ornery, but I'm stubborn like Mama. She taught me well. You know what I said about the beach being my refuge when I was a little girl? When I lived in Atlanta, a neighbor invited me to a Bible study, and I found another refuge there in the arms of the Lord. I'd never heard about it before I moved away."

"Why'd you choose Atlanta?" he asked. "For the record."

"The school there offered one of the best interior decorating programs in the country. In a big city, there were also more opportunities to lose myself in the mass of humanity. I wasn't conspicuous like I am here in Croisette Shores. I didn't have people scrutinizing my every move. The anonymity was wonderful." She shook her head. "Listen to me. I sound like a celebrity."

"You are to some people," he said.

"For all the wrong reasons. It's more notoriety. I love that verse from the Psalms that says '*Keep me safe, my God, for in You I take refuge.*' I've clung to that verse the past few years. I haven't gone to church the way I should have or helped others." She raised watery eyes to his. "But I've done what I needed to do to survive and keep myself sane. That's got to count for something, right?"

When Jackson smiled, her heart jumped to see the tears in *his* eyes. "You needed to take care of yourself before you could think of helping others. God understands that. The way I see it? You've helped more people than you know. It's not always about working in some kind of ministry. It's about kindness and goodness and giving of yourself, whether it's your time or your talents or whatever. Look what you're doing for your dad. Charlie and Maya are your biggest fans, and Kelsie admires you more than you know." He squeezed her hand. "Look what you're doing for me."

Her lip trembled. "What...what am I doing for you?"

"You've shown me unconditional love. Love as a friend that's not based on anything more than caring about someone and wanting the best the Lord has to offer. That's an incomparable *gift.*"

She sniffled again and he handed her another napkin. "You're too good to me."

He chuckled. "Not possible."

"Jackson?"

"Shhh," he said, leaning his head against hers, stroking her hair again. "Just let me hold you."

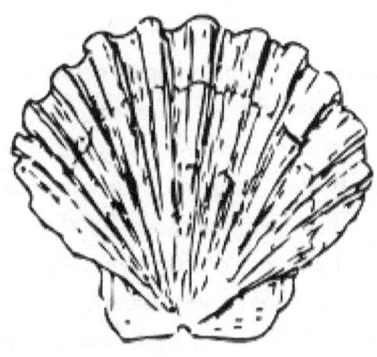

~CHAPTER 20~

*J*ackson drummed his fingers on the kitchen counter as he ate his breakfast the next morning. He hadn't fallen asleep until well after two a.m., mulling over Serenity's story. Like he'd told her after he first met her, he'd seen the way the ladies in the coffee shop responded to her, the way the older men looked at her in a fatherly way. Her family had lived in Croisette Shores a long time. With her dad a fireman and her mom a nurse, they were ingrained in the community. Some of those people in the coffee shop must have felt a keen sense of loss right along with Serenity when Danny was killed, their baby died, and then when her mother disappeared.

When Serenity first started telling him about Danny, it was clear she hadn't sought professional help to help her deal with the emotional pain. He'd seen it before in his clinical training with adult patients. Serenity's words had rolled out of her like a massive tidal wave. The way she'd been incapable of stopping clued him in she'd kept it bottled inside, but for almost five years? As impossible as it seemed, he knew in his heart it was true. She'd been through so much and only been married a few months when her husband was killed. A strong arrow pierced his heart.

Lowering his head, Jackson closed his eyes and prayed. "Lord, please give Serenity your peace," he whispered. The irony of her name didn't escape him and he wanted to help her, *needed* to help her. Not that he could explain it. It was more than physical attraction drawing him to this woman. That in itself could prompt him to do what he could to help Serenity, but not because he was trying to earn some kind of praise, reward or gratification.

Time for a reality check. *You're already falling in love with Serenity, but she can't be free to love you or anyone until she finds her answers.* He'd met a few young widows in the past and a majority of them still grieved their dead husband, no matter how long they'd been gone. Some never moved past it, especially when they'd been murdered like Danny, but Serenity seemed resolved to accept her husband's death. That in itself was a step toward healing. The circumstances of the marriage—how long they'd known each other, the strength of their bond, whether or not they'd had children together—all played a factor.

As bad a person as it might make him, Jackson was thankful she wasn't fixated on Danny like he was some kind of martyred saint and no other guy could ever compare. That scenario was difficult, if not impossible, to conquer. Dealing with her other issues might prove easier by comparison.

A lot of patients suffering similar heartbreak might have tumbled over the edge into mental instability. Danny's murder could have been enough, but the other tragedies that followed made it almost unfathomable to imagine the heartbreak she'd experienced, the pain she'd suffered. He'd witnessed an indomitable strength of character in Serenity sandwiched between the rare glimpses of vulnerability and insecurity. She'd learned to keep a tight rein on her emotions around most people, and that could prove both beneficial and detrimental. He was glad she'd shared her pain, and shed her tears, in his presence. If only he could absorb some of it and ease her pain.

To her credit, instead of becoming crippled by bitterness and anger, Serenity had faced life the best way she could. She'd distanced herself from her home and friends. Then she'd forged her own path and taken charge of her life. She'd earned two degrees in Atlanta, but then felt the pull to come home again. Her loyalty to her father was admirable. Based on what she'd told him, her faith was fragile and new. While he wanted to encourage her, invite her to church and tell her about his relationship with the Lord, he didn't want to scare her away by shoving "religion" down her throat.

His older brother, Chad, constantly criticized what he termed Jackson's "Good Samaritan" philosophy. "Nothing wrong with wanting to help people, Jax. I know that's what you do for a living—you nearly got yourself killed and earned a medal for it—but you can't get wrapped up in the problems of every single person who spills their guts or you'll drag yourself down and won't be able to help all the other people who need it. Save enough of yourself to spread it around."

He had a unique way of expressing himself but Chad was right in certain respects. Jackson had mastered techniques to divest himself from the troubles of others and show compassion while still standing firm in neutral territory. Not revealing he was a psychologist outside the office unless asked was best. Perhaps God in His infinite wisdom positioned him in certain places—in His perfect timing—for that very purpose. Like standing in the grocery line behind the older woman whose granddaughter was in drug rehab or the guy at the dry cleaners who'd returned from the war and had to readjust to civilian life, working out at the gym beside singles fed up with breakups and swearing off dating and marriage...the list could go on and on. Seemed even a small town the size of Croisette Shores had its share of trauma and drama. At heart, most people wanted someone to listen, simple as that. If he could fulfill that need, so be it.

And just when Jackson thought he'd heard it all, along came Serenity. She of the dazzling smile and gorgeous blue eyes that held sadness and heartache that drew him in and tempted him to toss everything to the wind and follow her anywhere. He'd never felt this way about Laura or any other woman. In record time, no less.

The cell phone beside Jackson on the counter startled him when it played the theme song of "Mission Impossible." He glanced at the display. *Kyle.*

"Hey, little bro." Jackson scarfed down the last of his over-easy eggs.

"You must really like this woman to ask me to do some detective work about her mother. It's about time you jumped back into the dating pool with both feet. I'd suggest playing the field, but you've never been one to do that, have you? Even when you *had* women throwing themselves at your feet." Kyle laughed. "What it must be like to be you."

Jackson frowned. "At this point, Serenity needs a friend more than anything else. She's got a lot going on in her life." He sounded like a clone of Charlie even if it was the truth. "So do I."

He heard Kyle's prolonged sigh through the phone. "Man, please tell me you're not attracted to this one because she's a wounded bird?"

His ire rose, but Jackson tamped it down. Kyle was beginning to sound like Chad. "You don't know what you're talking about, runt." By using a childhood nickname Kyle hated, he hoped it would distract him and he'd change the subject.

"Come on, Jax. Let's examine the facts. Laura was a mess, and you swooped in and took care of her. Once you'd worked your magic, she set you free. In case you can't see it for yourself, you tend to take on women with issues. It's like this insatiable need you have to make everything right, or else it's a carryover from your professional life."

Jackson shut his mouth, swallowing his sharp response. *Is that what I'm doing with Serenity?* Sure, she had problems, admittedly more than most, but who didn't have at least the equivalent of a carry-on of emotional baggage? Unlike Laura's case, Serenity's problems weren't of her own making. They were the result of unfortunate circumstances, God's will or whatever. He knew it wasn't theologically correct to think that way, but life had thrown Serenity some very unfair curveballs. Denying it didn't make him any more or less pious. From what he'd heard, Laura was doing well now, still in Chicago and teaching high school English. She was a good woman and deserved love and he'd prayed she'd find it...with some other guy.

At times, he wondered why one person should suffer so much when others existed with a poor excuse for a life yet encountered very little difficulty. Then again, he knew it wasn't *his* place to question God's motives. A life worth living was about taking risks. From what he knew from his studies and experience, the majority of those who'd loved and lost said they wouldn't change a thing given the opportunity for a "do over" in life. He'd always found that interesting. Of course, the answer again depended on circumstances. Nothing about Serenity's particular case was normal in any sense of the word.

"You still there, Jax? Speak to me, bud."

"Yeah. Sorry." He cleared his throat. "Tell me what else is going on in your life." He forced a brightness into his voice he didn't feel, wanting to change the subject. Chewing his toast, he listened as Kyle told him about their parents' latest jaunt to Europe and the opening of Chad's new Manhattan restaurant before telling him about his most recent coup in the corporate legal world. In spite of their differences, he was proud of both his brothers, but as he listened to Kyle's words, a sadness tightened around his gut. He knew firsthand the lure and temptations of the world and didn't want his younger brother to fall in the traps, but feared it was too late.

"Been to church lately, Kyle?" He winced. The question came across as a holier-than-thou, superior attitude. No wonder the kid didn't listen to him. Although he wanted to know the answer, he wished he could withdraw and rephrase.

Sure enough, Kyle snorted. "Organized religion and my lifestyle don't exactly mesh right now. I'm having too much fun. Jesus would cramp my style. I guess you're getting ready to go to church, huh? Remember when you were my age. You had your fun, buddy, so now it's time to let me have mine. Still, I have to admit, you sound...settled. Content almost. Leaving Chicago was probably a good thing and that little South Carolina town is good for you. Does your pretty new friend know about your illustrious past?"

Jackson shoved his empty plate aside with more force than he intended and had to catch it before it toppled over the edge of the counter. "No, and there's no reason to tell her. It's nobody's business but mine."

"You always were humble. If you don't want that medal of yours, ship it to me. I could probably score big time with that thing draped around my neck."

Jackson shook his head in disgust. "Don't be a pig, Kyle."

"Hey, ladies love a hero. If I were you—"

"That's just it. You're not me, Kyle. You probably don't want it, but I'm going to give you some advice, so listen up."

"Okay, lay it on me."

"Work hard at your job and have fun when you can, but be a man of honor enough to respect the women you date. Remember those words the next time you bring a woman home. Work on the inside of you as much as what the rest of the world sees. Trust me, it'll help you sleep better at night." He wondered if Kyle had an overnight guest tucked in his bed right now. More likely, he'd left one somewhere in Seattle when he'd snuck out of her place in the middle of the night. The one nice girl he'd dated for more than six months had her heart shattered when Kyle cheated on her. He'd already throttled him at Christmas for that one. When would he realize all the emotional damage he was doing? Jackson ran a hand over his brow, more determined than ever to pray for his brother.

"Yeah, well, thanks for the lecture, Dad." Their dad would never tell him those things, and they both knew it. Even if he did, would it change Kyle's lifestyle? Probably not. Like he'd found his own way, now it was Kyle's turn to navigate life, regret his mistakes and celebrate his personal triumphs.

"When you look in the mirror ten years down the road, I want you to respect the man you see."

"Speaking from experience, are we?"

Jackson sighed. Kyle had an annoying habit of throwing everything back in his face. "In some respects, yes. I've found my peace, but it's my prayer you'll find yours without making some of the same mistakes I did." Contrary to what Kyle probably believed, he'd always been a one-woman man, never a player when it came to relationships. Not that he'd been a poster child for clean living. Sure, he'd made errors in judgment, some pretty big, but thanks to a football coach who'd believed in him and the Almighty, he now lived a better, straighter and more fulfilling life.

"I'd say you've done pretty well, Jax. Don't sell yourself short. Any man who earned a..."

"I don't need to hear you trumpet my accomplishments, but thanks. That's all in the past. People tend to forget quickly, and I've got more important things to do. I know I ride you hard, little brother, but somebody's got to do it. Take it easy, runt."

"You, too."

Before he hung up, Jackson gave Kyle the pertinent facts he'd gotten from Serenity about her mother. It might not give them anything to go on. Then again, it might bring some definitive answers. The Lord knew that's what he wanted more than anything—help the woman he was falling in love with find what she needed most in her life.

Blessed, sweet serenity.

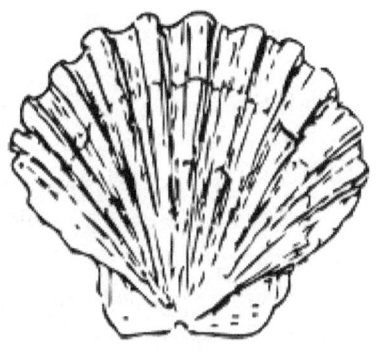

~CHAPTER 21~

"*Y*ou're a great assistant." Working side-by-side at the church picnic, Jackson smiled as he manned the grill and Serenity handed out paper plates and hot dog or hamburger buns. She got reacquainted with a few members of the church she'd known in the past and Jackson introduced her to everyone. She liked how he poured himself into the community and made a serious effort to get to know the townspeople, learn about their lives and show a genuine interest.

"Michael, good to see you," Jackson said when a curly-haired boy who looked to be about eight approached. "Want a hot dog, buddy?"

The boy's dark eyes widened and he bobbed his head up and down. "Yes, please. Is there ketchup? I gotta have ketchup." Serenity opened a bun and Jackson plopped a hot dog in the middle.

"Here you go. Condiments are on the picnic table right over there. Hey, David," Jackson said as a tall, blond man walked up to them. "David Marsh, I'd like you to meet Serenity McClaren. She's keeping me straight so I don't crisp the meat beyond recognition. Serenity, this is Michael's dad."

David smiled. "It's nice to meet you, Serenity. I'd shake your hand, but I see you already have your hands full."

"I take it you're talking about this," she said, lifting a plate, "and not Jackson."

David's laugh was hearty, and Jackson gave her a wink. "I think you've met your match, Doc Jack."

Jackson breathed out an exaggerated sigh. "That's what I keep telling her. What'll you have?" Jackson asked, rolling over a couple of the hot dogs. "I've got brats, hot dogs and burgers." The grill sizzled and Serenity hoped neither of them heard her stomach rumble. Who knew the smells of grilling meat—not vegetables—would make her so hungry?

"Great. I'll take one brat and one hot dog." David thanked her when she handed over two buns on a plate. A lovely woman walked up to stand beside him. "Carmen, this is Jackson and Serenity." With her long, dark hair and olive skin, she was exotic and very pretty.

As the two men exchanged small talk, Serenity turned to the other woman. She appeared to be a few years older, in her mid-thirties or thereabouts. "Are you new in town?" A weird feeling came over her, like she'd seen Carmen somewhere before.

Carmen accepted the hot dog David handed her and Serenity walked with her to the condiment table. "Is it that obvious? New in town, new relationship..." Although she spoke with a slight accent, her English was perfect. Tucking a dark curl behind one ear, Carmen gave her a small smile. "You?"

"I grew up here but went to Atlanta to study. I moved back a few weeks ago."

"What do you do?"

"I started an interior decorating business here in town called Inner Serenity. If you're in the market for some decorating help, let me know and I'd love to help. I also make a mean cup of tea or coffee if you'd like to stop by and chat sometime." After Carmen asked for her business card, Serenity told her the cross streets closest to her office and dug a card from her pocket. "It's in the heart of the downtown district."

"Your name is so unusual," Carmen said, glancing at the card. "Very pretty."

"Thanks. It's courtesy of two free-thinking, New Age parents. For a beach town like Croisette Shores, it seems to fit."

"Growing up in Miami, I always had a few other girls with my name in my classes, so consider yourself lucky."

"What do you do?" Serenity asked as the other woman squeezed mustard on her hot dog. The deep red color of her fingernails reminded her of something. *The woman in the hospital cafeteria.* Serenity lowered her gaze, unsure what to think or whether to say anything. What *could* she say? Nice to meet you, but have you been following me?

David called to Carmen, and Michael stood beside him. "I'm a flight attendant, but I retired a few months ago. I'd better go, but it's very nice to meet you."

"You, too." Serenity watched, puzzled, as they headed toward a picnic table.

"David's wife died in a car accident a few years ago," Jackson said when she rejoined him by the grill. "Michael took it really hard, as you can imagine, and he's having a little trouble adjusting to his dad's new relationship. They moved here for a fresh start, and David's the history teacher at the high school."

Without Jackson actually saying the words, Serenity understood Michael was one of his patients. "I hope it works out for all of them," she said.

Jackson nudged her shoulder, an action that was becoming more frequent. Not that she minded. "I think *you're* nice. I heard your invitation to Carmen."

"Just being neighborly."

"Well," he said, "here's an idea. How about the two of us get neighborly later tonight?"

Her mouth dropped open. "Dr. Ross!" She didn't know what to think, but against her better judgment, the idea sounded better all the time.

"Now, see? *This* is the real Serenity. The fun-loving, genuine, giving—"

"I get your point," she said. "Don't spoil the moment by reminding me of my shortcomings."

"Point taken." He started whistling and she moved over to straighten the condiment table. No wonder he'd more or less accused her of being hot and cold. It's how she'd survived the past five years and it would take some time to work it out of her system. If she *ever* did.

A half hour later, the crowd seemed to wind down. Another guy came over and told Jackson to go eat and he'd take over the grill duty. "Time to live dangerously," Jackson said, plopping a sizzling hot dog on her plate.

"Right," she said, giving him a mock frown as she grabbed a bun. "But don't put any chips on my plate or you're in big trouble, mister."

"I'm shaking in my shoes."

After loading her plate with salad and an ear of corn, Serenity canvassed the park for a table. Most were already occupied, but seeing Mrs. Marciano waving to her, Serenity led the way to a table occupied by a young couple, Mark and Sarah Coltrane, and their three kids. Friends of Deidre and Wes, she'd known them before they were married. Life moving on as it should. In some ways, seeing their children made the pain of losing Liam all the more real.

"A word of warning," she said, whispering in Jackson's ear after they'd climbed over the park bench and sat down side-by-side. "Dustin's a prankster. He's the one to your immediate right." Jackson smelled so good, his skin warm.

"Bring it on." She giggled and bowed her head as he took her hand and said a quiet prayer.

The first few minutes, Mrs. Marciano asked Jackson questions. "Why do I feel like *I'm* the one getting grilled?" he whispered, leaning so close his lips touched her ear, sending shivers everywhere.

"I can tell Mrs. Marciano likes you."

He chuckled, low in his throat. "Better than the quarterback?"

"Most definitely," she said, doing a little nudging of her own with her knee beneath the table. Jackson's surprised glance told her how much he enjoyed it when she initiated the flirting.

"Haven't you ever eaten a hot dog before?" Ten-year-old Katelyn watched as Serenity surveyed her hot dog, turning the bun in her hands, debating which end to nibble. "You're looking at it like you don't know what to do." Katelyn would faint if she told her she'd never consumed macaroni and cheese from a box mix or tried a Pop-Tart.

"My mom wouldn't let me eat them when I was your age," Serenity said. "I've never had one with mustard. Normally, I like ketchup."

"Then how come you put mustard on it this time?" Katelyn asked. Leave it to kids to ask the hard-hitting questions.

"Because I want to eat it the way Jackson likes it." Without looking at him, Serenity sensed Jackson's satisfaction with that statement.

"How come?" The girl seemed fascinated with the way she picked off a section and sampled it instead of digging right in and chewing a big bite. "My mom says you gotta do things your own way or you're a copycat. If Jackson jumped off a bridge, would you..."

"That's quite enough out of you, young lady," Sarah said. "Serenity has a right to eat her hot dog any way she wants without any comment from you."

"Yeah, it's a free country." Peyton scrunched his nose in his sister's direction.

"You see, Katelyn," Serenity said, tossing a glance at Jackson, "I don't look at it as copying, but more like an experiment." Taking a bigger bite for emphasis, she chewed slowly, savoring the taste.

"Whaddya think?" That from Peyton, watching for her reaction.

She wiped her mouth with the napkin and grinned. "Not bad at all."

Doubling over beside Jackson, Dustin clutched his stomach and gagged. It only took a second to figure out what was happening. Jumping up from the bench, Serenity ran to Dustin, wrapped her arms around the boy and hauled him off the bench from behind.

"What's she *doing*, Daddy?" Katelyn's question barely registered as Serenity performed the Heimlich with swift, sure thrusts. A piece of hot dog spewed out and landed on Katelyn's plate.

"Eww! Gross!" Squealing, Katelyn scrambled down from the picnic bench and threw herself into her mother's arms.

Dustin crumpled and cried as Mark reached his side. Peyton stared at the scene with wide eyes and then looked over at her. "Wow. That was way awesome."

"Thank you, Serenity," Mark said, and Sarah echoed the sentiment as she released Katelyn and moved around the table to gather the now whimpering Dustin in her arms, sitting on the bench and rocking her younger son back and forth.

Serenity nodded, embarrassed. "I'm glad I could help."

Mrs. Marciano sat watching the scene, appearing stunned, but she quickly recovered. "I always knew that girl was special," she said to Peyton, gesturing to her, "but I had no idea she could actually save somebody's life. Good neighbor to have, wouldn't you say?" Peyton nodded with enthusiasm.

"You're my heroine," Jackson said as he finished cleaning the grill and Serenity repackaged leftover buns a short time later. "What you did for Dustin was amazing and Peyton's crushing on you big time. Where'd you learn how to do that, anyway?"

"Mama made sure I learned the Heimlich by the time I was in middle school." She gathered leftover packages of buns and supplies, noticing Jackson's muscles on full display as he used serious elbow grease on the grill. Her mother always said a good man worth having was one who wasn't afraid to roll up his sleeves and work hard. Funny how her mother kept coming to her mind lately.

"Good to know in case I'm ever choking."

"Surely working with children, you know it, too."

His cheeks flushed, a rare sight. "Yeah, I do. But unlike you, I've never had to use it, thank the Lord." He grinned. "I know you're better at the Heimlich than you are at eating a hot dog. There's an art to it, and I think I'm going to have to teach you."

She sniffed. "No, thanks. A hot dog-free existence is fine with me, especially after what happened today." A few minutes later, finished with their task, she prepared to leave. "Ready to go?"

The look he gave her could only be described as sheepish. "Some of the guys are planning a game of touch football. Only for an hour or so. Do you mind?"

"Of course not. Why should I? Go. Have fun."

"Thanks." He grinned like a little boy. "Want to come and be my personal cheerleader?"

"I'm sure some of the other ladies will watch from the sidelines. I need to take Mrs. Marciano home."

Digging in the pocket of his shorts, Jackson pulled out his car keys and tossed them to her. "Take my car. It's parked closer than yours."

Serenity eyed him. "Are you sure?"

"It's hot and too far for Mrs. Marciano to walk."

She meant more as a matter of Jackson trusting her to drive his expensive car. "Thanks."

"Welcome. Coming back, I hope? You know, to return my car."

"Wouldn't miss it."

"Serenity?" Jackson stepped closer.

She turned. "Yes?"

"It's a British import, remember. Steering wheel's on the right."

"I've been in your car before."

"But you haven't *driven* it before. Big difference."

"I'll just take my car then," she said. "No big deal."

"No, no," he said, raising his hand. "I trust you completely."

"Do you have a name for your car? I mean, I understand that's what guys do."

He laughed. "Believe it or not, I haven't named it." Tilting his head, he grinned. "I'm thinking about Prudence."

"Right," she said, giving into her laughter. "I must be going now. To drive that ridiculously expensive import of yours. I sure hope I can remember the rules of the road and not drive on the wrong side or something."

"Serenity?"

Dropping one hand to her hip, she whirled around. "*Yes?*"

His smile was incredible and seared straight through her. This man was getting to her.

"Peyton's not the only guy crushing on you."

Her heart took a flying leap. Curling her fingers around the keys, she gave him her best smile. "I'll be back."

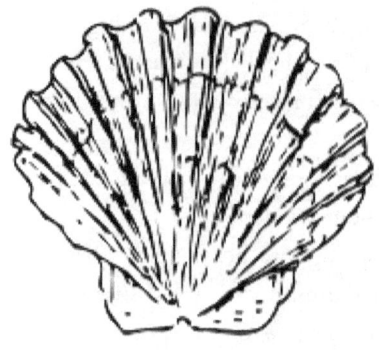

~CHAPTER 22~

*A*lthough he tried to hide it, Serenity caught Jackson's wince as he dropped down beside her on the grass an hour later. The man played hard, and from her limited experience, even she could tell he was better than most at the game of football—agile, fast and powerful. Now, he'd pay the price for all that diligence. Why men did it to themselves, she'd never understand, but they always seemed to have something to prove, one way or another.

Jackson rubbed his right knee with his hand in a back-and-forth motion too precise to be random. The fall he'd taken had been hard and a direct hit. Most of the other players had already departed and she knew he'd waited, smiling through clenched jaws as if nothing was wrong, not willing for them to see his pain. Leaning back on both elbows, he stretched out his legs, the muscles around his mouth tight, his lips pressed firmly together.

"What can I do to help you, Jackson?"

"Sit here with me and hold my hand for a minute. And then I'll probably need some help getting into the car and into my house. This one's going to take some time getting over."

"Should you go to the emergency clinic?"

His brow creased. "No, I don't think it's necessary. They'd only charge me a hundred bucks to tell me to do the very thing I'll do when I get home. I've had surgery. It helped for a while but then the pain returned."

Squeezing his hand tight, Serenity sat in silence, hoping her presence would give him even the smallest measure of comfort. He made a sound when he shifted, and bit his lip. Positioning herself beside him, she placed her palm over his right knee, leaving it there. She didn't know the first thing about knee injuries, but wanted to ease his pain in some small way. "Old football injury?"

For a fleeting second, something flickered in his eyes. "Something like that, yes."

"Is there anything I can do to make it feel better? I can tell it really hurts."

He drew in a couple of deep breaths, grimacing. Something about his obvious discomfort drew her to him even more. Although she hated to see his pain, it somehow made him more vulnerable, and that strangely appealed to her. For a change, Jackson needed *her*. "I'll show you." Placing his hand overs hers, Jackson moved them in a small circular motion, slow and steady. "Exert a little pressure, but not too much. The warmth of your hand helps as much as anything else."

"Lay back and relax," she said. "Just tell me when to stop."

"How about never?" Crossing his arms behind his head, Jackson stretched out on his back.

She continued moving her hand in the circular motion, pressing down and kneading slightly every now and again. Jackson's eyes were closed, his lips parted. As she worked, she was overwhelmed by a swell of emotion. It frightened her, but thrilled her, all at the same time.

Bending at the waist, she planted a soft kiss on his knee and allowed her lips to linger. *Lord, I hate to see him hurt. Let my ministrations help him in some small way.* Closing her eyes, she rested her cheek gently against his knee.

Jackson ran his fingers over her hair. "Come here. You're too far away." His voice was husky, full of tenderness.

Crawling beside him, Serenity cradled his head in her lap, stroking his hair, sifting through the silky strands. "You have the most gorgeous hair in the world," she said, admiring the natural highlights. "A lot of women pay tons of money for highlights like these."

"How do you know I don't?"

"Because you wouldn't. Would you?" She paused her fingers. *Please say no.*

"No, so you can release that breath you're holding." He winced again. "I can think of much better ways to spend my money, but thanks for the compliment. I think."

"Does your knee hurt often?"

"Often enough to remind me it's there. A direct hit tends to exacerbate it."

"Sorry. Want to talk about it?"

"Not particularly, Doc Serenity. I'd rather talk about anything else in the world, if you don't mind."

"I thought you liked talking about wounds."

"Other people's wounds fascinate me, not my own."

"Maybe we should examine why that is, counselor. We need to get you home, and I still have your car keys. Do you want me to bring the car closer to the field or do you think you can walk?"

"Depends. How far away did you park?"

"About five hundred yards."

He blew out a sigh and struggled to sit up beside her. "With your help, I think I can walk. Make that limp." Taking his arm, Serenity wasn't sure if she helped or hindered his effort.

"Thanks for catching me when I fall," Jackson said, his breathing heavier than usual and coming out in spurts.

"It's my honor." She assisted him into the car as best she could. He grunted and grasped the top of the car as an anchor as he swung his long legs into the vehicle.

Ten minutes later, she pulled in front of Doc Rasmussen's cottage. Coming around to the passenger side, she assisted him out of the car as best she could. With his arm draped around her shoulder, he hobbled beside her to the front door. Leaning on her, he seemed taller and bigger. Jackson rested against the wall as she inserted the house key. Once inside, he picked up speed as he made his way across the living room and collapsed onto the sofa. Closing the front door and putting his keys on the small table beside him, Serenity hesitated, not sure what to do first.

"Help me get these tennis shoes off, if you don't mind."

"Sure. Anything you need." Kneeling by the side of the sofa, Serenity unlaced his shoes. After tugging them off, she left them on the floor beside the sofa. "I'll get you a glass of water. Be right back." Bringing it to him a couple of minutes later, she pulled a coaster from the coffee table and put the glass on the end table beside him. Small beads of sweat dotted his forehead. This situation was awkward. She was afraid to touch him, but she wanted to help ease his pain. "Do you need an aspirin or ibuprofen?"

"That would be great." Jackson leaned his head against the back of the sofa and winced. At least he wasn't afraid for her to see how much it hurt. "Kitchen drawer, second drawer to the right of the sink. I think. Just grab a bottle of pain killers. I'm not picky."

Returning to the living room, Serenity shook three pills into her palm and waited as he downed them with water. "Do you want a couple of pillows from your bed? Would that help?"

"That would probably be better. Thanks. You're a great nurse."

"Maybe my mom being a nurse influenced me more than I know. Not that I ever wanted to be one."

"Well," he said, grimacing through his attempt at a smile, "you can be mine anytime."

"Flirt. Be right back to fluff your pillows."

"Even better. Thanks. The bedroom's down the narrow hallway, first room on the left, across from the bathroom."

Expecting to find an unmade bed and scattered clothing strewn on the floor and across the furniture, Serenity was surprised to find the bed made with no clutter or piles. She wouldn't be surprised if he employed a part-time housekeeper. Grabbing two pillows from the bed, she hugged them, inhaling Jackson's musky scent. She felt a little heady and silly. Jackson would love it if he knew she'd smelled his bed pillows, but she didn't need to suffer the embarrassment.

As she turned to leave the bedroom, something on the dresser glinted in the sunlight streaming through the slatted windows. Stepping closer, she gasped. *A Purple Heart medallion.* Although she'd never seen one of them before, her instincts told her that's exactly what this was. Picking up the heart-shaped medallion by the wide purple ribbon edged with white, she cradled it in her palm. She ran her finger around the outer rim, over the profile of George Washington and then the shield, stars and spray of green leaves. Turning it over, Serenity read, "For military merit." *Does this belong to Jackson?* From what little she knew of them, they were awarded for some kind of injury suffered in the line of duty. He'd never said a word about serving in the military. She returned the medal to its place, lost in thought.

Pushing what she'd seen to the back of her mind, Serenity returned to Jackson's side. Freud was on the floor beside the sofa, looking forlorn. "Oh," she said, surprised, holding the pillows against her chest as if they were a protective shield. "He's not going to rush me, is he?"

"Nah, I doubt it. If any male's going to rush you, it'd better be me."

She'd ignore that one. "I almost forgot about Freud," she said, plumping the pillows behind Jackson's head when he sat up long enough for her to arrange them.

"Careful or he *might* rush you for saying that. Come on, Serenity. How can you forget a dog named Freud?"

"You haven't mentioned him much."

"Well, we've had enough to talk about. I guess you could say Freud's one of my hobbies, too, since we spend a lot of time on the beach together."

"Now that you mention it, you're developing quite a nice tan," she said. "Doc Rasmussen has a great place here."

"Yep," he said, grimacing a bit. "It's perfect until I can find a place of my own." After taking a sip of the water, he released a prolonged sigh and settled further into the sofa.

The Purple Heart must belong to the older man. Although Serenity was aware Doc Rasmussen had served in the Armed Forces, it seemed odd she'd never heard about the honor. "Tell me what else you need. How do you treat a knee injury? Heat or cold?"

"Rice."

"Excuse me?" Serenity shook her head. "You're hungry? For rice?"

"Rest. Ice. Compression. Elevation. R-I-C-E."

"Clever. Do you have an ice bag, or an ice pack or something?"

"In the freezer."

Her brows rose. "I take it this happens often?"

"No, but you never know, so I always keep one ready. It's been in there since I moved, so it should be good and cold."

"What about the compression part?" Serenity asked after she applied the ice pack to his knee, handing him a kitchen towel to keep nearby.

"If you go in the bathroom, I keep a big elastic bandage somewhere in the small closet," he said. "I think it's on a shelf near the top. I think you'll be able to recognize it. It used to be white, but it's been used a few times. And don't judge me on the condition of that closet."

She grinned and winked. "I've already seen the bedroom, so after that, I can't imagine anything that will shock me. It's insanely...neat."

"I have a housekeeper who comes in a couple of times a week."

Serenity laughed. "Thank goodness. I was a little worried."

"Funny." She dodged one of the sofa pillows he tossed at her.

When she returned, Jackson's eyes were closed again as he reclined lengthwise on the couch. Pain didn't register on his face at the moment and he seemed so peaceful, she hated to disturb him. Opening his eyes while she debated what to do, he blinked hard a couple of times as though seeing a vision.

"Are you okay? You look...dazed. You're not going into shock or anything, are you?"

"No, no." Jackson shook his head, but still appeared somewhat shell-shocked. "At least I don't think so."

"Are you hungry? It's been a few hours since we ate. How about a sandwich?"

"I can eat, but don't feel like you need to wait on me, Serenity."

"Nonsense," she said. "You're in no condition to be up and moving around. You rest and let me go see what I can find."

"You're the best," he murmured, closing his eyes again.

A few minutes later, Serenity brought him a plate with a ham and Swiss on rye sandwich and settled herself in the armchair next to the sofa. The creases on his forehead had eased, and it appeared as though the over-the-counter medicine had finally taken effect.

"Thanks. I realized I'm starving." Positioning one of the sofa pillows on his lap, he put the plate on it. "Why didn't you make yourself a sandwich? I hate to eat alone."

"I'd rather watch you eat." She shrugged at his frown. "I'm not hungry."

Jackson lifted the corner of the bread. "Nothing was green, right?"

Her laugh escaped. "Not even close. The dates are all still good." She waited as he bowed and said a quick prayer. "I hope you noticed my concession."

"Ah, yes, the potato chips." He gave her a grin as he chewed a bite of his sandwich and gave her a thumbs-up. "My compliments to the chef."

"You're most welcome."

He bit into a chip and offered one to her.

She hesitated. "Oh, why not?" The chip was salty and tangy. She hadn't enjoyed a potato chip in as long as she could remember, and it tasted *great*.

"Good, huh? Bet you can't eat just one." When Jackson smiled, she melted a little bit more. All it took was sitting in the man's living room, watching him eat a ham sandwich. This was getting seriously dangerous. The man was addictive.

"Oh, all right. Give me another one, please." Serenity held out her hand, and he obliged, giving her three more.

He seemed to enjoy watching her eat. "Glad to see you walk on the dark side every now and then. It's strangely alluring."

She rolled her eyes. "You're delusional." Hearing a knock on the front door, Serenity startled. There it was again, more insistent. "Shall I get it?"

"I'm not expecting anyone, but sure. Thanks." Jackson sounded rather annoyed.

"News must travel fast." She felt his eyes on her as she crossed the room. Opening the door, she couldn't miss the obvious disappointment on the young, dark-haired visitor's pretty face.

"Oh, hi Serendipity. Is Jackson here?"

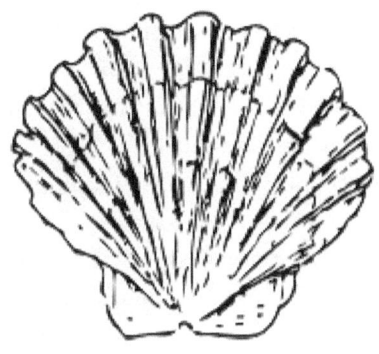

~CHAPTER 23~

*L*eaning around Serenity, Hayley checked out the living room, not bothering with subtlety. Her blue eyes lit when she spied Jackson.

"Jackson! Are you hurt? What happened, sugar?" Hayley flew to his side in a matter of seconds, dropping to her knees and putting a hand on his forearm.

"Got a little too involved in a game of touch football. I'm fine." He shifted his gaze to hers and moved his arm out of reach of Hayley's fingers which now caressed his arm. "Serenity's taking great care of me."

Well, wasn't he magnanimous? At least he hadn't called her Serendipity. Oh, sure, that "sugar" endearment from Hayley irked her, but why should it? She had no claims on Jackson. But like seeing them talking outside the church, it *did* bother her. Could be the exaggerated southern accent or the way Hayley couldn't stop touching him. The woman was incredibly pretty and employed her femininity to full advantage. This was a woman who knew how to find a man's weakness and play right into it. Jackson deserved credit for making a concerted effort to avoid her overly-familiar gestures. Whatever it was, all this fawning turned her stomach sour. If she saw or heard any more, she might say or do something she'd regret. Best to leave now.

"I'll say goodbye." Serenity deep-breathed so she wouldn't voice the childish thoughts that would betray her. Not to mention make it sound like she was consumed by the green-eyed monster. She'd wanted to voice her concerns to

Jackson about someone—Carmen?—either spying on her or following her. That sounded crazy in her own head. It'd probably only serve to convince the psychologist she was delusional, so she'd hug that thought to herself for now. If it happened again, then she'd say something.

"You don't need to go, Serenity," Jackson said, pushing himself up on the sofa.

Serenity grabbed her purse and pulled it over her shoulder. "I think I do."

"Thanks. For the sandwich and everything. I'll give you a call tomorrow." The regret in his voice didn't escape her. From the corner of her eye, she noticed his eyes held a *don't leave me alone with Hayley* look. Jackson was a big boy and could take care of himself. After all, the man held a doctorate in figuring people out. As it was, she'd been way too obvious in her reaction to Hayley's arrival.

Serenity paused with one hand on the doorknob, trying to ignore Hayley's smug smile. *Say your goodbyes and depart.*

"I'll take over now," Hayley said. "Thanks for taking care of Jackson until I could get here."

Lord, hold my tongue. It was all she could do not to huff. The expression on Jackson's face was pretty entertaining. Maybe the good doctor's higher learning hadn't included the lesson on wily women. Yes, this woman wanted Jackson and was unashamedly staking her claim.

"Any time."

"I mean," Hayley said with an odd but suspicious lilt to her tone, "I'm sure you need to get back to your dad now. He needs you more than ever, and—seeing as how he's the only man in your life—you should want to spend as much time with him as you can."

That does it. "That's true," Serenity said, measuring her words carefully. "Hayley, do you know Spencer Walton, by any chance?"

"You mean the quarterback from high school? *That* Spencer Walton?"

"The same."

"Sure. Who doesn't? Why do you ask?" Hayley brushed Jackson's bangs off his brow, her fingers lingering on his face.

"No reason other than I think the two of you might really hit it off. He's actively seeking a woman to settle down with and, like you, Spencer's a—oh, I don't know—a very *hands-on* kind of person." *Lord, forgive me.*

Hayley stopped her hand mid-stroke up Jackson's arm and stared at her. Trying to suppress his laughter, Jackson pulled his arm away from Hayley's reach and coughed into his fist.

"I'm off to see Dad now."

"Take my car again, if you want," Jackson said, picking up the keys from the table and tossing them to her. "I won't be driving it for a while and you left yours at the park." The look on *Hayley's* face this time around was reward enough.

"I appreciate the offer, Jackson, but I can't in good conscience take something that's not mine." Serenity tossed the keys back to him and it took everything in her not to glance at Hayley again. "A long walk sounds really appealing right now, anyway." She gave him her best smile. "Feel better, sugar."

After fixing a quick, healthy lunch for her dad on Monday, Serenity met with the part-time nurse who'd be helping for the next couple of weeks, going over the instructions for his daily schedule, diet and care. Her Dad waved her off and encouraged her to keep her planned lunch date with Deidre. Of course, all her friend could talk about was the upcoming dinner date on Saturday night. After protesting and telling Deidre it wasn't a date—at least not in the traditional sense—she finally gave up trying. After Serenity vetoed The Black Oyster, they'd agreed on Melvin's, a nice but not overly pretentious restaurant.

"Just think," Deidre said with an exaggerated sigh, "you'll get to see Jackson in a suit."

"It's not the prom, so please don't suggest he bring a corsage."

Deidre pouted. "Shall I come over and help you get ready?"

"I think I can manage, thanks," Serenity said, taking a sip of her water with lemon. "As soon as I figure out what to wear." All it took was a raised brow for Deidre to read her unspoken suggestion.

"That settles it, girlfriend. Thursday after work, we're going shopping downtown. Clara's Boutique is open late. We'll find an absolutely gorgeous dress you can't resist...and Jackson—"

"I really shouldn't spend the money," Serenity said, frowning. "I'm sure I can find something in my closet that will work. Or I can spruce it up with a pretty pin or scarf or something."

"No offense, honey, but a khaki skirt and cotton top isn't going to do it this time. And a scarf? The way to a man's heart isn't in how you can knot a scarf, trust me on that one." Chewing a quick bite of her salmon, Deidre speared asparagus and waved her fork at her. "I mean, the way you dress is fine for your run-of-the-mill, nine-to-five business meetings, but you need something flirty that will knock the good doctor right between the eyes. Show a little—"

"I'm not showing anything I shouldn't, Deidre. But sure, I'll knock Jackson out, figuratively speaking, and then Hayley Foster can swoop in, dripping with all that ingratiating southern charm and take care of the handsome doctor."

Deidre eyed her above the rim of her coffee cup before lowering it to the saucer. "You're not honestly worried about competition from Hayley, are you? Mark my words, that girl's a clinger. Why do you think she's not married? As pretty as she is, that girl's got attachment issues. Big time."

Serenity shook her head with a grin. "No, I'm not worried because it's not a competition."

Dabbing her lips with her cloth napkin, Deidre shook her head. "Let me see if I've got this pegged right. You're not ready for a relationship—a romantic one—but you don't want to see Jackson in a relationship with anyone else, either."

"No, that's not it," Serenity said. "I'd hate to see Jackson in a relationship with...well, Hayley Foster." *Or anyone else.* When Deidre watched her, as if waiting for more, she relented. "Okay, I don't want him to date anyone else. Satisfied? I can't believe I'm even talking about this. It's not fair to Jackson to give him false hope."

Deidre's lips curved. "Oh, I think you've already got the psychologist hooked, sweetie. All you need to do is say the word and he's yours to reel in."

Serenity frowned. "That's just it, Deidre. I'm not fishing. I shouldn't *be* fishing."

"I'm not buying *that* for one little second." Deidre took another bite of her asparagus. "Protest all you want, but you're only deluding yourself."

Walking to her office a short time later, Serenity chastised herself. How could she have left her dad so soon after his release from the hospital? Stopping and sitting on a park bench a few blocks from her office, she called him. "He's fine," the part-time duty nurse told her. She could hear her father speaking in the background. "Clinton said to tell you he's fine. Stop worrying."

"Tell him I'll be there in a few hours to fix his dinner." She told the nurse to call if he needed anything. When she lived in Atlanta, she rarely worried about her dad. One medical procedure later and she'd apparently turned into a certified mother hen? Perhaps a close brush with mortality *does* put an entirely different slant on life. In the back of her mind, she'd known he wasn't well and that was another underlying reason she'd come home again. If it was within her power, she'd do anything to keep him healthy and safe as long as she could.

"Who's your new friend?" Kelsie thumped a pencil on her desk and shot a wry grin in Serenity's direction when she walked into Inner Serenity a few minutes later, lost in thought. If Kelsie hadn't spoken and waved her hand to get her attention, she might have breezed right past her.

She gave her assistant a blank stare. "Other than Jackson, I don't know who you're talking about." Picking up her mail on the corner of Kelsie's desk, Serenity walked into her office and dropped her purse beside the desk.

Following her, Kelsie stood in the doorway. "Not Jackson. The other guy."

Serenity's frown deepened. *Please don't tell me Spencer's come back for round two.* "I don't know who you mean. A potential new client? Did he leave a name, a card or anything?"

Her assistant pushed her shoulder-length dark, wavy hair behind one ear and gave her a skeptical glance, as if she suspected she wasn't being entirely forthcoming. "No, he didn't give me a name or a card. He was overdressed for

Croisette Shores, but he looked sharp. Dark suit and fancy silk tie. Nice looking, shorter than Jackson, but then, most men are. Brown, straight hair. I couldn't see the color of his eyes. His voice was masculine, but not as deep as Jackson's."

Serenity moved a hand to her hip. "Must you compare every man to Jackson?"

"Yeah, I kinda do," Kelsie said. "He's more or less the measure of a man around Croisette Shores. Your doctor friend's caused quite a stir among the womenfolk in the village."

"That's really none of my business. While I admire your powers of observation, Kelsie, I really can't think of anyone I know who matches the description of this man. Let me know if you see him or if he comes into the office again." Shaking her head, Serenity dropped the junk mail in her trash can and dumped the rest on her desk, feeling a sense of relief when Kelsie departed without another word. Although she appreciated her assistant's sunny disposition, she wasn't in the mood today. After making a few phone calls to her father's health care provider and confirming the ongoing arrangements for his care during the upcoming week, she pushed away from the desk and walked back to the outer office.

"Kelsie?"

Her assistant swiveled in her chair. "I knew it! You're going out with *two* guys, aren't you? Not a big surprise, really. If I looked like you, boss, I'd never need to buy groceries." A smile tugged at the corners of her mouth.

"For the record, I'm not even going out with one," Serenity said. "And you're a lovely girl. You'll meet the right guy when the time comes."

Skepticism was written all over the younger girl's pretty face. "Thanks, but don't change the subject." She laughed when Serenity waved her hand. "The way I see it, you might not think you're going out with Jackson, but *he* believes you are."

Crossing her arms, Serenity frowned. "Yes, we do things together, but only as friends and business acquaintances."

"Denial is a sin, boss."

"So is idol worship, but I'm not engaging in either one." Dumb comment, but Serenity couldn't come up with anything better. She headed back into her office then thought of something else and turned around again. "So, this other man came into the office? When was that?"

Kelsie smirked. "I thought you weren't interested."

Serenity blew out a sigh. "I sign your paycheck. Give it up, Kelsie."

"He came in right before lunch and asked when you'd be in. I asked if he had an appointment and he said no. I gave him your business card." Her eyes widened. "That was okay, right?"

"Sure. That's why they're on your desk. Did he mention needing an interior decorator?" Serenity tried to control the rapid acceleration of her pulse, but it wasn't working. Why was some man in a suit at her place of business and asking about her? "Did he say anything else?"

Kelsie thought about it a moment before snapping her fingers. "No, but he did something I thought was kind of odd, now that I think of it."

Serenity was almost afraid to ask. "What was that?"

"He walked over to that photo on the wall. He didn't ask any questions but stood there, staring at it like he was trying to take a mental picture or something." Serenity didn't need to follow the direction of Kelsie's finger. She knew very well which photo. The one she debated whether to mount on the wall, a constant reminder of her past. But it was also part of her heritage, so there it was, on the side wall, not visible to everyone unless they walked closer to her office. She moved her gaze across the room and landed squarely on the smiling but immovable eyes of her mother.

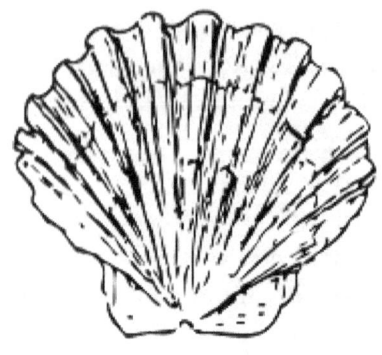

~CHAPTER 24~

Serenity watched with interest as Jackson and Deidre's husband, Weston, hit it off like old pals at Melvin's on Saturday night. The two men kept up a steady stream of conversation punctuated with frequent laughter. You'd think they'd known each other for years. Of course, Wes peppered Jackson with questions about his car. All Serenity could think about was how gorgeous Jackson looked in his dark suit, white pin-striped shirt and red silk tie. The man cleaned up extremely well.

"What are you two frat boys yakking about now?" Deidre teased. "You'd better calm down or they'll send the waiter over here to shush you up. Melvin's is a sophisticated, upscale joint and you're embarrassing us."

"Why send a waiter over when *you* do it quite well? The shushing, that is," Wes said. "You're never embarrassing." He planted a kiss on his wife's cheek. "You ladies will be happy to know we've come to an agreement on the landscaping of the playground," Wes said, pride lacing his announcement. "I'm donating my professional services in exchange for some free shrinking for our kids."

Serenity shot a grin at Jackson. So much for gathering bids. Wes had this one wrapped up in less than an hour. He *was* good. No wonder he and Deidre were an unstoppable team in their business endeavors.

"Shrinking?" Deidre laughed. "Is that what the Freudian set is calling it these days, Jackson?"

"It's an unofficial term," Jackson said, smiling, "but contrary to what Wes says, I imagine your kids are very well-adjusted. Of course, I reserve the right to change that assessment once I meet them."

Deidre winked at Serenity. "That's debatable in light of recent events. Stephanie's threatened to chop off her gorgeous long hair in support of some new environmental cause and Paul's decided to collect coats for the homeless."

"Both worthy causes, especially for kids so young," Serenity said, sipping her water with lime and meeting Jackson's admiring gaze over the rim of her glass. The pale blue silk sheath she'd found on her Thursday excursion to Clara's with Deidre was the perfect fit, color and price. When he'd picked her up at her door, Jackson kissed her cheek and told her how lovely she was. The compliment meant more than he could know. She hadn't *felt* lovely in a long time, either inside or out.

"You think so?" Deidre asked, startling her from her daydreaming. "Tell me how my well-intentioned but misguided daughter chopping off her long, beautiful hair is going to further the cause of some endangered spider in the rain forests because their webs can be used as a cure for some rare, tropical disease. What?" Deidre said as Serenity nudged her arm. "Okay, I know there's no such thing, but I said it to prove the ridiculousness of it all." She raised her hands in a helpless gesture as the others hid their grins.

"Donating her hair to cancer patients would be a good solution," Serenity said.

"Now, there you go!" Deidre sat back with a satisfied smile. "I can get behind *that* idea."

"Honey bunny, you know our kids." Wes's voice was soothing as he covered Deidre's hand on the tabletop and squeezed. "By next week, they'll be focused on some new pet project. We can take heart in the fact they're thinking outside the box and expressing a desire to help someone other than themselves. Like our friends Jackson and Serenity here with the playground."

Deidre leaned her head on her husband's shoulder. "Are you saying we actually did something right?"

"I'd say I did the right thing by marrying you," Wes said. "Still, we should keep the free shrinking offer on the table. Once Steph and Paul get to college, anything's possible. Now, let's talk some more about the landscaping for the playground."

"Sounds like a plan," Jackson said, raising his glass in a toast, winking when he touched his glass to hers.

"So, honey bunny, that was a fun evening." Jackson sat beside her on the top step outside her front door three hours later. It was a gorgeous night, balmy but not too humid. The stars winked at them in the clear night sky. With him sitting so close, his elbow resting lightly against hers, Serenity's breathing grew shallow with the exhilaration of heightened awareness. The musky scent of his aftershave was heady and masculine. He'd removed his suit jacket and tie, his sleeves were rolled and he'd unbuttoned the top of his shirt.

"Jackson, tell me something." She stretched out her legs, crossing one ankle over the other, fully aware Jackson watched every move. The sparks flying between them tonight were palpable.

"Anything."

"Have you ever called a woman a pet nickname?"

His eyes met hers. "I called someone sweetheart once. Not very original, but she wasn't really a *honey bunny* kind of gal."

"What happened?"

"She decided she'd rather be someone else's sweetheart."

"How old were you at the time?"

"Twenty-one and still in college. I had stars in my eyes. We both did."

"Did you date long?"

"A little over a year. Long enough to put a ring on her finger and ask her to join me in marital bliss."

"I'm sorry."

He shrugged. "Don't be. We both had some growing up to do and the relationship taught me a lot. Breaking it off was the right thing to do, although it took a while to get over it. I'm thankful Laura had the foresight to see it wouldn't work out between us for the long haul before we made a colossal mistake. Neither one of us was a Christian, either, and I think in some ways, it was the Lord's protection, saving us both from future heartache. After that, I dated a lot, but nothing serious. I pretty much concentrated on my career and establishing my practice."

Serenity reached for his hand and leaned her head on his shoulder as they sat and talked. Time lost all importance as they shared childhood memories and traded fun stories of school antics and accomplishments. At one point, Serenity heard Mrs. Marciano calling for Mr. Darcy to come inside. From the corner of her eye, she knew her neighbor watched them.

"That you over there, Doc Jack? Keeping Miss Serenity company on such a fine night?"

Jackson chuckled and they both waved. "Nice to see you again, Mrs. Marciano." He turned to her when the elderly woman went back inside her house. "Have I told you how great you look tonight?" he said.

"A few times, yes. If nothing else, you're very good for my ego."

"I want to make sure you know I'm thinking of you when you go to bed tonight. And ditto when you wake tomorrow morning." They were venturing into dangerous territory. Jackson brought out emotions and feelings she'd believed long buried.

When Jackson stood up and held out one hand, Serenity allowed him to pull her to her feet. Her gaze fell on the large Tuscarora Crape in the front yard. With its coral-colored blooms, majestic and beautiful, the tree served as a protector of sorts, giving her privacy in her little house and shielding her from the rest of the world.

"*Trust in the Lord with all your heart, and do not lean on your own understanding,*" he whispered, his warm breath against her skin, his lips brushing against her temple. "*In all your ways acknowledge Him, and He will make your paths straight.*" Jackson moved his lips to her brow where he planted a light kiss. Even as she leaned into it, Serenity sensed he wanted to say more, desired more than a soft kiss on the forehead. Such a gentleman, this man. "Thanks for tonight. I had a great time meeting your friends, and being with you."

"Wes and Deidre are quite the pair, aren't they?"

"I'm glad you have them in your life." He angled his head toward Mrs. Marciano's house. "Not to mention your sworn protector next door."

"Be glad Mrs. Marciano likes you. She wields a mean cast iron skillet."

"Thanks for the warning. I'll try to be good. Good night." He released her. Draping his jacket over his shoulder, he started down the front steps.

"Jackson?"

He turned around slowly. The way she felt in this moment, she'd be content simply looking at him the rest of her life. "Yes?"

"Am I...honey bunny material?"

That sexy, slow grin surfaced. "Oh, yeah. Good night, sweet Serenity." In the moonlight, his eyes caressed hers.

Warmth enveloped her as she watched Jackson climb into that fabulous car. It suited him well. Looking down at her hand, she marveled over how she missed Jackson's hand around hers. It suited her well, too. Climbing into bed a short time later, she understood Jackson waited on her cue to take their relationship to the next level. More importantly, he waited on the Lord's timing.

Reaching for her Bible, Serenity opened it, fingering the pages as if they were spun gold. This book was precious, yes, but she needed to read it. Absorb it.

She wanted the pages to be turned so often they became well-worn. Reading verses of scripture would help heal the frayed edges of her heart like nothing else. But first, she'd pray. Falling to her knees by the side of her bed, Serenity burrowed her head in the bedspread.

I want to be worthy, Father. Help me be worthy of Your love. I've done so many things wrong in my life, but I've tried to be a good person. I love how You see my heart and who I am inside and not on the outside. You've taken on all my faults and made me clean again. I don't deserve it, but I guess that's what mercy and grace is all about it. And, if it's not too much to ask, please help me be worthy of Jackson's love. He's a good man, and I only want the best for him. I never thought I'd be anybody's best. I'm willing to try, but I'm going to need You beside me.

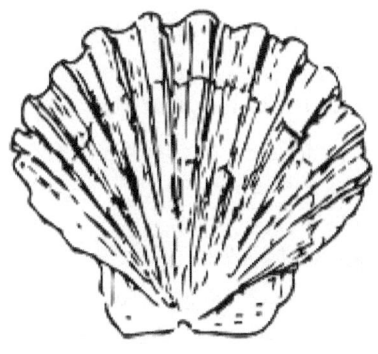

~CHAPTER 25~

"*B*ased on the results, I think we make a great team."

Jackson didn't pose it as a question this time, as he so often did. Turning in a slow circle from the middle of his office, Serenity surveyed their handiwork. "I think you're right, professionally speaking. Not bad at all, especially for a first effort."

He was standing so close, their shoulders touched. His nearness was unsettling in a good way as he turned to face her, his eyes bright. "You were spot-on about the chair rail, and the pale yellow above it is the perfect backdrop for all the great photos you helped pick out," Jackson said. "I like that you're a real *hands-on* kind of girl." His cheeks flushed and he ran a hand over his hair. "That sounded a whole lot better in my head. Sorry."

Serenity swallowed her grin at his thinly-veiled reference to what she'd said to Hayley. They'd never discussed that little episode, but perhaps it was for the best. "Isn't that what all good decorators do? Get personally involved in satisfying their client's needs?" She shook her head as he laughed. "You're a bad influence on me."

"In answer to your question," he said, "the good decorators hire someone else to do the dirty work *for* them. But the truly *great* decorators like you? They do it themselves because they pay close attention to detail and are insanely committed to their clients." He nudged her shoulder. "In case you missed it, that was a big compliment."

"They must teach you that in Faking People Out 101 in Shrink School. I was stuck on the insane part. On the other hand, it could be that some decorators are neurotic and control freaks and have this insatiable, compulsive need to make sure everything's done just so."

When Jackson laughed, she liked how the corners of his eyes crinkled, making him even more attractive. "Well, speaking for myself, I couldn't be happier, and I'm going to recommend my decorator to everyone I know. Which reminds me, I need more of your business cards."

"Thanks for all the free advertising. Much obliged." Retrieving her purse, Serenity opened a small case and placed a handful of her cards on the top of his desk. "You know, Jackson," she said, taking the bigger chair in front of his desk while he dropped into his desk chair, "I've lived in Croisette Shores most of my life, but I think you know more people than I do."

"Not true, but a lot of them seem to believe we're dating."

"Don't know why they'd think that." Her gaze fell on his business cards in the holder on the desk. It featured a simple cross in the background, like the one mounted on the wall behind his desk. Made by Jackson's grandfather, it served as the perfect focal point for his office. A beautiful reminder of the ultimate price paid to cover the sins of man.

"Probably because we've been spotted together all over town buying everything from stuffed animals to light fixtures and paint," Jackson said, interrupting her musings. "Going to The Summer Palace. The church picnic. Waiting at the hospital while your dad was in surgery. I think going to dinner with Deidre and Wes pretty much sealed the deal, though."

Time to change the subject. Twisting in the chair, Serenity nodded to the far wall. "Those watercolors of Croisette Shores we found at the antique shop are the perfect touch. I'm so glad we found them. It'll give the kids a sense of familiarity."

"That was my thinking. Glad you agree."

"I wish all my clients were as easy as you."

"Beg your pardon?" A muscle in his jaw twitched.

"Don't harbor any illusions, Dr. Ross. All I mean is, people can be unbelievably picky and some do what they want, anyway, so why bother hiring a decorator?"

"That's easy. Some people simply want a sounding board, whether it's a pastor, a psychologist, a bartender, a waitress or a decorator." He rose to his feet. "Come on, let's go. I want to show you something." Walking through the outer lobby to the front door, Jackson pulled it open and waited. He cocked a brow with an expectant expression.

She glanced at her watch. "I need to be back at my office for a two o'clock appointment."

"It won't take long. Promise." He placed a light hand on the small of her back as they exited the office. As they walked, Jackson told her more about the plans. "Because of Charlie's connections, we're getting the swings and jungle gym a lot sooner than expected, and the fencing is being donated and put together by Harry Maine's Hardware staff. Today I got a call from a local family who wants to donate a top-of-the-line sandbox. The Neiman-Marcus of sandboxes, if you will."

"That's great," she said, "but we still won't officially open it until next spring, right?"

"That's the thing," he said, slanting her a grin. "If everything goes as smoothly as it already has, we could be looking at sometime this fall. Things tend to move faster here in Croisette Shores, at least in terms of renovating playgrounds."

"I suppose that's a good thing...in terms of the playgrounds," she said.

"Answer a question for me. Why do the playgrounds in Croisette Shores even *have* a sandbox, especially when the real thing is only a few blocks away?"

Serenity flinched at his words, a reminder of Danny. He used to say the exact same thing. "I think some moms get nervous with the ocean being so close, and they feel their kids are safer at a playground. It's a contained area."

When they reached their destination, Jackson waved his hand.

"They've already resurfaced? It looks great."

"It's that new stuff—forget what it's called—but it doesn't get too hot in the summer and stays naturally cool," he said, crouching and testing it out. "They're right."

Like she'd done in Jackson's office, Serenity twirled in a slow circle, envisioning how it would look once all the renovations were done. "I ask you, what kid could resist a new playground? When it's finished, kids from other areas of town are going to want to come here." She stopped. "What you're doing is a great service for Croisette Shores. For the children, the parents, the town. Thank you. I'm honored to be a part of the project."

"You're welcome, and thanks for being willing to help."

"I haven't done much."

He shot her a look. "That's not true and you know it. Coming from the woman who won't even accept payment for all her hard work on behalf of the renovation."

"Consider it my donation to my community. I seriously doubt *you're* getting paid for your tireless efforts."

"Close your eyes."

She did as he asked.

"Wow, you didn't even question me that time. We're making excellent progress," he said, chuckling. Taking her hand, he led her across the playground before stopping. "Okay. You can open your eyes now."

Future home of the Daniel Marshall Kincaid Memorial Playground.

Oxygen drained from her lungs and Serenity's mouth dropped open.

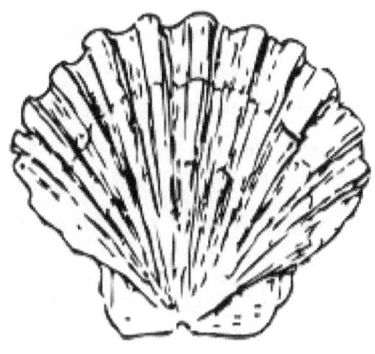

~CHAPTER 26~

"Serenity, have I done something to offend or hurt you?" Jackson's tone was full of concern mixed with confusion. How could he suspect she hovered on the edge of hyperventilating? Taking a quick breath, she willed the pounding in her head to ease. For her sanity, she needed to pretend the words on the sign hadn't seared through her heart, reminding her all over again of the deep-seated pain that might never go away.

"I've obviously upset you. I didn't know it would have this effect..." Jackson hesitated, and she darted a glance his way. The Adam's apple slid up and down in his throat. The deep concern in his eyes helped her summon the strength she needed. From his reaction, she could tell he didn't know Daniel Kincaid had been *her* Danny.

"Tell me how the name of the playground came about." She moved over to the end of the old sliding board and sat down, frowning when it bowed under her weight. She liked the idea of naming the playground after Danny. In truth, it made sense and would be a fitting tribute to him since he'd always been a kid at heart. He'd barely been more than a kid when he was murdered. How ironic Danny would remain forever young while she felt like she'd aged two decades in the last five years alone.

"Last week, I got a call from the town treasurer," Jackson said. "An anonymous donor sent a check with the specific request the playground be named in honor of Daniel Kincaid." Hesitating, he eyed her. "It's a very generous amount of money…and it costs more than people think to build a state-of-the-art playground with new equipment that meets all the safety requirements." Stopping, Jackson slapped his palm on his forehead and groaned. "For a guy who's supposed to be fairly intelligent, I can be unbelievably clueless. This is definitely one of those times. I'm sorry. I have no excuses and I hope you can forgive me."

"It's okay. There's nothing to forgive. You couldn't have known. So, you don't have any idea as to identity of the donor?"

"Only the town treasurer knows. How well do you know her?"

"Everyone knows Dora," Serenity said. "She'll never crack. She's loyal as anything, which is actually a very good thing. Dora will take the identity of the playground donor to her grave." She looked up at him. "I think it's time to tell you more about Danny."

For the first time since she'd met him, Jackson seemed uncertain. "Sure."

"Let's go sit on the bench and hope it holds the weight of both of us." Her attempt at humor didn't seem to work since he still seemed bothered when he held out his hand and helped her to her feet.

"Wait. Let me test it out first," he said, putting his hand on her arm to stop her when she started to sit on the bench. A couple of seconds later, he gave her a nod.

"Danny grew up in this neighborhood, too," she said, sitting beside him. "He was a year ahead of me in school, and I knew him from the time we were in the same preschool." Serenity's eyes misted as she took in the rusty equipment, the leaning chain link fence, the broken swing. She pointed to one corner, overgrown with unruly weeds. "The sandbox was in the far right corner and we'd play there for hours. Danny learned early on not to throw sand in my face or dump it over my head."

Shifting his position, Jackson turned to face her. The wind sifted through his hair, and for a brief moment, she glimpsed the little boy he'd been once, sitting at the feet of his mother or a teacher, listening to a story.

"Danny tried to kiss me under the finger painting table in preschool. Then in fourth grade, he caught me unaware in my classroom and kissed me behind the coat rack. That was my first kiss. He surprised me, and I was mad as anything. I retaliated by kicking him in the nose. Hard. I never knew a nose could bleed so much. The teacher demanded to know who'd *assaulted* Danny, and he had to go to the emergency room. I was scared to death I'd killed him and the police would storm into the school, put me in handcuffs and haul me away. On death row by the time I was nine. Not one of the kids told on me, but about an hour later, I finally couldn't take the guilt and owned up to being the aggressor."

She paused as she saw the corners of Jackson's mouth upturn. "Then when we were in middle school, he wanted to be cool and acted like he could barely tolerate me. He teased me and called me silly nicknames, but he usually walked me home when he didn't have track and field practice." Serenity brushed aside a tear. "Danny wasn't very good in math, and he told everyone he was only walking me home because he needed my tutoring skills."

Jackson smiled. "Why do I have the feeling that endeared him to you even more?"

"You're right. It did." Not that she'd thought about it before. No wonder Jackson was a psychologist. Understanding the way people think was a gift, but perhaps some were born with more of an innate understanding of human behavior than others. "In high school, he turned his attentions to a few other girls. But when it came time for the school dances, Danny always came back to good old, reliable Serenity. We dated off and on, but pretty much exclusively his senior year. From that point on, it was pretty much a given that we'd marry."

Jackson shifted his position on the bench. "Was anyone ever arrested for his murder?"

"No," she said, shaking her head. "The police classified his death as a random act of violence. I've never believed it, but I can't explain it and I have no way of proving otherwise. My heart tells me there was nothing random about his death."

"Tell me why you think it might not have been random."

"Danny was smart in some ways, but when it came to human nature, he was too trusting and naïve. He always wanted to believe the best in people. I'm not saying that's not a good way to live, but in his case, it might have gotten him killed. Unfortunately, we might never know."

"As exhibited by my ignorance a few minutes ago, I think being clueless is indigenous to the male species. Was there a formal investigation into his death?"

"No," she said, shaking her head. "Only a rudimentary one. No one ever pushed for it." Her hands trembled and belied the calmness in her tone. "I thought my dad might try to find out more. There's only one reason I can think of why he hasn't."

"Because he's afraid of what he might find."

"Exactly. The same as with my mom." She blew out a breath and glanced over at him. "When there's a missing person—especially for this long—there's a good possibility there's not going to be a good outcome."

Jackson nodded. "I talked to my brother and asked him to run your mother's information through the system. Knowing Kyle, he forgot. If he doesn't call me back by tomorrow, I'll call him again and remind him."

Serenity's heart raced. "Thanks. Call as soon as you hear anything?"

He helped her to her feet. "So, you're okay with the playground being named after Danny?"

She smiled. "Once I recovered from the initial shock, I think it's a great idea. Danny would have loved it, too. I only wish Liam could play here one day."

"Do you think about Liam a lot?"

"Yes, but not as much as I used to. I'm not sure if that makes me a horrible mother or if it's a natural part of the grieving process."

Jackson took her hand and covered it with his. "You'll have other children someday, Serenity. I realize no one can take the place of Liam, but each child will be special to you, a part of you and settled in your heart."

She nodded, unable to speak, touched by his sweet sentiment. After losing both Danny and Liam, she hadn't entertained thoughts of remarrying or having more children. Jackson was the first man she'd even considered *dating* much less anything else. Did he look at her as a potential wife? No, how could that be possible with all her emotional baggage?

"Jackson, you know everything about my life, but I know very little about yours," she said as they reached her office.

"You didn't ask."

When she started to turn away, he touched her arm. "I understand, Serenity. Like I said before, you've concentrated on taking care of yourself for so long, you've erected walls. It's not selfishness, it's self-protection, pure and simple. It takes time to build up those walls, so it'll take time to bring them tumbling down."

"Like the walls of Jericho?" She gave him a small smile. "Still, you don't have to sound so clinical about it."

His chuckle was low in his throat. "Sorry, I'm afraid it's instinctive."

"Problem is, you're right." She glanced up at him. "Forgive me?"

"For what?" He seemed genuinely puzzled. "Have lunch with me tomorrow and I'll tell you everything you want to know about my family. Anything. Feel free to bring Clinton."

"The nurse'll be with him tomorrow and I've already stocked his fridge," she said. "I'd love to have lunch with you."

As he waved and headed in the opposite direction, back to his office, Serenity realized how much she'd come to enjoy his companionship, his friendship...and the incredible smile that reached deep into her heart and grabbed hold with a silent promise to never let go.

~CHAPTER 27~

"Speak to me, Doc Jack," Serenity said. "Time to tell me about your family." They'd enjoyed a great, casual lunch of clams and scallops at Hermann's on the beach and shared a slice of carrot cake afterwards. For whatever reason, neither one of them brought up the subject of his family during their meal. Somehow she sensed it might be a difficult topic for Jackson.

"As you wish," he said, crossing his arms over his chest. In his deep red T-shirt, it only emphasized those distracting muscles. "I was the middle son of three boys, so I didn't suffer any high expectations for greatness." Jackson's smile was half-hearted, but the tautness around his mouth spoke volumes. "You know, the middle child syndrome."

"A stereotype," Serenity said. "Where are your brothers now?"

"Chad's three years older. He was the golden boy and graduated at the top of his class at Harvard Business School. Classic overachiever, but the guy's brilliant. As expected, he got a top job and worked as an investment banker in New York for Goldman Sachs. *Was* being the key word. Chad lost most of his colleagues on 9/11, and to be honest, I'm not sure he'll ever fully recover."

Hearing the pain in his voice, Serenity reached across the table for his hand, overwhelmed with the need to touch him. She wanted him to know she was there for him in the way he'd been there for her so many times. "I'm sorry, Jackson." No wonder he might be reluctant to talk about his family.

"He was supposed to be in a meeting in his office that morning, but my sister-in-law had a doctor's appointment and asked him to go with her. So, Chad sat in a doctor's office and lived to mourn his coworkers and friends." When Jackson met her eyes, they were damp with emotion. "Chad's had a tough road. He withdrew from life for a while and took off on an extended trip to go *find himself.*" Tracing circles on the tablecloth with his finger, Jackson was quiet for a long moment. "He finally came around and realized his wife and two daughters needed him and that's where his heart lies."

"I can't even imagine," Serenity said, "but I'm sure you helped him however you could."

"I've tried. The best thing I can do for him is pray, but he's resistant to the point of being adamant against Christianity. Chad's of the opinion a loving God wouldn't have destroyed the innocence of a nation on 9/11. He can't understand my belief in a higher power who could allow it to happen. Even though my family's heard the story of how God found me, and even though I pray they can see I've changed for the better since I became a Christian, they're so set in their behaviors and habits, they can't open their narrow minds to something beyond the scope of their limited understanding."

The regret in his eyes touched her deeply, and Serenity squeezed his hand. "I love how God has a way of bringing us into His presence even when we're not consciously seeking Him."

"That's a beautiful truth. Chad"—when Jackson hesitated, she heard his voice catch—"likes to pick stupid fights with me. The primary reason I go home at holidays is for my mom. It's important for her to have us all gathered around the table." Frowning, he took a quick sip of his iced tea. "Doesn't matter that it's tense and only a matter of time until the verbal sparring match begins."

"I always wished for a sibling, but I think I see it through rose-colored glasses," Serenity said. "More someone to share the burdens and responsibilities as opposed to someone I might be at odds with. I really wanted a sister. I begged Mama, but she finally told me she couldn't have more kids."

"Sorry," he said. "I have times when I wish I was an only child, as bad as that sounds. But, in *your* case, I think Deidre's as close as a sister, am I right?"

She nodded. "She's part of me, so yes, you're right."

"I'm not saying we didn't have good times growing up, because we did."

"Does Chad still work as an investment banker?"

"Funny you should ask. He always used to call himself a weekend cook. After the initial aftershocks of 9/11 wore off—and some extensive therapy—he quit his six-figure job and went to work as a sous chef in a top New York restaurant. Now he's happier than he's ever been. In that regard, I'm happy for him, but I wish he'd ease up on the criticism of something that's so important in my life. Mom and Dad always admired Chad and now they're trying to accept him as a chef. They dote on his kids, though, and that's great to see. In spite of everything, they're great kids, due in large part to Chad's wife, Leslie, and how grounded she is. She's a full-time, stay-at-home mom and filled the void when Chad decided to go off on his little expedition."

"What about your dad and mom?" she asked. "Are you close?"

"We talk, but it's mostly surface stuff and nothing deep." He smiled a little. "Nothing like the discussions I've shared with you. Dad's the most passive of us all. He worked as an accountant and is now happily retired, fishing and golfing as much as he can. Mom stays busy with all her charity and social events. Financial success equates with personal worth in my parents' eyes, unfortunately."

"And your younger brother, the lawyer?"

"Kyle's being groomed to be the youngest partner in the history of his prestigious law firm in Seattle. I call him *runt* and he hates it. Good guy, but I'm afraid his ego is inflating along with his rising status in the firm. We're pretty close—closer than I am to Chad—but Kyle's committed to breaking a few hearts on his way to the top. I just don't want to see him sitting in that big corner office in a few years, surrounded by his awards and material gain, lamenting the fact he has no one to go home to at the end of the day. He's still young, though, and he's got a lot more growing up to do." He frowned. "Not that I'm an expert on anything. Far from it."

After settling the bill, Jackson put his arm around her waist and steered her out of the restaurant. "Do you have time for a walk on the beach?"

Seeing the hope in his eyes, Serenity hadn't the heart to tell him no. "I have an appointment with a new client later this afternoon, but I can definitely spare more time with my favorite client." The warmth of his smile filled more holes in her slowly mending heart. Never would she have thought she'd meet a man after God's heart like Jackson. When he moved his arm to her shoulders, she didn't protest. The action seemed an unconscious gesture on his part. The unconscious, little gestures were those she hugged close in her heart.

Removing their shoes, they carried them as they skirted the edge of the waves lapping on the shore in the low tide. The sun was partially hidden by the clouds and a light breeze stirred the air. "For a long time, I didn't feel like I measured up to my parents' ideal of a career," he said. "In spite of the fact that I..." Scratching his head, he paused, making her wonder at his open-ended sentence.

"I'm sure your parents are very proud of you."

"Let's say the jury's still out on that one." He didn't sound bitter, but he *did* sound hurt. The muscles in his jaw twitched. "I'll tell you one thing. If I'm blessed to have children one day, I'm going to accept them, no matter what they do." His eyes took on a faraway glaze. "If my son wants to work on a dude ranch, be a beekeeper or deep sea fish off the coast of Newfoundland, then that's great. If my daughter wants to ride in the rodeo, be a fire...person, the head of a multi-national advertising firm, a shepherd or a horse whisperer, that's perfectly fine, too." He paused when she laughed. "Did I say something funny?"

"Those are very interesting professions. But I understand what you mean," she said, slipping her hand into his again. "I'm sure your children will be strong, good, law-abiding and true to the Lord, no matter what they choose to do." Feeling awkward at this turn in the conversation, Serenity started to withdraw her hand, but he wouldn't allow it and held on tighter.

"I have a nickname for you," he said as he nudged her shoulder and they resumed walking.

"Should I ask?"

"Beautiful pretty. I know it doesn't make much sense, but it describes everything about you. I've never met a woman like you."

Serenity lowered her gaze as Jackson swung her around to face him. Removing his hand from hers, Jackson caressed her cheeks with both hands. Closing her eyes, she relished the feel of his light touch on her skin, warming her. *Thrilling her.* With a gentle hand, he tilted her chin so she'd look up at him. What he did next surprised her even more. He kissed one eyelid and then the other. Opening her eyes, she shivered. What she saw in the depths of his gaze was something she'd seen in Danny's eyes, at least early on in their marriage. Desire, yes, but so much more. "Don't say it, Jackson. Please don't say it."

He leaned his forehead against hers, his lips dangerously close. All she could do was stare at those full, sensuous lips, wondering how they'd taste. How'd they feel on hers. All it would take was a tilt of the head and their lips would meet.

"You don't know what I was going to say." His voice was husky, low, sensual.

"I have a pretty good idea."

Jackson tucked her into his chest. She felt his heart beating beneath her hand resting on the thin cotton of his T-shirt. "You can't run away forever, baby." He brushed his warm and achingly tender mouth over her temple. "One day, you'll want to let someone in again."

"I promise you one thing." Pushing back, Serenity breathed him in, this man.

"What's that?" Flecks of honey warmed his eyes.

"If I let someone in, it'll be *you.*"

A smile eased his handsome features, making her heart sing. "Thank you. That's all I need to hear." Taking her hand, they walked, content in the shared silence.

Surely the man knew he was already *there.*

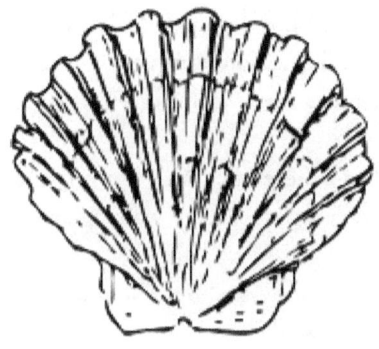

~CHAPTER 28~

As they left the beach and reached the sidewalk, Serenity spied a woman a few hundred yards away. *Carmen*. Wearing a hat, sunglasses and nondescript clothing. Gripping Jackson's arm, she squeezed it hard. "That's her," she hissed, easing her hold and ruing the white marks left by the impression of her fingers on his arm. "Sorry for mauling you, but come on."

"It's hardly mauling and I'm happy to be needed, but who are you talking about?"

Serenity pointed to the figure walking ahead of them on the same side of the street. "Okay, I know this sounds crazy, but I think that woman might be following me. Or keeping watch on me or something. And...I believe it's Carmen."

"Carmen? You mean David's friend, Carmen?"

"How many Carmens do you know? Yes, *that* Carmen," she said, tossing him a sidelong glance as she tugged on her shoes and he did the same. "She wore hats and sunglasses the first couple of times, so it was hard to determine her hair or eye color, but she has the same frame. The deep red color of her fingernails was the tip-off." They started walking. "Plus it's the way she moves. It's all in the hips. Maybe it's a Latin thing, I don't know, but it's distinctive and the woman really knows how to work it good."

"Whoa. Hang on a red-hot second." Jackson stopped and held up both hands. "You believe you're being followed and you didn't tell me?" Judging by his expression, that statement made him none too happy. "And you think it's Carmen?"

At least he seemed to believe her. "Yes, but not in a sinister way. More like she's spying or keeping an eye on me. Keep walking and I'll tell you what I know, which isn't much."

"I hate to point out the obvious, but she must not be following you now since *she's* the one being followed."

"Right. I can't explain it, but I have a need to follow her and see where she goes." She tossed him a glance. "So, are you with me or not?"

"Do you even need to ask?"

Keeping the other woman in sight, Serenity hastened her pace. While they walked, she told Jackson about seeing her the day he left her office with the stuffed giraffe and Arnie. Then when she spied her again in the hospital cafeteria. "When I met Carmen at the picnic, I had that weird déjà vu feeling you get sometimes. Like I'd met or seen her somewhere before. She told me she'd been a flight attendant but had recently retired. I'll say one thing. If she *is* following me, she's not very good at it."

"I'll bite. Why not?"

"In trying to be inconspicuous, she accomplished the exact opposite effect and stuck out like a sore thumb. I mean, really, who goes around with their hair covered and wearing sunglasses? Okay, sure women wear hats and sunglasses here all the time because we're near the beach, but not usually inside a hospital cafeteria. That's the one thing that made me really notice her, even though I was distracted at the time about my dad and your whole Jesus-in-a-potato-chip spiel."

"Why didn't you tell me any of this at the picnic? If it's true, we could have confronted her then, or I could at least have talked with David and tried to find out something. I don't want to think there's anything shady going on since he's involved with her."

"I haven't ever felt threatened or I would have told you. There wasn't an opportunity to tell you at the picnic with the whole hot dog spewing incident and then you got hurt and the timing was never right."

"You couldn't you have told me *after* the picnic?" Now he sounded disgruntled.

"Right," she groused. "How could I do that with Hayley fawning all over you?"

She heard his deep sigh. "You could have told me *since* then. And, trust me, Hayley's done fawning and touching me or whatever you implied with your little speech about Spencer what's-his-name. I set Hayley straight right after you took off and left me alone with her. Is there anything else I should know that you haven't told me?"

"I'm curious as to how you set Hayley straight, but thanks."

Jackson's gaze—the bone-melting, soul-searching kind she'd always heard about but never knew until Dr. Ross walked into her life—bore into her now. "I'm pretty sure you can figure it out. Not going to spell that one out. Tell me what else you know."

Still lost in the intensity of his eyes, Serenity snapped to attention. "The only other thing I know is a man came into Inner Serenity the other day and asked Kelsie a few questions when I wasn't there. She said he was very well-dressed in a suit—not that it has anything to do with anything—and asked a few questions about when I might be back in the office. Then he stared at Mama's photo for a minute or two before leaving."

"You finally hung it on the wall? I'm happy to hear it."

"I did, but not where everyone can see. It's hanging on the wall leading into my office."

"Then how'd Mr. Nice Suit see it?"

"Probably because he was by Kelsie's desk," she said. "I know she handed him my business card. If he was standing at the right angle, he'd have a good vantage point."

"Any theories on why he'd be interested in the photograph?" Jackson retrained his focus on Carmen. "That's kind of weird."

"Haven't a clue."

"And he hasn't come back to your office since? No further sightings from Kelsie?"

"No, and you and I both know she'd tell me if she did. One thing that girl's *not* is shy."

Jackson nodded and they turned the corner, being careful to stay behind Carmen. If she turned around, she'd see them, and Serenity wasn't sure what they'd do in that case. It wasn't like she'd been followed—or followed anyone—before in her lifetime.

"Should we just march up to her, confront her?" she asked.

"I'm game if you are." Judging by his expression, Jackson wouldn't hesitate. "Say the word."

She considered it for a half-second. "For now, let's follow her and see where she goes. In case I'm sorely misguided, I wouldn't want it getting around town that I'm certifiable on top of everything else."

"As you wish," Jackson said, "but if you ever feel threatened, you'd better call me."

"Aye, aye sir. Looks like she's headed to the library."

"Then it's time to pick up a new thriller." With his focus trained on the woman, Jackson started up the front steps of the library. "Tell me how you want to play this out."

She gripped his arm, stopping him. "Let's wait here and give her a head start of about thirty seconds before we head inside. Let's see what she does, if she speaks with anyone, where she goes."

Jackson chuckled under his breath.

Serenity darted a glance his way. "Something funny?"

"With that whole Jackie O. thing she's got going on, it's more than obvious she doesn't want to be recognized. It didn't work for Jackie, either. If anything, that getup's a clear giveaway she's trying to hide her identity."

"You don't think she's a celebrity in hiding, do you? She *is* very pretty, after all."

"I'm not agreeing or disagreeing with that statement."

"I'm not the jealous type."

"Could have fooled me, Serendipity," he said, tugging on her hand and pulling her up the stairs. "Thirty seconds are up, and we don't want to lose her."

She should have known he'd throw that nickname in her face at some point. Serenity nodded toward a section by a side wall. "She went over to the fiction area. That hat's so big you can't see her hair color."

"Dark. Like Carmen's."

"How can you tell?"

"Long strands peeking out beneath the hat. Look at the back of her head. The nape of her neck, to be more specific."

Her breathing grew shallow from the warmth of his lips as he whispered in her ear. She shivered. This was getting ridiculous. "Your eyes must be sharper than mine."

"I did a little surveillance in the..." He stopped. "I know where to look."

"You're a man of mystery, Jackson Ross." It was ridiculous to feel like a giddy schoolgirl because a handsome man stood beside her. But it was wonderful because it was *Jackson*. She certainly didn't allow any other man to stand so close to her much less breathe on her. Inhaling a quick breath of her own in a vain attempt to steady her equilibrium, Serenity shifted from one foot to the other. "What else can you tell about her, my brilliant detective?" She found his thought process fascinating in itself.

"Well, let's see." It was both a source of sadness and relief when he pulled away, rubbing his fingers over his chin as he studied the woman. She leaned against a tall bookshelf, a book between her hands, her purse by her feet. The corners of her lips upturned, but she shifted to one side, making it more difficult to get a decent glimpse of her facial features. "I wish she'd turn back this way so I can get a good look at her face. She's always turning her body one way or the other so you can't really see her. That's a clue in itself she doesn't want to be noticed or recognized. Classic avoidance tactic."

"How do you know that? The surveillance training or whatever?"

Jackson chuckled under his breath. "I don't, really. Sounded good, though, don't you think?"

Serenity rolled her eyes. "Get on with your assessment, please."

"Judging from the book she's reading, she likes romances. The, um, spicy kind."

"And how would you know it's spicy?"

"Don't form any judgments, Miss McClaren. Think about it. When you see a half-naked man and woman on a book cover, they're not vertical and locked in one another's arms, that's a pretty decent clue, wouldn't you say?"

"Wow, you really *are* eagle-eyed, but you're right. As usual," she grumbled. "Either that or you're familiar with that particular book."

"Yep, that's me," Jackson said under his breath, "the Christian psychologist, closet erotica reader. If that got around, it'd kill my career in ten seconds flat."

Serenity swatted him on the forearm and he twisted his lips, probably to quell his laughter. "I'm learning new things about you every day. What else do you see?"

"She obviously takes great pride in her appearance. Like you said, she's got deep red fingernails. Matches the polish on her toes."

"Red's not an easy color, either." When Jackson gave her a funny look, she giggled and then clamped a hand over her lips. "The color's vibrant, which makes it hard to correct if you mess it up because it stains the skin..." She stopped when he shook his head.

"I do believe you and I could talk about nothing for an entire day without stopping and it would be the most fascinating conversation of my life."

"You're distracting me again. Stop flirting and get on with it, please."

"As you wish," he said. "All right. She might not be used to spying on someone but neither is she used to being observed. She's way too involved in that book or else she'd have spotted us over here, conspicuous as anything, gawking at her."

"Agreed," Serenity said. "Your conclusion, my good man?"

"She either doesn't want to hide or else it doesn't come easily or naturally for her."

"Well, I shouldn't think spying comes naturally for *anyone*, Jackson. I guess the biggest question in my mind is why she would spy on me in the first place, if that's even what she's doing?" Serenity met his eyes briefly before returning her focus to the woman.

"I have no idea, but if she doesn't leave soon, we might as well go," he said. "Seems to me she's on her own time and, to be honest, I'm starting to feel pretty silly standing here watching a woman reading a smut novel."

Carmen snapped the book closed and replaced it on the shelf. She turned in their direction and pushed the sunglasses further up on her nose with one red fingernail. Her heart thumping in her chest, Serenity turned and grabbed a book from the nearest shelf. She shifted her weight onto her other foot, gasping as Jackson swept her into his arms and crushed his lips down on hers. Off-balance, she grasped both his arms. Catching her, he pulled her against him, so close she could feel his heart racing. Or was it hers?

"*Wha...a...t?*" she sputtered. *I'm protesting this why?*

"Relax and kiss me," Jackson murmured. "Go with me on this."

"If you insist." Sighing against his lips, Serenity reveled in how perfectly they fit, the feel, the texture, the slight roughness of his chin. She moved her hands over his firm chest, up to his shoulder blades and then around to the back of his neck, her fingers lightly touching the curls on his collar. A quiet moan escaped from somewhere inside her, but she didn't care. Or was the moan from Jackson? Could it be tandem moaning?

She hadn't been kissed in so long. Hadn't been held and caressed. Even so, with Danny, it was never like *this*. Then it was over. Dropping his arms and releasing her, Jackson turned away just when she was starting to get the hang of it. The kiss was so unexpected, and there was definite, scorching heat. Undeniable *passion*. Serenity moved one hand over her mouth and stared at him, unsure what to say. What just happened?

"Come on!" he said, his voice barely more than a whisper, motioning with one hand as if she dawdled. "Hurry up, so we can follow her some more."

Too dumbfounded to speak, Serenity tugged her purse strap over one shoulder and headed out the door of the library behind him, ignoring his outstretched hand. Talk about a deflated ego. What a fool she was. Like she was a big, helium-filled balloon, and someone stuck a pin in her as the air slowly filtered out. Shaking, she moved one hand over her stomach and deep-breathed a couple of times in an attempt to regain her equilibrium.

Their first kiss and it was all for show. Jackson Ross sure knew how to flatter a girl.

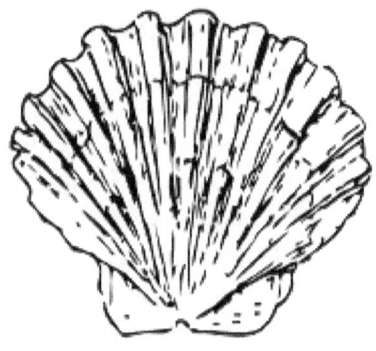

~CHAPTER 29~

*T*hey followed about twenty paces behind Carmen as she walked down the street. Serenity's steps faltered and Jackson tossed a look over one shoulder and made that annoying gesture with his hand again.

"I'm coming," she muttered, quickening her steps to reach his side. They walked in silence, slowing when Carmen slowed and keeping pace with her.

A couple of minutes later, she entered a small apartment building two streets over from Inner Serenity. Jackson walked a few steps ahead of her. Catching up to him, Serenity refused to look his way, still befuddled by what had transpired.

"I'll find out who owns the building and see if I can learn anything else." Putting a gentle hand on her arm, he steered her away and turned in the opposite direction. "Good thing she didn't seem to pick up on the fact she was being followed. Like I said, she's not very good at hiding, if that's her intent." Jackson stopped and his eyes widened. "You're not saying anything and you've got kind of a wild look in your eyes. What's wrong? Speak to me."

Serenity turned away. "It's nothing."

From the corner of her eye, she could tell he raked his fingers through his hair. Next he'd be rubbing his hand over his chin. She was getting rather used to his habits and found them all endearing.

"Not buying it. Tell me."

"I can only imagine how you're such an expert, Mr. Psychologist. Knowing how women tick and all." She cringed. That didn't sound pretty, and the only guarantee was that it irritated him. It annoyed her even more that his statement sounded like something her father would say.

"Look, if this is about me kissing you..." Sure enough, Jackson rubbed his hand over his chin with a frown.

Her hands traveled to her hips. "You'd better believe it's about the kiss!" Frustration bubbled up inside her when the corners of his mouth lifted. "I don't find anything funny about the fact that you played with my emotions."

"Serenity, baby, you've got it all wrong." He frowned. "Don't get mad. It couldn't be helped."

She took an involuntary step backward as he came closer. "Don't *baby* me." What was it about men and that particular nickname? "Did your lips just *happen* to fall on mine? I'm a party to the entire kissing scenario. Or was it that my lips were the nearest ones handy to satisfy your...primal urges?"

He laughed but stopped when he saw her frown. "Oh, come on, Serenity. What's got you more upset...the fact that I kissed you in public the first time or the fact that I broke it off so abruptly?" His grin broke through. "If it's any consolation, I really enjoyed it. Loved it. Want to dance on a rooftop and shout to the world about it. It ended all too soon. I thought we fit pretty well together, but that's another thing I suspected all along."

"Oh...you!" She seethed, but part of her wanted to laugh. The tension was getting to her. She needed to go to the beach and take a long walk, feel the wind whip through her hair and clear her head. Get Jackson Ross and that kiss out of her head. How pathetic was she if all it took was one pretend passionate kiss to get her so stirred up?

"What did you expect me to do?" he asked. "The woman—Carmen—was headed straight for us, and no offense, but you looked like a sitting duck. You couldn't be a detective if your life depended on it."

"So," she said, twisting her mouth not to give into a threatening grin, "your best solution was to grab and kiss me like some kind of sex-crazed man so the woman wouldn't notice we were watching her?"

"Well, yeah, that's pretty much it."

"If anything, you probably called even more attention to us. Ever think about that?"

"We might never know. If she *is* following you, we gave her something to see, right?" When she shook her head, he shrugged and started walking again. "You're really cute when you're all feisty and flustered. So, did the kiss do anything for you?"

Serenity blew out a sigh. No sense in sparring with him. She was tired and wanted to go home. "It was good." Much better than good, but it was all she could muster.

When she stopped, Jackson backed up a few steps to stand beside her. "Care to share?"

"Did you say the *first* time?"

Tilting his head to one side, he appeared puzzled. "I have no idea what you're talking about."

"The kiss. You said something about it being the *first* time."

That slow, lazy grin surfaced. "Yeah, I guess I did."

"Which would imply there's going to be a second time, and..." *Stop talking now.*

Jackson took a step closer. "Would you like a repeat performance right here? Right now? I'm willing if you are."

She whirled around and started walking. "That won't be necessary." When he was beside her again, she darted a glance his way. "I like my kisses private."

Shaking his head, Jackson chuckled under his breath. "I'll keep that in mind for future reference. And, I realize I'm probably pushing my luck here, but what was the hip action you mentioned?"

"What?" She shook her head.

"When you were telling me how you knew it was Carmen and you said something like, 'It's all in the hips.'" Oh, his grin hinted of mischief, dimple and all. "Should I ask for a demonstration? That's bound to be interesting."

Well, fine, she'd give the man a show. "All right, mister. You asked for it." Glancing around, relieved no one else was around and they were alone, Serenity demonstrated, feeling foolish but doing her best to duplicate the gentle sway of her hips. "This is how Carmen walks. I noticed it at the picnic." She sighed and stopped. "You can't tell me you didn't, Jackson. You're a man, you're breathing and you're not blind. It's the calculated kind of move designed to attract every red-blooded man on the planet."

He laughed and crossed his arms over that distractingly taut chest. "Remember, I'm a blue-blooded male. I'm different."

"Yes, you are definitely that last part. I'll give you that much." They started walking back in the direction of her office.

"By the way, that little hip action thing was pretty sexy," he said. When he reached for her, Serenity slipped her hand in his. "You can do it anytime you want, but in private, if you please."

Serenity felt her cheeks flush. All she could do was give him a goofy smile and keep walking, but maybe with a little more hip action than usual.

*T*rue to form, Justin marched in Jackson's office for his appointment the following Tuesday morning. Waving to Arnie on the shelf, he stopped at the terrarium to pay his respects to Señor Igor before plopping in the small chair opposite his desk. "You're playing Mozart."

"That's right," Jackson said, not bothering to hide his surprise. Ever since he'd heard Mozart in Serenity's office, he'd developed more of an appreciation for classical music. "It's Symphony Number Ten in G—"

"Symphony Number *Five* in G Minor." Mrs. Johnson came into the office, closing the door behind her.

"You're right," Jackson said. "My mistake." As usual, the woman's expression was stoic and noncommittal. What were the odds she'd know it by name, the *exact* same symphony he'd heard playing in Serenity's office?

"Grandma takes me to the symphony in New York sometimes," he said. When talking with this child, he had to remind himself this patient was only a four-year-old boy. In terms of certain aspects of his life, Justin was more on-par with a *twenty*-four-year-old man. He appreciated how Mrs. Johnson dressed him age-appropriately in shorts and T-shirts instead of like a miniature corporate executive. No doubt, this child would grow up to be a fine man in spite of the apparent lack of parental presence in his life. He'd seen a lot of families where grandparents—one or both—had become the primary caregivers for their grandchildren for any number of reasons. Most accepted the responsibility with grace, and some even fought for the right to raise them.

"That's wonderful, Justin. Your grandmother wants to make sure you learn about all kinds of things. Music and the arts are important and help us better understand the world around us." Jackson tried not to smirk at the pompousness of that spiel, but it *was* true. Sure, he'd appreciated cultural things in the past, but he'd never thought much about attending the orchestra although he'd seen a few Broadway plays. Even then, he'd gone primarily because his date wanted to go, but he'd drawn the line at musicals.

Returning his focus to his patient, irritated by his own lack of concentration, Jackson cleared his throat. The drawing. Justin mentioned it in the last session and Mrs. Johnson promised to tell him more about the mysterious relatives in Croisette Shores. "I understand you have something you want to show me today?"

"Yep. Nana has it." Sliding out of the chair, Justin walked over to her, leaning against her knees and swaying back and forth while he waited. The boy's body language reinforced the inherent trust and affection shared between him and his grandmother. Outside of the office, Jackson imagined she was loving and giving, unlike the cool and distant woman she presented in their sessions.

Opening her purse, Mrs. Johnson pulled out a piece of heavy white paper folded in quarters and handed it to Justin. "Go show Dr. Ross your nice drawing, sweetie."

Jackson sat up straighter and his pulse picked up speed. Reaching for the paper, he unfolded it, but didn't look at it. Not yet, although it took restraint. "Can you tell me about your drawing?" Walking around the desk, he pulled a chair next to where Justin sat in the smaller one. His knee bothered him more than usual and he tried to hide his grimace. "Who's this?" He held up the drawing of four figures and pointed to the tall, thin figure of a woman. Jackson hid his smile when he realized the dark circles over the eyes represented sunglasses.

"That's Nana." Based on Justin's expression, that question was a dumb one.

"And this?" The figure was as tall as the rendering of his grandmother, but she wore a long, flowing pink gown. He'd colored her hair yellow and her big eyes bright blue.

"That's my mama." The boy's tone sounded somewhat wistful and he touched the drawing, his finger lingering on the figure for a few seconds.

Jackson searched for the right questions and his mind raced almost as fast as his pulse. "Your mama looks very pretty."

He nodded. "She's beautiful." He glanced at his grandmother. "Right, Nana?"

"Yes." One word, but tinged with an edge of raw emotion he'd never heard from her before.

Jackson pointed to the figure of a child wearing pants. "This is you?" Behind the figures were wavy lines colored in blue. "And you're standing by the ocean?"

Again, the boy nodded. One figure—a taller man in pants—stood to the side of the other figures.

"Who is this? Is this your father?"

"Nope." He shook his head. "That's my grandpa."

Jackson swallowed hard, his head spinning. *Keep the conversation flowing.* As much as he wanted to face Mrs. Johnson to gauge her reaction, he kept his focus trained on the drawing. In the span of only a few minutes, they were making more headway than in any of the previous sessions combined. He bit his tongue not to ask Justin where his father was. The fact he wasn't depicted in the boy's drawing was significant enough.

"What's this over here?" Jackson pointed to a brown, rectangular design near the bottom right corner of the drawing.

"Oh, that's a sand castle. See," he said, pointing to another smaller object on the beach in his drawing, "that's the sand pail and scooper thing." When Justin leaned close, Jackson caught a whiff of a sweet-smelling perfume lingering in his T-shirt, probably from when he'd been hugged by his grandmother. Something about it jogged Jackson's brain. One of his teachers used to wear the same scent. Some flower that used to grow in the summer near the house where he grew up.

"Have you been to the beach much since you've been here in Croisette Shores?" Jackson forced himself to ask. He needed to garner as much information as he could before Mrs. Johnson cut him off. She'd done it both times before, so why should this session be any different? With this woman, it was only a matter of time. To her credit, she kept coming back with Justin, but she made it clear she also wanted to be in control of the discussion. He could live with it as long as she understood it would take longer to help the boy if she stifled his answers and repeatedly cut their sessions short.

"We go to the beach on Friday mornings," Justin said.

"Do you play with any of the other children?"

Mrs. Johnson coughed. Was that a signal to discontinue his current line of questioning? If it was, how was he supposed to know? He'd keep going until she cut him off again.

"Sometimes."

"There's a little girl named Maya that's about your age that goes to the beach with her grandfather a lot," Jackson said. "Dark brown curly hair and green eyes. Have you met her?"

Justin shook his head. "No. I don't think so."

Sneaking a glance at Mrs. Johnson, Jackson saw her twisting her hands in her lap. For whatever reason, that particular question struck a nerve. Clutching her purse to her chest with both hands, her fingers turned white.

"Tell me more about your mother. What else can you tell me?"

"I don't know."

That answer came as a shock. "What do you mean you don't know?"

"He doesn't know because he hasn't met her yet," Mrs. Johnson said, her words clipped.

"Never?" His jaw went slack, and it took him a moment before he could continue. Justin swung his legs and waited. Patience was one of the boy's many virtues, especially in one so young.

"You're here in Croisette Shores to meet your mother for the first time?" Jackson finally managed. Was Justin adopted? Given up at birth?

Justin nodded and his brown eyes looked so sad, Jackson longed to hug him. If the boy's forbidding grandmother wasn't sitting in the same room, glaring at him, he'd probably do it.

"I know one thing," Justin said finally.

"What's that?" If Jackson wasn't mistaken, Mrs. Johnson strained forward to hear the boy's words. She was probably afraid of what he'd say, but at least she didn't jump to her feet, abruptly end the session and haul the child away.

"She's a princess."

"A *real* princess?" His thoughts immediately went to Serenity.

"Nana calls her that sometimes."

Jackson's head pounded with the suspicions forming in his mind. "Do you know your mommy's name?"

"No names, please. Not yet," Mrs. Johnson said from across the room. "Justin, remember what we talked about."

Jackson sat back in the chair, rubbing a hand over his brow. Inside, he seethed at the fact this woman wouldn't permit the boy to answer without imposition. "Tell me this. Is there anyone else you're here in town to meet?"

Justin glanced at Mrs. Johnson and then back at him again. He nodded as if in slow motion.

Leaning his arms on his thighs, Jackson leaned closer. Inches away, he looked him directly in the eye. "Tell me, Justin. Besides your mommy, who else are you looking forward to meeting for the first time?"

"Grandma says my gr—"

"Your grandpa, right? The one from your drawing?"

"That's enough for today." Mrs. Johnson rose to her feet. She gave Jackson a pointed glance. "We'll see you again next week, Dr. Ross."

Jackson closed his eyes for a few seconds, trying to maintain his calm. He couldn't lash out at her in front of the child. Why was she dragging out this process? He'd never been a fan of the Big Reveal, as he'd termed it. Too much mystery and for what purpose? In some ways, it was more harmful to bring Justin and then slow everything to a snail's pace. If he demanded answers, it'd be the kiss of death with these sessions if not his entire practice, at least here in Croisette Shores.

Lord, grant me patience.

Justin went out to the waiting room to speak with his newly-hired assistant and receptionist, Audra Toomey. Rising from his chair, Jackson was surprised when Mrs. Johnson paused in the doorway. "I know you're upset with me for interrupting. Perhaps that was wrong, but I have my reasons for the timing of the introductions to Justin's relatives. Everything I've done is for his own protection and for that purpose alone." She blew out a sigh.

"So you've said before. I believe you."

She nodded. "I appreciate that."

"Tell me this. Did you adopt him?" Standing in front of her, he kept his voice low.

Her mouth downturned. "No, not exactly."

What kind of answer is that? Her latest version of evasion, apparently. This was becoming increasingly maddening with every new session. The concept of one step forward and three back certainly applied to this situation. Jackson's frown matched hers as he stared her down. Tired of the guessing games, he needed some solid answers.

"Dr. Ross, I guarantee you've never heard a story like ours."

"One I hope to hear sooner than later." That sounded rude, but it was honest. "I understand your concern for Justin and wanting to take things slow. My observation is that he's fine, but I'm beginning to wonder if *you're* the one who's worried about what may happen."

"We'll see you again next week." Mrs. Johnson turned to go, but not before she squared her shoulders and tensed. Just like he'd seen Serenity do when she was bothered yet determined. When the woman lifted her chin, he almost gasped.

Lord, what's happening here?

"Bye, Doc Jack!" With a small wave, Justin skipped beside his grandmother as they departed.

*T*wenty minutes later, Jackson sat at his desk, staring into space. A hundred different thoughts swirled in his mind, warring for precedence in his cluttered brain. He hadn't even been able to formulate his thoughts for his report yet.

"Dr. Ross?"

He pushed the intercom. "Yes, Audra?"

"Your brother's on Line 1."

"Kyle or Chad?"

"Kyle."

Good. "I'll pick up. Thanks." He reached for the receiver and swung around in his chair, staring at the cross on the wall. "What's the good word, little brother?"

"I got that report you wanted. You want me to send it email or fax?"

"Email. Same address as before."

"Sure thing. Will do in a sec. Hey, you okay, Jax? You sound a little strange."

Jackson forced a laugh, knowing full well Kyle wouldn't buy it. "No more than usual, I'm sure. Thanks for getting the report, bro. I owe you one."

"Don't think I won't make good on that offer. I'd hide that medal if I were you."

"Talk to you later. Send me that report before you get too busy and forget about it."

"You know me too well. Patience, big brother. I just clicked the SEND button."

Jackson swung back around to the computer and clicked on his email account. "Got it. Thanks, Kyle. Talk to you later."

Disconnecting the call, he clicked on the message and quickly scanned the attached report. As he suspected, there wasn't much to go on, but his eyes widened when he saw the last known address for Elise McClaren. *Long Island, New York.* Fingers shaking, heart pounding, he opened his drawer and grabbed the paper where he'd written the social security number Serenity gave him. Sure enough, the numbers matched. Something else that might be significant? He stared at her middle name displayed on the screen.

Rose.

He'd never had a reason to ask Serenity about it, never thought to ask. If what he knew in his heart was true, then Justin's given first name was...

"Liam," he said under his breath, lowering his head to his hands for a few seconds.

"This can't be happening." Jackson closed out of the email and turned off the computer. Swinging out of his chair, he rushed for the door, not bothering to close it behind him. He should stop and pray, but he couldn't. His one-track mind took over and nothing—not even the Almighty—was going to stop him.

Sorry, Lord, but I've got to get some answers. Now.

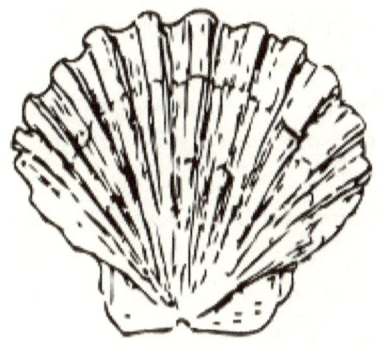

~CHAPTER 30~

*D*ropping by the house to check on her dad during her lunch hour, Serenity was surprised to see a book by a well-known, popular Christian author and speaker sitting on the table beside Clinton's recliner. She picked it up and glanced at the photo of the author—a handsome, dark-haired man in jeans and a white shirt, perched atop a stool—then thumbed through the book. She'd seen his name and those deep smile lines gracing the cover of a magazine or two at McHenry's Market. Based on the chapter names, the primary emphasis centered on becoming a Godly husband and father. Why would her father read a book like this?

Clinton carried an open container of yogurt with a spoon and a pear as he came around the corner from the kitchen. He grinned when he caught her smile. "Yeah, I'm eating this stuff, and not because you're here to see me do it, either. It's not too bad." Thank goodness, he seemed to be taking the advice of Dr. Saunders to heart. The whole healthy living plan might actually be carrying over into other aspects of his life. For one thing, he no longer lounged around the house in his undershirts and shorts. Lately, he'd taken to wearing decent shorts and shirts. Nothing that pulled over his head, though. Only shirts with buttons, the way he'd always preferred.

Serenity held up the book. "I'm curious. Where'd you get this book?"

"Your friend Dr. Ross gave it to me."

"When did you see Jackson last?" Although she kept her tone casual, she wasn't fooling her dad. Leafing through it a few more seconds, her mind worked overtime. All kinds of changes were taking place with her dad. *Good* changes.

"He comes around sometimes." He shrugged. "Earlier in the week. Monday, I think."

She looked up at him, startled. "Jackson just...drops by the house? To chat?"

"Sure. Here, sometimes the coffee shop, the park. He's a good man. We talk." Settling in his chair, he pretended to watch the game show. Some things never changed.

Serenity sat in Mama's chair, still holding the book. "This book is about being a better man, husband and father. You're aware of that, right?"

Watching her, Clinton spooned mixed berry yogurt into his mouth before answering. Licking his lips, he appeared to be formulating an answer. "Yeah, I'm aware. Don't look so shocked. That book has good advice. Like you said, tips for how to be a better father." He darted a glance at her before returning his focus to the television. "Might be a little late, but you'd probably be all for that, wouldn't you, girl?"

"Did I ever complain? You could try not calling me 'girl,' though. *That's* annoying." Why was she so defensive? He'd never been much of a reader and she was more surprised by that than anything else. A *Christian* book, no less. Mama was the one who'd always devoured every new thriller within a day or two of its release. She'd never understood how Mama could love medical thrillers when she worked around life and death every day. Much like she couldn't understand how a man who'd fought fires for a living had ever smoked cigarettes.

"Well, thanks for telling me after fifteen plus years," Clinton muttered with a scowl, shoving another spoonful of yogurt in his mouth. "Old habits die hard."

"I know, and it doesn't bother me that much. Does Jackson talk with you about God?"

An ad came on the television, and Clinton surveyed her with lowered lids. "Why don't you ask what you really want to know?"

"I really want to know if Jackson talks with you about God."

"You're holding the book. What do *you* think?" When he laughed, she was surprised how white his teeth appeared. Had he had some cosmetic whitening done? *Impossible.* Something was definitely afoot. Had Karen Gorham finally convinced him to take her on a date? *Surely not.* That thought brought a frown. After seeing how Spencer's dad had moved on, she'd wished her father could do the same. Still, there was a difference. Spencer's mom had died. Even if they found out Mama was gone forever, she doubted her dad would entertain the notion of dating another woman. Now, his loyalty pleased her. *How fickle am I?*

Serenity snapped out of her reverie. "Have you learned anything from this book or your talks with Jackson?"

Although he shifted in his chair, Clinton didn't appear uncomfortable with her continued questions. "A few things, yeah. But I also learned more about Jackson's family and growing up in Illinois. Guess he got full of himself when he was in college. I pegged him for an athlete, and I was right." He shot her another grin. Two in the span of five minutes? "Bet you didn't know your boyfriend got drafted into the NFL straight out of college."

The book slipped out of her hands and fell to the floor. "Jackson's not my boyfriend, but he what?" Her question came out somewhat garbled. "He *what?*"

"Yep. Went through the training camp, passed it with flying colors and was all ready to suit up. But then he turned them down and walked away. Chose another life. Stunned the spit out of his family and the Bears. They thought he was crazy. Patriotic, but still nuts. You've gotta admire a man who sticks up for his beliefs."

She gulped. "The Bears? The *Chicago* Bears?"

Clinton chuckled. "No, the Bad News Bears. Yes, girl, the NFL team."

Flabbergasted, she sputtered, "I had no idea." When Jackson told her about his family, he said nothing about a professional football career. Not even a hint. Then again, he really didn't reveal much about his life other than his relationship with and issues with his family. That's all she'd asked about, and it seemed the man wouldn't freely offer information. He needed to be asked. Dazed, she shook her head. For one thing, an athletic career would put his attention to physical fitness in perspective and might explain the on-and-off pain in his knee.

"What do you mean he chose another *life?*" He'd better not make an open-ended statement like that and then clam up on her.

The television program came back on and her father returned his attention to the screen. "That's a question you should ask Jackson. Better if you hear it from him." Catching her chastising look, Clinton blew out a breath. "Look, it's all fine. Nothing to worry about. Like I said, he's a good man. With a mighty interesting story."

"I'll be sure and do that." Rising from the chair, Serenity retrieved the book from the floor and put it back on the table before hurrying through a few chores—dusting in the living room and folding laundry before putting a casserole in the oven for his dinner. The whole time she worked, questions ran through her mind. She couldn't wait until she talked again with Jackson, but she'd have to be careful and not pummel him with questions. The man was humble, yes, but this was ridiculous. Not that it would change anything about their relationship, but why hadn't he told her?

"I need to run," she called to him, retrieving her purse in the kitchen. "I'll talk with you later."

"Serenity?"

She turned in the doorway to the family room. "Yes?"

"I hope you know that man loves you."

Tears filled her eyes even as she shook her head. "I hardly know him." That was a bald-faced lie. She already knew Jackson better than she'd known Danny, a man she'd grown up with and played with in the sandbox. He'd dribbled sand in her hair when she was in kindergarten and thrown spit wads on her head in the auditorium during an assembly in grade school.

"You're preaching to the choir on that one." The smile she used to adore as a little girl stretched across her daddy's face. How she'd missed it.

Telling Clinton goodbye and closing the front door behind her, Serenity leaned against it and deep-breathed. Maybe there was hope for them, after all.

*M*rs. Toomey opened the front door of the office and called after him. "Dr. Ross!"

Swallowing his mounting frustration, Jackson turned and forced calm into his tone. "Yes, Audra?"

"Don't forget you have that meeting with the Town Council at nine on Thursday morning to sign the contracts for the playground. I need to RSVP for you."

"It's on my calendar. Oh, and please call Serenity McClaren and remind her. Thanks, and I'll see you tomorrow." With a quick wave, he ducked inside the car and heard her call to him that breakfast pastries would be served. Bless her heart, the motherly receptionist always made sure he was fed. If she kept up her daily ritual of bringing him something sweet, he'd need to step up his workouts to counteract the extra calories.

Jackson walked through the open doorway of the Vital Records Office in Town Hall less than ten minutes later. A clerk sat at a desk across the room, clicking away on her computer keyboard. When he cleared his throat, she jumped.

"Oh, mercy me. I didn't know anyone had come in." She pushed away from the desk and hurried over to where he stood by the counter. Tall and thin, this woman reminded him of his socialite mother—perfectly-groomed hair and clothing—although she appeared more accommodating with strangers. "I'm Jillian Montgomery. What can I do for you, handsome stranger?" Brushing aside a stray strand of dark hair from her otherwise stylish haircut, she gave him a warm smile.

"I'd like to look up a birth and death record, if that's possible."

"Well, you've come to the right place. Let's start by getting some information. I'll need the person's name and either the year of their birth or death, if you know them." She picked up a pen and poised it above a legal pad on the counter.

"Actually, it's an infant. From what I know, he was born at Croisette Shores Hospital but died either the same day or the next day." He was determined not to give her a name unless she pushed.

"Well, now, that's awful sad," she said, dropping the pen and crossing her arms on the counter. "Enough to break my heart. I moved here from Beaufort and took over when Luellen Mays retired last year. I don't remember hearing anything about a baby. How long ago are we talking?" She drummed a slow march on the legal pad with her pink fingernails.

"About five years ago, right around this time of year."

Jillian stopped midway to the computer. "Ah, hon, I'm afraid that information's probably not available yet. Records that recent are still closed to the public." She shrugged. "Rules, you know. Luellen said they used to wait five years, but for whatever reason, they wait seven years now."

"I see." Jackson swallowed his disappointment. "I appreciate your help."

"If you ever need any more information, you call on me. I'll be happy to help."

"I'll keep that in mind, Jillian. I'm Jackson Ross, by the way. Nice to meet you."

Her dark eyes grew larger. "*You're* Dr. Ross? Forgive me, sweetie. I've heard about you moving to town, of course, but to be honest, I expected someone twenty years older and at least twenty pounds heavier with a whole lot less hair on top." She broke into a wide grin. "You're sure a long tall drink of water if ever I've seen one. You married?"

"No, ma'am." He felt a slow flush crawl up his neck.

She waved her hand. "Fine looking man like you, I'm sure the women of Croisette Shores will help you out with whatever you need. Okay," she said, giving him a sidelong grin, "I can see I'm embarrassing you, so here's what you need to do. Go to the website for the *Croisette Shores Daily News*. I'm not sure how far back their online records go, so you might need to look at the paper on microfilm at the library. Ask for Myrtle and tell her I sent you. She'll take good care of you and get you all set up. That should give you what you need to know." Jillian tilted her head, brow furrowed. "If you don't mind my asking, what exactly are you hoping to learn about that poor child?"

Jackson's heart palpitated as his mind raced for an answer that might satisfy her curiosity. He should have left the office when he had the opportunity and before he'd revealed his name. The way the grapevine worked, if she'd heard he was friends with Serenity, she'd probably figure out why he was interested. She'd mentioned she was new to the area, so that might be his saving grace. In a small town like this, everyone knew everybody's else's business. He imagined it was a mixed blessing.

Assuming what he hoped was a neutral expression, Jackson shrugged. "In my profession, I've found it's best to verify every fact for confirmation and accuracy." Hopefully, she'd buy it and not ask any more questions.

"Yes, I see your point. It never hurts to be too careful." Jillian blew out a sigh. "Trust me, working in this office, I understand how important it is to get things right. Good luck with your research, Dr. Ross. Hope you find what you're looking for."

"Thanks again, Ms. Montgomery. I appreciate your help." With a wave, Jackson departed.

He needed to call Serenity, but what could he say? Inner Serenity was only a couple of streets over, and—as it always did—the urge to drop in at her office and say hi was overwhelming. If he stopped by today, though, he'd invariably say something out of place. As smart as Serenity was, she'd quickly pick up on the fact he was hiding something. He'd always been a terrible liar, an even worse actor. Best to stay away from her for now.

As he walked to his car, Jackson thought over the session with Justin, recounting everything he could recall from memory from their previous sessions. Things were starting to simultaneously add up and bother him. When he got home, he'd make a list. At least as of two years ago, her mother was alive and living in Long Island, New York. And today? She might be right here in Croisette Shores with a boy who may—or may not—be Serenity's son, Liam.

Walking back to his car, Jackson passed a ladies boutique. He paused, feeling silly, but pushed the door open and went inside. Soft music played and he heard laughter from the back of the store. One customer browsed through racks of clothing and another did the same by a display of shoes and purses.

"May I help you?" A blonde woman wearing too much makeup and about a hundred jangly bracelets on one arm moved toward him with a friendly smile.

"Do you have any perfumes or bath...things?" he said, feeling ridiculous.

"Yes, we have a line of products if you'd come over here with me." He followed as she led him to a back wall. "Is there a particular scent you're looking for?"

"I can't think of the name of it, but it's honey something-or-other. Grows on bushes during the summertime? I think it's yellow or white?"

"Oh, you must mean honeysuckle," she said, picking up a bottle on the display rack to read the label. "We usually have that one in the summer, so let me see what I can find." He waited while she called to someone else. "Darla, do we have anything in honeysuckle?"

Jackson shifted from one foot to the other, hoping no one he knew came into the store until he could escape. If pressed, he wasn't sure he could come up with a plausible explanation for being here. When he was a boy, his mother sometimes dragged him into places like this on occasion while she shopped, and it drove him crazy. Shopping had to have been invented as a punishment for men. The only thing that would make it tolerable would be shopping for Serenity. He shoved that thought aside and tried to concentrate, although he realized he'd probably missed her birthday. The Newport Jazz Festival when her parents met would have been in August, and nine months later would have been May. Sometime in the last few weeks.

"I think we have a body lotion in honeysuckle." An older woman emerged from the back, wiping her hands together and swallowing. "Sorry," she said to him, "finishing up a snack. Let's see what we can find. Another lady came in the other day asking about honeysuckle, too." She gave him a quick once-over. "Maybe you know her? Tall, thin, short red hair and speaks with a more northern accent?"

His pulse quickened. "Did she wear sunglasses?"

The woman laughed. "Yes, she did, as a matter of fact. At least until I brought her back here. As you can see, the lighting's not the best in this back corner, so she took them off."

Jackson's mind raced as fast as his pulse. How could he find out what he wanted to know? "Did you, um, notice anything odd about her eyes?"

She tilted her head. "What do you mean?"

Say anything. "Well, she's had a problem with her left eye and the ophthalmologist advised her to leave the glasses on." He lifted his shoulders and gave her a smile. "Checking to see if she's following the doctor's orders." *Forgive me, Lord.*

"Well, she seemed okay and read the label fine," the woman said. "As a matter of fact, I noticed how blue her eyes were. They were really piercing and pretty and stood out against the color of her hair. As I recall, she bought two bottles of the honeysuckle lotion and I think this display tester bottle is the last one."

"Here's the body lotion," the first salesclerk said, pulling out a bottle and lifting the top. She offered it to him. "Take a whiff."

As soon as he inhaled the sweet scent, Jackson recognized it. The same one Mrs. Johnson wore. The same as lingered in Justin's T-shirt. Honeysuckle.

The same scent Serenity said her mother always wore.

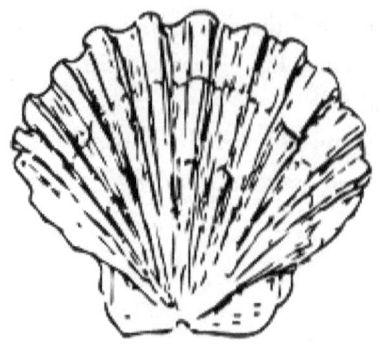

~CHAPTER 31~

*S*erenity dropped to her knees beside where Jackson planted flowers on the church grounds—a row of pretty petunias in various shades of pink, purple, white and lavender. What an intriguing contrast to see such a big, strong man lowering the delicate blooms into the earth. Petunias were hardy, and so was Jackson. Removing a pink one from its container, he placed the flower in the hole he'd dug in the ground, taking great care to position it evenly in the row before spreading the soil around it.

He sat back and swiped a glove-covered hand over his brow. Interestingly enough, the glove was pink and white with a paisley pattern.

"First of all, you should have a cushion beneath your knees," she said.

"I'm not a girl. No offense." His brow was furrowed, his jawline tense as he continued his work.

"Someone's in a good mood." Serenity handed him a pink petunia but switched it out when he motioned at a white one tinged with pink.

"I have a pattern going," he said, glancing at her. "Probably what a decorator calls symmetry."

"You were right the first time. It's more of a pattern. To be honest, if you're worried about looking like a girl, then you definitely shouldn't be wearing that girly glove."

"Hey, I borrowed them from Sue Martin and it's all she had left. The manly gloves were all taken." He grunted and positioned the next plant in the ground. "I'm not too proud to be seen in pink and white. Doesn't offend my masculine sensibilities or whatever."

She laughed. "I was referring more to the paisley pattern."

He shook his head, but she caught a glimpse of that adorable dimple. "Are you here to work or insult me?"

"Both." She grinned. "You seem contrary today. Which color's next?"

"You tell me," he said, "since you're so color conscious today. Or pattern conscious. Whatever." Reaching to the ground behind him, he tossed the matching glove at her. "Here. Better put this on so you don't get dirt under your nails."

"Thanks, I think," she said, tugging it over her hand. "I'm very cognizant of colors all the time, not just today. Because that's what we decorators do." She handed him a purple flower, pleased when he gave her a nod of approval.

They worked in silence for a few minutes, planting the flowers along the low row. He dug the holes while she lowered the petunias into the ground and they alternated filling in the holes with dirt. A couple of times their hands touched and he playfully swatted her away and then she did the same. In a way, it reminded her of the way she and Danny used to play together. Silly fun stuff.

Finally, he seemed to relax and initiated conversation. They laughed and talked about nothing in particular, enjoying the warm sunshine, slight breeze and one another's company. She'd wait until they were done and she had Jackson's full attention before hitting him with her questions. As it was, she was still trying to figure out how to raise the subject without just blurting it out.

When Serenity noticed he'd stopped working, she glanced over at him. "Lazing about on the job, are we?" Laughing, she swiped a dirt-covered finger over his cheek. He mock-gasped, so she repeated it, rubbing more dirt into his tanned skin and smearing it around. She lowered her gaze, not wanting to stare at him. Breathe him in was more like it. Jackson's bright blue tank was soaked in completely male, strategic places, and he wore shorts that showed his muscular legs to full advantage. A faint line of sweat peppered Jackson's forehead and the skin on his shoulders glistened. She felt a bit overheated although not necessarily from the rising humidity. Sweat on a man never looked so absolutely...attractive.

"You're not playing fair." His tone wasn't teasing this time.

"Neither are you," she whispered. When his eyes met hers, Serenity held her breath.

With one hand, he smeared a slow line of soil on her bare arm near her shoulder. That's what she got for wearing a sleeveless top. Brilliant move.

She hadn't expected to be so sidetracked. They worked in silence again until they finished planting the last row of flowers. After Danny's death, she never imagined she'd find another man to love. From the time she was a teenager, he'd been her world. Now she couldn't stop thinking about Jackson with his confidence, his strength and his ability to make her believe everything could one day be "normal" again. A different kind of normal from what she'd shared with Danny, but a new normal.

"Want to know why I didn't smear dirt on your *face?*" Jackson tugged off his glove and gestured for her to remove the matching one she wore. "I have to say, it was mighty tempting. Took everything in me not to do it."

"Only if you're dying to confess."

"You ponder that and I'll be right back with water bottles." Sprinting across the yard to a cooler beneath a tree, he chatted with one of the ladies and then left the gardening gloves on a table near the back door of the church. Serenity waved to a few of the others scattered about the yard and smiled when she spied Charlie trimming hedges. He waved and gave her a big smile as Jackson came back and handed over one of the cold bottles. She liked how he always considered her needs.

"Want to go share a tree and some conversation, Miss Serenity?" Twisting off the cap of his bottle, he took a long swig, nearly draining the bottle.

"I'm done pondering, so sure." Grabbing her hand, Jackson pulled Serenity to her feet.

"So, did you come to any conclusions?" he asked, walking beside her as they crossed the church grounds.

Unwittingly, he'd given her the perfect segue. "Yes. I concluded there's some things in your past I know nothing about. Things I'd like to know."

"I'm happy to tell you," he said. "Whatever you want, especially since you asked."

Reaching above her head, Serenity pulled down one of the sturdy evergreen leaves of a magnificent southern magnolia tree and inhaled the scent of an off-white bloom. "Bet you don't have trees like this in Chicago. Here, take a whiff."

Jackson leaned closer. "Smells like lemon. That's a surprise."

"I know. Kind of like sugary lemon," she said. "Rich and sweet."

"Like you said, there's a lot to love about Croisette Shores."

She couldn't miss the implication of his words, but she avoided his gaze. "It's a much slower pace of life, but that's one of the reasons I love it so much."

"Yep," he said, sliding down to sit at the base of the tree, leaning against it. "Just the way I like it." He darted a glance at the ground beside him before tugging on her hand, catching her off-guard. Serenity tripped and landed in an awkward position on Jackson's lap, and she cried out in surprise. Ignoring his soft laughter, she slid down to the ground beside him, her cheeks flushed with warmth.

"Way to be subtle, Dr. Ross. Hope you enjoyed that little thrill."

His smile was so inviting with all those white teeth and that dimple winking at her. Charm could be a dangerous quality and Jackson had been blessed with more than his share.

"Sorry. Guess I don't know my own strength."

"Sure you do." Leaning against the broad base of the tree, Serenity wrapped her arms around her propped knees. "Talk away. I've got time. My dad tells me you have quite a history, but he said I should ask you since it's your story to tell."

Stretching out his long legs, Jackson rested beside her. The pain didn't seem to bother him today, although she'd think being on his knees to plant flowers would be hard on them. She'd prayed for his knee since that touch football game at the picnic.

"How much did Clinton tell you, exactly?"

"Is it true you were drafted into the NFL straight from college?"

Jackson chuckled. "Yep, unbelievable as it sounds."

"What position?"

"Wide receiver, same as in college. Let me back up a minute and give you the whole picture. I made the first-string football squad as a freshman in high school and played all four years and then got a scholarship to one of the powerhouse football schools in the country. They worked us to death, but I loved it. Expectations for the players are extremely high, to say the least. Even higher than my parents' expectations, and that's pressure enough to make anyone blow." Propping his arms on his bent knees, Jackson shook his head. "The training was relentless and I was exhausted in my *bones*. I fell into bed fully-dressed most nights, no dinner, nothing. It's a miracle I had any energy left to study."

Serenity smiled. "I'm still stuck on you not eating dinner. That's serious business."

He laughed. "You're not kidding. I'd grown really close to this cool older guy on the coaching staff named Gus Michaelson. Gus took some of the guys on the team, including me, under his wing. Taught us a lot, yelled at us a lot, but he made us better players. He'd been with the Bears for over twenty-three years, but he wanted to go back to college coaching the last few years of his career. Gus poured his all into the players. I mean, he was more than a mentor. That man cared for the heart and soul of each man and not just because it'd be good for the team. He was a great man and cared for the *entire* player, and he wanted the players to see the team was the sum of its parts. Some guys got too arrogant and pushed him aside. Once he helped get them where they needed to be, they forgot about old Gus."

When a strong, brisk wind blew a few wayward strands of hair across her eyes, Jackson tucked them behind her ear. His fingers brushed her cheek as he lowered his hand.

"But *you* never forgot him, did you?"

"No, I didn't. He's also the one who led me to the Lord. Believe it or not, it started at the dinner table one night. His wife, Helen, invited me over to their house at least once a week."

She laughed. "I can see it now. Pass the potatoes, please. Jackson, did you know the Lord loves you like you love mashed potatoes? This explains so much. Maybe that's where the whole idea of seeing Jesus in a potato chip began."

"Could be." He laughed with her. "It's not really anything overly dramatic, but never one to pass up an opportunity to share about spiritual things, he seized the moment and laid out the plan of salvation. He grabbed his pen and drew on his napkin, kind of like a game plan in the locker room."

Jackson's smile sobered. "My story turned ugly. You can't sugar coat it, any way you look at it."

She met his gaze. "If you *didn't* have any skeletons in your closet, I doubt you'd be sitting here with me now. Nothing you can tell me will change my opinion of you." The softening in his eyes matched what was happening in her heart.

"That means more than you know." Jackson shifted his position and blew out a long breath. "My junior year in college, a couple of the guys started taking performance enhancing drugs to keep them strong. They found ways to get around the testing and convinced me to try them. I was low on my game one day, and—like an idiot—I tried them. Problem was, I liked it and kept taking them for a few months. My game improved and I had some stellar performances. We won a lot of games, all based on stupid lies." Staring at the ground, Jackson picked at the grass between his propped legs.

"What happened?"

"*Gus* happened. He hauled us into the locker room and reamed us out. I'd never seen him so mad. His cheeks were flaming red, his eyes bulged, and I was afraid he'd blow a gasket or fall dead on the spot from a massive coronary. Most of the guys laughed in his face and walked away, telling him to mind his own business, and I think some even threatened him to keep quiet. Before I knew it, I was the only one left in the locker room." Jackson glanced over at her. "I couldn't leave him there. Not after what some of those idiots said to him. He deserved better."

"How did Gus find out?"

"He'd been cleaning around the locker room one day and found evidence. When he calmed down a little, he fell onto the bench beside me and asked me point-blank about it. I broke down and confessed everything. Then the other players made up a pack of outright lies and got Gus fired." That last part came out almost a growl and Jackson's eyes sparked with anger. "I wanted to defend Gus to the school board and tell them about the drugs, but Gus convinced me it wasn't worth it, and intimated the other coaches knew about it but were willing to cover it up. He told me to stop doing the drugs, pray about it and let God handle the rest." He shrugged. "So, I did. To this day, I still wonder if it was the right decision. A few like me got drafted into the NFL, some suffered career-threatening injuries, others got fed up with the relentless pace or left for other reasons."

Jackson lowered his head to his hands. When he raised his head a few seconds later, his eyes shimmered with raw emotion. "My parents weren't perfect, but they raised me better than to stoop to using an artificial crutch to be a better football player. I not only shamed myself, but I shamed them, the team, everyone. At the time, I was one of those holiday churchgoers and didn't have any kind of personal relationship with the Lord. No two ways about it, I was not only a sinner, but I was a coward." His voice took on a defiant tone, and he shook his head. "I should have marched into the school board meeting and told them about the drugs. But I took the easy way out. Gus knew I wanted to play professional ball, and he told me I wouldn't stand a chance if I blew the scandal wide open."

"So, then what happened? If you feel like talking about it."

"Long story short, I cleaned up and never touched another drug and by the grace of God had a great final college season and got drafted by the Bears. To this day, I think Gus had something to do with it but he'd never admit it. Helen winked at me at graduation, and that's when I knew in here." Curling his fist, Jackson thumped it on his chest. "I started training camp and passed, got my uniform and started all the preseason rookie publicity stuff and then decided I couldn't do it."

Serenity turned to face him, sitting cross-legged on the grass. "Couldn't do...what?"

"The whole thing. I wanted more from my life, but I wanted to *do* more with my life. I wanted to make a difference to someone like Gus made in mine, I guess. I thought about coaching, but knew that wasn't it, either. So, I quit the team and joined up with the Army and shipped off to Afghanistan as soon as I finished my leadership training."

Her jaw gaped and she couldn't speak. She motioned for him to continue.

"I was a little long in the tooth since most of the kids were barely old enough to shave. All the physical conditioning I'd done in the past paid off and I rose quickly in the ranks and earned a modicum of respect from my superiors, at least in terms of my willingness to follow orders and pay them due respect. As much as anything, I learned from Gus to respect others, no matter their weaknesses, and to appreciate their strengths. Long story short, one morning I was in a jeep with a couple of my commanding officers and we were attacked by an IED."

"Oh, no," Serenity said, grabbing his hand. "Is that how your knee—"

"Yeah. I know you've noticed the scar but were too polite to ask."

"It looks painful, and I didn't want to bring up anything hurtful. You were in enough pain."

Taking her hand, Jackson guided it to his knee with an unspoken invitation in those soulful eyes. Serenity ran a light finger along the length of the scar—running jagged and horizontal across his right knee—lighter than the tanned skin around it. As she'd done before, she bent and planted a soft kiss on his heated skin.

"It's not the actual scar that hurts, you know." His voice was as quiet as she'd ever heard it and brimming with emotion. "One of the guys, Damon Marshall, lost the bottom portion of his right leg. He came back home and decided three days later he couldn't cope with life as an amputee. So he waited until his wife went to the grocery, fashioned a noose out of bed sheets and made her a widow."

She gasped. "That's horrible! I don't know what to say. I'm so sorry." Lacing her fingers through his, Serenity leaned her head on his shoulder.

The Purple Heart. "Jackson, when I went into the bedroom at Doc Rasmussen's to get your pillows, there was a Purple Heart medallion on the dresser. I wasn't being nosy, but the sunlight caught it. I wanted to see what it was. When I realized what I held in my hands, I assumed it belonged to Doc since he'd served in the military. I remember thinking how—being born and raised in Croisette Shores—I should have heard about it." She touched Jackson's jaw, turning his face toward her. "The Purple Heart belongs to you, doesn't it?"

He nudged her shoulder. "You're finding out all my secrets today."

"Why should something so honorable be kept a secret?"

"Because I might have saved Damon's life, but I didn't save his soul."

His statement stirred her anger. "I know I haven't been a Christian long, but from what I know, that's not *your* responsibility. Damon was responsible for his own eternal security or whatever. Not you."

"But neither did I share the gospel with him. I dragged Damon and Sean out of the jeep and tended to their wounds. I prayed the whole time, but I didn't ask them to pray with me."

"How do you know they didn't pray in their hearts? I mean, if you were laying there with half your leg gone like Damon, or bleeding profusely like Sean probably was, would *you* be in any conscious frame of mind to do anything?" She caught his look. "You can't take on the wounds of the world, Jackson. You did what you could. I might not know much about the Purple Heart, but it's an honor you earn not only for being brave, but doing something selfless and heroic and being wounded in the process."

Sitting up on her knees, Serenity cradled his face—hot, sweaty and with a couple of dirt smudges on his cheek, but the most handsome face she'd ever seen. "What happened?"

"We were on the fringe of a roadside bomb, close enough yet just far enough away. Flying shrapnel showered the Jeep, but trust me, I suffered the least. I was driving and"—he paused and his eyes were wet—"the officers were in the backseat."

"What happened to Sean? Where is he now?"

"He's had several reconstructive surgeries on the right side of his face and he'll never walk again without a serious limp, but he's home in Tennessee with his wife and kids. He's *alive*. I talked to him last week. He's doing well and owns an express delivery company in Nashville." Jackson stared straight ahead and blew out another sigh. "Remember that napkin I told you about? The one where Gus laid out the plan of salvation?" He waited until she nodded before continuing.

"Believe it or not, I still have it to remind me how low I'd sunk and how Christ lifted me up from the literal muck and mire of my sin." He rubbed his fingers over his chin. "There's something about lying face down in the mud with a 200-pound linebacker on top of you to make you face your spiritual condition. Then sprawled on the ground and watching your commanding officers almost bleed to death, grown men screaming for help, that makes you realize how small and helpless you are in the universe. And makes you realize something else." Shifting his body, Jackson turned toward her.

"What's that?" She'd never been more aware of him.

"How important it is to have someone in your life to care about and that hopefully cares about you." Warm chocolate eyes melted into hers, then swept down to her lips. As Serenity sank onto the ground beside him again, Jackson leaned over her, all six-foot-three of masculinity affecting her in untold ways as his face hovered inches away from her and the air slowly drained from her lungs. She couldn't breathe but didn't care. His smile—slow and easy—inched its way further into her heart, softening and opening it even more. With the softest touch imaginable, Jackson brushed his thumb across her lower lip. "Pretend I'm smearing dirt there, beautiful pretty. And if I did *that*, care to guess what I'd do next?"

Cupping his face between her palms again, Serenity drew him close and planted a sweet, soft, lingering kiss on his lips. "Something like that?" she whispered, her own voice raspy.

"Exactly."

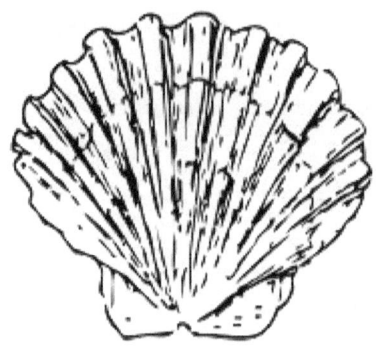

~CHAPTER 32~

Mrs. Johnson and Justin stopped by unexpectedly on Wednesday morning and asked if Jackson could meet with them. What a pleasant surprise. Must be a God thing, especially since he'd met with them the day before and his schedule was free. Maybe she, too, was finally growing anxious and wanted to move this process along at a faster pace.

"Justin, what's your favorite fruit?"

"Bananas. I like to eat them with peanut butter. On bread. Like a sandwich."

Jackson tried not to stare. Hadn't Serenity mentioned liking peanut butter and banana sandwiches, too? His pulse raced at an almost uncontrollable level and he could feel the sweat already beading on his brow. Clearing his throat, he dug deep to find his voice. "Why don't we ask your grandmother about *her* favorite fruit?"

Even with the glasses, the set of Mrs. Johnson's jaw and the firm line of her lips conveyed she wasn't happy with the current line of questioning. "I hardly see why that matters."

"Nana likes pears," Justin said, giggling. "She says they make her happy."

Jackson reeled back in his chair as though he'd been slapped. Surely his cheeks burned as though he'd been physically struck. *Lord, is it possible? How can it be?* Too many things were adding up now. "Is that right?" He wasn't sure how he choked out the question, but never in his life had he struggled so hard to maintain his calm and sense of decorum. Certainly nothing in his training could have prepared him for the growing suspicions forming in his mind. The similarities between what he knew of Elise McClaren and Violet Johnson, and what they'd said about Justin's mother in comparison to what he knew of Serenity, were uncanny. No way could every one of them be explained as coincidence. Jackson moved his gaze to Mrs. Johnson. Everything in him wanted to blast her with questions and demand answers. The muscles in his jaws flexed so hard he thought surely they'd snap.

He forced another question. Anything to keep the conversation flowing. "Why don't we talk more about your mommy today, Justin. Is that okay with you?"

"Yep." The boy started swinging his legs.

From the corner of his eye, Jackson noticed Mrs. Johnson reaching for a tissue and dabbing at her eyes from beneath the sunglasses. He'd started conjuring ideas about how to get them off the woman, but so far he'd come up with no viable plan. "Once you meet her, what kinds of things do you want to do with her?"

Justin pondered the question, the only sound the ticking of the wall clock. "I hope she can teach me to ride a bike, and read Dr. Seuss with me. I'd really like to get a puppy." He darted a glance at Mrs. Johnson. "Do you think she'll let me have a puppy?"

"We'll have to ask her, and make sure you're not allergic since you've never had a pet before."

Justin scrunched his nose and cocked his head to one side. "What's *lergic* mean?"

"It means something you eat—or something you're around—makes you sneeze or break out in hives. Your throat might feel scratchy. Like from the inside out," Jackson said. "What else would you like to do with your mommy?"

"Maybe she can buy me a backpack and walk me to school. Or I can ride a bus like the big kids."

"You'd like that, huh?" Jackson smiled.

The mop of curls bounced as Justin nodded in an exaggerated manner. "I think so. Never done it before." He frowned for only a second before brightening, his ready smile never far away. "She can make me peanut butter and banana sandwiches to take to school for lunch."

"A lot of schools won't let you take peanut butter to school, honey."

"Why not?"

Jackson cleared his throat. "It has something to do with that *lergic* thing. A lot of kids can't eat peanut butter or be around it."

Crossing his arms over his chest, Justin shook his head and slumped against the back of the chair. "Then she can make them for me to eat at home. Can I take my gummi worms to school? Are people *lergic* to gummis?"

Both Jackson and Mrs. Johnson smiled. "I don't think so," he assured him.

"I made a card for my mommy." When he darted a glance at Mrs. Johnson, she reached into the outside pocket of her purse and pulled out a bright yellow piece of folded construction paper. When Justin bounded out of his chair, she handed it to him.

It was difficult to maintain his composure as Jackson studied the drawing of a small boy with curly hair walking beside a taller figure, a woman by the high heels and long hair. He'd drawn a large, red heart on the woman and drawn a line from her heart to the general area of the child's heart.

"What does this mean?" Turning the card around, Jackson held up the card and pointed to the line connecting the two figures.

"My mommy and me are connected."

Jackson swallowed hard. "Do you feel connected to your mommy *now*, Justin?"

The brown eyes grew wider and he looked over at his grandmother. She nodded. "It's okay. Tell Dr. Ross how you feel. He's here to help you."

Justin kicked his legs back and forth again and rubbed his hands up and down the arms of the chair. Finally, he shrugged. "I don't know."

Jackson smiled to reassure him. "That's a very honest answer and I'm glad you told me how you feel. I know you might not understand some things until you meet your mother." He glanced at Mrs. Johnson.

She shook her head. "Not yet. Soon." Something about her slight smile struck him as familiar. *Serenity* familiar. His pulse pounded, his head throbbed.

Jackson nodded, forcing another smile. Justin saved him for the moment. "Maybe you can go with me when I meet my mommy, Doc Jack. You can tell her how we're connected."

Mrs. Johnson spoke up. "I think she'll know, Justin."

He stopped swinging his legs and looked over at her, his brows raised. "How?"

"She'll know." Curling her fist, she placed it over her chest. "In here. A mommy always knows her child." Judging by the unusual and unexpected emotion in her shaky voice, and the tautness of her drawn lips, Jackson wondered if tears might be in those eyes hidden from his view. Sure enough, she raised the tissue and dabbed behind those infernal glasses.

"I'll take my gummi worms when I meet her. Do you think she'll like that?"

Jackson swallowed hard. "I think she'll love them, especially because they came from you."

Uncrossing her legs, Mrs. Johnson rose to her feet. "Justin, we should leave now."

Had the woman read his thoughts? He wasn't very good at masking his emotions. As it was, saying good night to Serenity the night before had been tortuous enough. So, like the coward he was, he'd taken off before he either told her everything he'd discovered or kissed her until the morning. That kiss under the tree on the church grounds, of all places, had been incredible. But like a greedy man, he'd wanted more. Craved more. But he didn't take more, neither did she offer. And it was enough. For now.

Still, it would be increasingly difficult to be around Serenity and not want to take her in his arms. Surely she knew how he felt. To his detriment, he'd always been obvious with his feelings for a woman. Finding her answers and then figuring out how to tell her without jeopardizing his practice was the best way to meet that goal.

Focus. "You still have ten minutes left in your session," Jackson said, keeping his tone as even as possible. As it was, Justin eyed him. The boy was smart and missed very little. Revealing he was upset in front of the child wasn't good.

"Justin, you have a birthday coming up soon, don't you?" They'd talked about it during the last session.

That brought back the child's easy smile and he nodded. "Nana's taking me to the beach."

Jackson swallowed. "It's Friday, isn't it?"

"Yep. We'll make sand castles and play in the waves. I'm supposed to meet someone."

If he knew nothing else, Jackson knew he'd be on the beach on Friday morning.

Serenity's mother took her to the beach on Friday mornings.

"Come on, honey." By this time, Mrs. Johnson was already by the door, one hand on the doorknob, ready to take flight. He'd unnerved her. For once, Jackson understood what wanting to jump out of your skin meant.

Justin scrambled down from the chair. "Bye, Doc Jack."

"Here, take the whole bag of cherry gummis. Call it a birthday present. I trust it's okay that Justin takes them since he likes the cherry ones so much...Mrs. Johnson?"

She nodded, and it was slow and methodical. He'd love nothing more than to yank those sunglasses away from her face and blast her with questions. If this *was* Serenity's mother, was it possible that Justin was Liam? The enormity of it threatened to overwhelm him. At the moment, he couldn't begin to wrap his head around such a concept. Everything he'd heard about Elise McClaren was positive—how loving she was, how kind, how protective...

"My mommy likes the red ones best, too," Justin said, pulling one from the bag and slurping it into his mouth. In a way, it was good to see him act like a normal kid enjoying a treat. He giggled and looked up at his grandmother. "Nana told me."

Without another word, Mrs. Johnson put a hand on her grandson's shoulder and steered him toward the outer office. The set of her jaw, the lift of her chin and shoulders...the same mannerisms mirrored in Serenity. He'd spent enough time with her to recognize them. *Why haven't I seen this before, Lord?*

All the things they'd said about the boy's mother, every last one of them, added up to a woman fitting Serenity's description. After this session, he could add the love of banana and peanut butter sandwiches. Combined with the love of that Mozart symphony, the cherry gummi worms, the honeysuckle...*everything.* He didn't need to look at any list.

Jackson rose from his chair and quickly crossed the room, reaching the outer office as Justin and his grandmother departed out the front door. "Justin? Who are you supposed to meet at the beach on your birthday?"

Stopping, he gave him a curious glance. "Grandpa."

A chill ran through him as Jackson lifted his hand in a feeble attempt at a wave.

"She didn't make another appointment," Audra said, pausing when she saw his face. "Are you okay, Dr. Ross? You look really pale. Kind of like you just saw a ghost."

"I think I might have, in a manner of speaking," Jackson said, half-stumbling back into his office. Closing the door—being careful not to shove it hard although he wanted to slam it in his frustration—he paced back and forth, immensely thankful he was free the rest of the afternoon. Glancing up at the cross behind his desk, Jackson fell to his knees. "Okay, this won't work," he said a few seconds later, pushing himself off the floor when his knee throbbed. His appointment with the orthopedic surgeon couldn't come soon enough. Stumbling to the chair—the one usually occupied by Mrs. Johnson—he dropped into it. With his elbows balanced on his thighs, he buried his head in his hands.

Jackson's shoulders heaved with the force of his breathing as he dragged his fingers through his hair. Through all the sports practices and games in his life, he'd never hyperventilated, but he was pretty close to it now. Jackson suppressed the groan stirring in the inner core of his being. If Audra weren't right outside the door, he'd release his frustration full force. Roar like a lion. He couldn't even put a name to what he was feeling, but the one thing he *did* know? If ever he needed the Lord beside him, it was now. In this very moment.

Father God, am I right in thinking this woman might be Serenity's mother? And Justin is Liam, her son? Is that possible? How can it be? Why? Help me find the answers, Lord. I know it could be the key to unlocking the mystery of Serenity's past and give her what she needs in order to move forward with her life.

As he prayed, the undeniable truth hit him. Even if he discovered the truth and it confirmed his suspicions, he couldn't tell Serenity. Yet it was his first instinct since he'd met her. He couldn't deny the truth. *Lord, I love her.*

When he'd become a psychologist, he'd taken a sacred oath before God and man. Justin was, first and foremost, his patient. And to breach that bond between them would be a violation of his ethics as a Christian and a professional psychologist. Overwhelming helplessness seized him unlike anything he'd ever felt. He prided himself on being a man of truth and honesty, but how could he be around the woman he loved and not tell her what he knew?

Jackson's shoulders slumped as yet another, equally painful truth, hit him. Once Serenity found out he knew, and that he'd kept it from her, she might hate him or banish him from her life. The thought of that happening slammed hard against his chest, crushing him under the weight of such an unbearable burden. He was in the worst possible situation he could imagine—in love with a woman wounded and torn apart by secrets. And he was a man held prisoner by the truth.

"Oh, Lord," he said, collapsing in the chair, "what am I supposed to do now?"

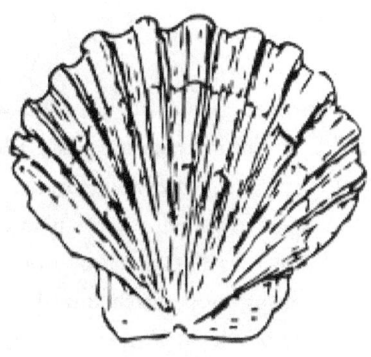

~CHAPTER 33~

*D*uring the morning meeting with the Town Council, Jackson was inordinately distracted. Of course, Serenity picked up on his mood and asked if everything was okay. He liked how she could "read" him but it also made him wonder how long he'd be able to hide what he knew. The whole situation was repugnant and churned his stomach.

After signing the contracts for the playground, they walked out of Town Hall together and Jackson listened as Serenity told him about the plans for the fall gala to raise additional funds. They'd discussed it a few times and he'd been impressed by how she'd recruited Deidre and some of her well-connected friends. From what she said, a special planning committee was already making plans. While the generous check from the anonymous donor would pay for all the playground equipment, more funds would be needed for the ongoing landscaping and maintenance costs.

"Thank you for making this a reality, Jackson," Serenity said. "It means a lot to me that you'd do this for my old neighborhood and especially that it's named for Danny." Her shy smile socked him right in the gut and made him feel like the worst kind of friend for not being straight with her.

Secretly thankful she was busy most of the day, he made a flimsy excuse about needing to get back to his office for an appointment. While true, he hated keeping her at arm's length. Ah, the sweet irony. The one person he wanted to share something with was the one person on the planet he *couldn't* tell. "Call me later?" Serenity said.

The significance of that question was huge since it was the first time she'd ever asked him. He wanted to groan in frustration and all he could manage was, "I'll be in touch." Stupid thing to say. A fleeting glimmer of hurt surfaced in her eyes before she nodded. Giving him a small wave, she hurried to her car, leaving him standing on the steps of Town Hall with a dumbfounded expression.

Returning to his office, inspiration seized him. He'd send Serenity a card and ask her to meet him at the beach on Friday morning. After a late morning appointment, he walked to the nearest store selling beach supplies and toys. Coming back into the office a few minutes later, he handed the pink plastic sand pail to Audra, practically begging the woman to see if her daughter, Gina, would gift wrap it for him. After all, his assistant was always singing the praises of the gift boutique Gina owned a few doors down from Inner Serenity.

"Tell her to use the best paper, bow, flowers. Whatever she thinks will make it look elegant and sophisticated," he said. "Fit for royalty." When he pulled out a fifty dollar bill and offered it to Audra, he chuckled when he glimpsed the excited spark in her eyes.

"Let me make sure I understand," she said. "You're willing to pay a lot of money just to have a plastic sand pail gift-wrapped?"

"Don't forget the scooper thing," he said, giving her his best grin.

"I'm sure Gina can make it look real pretty," Audra said, taking the box from him. "You and Martha Stewart. It's all in the presentation, huh?"

"You got it," he said, starting back into his office. "Trust me, Serenity will appreciate the sentiment."

"Ah," Audra said, "I knew you were more than book smart, Dr. Ross. You understand what goes on in a woman's heart, and that's what makes you such a good doctor. And a romantic suitor." Even though they hadn't worked together long, Jackson adored this woman. Sure, she flattered him, but it was about more than inflating his ego. Audra was a straight shooter and told it like it is. If he ever stepped over the line, she'd be sure and tell him. Plus, how could he resist a woman who used the word *suitor*?

"I'm not sure how Gina will reconcile this on the books, but I'm sure she'll think of something."

"Tell you what," Jackson said, "buy something to justify the gift wrapping. When's your birthday?"

"July," she said, "but you don't—"

"Then call it an early happy birthday gift. Does the store offer delivery?"

Audra nodded. "The young man who works at the print shop next door makes deliveries during his breaks."

Thanking her, Jackson pulled out his wallet and handed her another twenty, but she waved his hand aside. "Please stop throwing your money around. It's only a few steps from the store to Serenity's office, and I'm sure he can handle it. Don't you worry. I'll give him a real nice tip."

"Call it an investment," he said, opening her palm and placing the money inside, curling her fingers around it. "Make sure the guy gets a really good tip for taking it as soon as it's ready."

"I'm only taking your money because you insist," Audra said, tucking the money into her purse.

Jackson regretted he wouldn't see Serenity's reaction when she opened the box. Thinking of it made him smile. Although not exactly sure of his intent with the invitation to meet her on the beach on Friday morning, the one thing he could tell her was Elise McClaren's last known address. That would confirm her mother *might* be alive but couldn't provide any guarantees. Otherwise, he'd wing it, enjoy Serenity's company and pray she wouldn't suspect anything.

As it was, during his last session of the day, he'd barely paid attention. It wasn't fair to his patient, but he couldn't help himself. The child had prattled on about something that wasn't going to scar him for life, and Jackson managed to ask questions when appropriate. A natural chatterbox, the patient was content to talk without being prompted. At least his comments and recommendations at the conclusion of the session seemed to please the boy's mother, and he was grateful for the presence of mind to jot down notes early in the session.

Turning to his computer, he typed in *CroisetteShoresDailyNews.com* and clicked the mouse on the tab for "Births and Deaths." Only a few recent announcements. When he clicked on the Archives tab on the far right of the website, it only listed births within the last couple of years, both in Croisette Shores and the surrounding communities as well as a few out-of-state births with local connections. With a frown, Jackson checked the obituaries, pleased to see the records dated back as far as six years. Sitting up straighter in the chair, he input what information he knew, starting with the bare minimum. Closing his eyes, he whispered a quick prayer. Nothing. He tried again, adding more information, knowing it was probably useless. Nothing. Listing a broader date range, he tried again. Still nothing. Next he searched for the last name "Kincaid" and then finally for "McClaren."

Sweat broke out on his brow and he typed harder and faster. As a last resort, Jackson attempted to search the birth records from five years ago. A message popped up saying notices published five years ago were not accessible via the website and to go to the library or check with the Vital Statistics Office. "Been there, done that," he grumbled under his breath. But Justin's—Liam's—records must somehow be "stuck" in cyberspace limbo.

"This makes no sense!" Exasperated, Jackson collapsed back in his chair and rubbed his fingers over his eyes. How could a child be born and then die with no evidence whatsoever in the public record? Were there rules against publishing such things for some unknown reason? He'd need to make a trip to the library.

Danny. If he couldn't find anything about Liam, surely he could find news about a murder in this little town. That would have been huge news five years ago in Croisette Shores. Sitting up, he clicked the mouse to search under the "Archives" tab. "Give me something to go on," he muttered. After typing in "Daniel Kincaid Murder" in the search box—repeating it three times because his fingers shook and he mistyped—Jackson sat back again, drumming his fingers on his crossed arms, his heart racing as he waited.

As he suspected, he generated a lot of hits with those keywords for his search. Quickly perusing the list, Jackson chose one at random. Clicking on the article, he waited a few seconds, nearly jumping with the frustration of it all. He didn't know what he expected, but he knew he was on the verge of discovery. But of what? Leaning forward, he tapped his fingers on the desk.

The website was unbelievably slow, but finally the article started to pop up on the screen, section by section. Jackson strained to see the photograph appearing on the screen, scrolling from the top down to the bottom. Staring out at him from the computer screen was a photo of Daniel Kincaid. Jackson's jaw gaped.

Same dark, curly hair. Same dimples. Same smile. Same...everything.

The same face as Justin.

The same face as *Liam*.

"He's alive, Serenity. Your son is *alive!*" Dropping his head to his hands, Jackson wept.

"**C**ome in." Working on the estimate for the Cartwright project, Serenity looked up when Kelsie grunted. Her assistant stood in the doorway, holding a medium-sized, square package. Wrapped in shiny, pale blue paper with pastel silk flowers and curling ribbon cascading down its sides, it was exquisite. "What's that?"

"You tell me. It was hand-delivered a few minutes ago." Kelsie held it up, turning and eyeing it from all angles. "Hope you don't mind, but I shook it. Doesn't sound breakable. No rattle, no roll, nothing." She laughed when Serenity raised a brow. "My dad got my mom something from Tiffany & Co. once and she freaked. In a good way, though. It was wrapped in paper just like this but without all the fancy froufrou."

"I'm sure it's not from Tiffany's, but it *is* gorgeous, isn't it?" Serenity pushed away from her desk and smiled when Kelsie bowed low, as though presenting the gift to a queen. "Thank you, my subject. Your loyalty will not go unrewarded," she said as Kelsie made a big show of presenting it to her. Light as air. "I'd hate to destroy this lovely work of art if there's nothing inside, but that wouldn't make any sense. Who delivered it? Was there a card, a note, anything?"

"Kenny from the print shop a few doors down brought it. He delivers stuff from stores all over town for tips when he's on his break. No card, but he said it was for Princess Serenity, thus the reason for my bow. You know, if it didn't sound totally lame, I'd say you have a secret admirer." Kelsie's eyes grew rounder. "Hey, maybe it's from that mysterious guy who came in the other day."

Serenity frowned. "He didn't come back, did he? You promised to tell me if he did."

"No, he didn't. And I keep my promises."

"Didn't mean to imply otherwise," Serenity said, putting the box on her desk.

"I sure hope you're going to let me watch you open it because the suspense is killing me." Reaching for it, Kelsie laughed when Serenity put a hand on her arm.

"I'll do it, thank you." Lifting the edges on one side, she repeated the same on the other side and slid the box out of the wrapping easily enough. It brought to mind Christmas mornings with Mama beaming and Dad snapping photos as she tore into her presents beneath the gaudy, over-decorated tree in the family room. This gift was wrapped much too pretty to destroy it.

Kelsie hunched forward in her eagerness to see as Serenity lifted the lid of the plain white box. No store name was emblazoned on the top which made it all the more curious. Digging through mounds of white tissue paper, Serenity's breath hitched and she cried out with delighted surprise when she glimpsed something hot pink and plastic. With something attached to the side.

As Serenity pulled the sand pail from its nest, Kelsie's eyes widened and her jaw dropped. "You've got to be kidding me. Why would someone give you a present wrapped like it's for a queen and then put *that* in it?" She stopped after Serenity shot her a look. "Okay, I get it. For reasons I'll never understand, this so-called gift really means something to you."

"Believe it or not, Kelsie, this is one of the most precious gifts I've ever received. Thanks for bringing it to me." Serenity couldn't stop smiling.

"Please tell me it came from Jackson. That man's your prince, I hope you know."

Momentarily unable to speak, Serenity nodded. Oh, yes, she knew. With a dramatic sigh, Kelsie departed the office, shaking her head. Waiting until she was out of the room, Serenity pulled out the envelope embossed with the initials JDR tucked inside the sand pail. Returning to her chair, she read the card several times. And then again. Moving her hand over her heart, she breathed a sigh borne of...what, exactly? Hope for the future perhaps and the idea that she might one day regain that elusive peace in her life. Nothing could replace the pain of the past, but Jackson's spontaneity and enthusiasm for life was having a profound effect on her. Every gesture, everything he did, showed a caring and sensitivity beyond anything she'd ever known in another man. Not just for her, either, but for everyone. Well, perhaps a *little* more for her than others.

"Lord, you knew I needed someone like Jackson Ross in my life, didn't You?" Feeling silly, she smiled. Of course, He did. That's what sovereignty was all about. The Lord could see the ugly parts inside her as well as the not-so-ugly parts. Although that used to make her worry, now it gave her an incredible comfort to think He could take her insecurities and help her face those fears to make her stronger. As far as Jackson, she didn't simply need someone *like* Jackson in her life. She needed *Jackson*.

Her gaze fell on the card once more:

> *Princess Serenity,*
> *Meet me at the beach tomorrow morning.*
> *Eleven a.m. Bring yourself and the*
> *sand pail. I'll bring the rest.*
> *Your Humble Servant,*
> *Jackson*

~CHAPTER 34~

*S*itting on the beach on Friday morning, Jackson's pulse was erratic and he was antsier than ever before in his life. More nervous than he'd been before taking his board certification exams. More nervous than when he'd asked Laura to marry him. Thankful the first worked out, grateful the second didn't, Jackson jumped to his feet and paced the beach, darting glances at his watch every other minute. At ten minutes after eleven, he figured Serenity would have called if she couldn't make it. The woman prided herself on punctuality.

Stopping, he moved his hands to his hips. Neither were Violet Johnson and Justin anywhere in sight on this stretch of beach. Jackson assumed they might come here since Serenity said it's where her parents always used to bring her, but they could have gone to another beach. If any of the information she'd given him on the new patient forms was true—something he was beginning to question—they were staying at an address the next town over to the east.

Another twenty minutes later, Jackson could stand it no longer. After dialing her number, he sat back and waited, listening as it rang a few times before he heard her voice asking him to leave a message.

"Serenity, it's Jackson," he said, trying to maintain calm in spite of his increasing concern. "I'm checking in since I'd hoped to meet you at the beach this morning." Was it possible the gift hadn't been delivered yesterday? Surely Audra would have told him if there'd been a problem. No, come to think of it,

Audra left him a message telling him it was delivered to Kelsie at Serenity's office and she'd said she'd give it to her right away. And she also mentioned how beautiful the package looked.

Signing off after asking her to call him, he pondered his options. He could call Clinton, Charlie or Kelsie. He opted for the latter, hoping she'd be in the office on a Friday morning.

"Inner Serenity. This is Kelsie."

"Hey, Kels. It's me, Doc Jack. How are you?"

"Great, Doc! Hope you're out squiring my boss somewhere on this lovely summer morning."

He chuckled in spite of his apprehension. Kelsie could always make him smile. "Matter of fact, that's why I'm calling. I sent her something yesterday with a note in it, asking her to meet me this morning at eleven, but she hasn't come yet. I thought she was delayed at the office or something."

"Well, your gift came and Serenity loved it. You should have seen the smile on her face."

"Glad to hear she liked it."

"Oh, that was *before* she opened the box. After she opened it, I could tell she was touched. Whatever that little plastic sand bucket represents to her, you nailed it. You know what I mean."

"I do. Thanks, Kelsie. If you see her, would you please have her call me?"

"Sure thing, Doc."

Jackson pulled his sunglasses from the glove compartment and positioned them. On the short drive to Serenity's house, he coached himself. Surely Serenity was fine. She could have overslept or gotten involved with something and lost track of the time. The fact she hadn't been to her office or even called Kelsie seemed odd and out of character. This whole business about possibly being followed lingered in the back of his mind and he couldn't shake it.

Lord, let Serenity be okay.

Less than three minutes later, he pulled up in front of Serenity's small house, feeling ridiculous for not walking. Hauling out of the car, he spied Mrs. Marciano working in her yard. She turned and waved. "Howdy, Doc!"

Jackson nodded and smiled. "How are you, Mrs. Marciano? And Mr. Darcy?" he said when he spied the cat sitting on the lawn with a sleepy-eyed stare trained on him.

"We're doing fine. Enjoying this beautiful morning before it gets too hot." She gave him a saucy smile. "I take it you've come to see my pretty young neighbor?" Her gaze slid to the Aston Martin. "Nice wheels, by the way. I knew right away how much you liked Miss Serenity seeing as how you gave her the keys to drive me home from the church picnic. Don't know many men who'd give up the rights to their car, especially one that's worth a pretty penny. Isn't this one of those James Bond cars or something?"

He grinned straight through his nerves. "Mr. Bond squired around in an Aston Martin in a few of his movies. It's a lot of fun and my one concession to excess." He chuckled. "Make that extreme excess."

Mrs. Marciano laughed. "Everyone's entitled. Question is, did you get it as a personal reward or to impress someone?"

Smart woman. "Would you believe both?"

She hitched her chin and met his gaze, brushing short strands of gray hair away from a thin face lined with wisdom. "The reward?"

"For getting my doctorate. Believe it or not, I wasn't trying to impress a woman."

"Then it's more you had something to prove to yourself or someone else. Am I right?"

"You're too wise for me," Jackson said, his smile resurfacing. "I think I'm the one talking to the psychologist."

"Wanna talk about it, Doc?" She slid one hand to her hip.

"Sure. Hop in the ejector seat right here and I'll tell you all about it."

The older woman laughed so loud Serenity probably heard her from inside the house. Darting a glance at the front door, he wondered if she might appear.

"I'll see you again soon, I hope, Mrs. Marciano."

"Hope so, too, Doc."

He started up the front walkway beneath the shade of the lovely, large tree with reddish-colored flowers. Inhaling a quick breath, his smile sobered. Standing outside the door, he paused with his fist poised, ready to knock. For whatever reason, he was relieved to see Mrs. Marciano go inside her house with Mr. Darcy. In case he needed to break down Serenity's door, he didn't particularly want an audience.

"*G*o away!" The pounding on the door matched the relentless pounding in her head.

"I'm not going anywhere until you come to the door and I can see you for myself!"

A loud groan escaped as Serenity rolled over in the bed. Why couldn't Jackson let her wallow in her misery for once? Wasn't a person allowed down time every now and then? Sometimes she wished she could be a little girl again. Grab her blankie or her teddy bear and crawl into her bed, curl into a ball, stick her thumb in her mouth and go to sleep without a care in the world.

"Serenity McClaren, I'm ready to break this door down, and I don't think you want that!" The pounding continued, and she cringed. Was that a cracking sound? Would the man really *do* that?

"Okay, okay. Hang on." Dragging herself from the bed and hurrying down the hallway, she crossed the living room as the pounding continued. "I'm coming!" she called, throwing open the door before he had the chance to totally obliterate it.

"About time." Jackson swooped through the doorway and she was in his embrace before she had time to think, time to breathe.

"Nice to see you, too," she mumbled against his chest, feeling like an idiot by burying her face in his black T-shirt. It smelled like Jackson mixed with laundry detergent, and the combination was better than nice.

"You didn't show up at the beach this morning, you didn't answer your phone, and Kelsie didn't know where you were." He crushed her against his hard chest.

"Jackson," she sputtered, gasping, "you're going to suffocate me." The man didn't know his own strength.

"Sorry," he said, releasing her. Pulling back, he held onto her arms, gentle but firm, his eyes searching her face. "Tell me what's going on." Bless his heart, he really *was* worried about her, and guilt pinched her insides. "Has something happened?" The corners of his mouth tugged down. "No offense, but you look pretty ragged."

"Well, thanks for that, Doc." The moment of closeness broken, she turned away from him, crossing her arms over her chest.

"Tell me what's going on, Serenity. No evasions. Be straight with me."

She frowned. "In spite of your noble efforts, this isn't a case where you can break down my door, swoop in here, play the hero and make everything all better." Serenity headed to the sofa, dropping onto it, staring absently at the floral pattern. "You shouldn't have come. I'm not decent company today." Curling into the sofa, Serenity leaned her head back and draped her forearm over her face, as if that could somehow make her disappear into the cushions.

Jackson blew out a sigh laced with exasperation. "I should call you Scarlett O'Hara with your theatrics. Do you have the vapors or whatever they're called?" He crossed his arms. "Time to stop acting like you're ten. I see it enough with my patients and I've never known you to wallow in self-pity."

She opened her eyes to find him staring down at her from a foot away. Stepping closer, he moved his hands to his hips. She couldn't look away if she tried, not sure if he was more angry or annoyed by her evasiveness. Serenity's mouth went dry, and she swallowed, afraid she'd cough.

"I'm not going anywhere, so start talking."

"You're pretty bossy sometimes, you know that?" At the moment, it was one of his most aggravating habits as well as his most endearing. Warmth invaded her cheeks. "Not to mention your infuriating ability to be right most of the time." Even after licking her lips, they were dry again seconds later. Serenity hung her head, gathering her thoughts, willing herself not to cry.

The sofa cushions dipped as Jackson settled beside her. His nearness surrounded her like a blanket on a cold morning, bringing to mind the way her mother would wrap her in a warm towel after her bath when she was a little girl. But she wasn't a little girl anymore, and Jackson certainly wasn't her mother. Awareness of him washed over her like the waves at high tide, crashing into her subconscious. Without touching her, Jackson awakened feelings she'd thought were long dead. What a lonely, needy mess she was.

Squeezing her eyes tight for a moment, she felt the prompt to tell this man. She'd shared everything else about her life, and he was here and cared about her.

Jackson sat quietly with his hands clasped together on his lap, waiting for her to speak.

"It's my anniversary."

Stealing a peek, Serenity noticed the lines circling his eyes, the tautness around his mouth.

He finally spoke. "If you want to talk about Danny, I'm here. Whatever you need."

She couldn't meet his eyes. "No, not *that* anniversary."

"Well, then what..." Jackson's voice faded and the muscles in his jaws tightened.

"I found my heart five years ago today, Jackson, and then lost it the next day." The tears started, and she didn't bother to stop them. Neither did she protest when he gathered her into his chest, brushing loose strands of her hair away from her face with his gentle fingers and then leaned his head against hers. He absorbed her shaking shoulders and her trembling body. She didn't know what he said, but his presence gave her comfort. But it was so much more than that.

"You need to talk about it." Their eyes met, but she lowered hers first. "It's been too long, honey. You can't keep this bottled up inside you. It's not healthy, and you can't move forward with your life until you come to some kind of resolution."

A small surge of anger sparked within her, and she drew in a shuddering breath. "For once I don't *want* to talk about it."

"Why?" He didn't even flinch and held her gaze.

"Because," she said, a small sob escaping, "if I talk about it, then it's like he's really gone. Don't you see?" Her voice broke. "My baby was the one thing in this world I managed to do right, Jackson, and I couldn't even hold onto him." The last part came out a wail, and she clamped a hand over her mouth as her sobs unleashed.

Her shoulders shook as she wept. They weren't hard, body-rocking sobs, but quiet, steady tears that she couldn't seem to stop. How long they sat there together, Serenity couldn't know. The right shoulder and half of Jackson's shirt was soaked with her tears. Finally, she disengaged from his arms and swiped beneath both eyes with her fingers.

"I'm sorry about your shirt."

"I'm not. Baby, you can soak a hundred shirts, and I wouldn't care."

Serenity cleared her throat. "I want to show you something. I'll be right back." Pushing off the sofa, she darted down the narrow hallway to the bedroom. Reaching into the top shelf of her closet, she pulled down a small plastic shoe box. She startled to see Jackson leaning against the doorjamb a few seconds later.

Staring at the box for a long moment, not moving, she crossed the room and sat down on the bed. She balanced the box on her lap. "I haven't taken this out in a long time."

Jackson watched as she lifted the lid and removed a tiny knit cap and a white, pink and blue striped receiving blanket. Draping the soft blanket over her lap, she smoothed her fingers over them. "They're so tiny. It's hard to imagine we were ever this little, isn't it?" She picked up the wrist bracelet and stared at it for a long moment, dangling it from her fingers.

"I was over ten pounds when I was born. My mother reminds me at every opportunity."

"Okay, Paul Bunyan," she said, appreciating his attempt to lighten the moment.

Reaching into the box again, she pulled out a birth certificate with Liam's footprint. She traced her finger over it. "He weighed over eight pounds. Danny would have been so happy and proud of him. He used to bring home little bouquets of flowers and put them in a glass on the kitchen table to liven up our dinner. He always made sure I ate well. Once he packed a picnic basket and whisked me away to the park." The thought made her smile. "He actually fed me grapes under a tree and read poetry. He didn't understand much of it, but that's what made it even more special. We shared a lot of laughter, and we shared Liam, at least when I was pregnant. I'll always cherish those memories."

"I'm thankful you can talk about them"—he tweaked her chin—"and smile."

"Me, too." Sniffling, she put the certificate back in the box. "We were planning on naming our child after Danny if it was a boy. But after he was born and I had to put a name on the death certificate..." She took comfort from Jackson's presence when he settled on the bed beside her. "I couldn't do it. I'd always liked the name Liam and it means guardian and protector." She heaved a sigh. "It's silly and makes no sense, really, but I promised Liam he'd always be the big brother protector when I have more children."

Sitting back and leaning on his elbows, Jackson surveyed her. "You realize what you said in subtext?" Returning to an upright position, he nudged her shoulder. "You want to have more children."

"I remembered what was so familiar about Dr. Saunders."

"What's that?"

"I'd never met him before, but he's the doctor who signed Liam's death certificate."

Jackson's eyes widened. She'd caught him off-guard, and for once, he'd been rendered speechless.

"I'm sorry," she said, wiping away another tear that escaped. "Leave it to me to add a little morbidity to your morning."

"Serenity, look at me." She raised her eyes to his. "Liam will always be in your heart. You know he's loved and he's safe, and that's what you'd want for him, right?"

She nodded and bit her lower lip. Although it still trembled, no fresh tears fell.

"Right," she whispered.

Liam's middle name is Justin. If any doubts lingered in his mind, they were eradicated when his gaze fell on that piece of paper. Struggling with a tumult of emotions as strong as he'd ever experienced—a tidal wave of elation tempered with extreme frustration all at the same time—Jackson forced himself to focus on the woman beside him.

"I only held him a couple of times, but I nursed him the second time, about an hour after his birth," she said, lowering her gaze from his. "I'll never forget that feeling of wonder and awe, inspecting every tiny toe and finger. I drank him in and kissed his soft skin. Told him how much his mama loved him. He was a miracle, *my* miracle. Liam was the best thing I ever did. Even though I didn't know Jesus at the time, I still believed in God. When the nurses told me he'd developed a lung infection and died, I was in a drug-induced haze but I clearly remember praying and asking God to take care of my little boy and watch over him until I could be with him again. I'd memorized his features and imprinted them on my heart."

Jackson enjoyed hearing Serenity's memories in spite of the pervasive sadness. Everything in him wanted to hold her close and murmur the words that would change her life. *Serenity, your son is alive. Your mother is alive. They're here in Croisette Shores.* In that moment, he resolved to confront Elise and demand she meet with Serenity as soon as possible. Reunite the woman he loved with the child she thought had died. What on earth happened in that hospital five years ago? Why was Serenity told her baby died? Was her mother involved? If so, what possible reason could she have for decimating her daughter's life like this?

"Jackson?" Her fingers, warm and soft, rested on the side of his face. "What are you thinking?"

Turning his head, he met her eyes. "One of the best ways to get over heartache is to face those fears and plunge right back in. Immerse yourself in the very thing that brought you sadness. Only then can you conquer it. Another child won't replace Liam, but it'll give you a contentment you might not think possible. I hope you're at least willing to consider it."

Serenity's gaze slanted over to his. "I know you're trained in psychology, and I'm sure it makes some kind of sense in the annals of clinical shrinkdom or whatever, but please tell me how—hypothetically speaking—a woman who can't swim can possibly benefit from jumping feet first in a river?"

"For one thing," Jackson said, measuring his words, "why would you want to deny yourself another opportunity to find love and happiness?" Not sure why he'd started this tangent of conversation, he felt powerless to stop. Subconsciously, did he need to know how she'd respond?

Refolding the baby blanket, Serenity tucked it back in the plastic box with the certificate and the knit cap. Turning on the bed to face him, Serenity appeared thoughtful, but she didn't seem upset. "I never said I didn't want another chance."

He gathered his thoughts. "The way I see it, if you fall in love and get married again, having another child is part of the natural progression."

"You mean the natural order of things? If you know me so well, then you'd know I don't follow the same path as most people. I do things my own way, for better or worse."

He couldn't leave it alone. Something inside spurred him on. "I know you love children. If you never have another child of your own, you'll be denying one of God's children a great mother."

At least that made her laugh. "That's one unique campaign for motherhood. You should be on the board of the local women's shelter. With passion like that, I'm sure they could use someone like you."

"I've got enough to do right now. And job one," he said, lowering his voice and looking her straight in the eye, "is taking care of the beautiful woman God's brought into my life. *She's* my passion."

Leaning toward her, Jackson waited. When she touched those sweet lips to his, desire shot through him like a red-hot branding iron. Lost in the moment, he covered her mouth with his. Cupping her face, he moved his lips over her cheeks, peppering her soft, supple skin with featherlight kisses. Every nerve ending in him ignited and he slowly moved with her as she fell back on the bed and his lips found hers again. When she arched her neck, he traced a slow, sensuous path of kisses from her jaw down to her neck, delighting when she moaned and whispered his name. Their bodies were close, inches apart. Oh, how he wanted...

You can't do this. In an abrupt move, he sat up and reached for her hand, pulling her up so they both sat upright again. He could tell she was surprised, but he dared not look at her until his shaky emotions were under control. Putting both hands on his knees, he remained silent and so did she.

"I'm sorry. That was wrong of me to take advantage of your vulnerability. We need to get out of here," he said, running a hand through his hair and jumping up from the bed. *Lord, forgive me.*

"It was the moan, wasn't it? It was too much. I shouldn't have done it."

"Baby, I loved that little moan, but that's the problem. You can't begin to know what you do to me." Sweeping her into his arms—taking care where he placed his hands—he started down the hallway and moved through the living room toward the front door. After leaning down to turn the knob, he threw open the door and walked outside into the warm sunshine.

Serenity squinted and squirmed in his arms. Her legs dangled and she moved her hands over his shoulders and around his neck. When she leaned her blonde head against his chest and snuggled closer, he felt his pulse accelerate at warp speed. He'd been preoccupied with thoughts of Serenity in recent days— ever since he'd met her, if he was honest with himself—and holding her like this brought out every male instinct he could imagine, some honorable, some not. As much as the pleasurable sensations pumping through him, he loved how she clung to him. Serenity trusted him.

"Where do you think you're taking me?"

"Somewhere way less tempting, for starters." He hesitated a second. "You're dangerous for me to be around."

She looked up at him. "Sorry?"

"No, you're not."

"Jackson." Something in her voice made him stop. Serenity angled her head toward what she was wearing—or wasn't—and raised a brow.

Lowering her to the ground, he grunted. "Do you have any appointments or pressing obligations today?"

"No. I cleared my schedule," she said, tugging down on the hem and tightening the belt on her robe. Hopefully the Lord would understand and cut him some slack. He was only a flesh-and-blood man with the thoughts of a man. Not that he'd act on them, but oh yeah, he'd be asking forgiveness for his thoughts. All the more incentive to help her solve the mysteries of her life, pray she wouldn't hate him and then get on with both their lives, one foot in front of the other.

"This day is always one of the hardest for me since I left Croisette Shores," she said, bringing him back to the present. "I'm sure you know by now that I'm a case in emotional instability. I really wanted to meet you on the beach this morning, and I had every intention of being there, but..."

"We'll go to the beach another day. I have somewhere else in mind for now." That wasn't the entire truth, and he hoped he'd come up with something while she went back inside and changed. Fun. Serenity needed a day to get away, relax and enjoy herself, but not the beach this time. *Charlie*. He'd call his friend. If anyone knew a place to suggest, Charlie would.

"While you're quite fetching in your cute little robe, why don't you go change into some *I'm going to have fun today* clothes. Shorts and tennis shoes. And think about retiring that robe but at least get some good dust rags out of the deal." It took everything in him to keep his eyes trained on her face. The thin, ratty cotton of her white robe accentuated the curves beneath it to great advantage and its short length highlighted her long, shapely legs. He almost let out a moan of his own but kept it in check.

Serenity absently fingered the torn belt, the expression on her face sad. What had he said now? "This robe was Mama's. That's why I haven't been able to let it go. I don't have much of her left to call my own. It doesn't smell like her anymore, though. For a long time, it did."

Jackson's eyes widened. "Then I think you should definitely keep it. I'm sorry. That was an incredibly stupid thing to say."

She shrugged. "No, it wasn't. You had no idea, and you're right. I guess I needed my mother today." Her eyes met this. "But then God sent *you*."

Tears stung the back of his eyes. So much he *couldn't* tell her, so much he *wanted* to tell her. What a horrible place to live. He hadn't even told her yet that he'd found the last known address for her mother and was surprised she hadn't asked.

Lord, please don't let her hate me.

Her eyes bright, Serenity touched his forearm as she headed back toward the house. "Give me five minutes to change."

Reaching for his cell phone, he nodded. "Sure. Take your time."

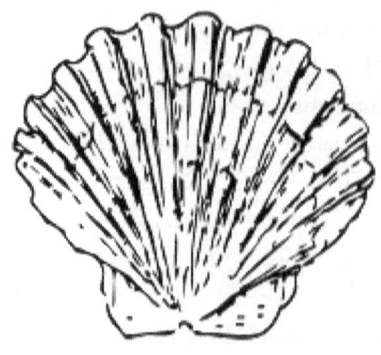

~CHAPTER 35~

*U*ntying her robe, Serenity slipped it off her shoulders and tossed it on the bed. She darted into her closet and grabbed a pair of khaki shorts and a light blue cotton top. Dressed less than two minutes later, she headed into the bathroom, washed her face and then applied a couple of light coats of waterproof mascara, the latter being one of Deidre's best suggestions. The thought made her smile. After brushing her teeth, Serenity slicked a light pink gloss over her lips and frowned at her reflection in the wall mirror. Faint circles lined her eyes, evidencing her lack of sleep the last few nights and her features appeared more pale than usual.

"Look lively, girl, and get ready to enjoy the day. No more wallowing." She combed her hair and secured it in a twist in back with a plastic clip.

Next she rummaged through her closet for her most comfortable pair of athletic shoes. They were well-worn but hopefully they'd suffice for whatever Jackson had in mind. She suspected he might be winging it and hadn't planned on whisking her off anywhere today. How could he have known he'd walk into the den of emotional instability when he almost broke down her door? As usual, he was being compassionate, sensitive Jackson. One of the things she admired most about him was his ability to sense her moods and not push her. Today, he knew she needed company and fun. He really was so good to her, so good *for* her. Not many men would be so patient and kind. Danny might have been the one she'd played with in the sandbox as a child, but Jackson was the one she felt like she'd known forever.

Stuffing the tube of lip gloss in the pocket of her shorts, she reached for her purse on the dresser. After removing her driver's license and a credit card from her wallet, she detached her house key from the butterfly key ring, a gift from Deidre on her last weekend visit to Atlanta. "Honey, one of these days you'll emerge from your cocoon and you're going to sail through the air like the most beautiful butterfly. You'll soar like you're meant to do."

As she left the house, Serenity spied Jackson leaning against his car, facing her, his cell phone at his ear. A huge grin spread across his face when he spied her and he gave her a thumbs-up sign. After locking the door, she pocketed the key and headed down the front walkway to meet him.

"Charlie sends you his best regards," Jackson said, finishing the call. "Said to tell you he's thinking of you today."

Dear Charlie. He knew today would be a hard one for her. He'd left her a voice mail on her phone but she hadn't listened to it yet. For a fleeting moment, she wondered if she'd hear from her dad. Ever since Liam's death, he hadn't let the day go by without contacting her in some way. "Thanks. And where are you taking me today, kind sir?"

"I'm kidnapping you."

"Excuse me?"

"You heard me. Okay, first I have a confession." After stuffing his phone in the pocket of his shorts, he held up both hands with an adorably sheepish smile.

"You don't look especially repentant." Her attempt to frown didn't work. The man was irresistible.

"I called Charlie since I figured he'd know the perfect place to take you, but I'm not telling. You have to wait and see. After you, Princess Serenity." Opening the car door, Jackson ushered her inside.

"You realize there's a high penance to pay for kidnapping royalty," she said as he slid behind the wheel.

"I'll pay whatever the price for the pleasure of your company."

She couldn't even muster a comeback. The man was certainly smooth like the engine of his car as it purred to life. Serenity's stomach rumbled, reminding her she hadn't eaten anything. "So," she said a mile down the road, "I hope you're planning to feed me."

He tossed her an amused glance. "I heard. Whatever your heart desires—or make that your stomach—shall be yours once we reach the kingdom."

"And which kingdom are we traveling to today, kind sir? Please don't say Burger King."

His laugh made her heart spiral. "The kingdom of Serenity, of course."

This man is a gift.

Serenity settled into the seat as Jackson headed onto the highway. She hadn't even ventured out of Croisette Shores since her arrival, and it was good to hit the open road. It brought a sense of freedom even though she never felt confined in her small town.

"How about some music?"

"Sure." A few seconds later when he turned on the CD player, she turned in the seat to face him. "You listen to Mozart?"

"Don't sound so surprised. I guess you could say I'm developing more of an appreciation for it." Reaching for her hand, he gave it a quick squeeze.

"I'm not surprised," she said, leaning her head against the seat, admiring his rugged, handsome profile. "Just...very pleased."

Twenty minutes later, Jackson pulled the car into the large parking lot of Faire Kingdom, an amusement park catering to the preteen and younger age group—complete with a small castle, moats, dragons and attendants in medieval costumes. She glanced around in wonder. "I haven't been here in a long time. I'd forgotten all about it and didn't even realize it was still here."

As Jackson helped her out of the car, she planted a kiss on his cheek and slipped her hand in his. "I love it. Thank you. I can't tell you how much this means to me."

He dipped his head to capture her eye contact. "Sure you're okay? You looked sad for a minute there."

"Being nostalgic. My parents brought me here a few times. I have lots of fond memories in Faire Kingdom." She met his gaze. "Honestly? It's absolutely perfect for today."

"Then let's go have some fun. But first order of business is to get you something to eat."

She laughed. "Let's wait until after we ride the roller coaster."

*F*our hours later, Serenity collapsed on a park bench beside Jackson. "I haven't had this much fun in as long as I can remember."

"You realize those little girls over there have been following you around for about an hour."

Although she'd noticed them a few times during the day, she hadn't thought twice about it. "Why do you think they're following me? They probably think *you're* someone famous. Face it, Jackson. You have a certain quality or whatever about you, and that car you drive is pretty awesome."

Relaxing against the back of the bench, Jackson draped one arm around her shoulders. "I think it might have a little something to do with that glittery thing perched on your head."

Serenity touched the rhinestone tiara he'd bought for her in one of the stores on Palace Avenue. She'd always loved them as a child. Somewhere, at the back of her closet, she still had the one her dad bought her at Faire Kingdom for her seventh birthday.

"A tiara does not a princess make, you know." Jackson's smile sobered a bit. Those deep chocolate eyes bore straight through to her soul. He already knew her mind more intimately than Danny. Her husband hadn't been as much concerned with anything intellectual as physical and tangible. In some ways, sitting on the bench beside Jackson now, her life with Danny seemed like someone else's life.

"Time for another confession," Jackson said. "Your dad called when I was waiting for our food earlier. He asked me to buy one for you. Dance, Princess Serenity, dance—"

"And all of God's riches shall be added unto you," she murmured.

"Oh, no you don't." Jackson rose to his feet and pulled her up with him. "No sad looks allowed. How about some cotton candy?" He left his hand wrapped around hers. "Come on, live dangerously." When he raised a brow, she laughed.

"Tempting. Only if you share it with me."

"Deal. Only question is which color."

"Pink, of course." Serenity smiled at the little girls as they walked past. When one of them tugged on the bottom of her shorts, she stopped with Jackson beside her. He released her hand as she crouched down beside the freckle-faced redhead.

"You look like a real princess."

"Of course, she's not, silly," another one of the little girls piped up, nodding at Serenity with a serious expression. "They sell those crowns at the gift shop."

"I've never seen a princess wear shorts and tennis shoes." That comment came from a dark-haired girl who looked a few years older.

"Sure they do," the red-haired girl said.

"I'm Serenity. What's your name?"

"Isabella. Serenity *sounds* like a princess name." She glanced up at Jackson. "Are you her prince?"

Playing along, Jackson bowed at the waist. In so doing, he captured more of her heart. "Prince Jackson at your service, Royal Miss."

All the girls giggled and it brought that sweet but rare flush of color to Jackson's cheeks that made him look all the more charming. With a smile, Serenity carefully removed her tiara, thankful her hair didn't catch on the comb. "I hereby crown you Princess Isabella." The awe in Isabella's bright eyes was unmistakable as she reached up with one hand to touch the tiara.

"Does this crown make me a princess?" The hope in the girl's voice was precious as Serenity helped her secure it in her hair.

Lord, help me say the right words. "I might look like a princess, but I'm really not in the eyes of the world. In God's eyes, you're a princess every day, Isabella. He's the true King and He wants you in His kingdom. It doesn't matter whether you wear this crown or not. All you have to do is invite Jesus into your heart and love Him. Talk to Him like a best friend. You'll always be a princess in His eyes." Serenity tapped a light finger on the tip of the girl's nose, prompting giggles. "And one day, *your* handsome prince will come along."

Isabella nodded before throwing her arms around her neck. "I think you're the prettiest, nicest princess I ever met."

"As if you've met any," the skeptic commented, rolling her eyes. "Come on, Bella. We've gotta get back or mom's gonna yell at us. You sure you want to give her that?" Defiant dark eyes stared at Serenity.

"Yes." She winked at Isabella. "It looks a lot better on you than me. Have a good time. Bye girls!" Serenity gave them her best impression of a royal wave, and avoided looking at Jackson. When the girls were out of earshot, she turned to face him. "Please don't tell me you spent a lot of money on that tiara. It was a pretty nice replica."

He gave her a coy grin. "I could buy you another one."

"That's okay. The thought was there and it was fun while it lasted, but there's so many obligations in the royal spotlight. I think I'd rather be one of the common folk."

"It was definitely worth every penny to see the look on Isabella's face. Even more so what you said to her about belonging in God's kingdom."

Serenity frowned even as she heard the admiration in Jackson's tone. "I don't usually say things like that and it was the first time. Not sure why I did."

"You're thinking more about the things of God's kingdom these days. I can tell."

She raised a brow. "Really? I've been making a conscious effort to do what Pastor Tom suggested about showing people God's love, even without words. This is the first time I've actually verbalized my faith." Her eyes met his.

"How'd it feel?"

Her grin escaped. "Amazing."

He stepped closer. "In case I haven't told you yet today, you're a beautiful woman, Serenity McClaren. And you're in no way, shape or form among the *common folk*. You're actually quite *extra*ordinary."

She couldn't hide her smile. "And in case I haven't told *you* today, you're..." She paused for dramatic effect.

"I'm...what? Don't you dare leave me hanging. You might as well learn now that open-ended statements drive me absolutely crazy. Bonkers."

Serenity touched his cheek with a gentle hand. Leaning into it, Jackson watched her, his expression curious, but full of optimism. "I think you're quite possibly the most wonderful, honorable man I've ever been privileged to know."

"I don't know about that," he said. Glimpsing the flicker of emotion in Jackson's eyes, Serenity could see how deeply her words affected him. "Thank you for letting me in, Serenity."

After a romantic carriage ride around Faire Kingdom, they poked in another one of the shops, trying on silly hats and acting silly. Leaving the amusement park, they stopped at a nearby diner. As they shared a burger and fries, they discussed the preliminary plans for the gala fundraiser for the playground. The thirty-minute drive back to Croisette Shores was quiet and Jackson kept his hand over hers most of the way. Yawning, Serenity fought the overwhelming urge to sleep.

"Wake up, Princess Serenity." Her eyes fluttered open to find Jackson's handsome face next to hers.

"What a wonderful way to wake up." She struggled to sit up and ignored his light chuckle. "You know what I mean," she said as he helped her out of the car.

"I do, but it sure sounded great." Stuffing his hands in his pockets, he walked beside her as she dug her house key from her pocket.

"Thanks for turning what could have been a horrible day into one of the best of my life, Jackson." Although she wanted to invite him inside, it was best they say good night now. If he came inside, the temptation would be too strong for him not to leave until morning.

"I know my limitations, and it's best if I don't come in, Serenity."

She lowered her gaze. The man's ability to read her mind was uncanny, but she was thankful he understood his limits and was such a man of honor. "I'm sorry about earlier today," she whispered, meeting his eyes again.

"I'm not." Scratching the beginnings of a beard, his grin was wry. "You tempt me without even trying, fair maiden."

The way Jackson looked at her set her heart afire although it was tinged with something she couldn't define. Not a sadness, exactly, but like he had words on the tip of his tongue he wanted to say but felt he couldn't. What, she couldn't imagine. Even with all the teasing and laughing during the day, she'd noticed that same look in his eyes several times. Whenever she tried to broach the subject, he'd turn the conversation around or ask her a question. Deflecting attention away from himself might be part of his training as a psychologist, but in any case, the man was very adept at it.

"Want to come to dinner tomorrow night at my house?"

"Are you sure..."

"I promise to be at my most chivalrous. Good fun and hopefully a halfway decent meal. I can pick you up around six, if that works."

Her heart raced. "Sounds great, but I can drive myself. What shall I bring?"

He kissed her forehead. "All I need is you."

Crawling into bed a short time later, Serenity felt more at peace than she had in a very long time. It's true what she'd told Jackson. What started out as one of the worst days since coming back to Croisette Shores had become one of the best ever. All because of Jackson.

"I have You to thank, Lord," she said into the darkness of her bedroom. "Thank You for bringing Jackson into my life." She'd been reading her Bible, trying to get in a few chapters each night.

She'd been surprised by how much of her life compared to the characters and their stories in the Bible—some sad, some unbelievably hard, some hopeful and others tragic. As Jackson had promised, the verses she read made her think and evaluate her own life. No matter what happened in the past, it wasn't because of anything she'd done. She hadn't caused Danny's murder. That was a random act of violence. Liam didn't die because of anything she'd done wrong. As always, though, it was her mother's disappearance that continued to befuddle and confuse her the most. For that, she had no answers and wondered if she ever would. She'd continue to pray for her the same as she'd continue to pray for her father. *Great is our Lord and mighty in power; His understanding has no limit.*

Reading her Bible gave her comfort, but a different kind of comfort from being held in Jackson's arms. No longer was she alone in the world. She had the greatest ally of all beside her to help fight her battles. The Lord wrapped her in the warm blanket of His love, the kind of soul-soothing, soul-satisfying love no earthly man could give her. Not even Jackson, as important as he'd become to her. *He heals the brokenhearted and binds up their wounds.*

Through faith, she'd been able to share about God's love with Isabella at Faire Kingdom. She wouldn't have been able to do that a month ago, even a couple of weeks ago. The light in the little girl's eyes gave her hope what she said might plant a seed of truth in her young mind. Most likely, she'd never see Isabella again, but she could pray for her. *The Lord delights in those who fear Him, who put their hope in His unfailing love.*

"Lord, help her know she's a princess in Your eyes," Serenity murmured as she turned over in the bed, pulling the lightweight blanket over her and closing her eyes.

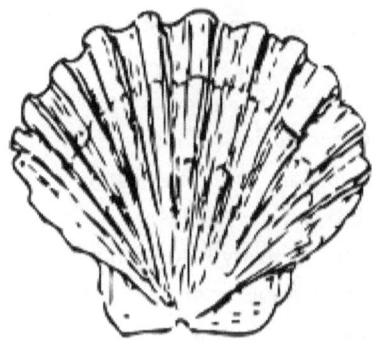

~CHAPTER 36~

Serenity awoke to pounding on her front door less than an hour later. Struggling to sit up, she pushed her hair out of her eyes and glanced at her clock on the nightstand. Almost twelve thirty. What was happening? Her heart raced and she put a hand on her chest. Closing her eyes, she said a quick prayer, willing the person assaulting her door at this unearthly hour to leave. She held her breath when the pounding stopped, but then it started again a few seconds later with even more force.

"Miss Serenity! Miss Serenity!"

Mrs. Marciano. She breathed a sigh of relief. Tossing the sheet aside, she swung her legs over the edge of the bed and reached for her robe. Pulling it around her shoulders, she lifted her hair out of the way and tied the robe in a haphazard fashion at her waist. "I'm coming, Mrs. Marciano!" She had to holler twice before the pounding finally stopped. Surely she wasn't using the skillet. If she did, the front door would be dented.

Out of habit, Serenity peered through the peephole before flinging the door wide and stepping aside. "What's wrong, Mrs. Marciano? Has something happened?" She stifled a yawn and ushered the elderly woman inside, closing the door behind her.

"You have a Sneaking Thomas." In her lightweight housecoat, fuzzy slippers and her salt-and-pepper hair half falling out of pink sponge rollers, her neighbor made quite a sight. Sure enough, she held the cast iron weapon at her side.

Swallowing the impulse to giggle, Serenity sucked in her cheeks and listened as she went on for at least three minutes. "I'm telling you," Mrs. Marciano said, gesturing wildly with her hands, "he's lurking around here somewhere, and you need to call the police."

"Slow down a minute." Serenity held up one hand. How could the woman talk so fast? "Why don't you come sit on the sofa and I'll fix you a cup of that soothing orange tea you like?"

An exasperated sigh escaped. "You're a sweet girl, Miss Serenity, but honey, you gotta wake up and smell the roses!" She didn't make a move toward the sofa and stood with one hand on her hip, one foot engaged in a constant up-and-down thumping. "You tell me, what kind of pervert sneaks around a woman's home at this hour of the morning?"

"It's not that late for some people, but I know you usually go to bed earlier. Why are you up, anyway?"

"Couldn't sleep since my arthritis is acting up again. I was watching an old rerun of *Who's the Boss.*"

Serenity stifled her yawn and smiled. "That's your favorite show, isn't it?"

"Sure is." At least it made her neighbor smile, relaxing her features. "I like that Italian, Tony what's-his-name. I think he used to drive a taxi in New York. He and that hoity-toity blonde boss lady are funny." She waved her hand in the air. "Always knew those two would end up together."

"On the show, of course," Serenity said.

"Well, yes. On the show." Mrs. Marciano arched a brow. "If you're *that* practical, you should be more worried about the man lurking outside."

"Where is he?" When Serenity turned back toward the front door, the older woman reached out to stop her.

"Are you crazy? Don't go out there now. You'd be opening up your life to a whole boatload of trouble."

"I really don't think you have to worry. I'm sure it's Mr. Herndon's cat or a dog chasing a rabbit into the bushes or something. This is a very safe, quiet neighborhood."

"Well," she huffed, "if you call tall and dark with lots of muscles safe, well, okay then."

Serenity's brows rose. *Tall, dark and handsome?* "Dark?"

"That's what I said. It's dark, you know?"

"What's dark? The night or the man?" Serenity shook her head at this inane conversation.

"His hair." Mrs. Marciano pointed to her head and rolled her eyes. "Dark. Wavy, I think."

"What was he wearing?" Okay, that sounded a little strange. Mrs. Marciano might think she was as much a pervert as the man outside. If that's what it—*he*—was.

She snorted. "Why does *that* matter? Can't really tell you except I think it might have been black on top and jeans." The crinkles in the corners of her neighbor's eyes deepened. "Do you know this pervert?"

"I think I just might. What did the…what exactly did he do?" She almost slipped and called him a pervert. Serenity hid her grin.

"He kept walking up and down the sidewalk out front. Then he'd stop and stare at your house. I'm not afraid of some Sneaking Thomas, and thought if I came over and made a racket, he might leave. You think we should call the sheriff?"

"No, I don't think that's necessary." Stalking to the front door, Serenity flung it wide and stomped outside on the front walkway in her bare feet. "Jackson!" she hissed. Something stirred in the bushes to the right of the front door and she jumped.

Moving behind her in the doorway, Mrs. Marciano put a hand on her arm. "You okay?" They both startled as another neighbor's cat scampered out from beneath the bushes and across the sidewalk.

"Well, at least it's not black," the older woman said under her breath.

Serenity looked up to see Jackson walking toward her with a sheepish expression, as well he should, at this ridiculous hour. Crossing her arms, she eyed him with a sleepy smirk.

"I forgot to give you something earlier tonight." Jackson nodded to Mrs. Marciano with a grin. "Evening, Mrs. Marciano."

"Young man, doctor or not, fancy car or not, unless you just got off a plane from somewhere, it's going on one o'clock in the morning. What kind of fool are you to be hanging around a single lady's house at this hour?" She planted both feet apart, fingers gripping the skillet with both hands like a baseball bat at-the-ready, a menacing expression creasing her face.

Jackson's mouth twisted with his effort not to grin. He held up both hands in surrender. "I assure you, I come in peace and mean you ladies no harm. Serenity, why don't you tell this lovely woman where we went earlier today."

"Delighted." Serenity graced Mrs. Marciano with her sweetest smile. "Dr. Ross escorted me to Faire Kingdom today."

"Did he now?" The skillet lowered and she stared at Jackson. "Son, that place is for kids." She eyed him up and down. "You ain't been a kid for a while now."

Serenity bit her lip not to laugh and darted a quick glance at Jackson. "My dad used to take me there. I haven't been in years and Jackson thought it would be fun. It was." She gave him a wink, and it was worth it for the smile that lit his face. Tiny shivers ran through her.

"Only the best for Princess Serenity."

Mrs. Marciano snorted again. "Princess Serenity," she harrumphed. "Sounds like a fancy cat name to me." She waved her hand. "You kids today are silly. Next thing I know you'll be telling me you wore a crown or something crazy. Serenity, you want me to stay with you tonight?" She tossed a chastising glance at Jackson. "You never know what kind of pervert might be lurking around."

"I think I'll be safe enough, but I sincerely appreciate your concern for me." She gave her neighbor a warm hug. "You're a dear to come over here and check on me, especially at this time of the morning. Jackson's a good friend and will protect me if there's any real danger."

Mrs. Marciano swatted Jackson's arm as she moved past him, her expression a combination of wariness and bemused curiosity. "I know what goes on with you young people nowadays," she said, wagging a finger in Jackson's face. "Miss Serenity's a good girl, Doc. You treat her right or you'll be seeing the bigger end of this skillet up close and personal. And that's no idle threat." She held up the skillet for emphasis.

"I'm a man of honor, and I'll be good. Promise." Jackson's warm smile and the sincerity of his words appeared to thaw Mrs. Marciano. "Let me walk you back home."

Mrs. Marciano paused on the grass and inclined her head. "Okay, then. Get a move on. Don't dawdle. And they say *old* people are slow." She crooked her elbow, waiting. Serenity smiled as Jackson took her arm and they headed across the lawn.

Closing her front door, she wasn't sure what to do. She suspected Jackson would return. But, he hadn't wanted to come inside earlier in the evening, when it was still a respectable hour. Darting into her bedroom, she pulled on her shorts and her favorite pink tee. After running a brush through her hair, she returned to the living room.

Hesitating for a few seconds, she opened the door and stepped outside. She'd sit on the top step and wait for her prince to return.

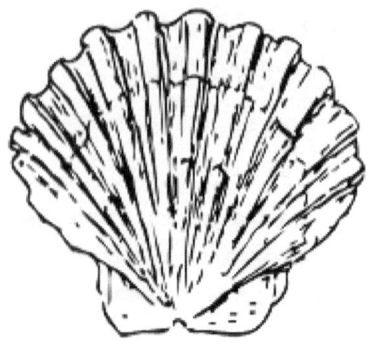

~CHAPTER 37~

"*M*rs. Marciano thinks you're a pervert." Serenity watched as Jackson settled beside her.

"Correction. She *did*, but I've managed to get back in her good graces."

Conscious of the way her shorts had ridden up on her thighs, Serenity tugged down the hem on both legs.

"Too late. You can't cover up the best view in town."

Her cheeks flooded with heat. "Do you make it a habit of hanging around a single woman's home uninvited in the wee hours of the morning?" She shook her head. "Wait a minute. That came out totally wrong. I retract the question."

Jackson's smile was enough to chase all coherent thoughts from her brain. "Only your house."

"You still haven't told me why you're here," she said. "I believe you said you forgot something earlier?" She suspected he meant a good night kiss.

Stretching out his legs, Jackson avoided her gaze. An inner voice whispered she wasn't going to get a straight answer. At least not right away. She knew him well enough to know he was leading up to something. What, she had no idea.

"If you thought I'd invite you inside—"

"This isn't anything like that." He sounded almost brusque.

"Okay." She shook her head. "Forgive me, but men don't usually show up on a woman's doorstep at this hour unless they're looking for...companionship."

He shifted his gaze back to hers. "You know me better than that."

"I know. You wouldn't even come inside earlier tonight."

"Yeah, sorry for the timing."

"Not that I'm not thrilled to see you, but couldn't you have called?"

"This is something I wanted to discuss face-to-face and I decided it couldn't wait. One of the main reasons I wanted to meet you on the beach was to tell you I got the report from Kyle."

Serenity inhaled a quick, sharp breath. "He found her? Is it bad?"

"No." His lips curved. "Unless you consider living in New York a bad thing."

"Manhattan?"

"Long Island. As of two years ago."

"Oh." A sudden coldness swept over her, making her shiver.

"May I?" When Jackson opened his arms, she snuggled in the curve of his warmth, resting her head on his shoulder.

"I used to wonder what would happen if she ever came back," she said. "Would she act the same? Would she be sad or happy? Heavier, thinner, blonder, darker or the same?"

"She looks a lot like you, right? Or the other way around?"

"Yes, like in that photo you like so much," she murmured. "Basically the same but with a few more lines around the eyes and a few pounds heavier."

"Your dad would be pretty happy if she came back, don't you think?"

"He would. Very much so. Even if she'd run away with another man—I'm not saying she did, but anything's possible—Dad would forgive her. But in my heart, I know there's no way she'd ever do that. They were soulmates, as much as any two people I've ever met." She pulled back to look at him. "Except for Charlie and Marcella."

Jackson absently stroked his fingers along her arm, up and down. She doubted he was even aware of what he was doing. "I met up with Clinton at McHenry's the other day and we talked."

"Oh, that's right," she said, "you've become best buds." That came out more sarcastic than she intended. "Sorry. I warned you I inherited some of my dad's cynicism."

"I really like your dad," Jackson said. "Beneath his crustiness is as soft a heart as I've ever known."

"I know." Her eyes misted. "Bet you didn't expect that, huh?" She shrugged. "You're good for him."

"We're good for each other, I think," Jackson said. "He dropped another clue, although I don't think on purpose. He said something about your mother being ecstatic when the little girl kidnapped from the slumber party in Georgia was found safe in Florida. The one where her best friend's father took her. You might remember the case. It was all over the news last week. He mentioned how Elise was always broken up when a child was kidnapped."

Serenity shook her head, confused. "I remember a case in California where that happened, but it was a long time ago and had a tragic ending. I don't remember a recent case in Florida. It's not like I've been glued to the news lately, though, since it's mostly bad."

"Let me see if I can remember something else about that case to jog your memory."

"It doesn't matter. I believe you," she said. "So, according to my Dad, my mother reacted to a news story about a little girl who was abducted but found alive in the last week?"

"Exactly. I honestly don't think he realized what he'd said."

Her frown deepened. "I don't know what to think." Curling her arms around her legs, Serenity leaned her chin on her propped knees. "Maybe he wasn't thinking and let it slip. Or, like we said before, it could be he's trying to drop little hints here and there, hoping we'll pick up on it and question him."

"Has he ever told you an outright, bald-faced lie?"

"No, at least not to my knowledge. Offhand comments or throwing questions back in my face is his preferred method of avoidance."

"I think he's either afraid to tell you, Serenity, or else he can't for some reason."

A slight breeze stirred the Tuscarora Crape tree. "Care to hazard any guesses?"

"From what you've told me about your mom, she was—is—a good woman and loved her family and her life here in Croisette Shores. I keep puzzling over what could have happened that would drive her away from you and your dad. From what you've told me, she wouldn't have left because she was consumed by grief over everything that happened. She wouldn't have abandoned you or your dad willingly."

"Right," she said. "That's why I wasn't buying into Dad's reasoning when he said she couldn't take the sadness. She wouldn't have left because of that. If anything, she would have stayed to help me." Tears stung her eyes.

"You get your strength from her, Serenity. The only conclusion that makes any sense is that either someone forcibly made her leave against her will or she did it in order to protect herself or to protect you and Clinton in some way."

She darted a sharp glance at him. "What makes you say that?"

"A feeling, I guess. I can't really explain it otherwise."

"Your instincts are very good," she said, her voice quiet. "I'm sure that helps in your work."

"I know something else," Jackson said, shifting and taking both her hands in his. "You're Clinton's world. He shared some memories with me about what you were like as a baby, then a little girl, a rebellious teenager and"—he tapped her chin—"as the gracious and lovely woman you've become."

Those words hit home and she blinked hard. "I wasn't that rebellious, but I'm not sure I'm his world. At one time, that might have been true, but not so much anymore."

"Tell me what kind of father kept a calendar in his desk drawer while his daughter lived in Atlanta, and marked off the days since he'd last seen her? Marked the days until he'd see her again when she came home? Kept every letter, postcard, birthday card and Father's Day card she'd ever made or sent to him? Told the nurses in the hospital about his beautiful daughter and how successful she is? If that's not a father who absolutely adores his daughter, I don't know what love is."

"How do you know all this?"

"I saw the calendar. Clinton had it out on the kitchen table during one of our visits, along with the stack of cards you'd given him through the years. He keeps them all in a big, wooden treasure box." Jackson chuckled. "I teased him and called it his pirate loot, and he made some comment about how it was his treasure. Come with me, please." Rising to his feet, Jackson reached for her hand. "We can't very well do what I have in mind if we're sitting on the steps."

"That's a provocative statement if ever I've heard one." Hesitating only a moment, Serenity placed her hand in his. Her heart soared when he wrapped his fingers around hers. "You're keeping me from my beauty sleep, you know, so you'd better get to it. This kind of behavior is getting to be a habit with you. Are you taking me to the beach?"

"A walk in the moonlight sounds incredible, but sorry. Not this time." With a strong tug on her hand, Jackson pulled her down on the grass beside him. Stretching out on his back, he settled himself on the lush grass and crossed his arms beneath his head. "Look up."

Mirroring him, Serenity moved her gaze to the night sky where dozens of stars winked at them. "They're so beautiful," she breathed. "I didn't think too much about God growing up, but how can anything like this be in the universe without being made by the Master Creator? It's so far beyond our comprehension, isn't it?" She felt Jackson's eyes on her. "You're not looking at the stars."

"Oh, I'm looking at one, and she shines brighter than she knows."

Her laugh was shaky. "I'm a disheveled mess, silly. Got anything better than that?"

Jackson reached for her hand, caressing the side with his thumb. His fingers were warm as he traced the lines on her palm. "A lover holds her hand like a precious jewel. A lover craves the presence of his love, wants to be near her, listens to what she says, hears what she's *not* saying. A lover hears with his big, silly ears," he said with a small grin, "but opens his heart wide open ... for *her*."

She giggled. "Where'd you get that?"

"Didn't like it?" He appeared slightly wounded.

"Actually, it's rather sweet. Not exactly profound, but very touching."

"In that case, it came from me. Straight from here." He thumped his fist against his chest.

Tears welled in her eyes and she turned her head.

"I think until you have some closure about your mother, you won't be fully free to love."

"Is that your professional opinion?" She lifted her chin to the sky as a light breeze caressed her cheeks.

"That, too."

Something inside her quickened at his tender sentiment. *Let him wait for me, Father, if that's Your will.* Biting her lower lip, Serenity willed herself to stay strong. This man was getting too close, too deep into her soul. Removing her hand from his, she closed her eyes and forced several deep breaths. "Jackson, you deserve more. You shouldn't wait around for me, hoping I'll eventually come around."

"Serenity." The mere whisper of her name held compassion beyond any she'd ever known. When had she let this man get into her bloodstream, into her heart? Jackson moved his loving gaze from her hairline, to her forehead, her cheeks and then slid down to her mouth. As one tear slipped out, then another, Jackson absorbed each one with his lips. He moved his arms around her, drawing her close. Here she was secure and safe from the world. Burrowing her head against his chest, she loved the way she felt when he held her. Loved *him*. He held her that way for a long time, so long the first rays of dawn peeked over the horizon. They didn't speak, but something between them changed. It wasn't just Jackson holding her. They were holding *each other*.

"Jackson, thank you for waiting," she said as he walked her to the front door.

He smoothed her hair away from her face with his big, gentle fingers. "Tonight you met me halfway, Serenity, and that's a significant *gift*."

"I—"

He moved two fingers over her lips, stilling them. "I know." Patting his fist over his heart, he kissed her forehead.

She watched as he walked back down the front walkway. Pausing at the end of the sidewalk, he motioned for her to go inside. Closing the door behind her, turning the lock so he'd hear, Serenity stood beside the front window until he was out of sight.

After tonight, Jackson Ross would never be far from her heart.

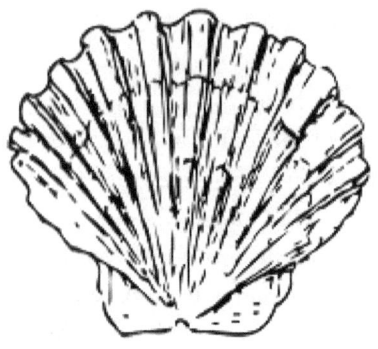

~CHAPTER 38~

*D*riving to Croisette Shores Cemetery a few hours later on Saturday morning, Jackson chewed on his lower lip, something he rarely did. If he hadn't needed a couple of hours of sleep, he would have driven this same road at the crack of dawn. He needed to see if there was really a headstone for Liam's grave. Not that it would really tell him anything new.

He'd never been to the small cemetery on the edge of town—and never had a reason—he knew it wasn't far. Spotting a sign for the cemetery, he turned at the next intersection, resisting the urge to floor the accelerator. Another sign told him it was a half mile down on the left. As he turned inside the well-kept entrance, Jackson wondered if Serenity ever came here. Would it comfort her or bring her more grief? He'd never understood the need of others to visit a gravesite, although he knew it gave a lot of people—his parents included—a kind of comfort. In a way, it was paying respect to a loved one who'd passed on. Perhaps it was one of those things he'd understand more as he grew older.

Driving as far as he could along the narrow, winding gravel road, Jackson slowed the car, looking left and right, searching for a headstone appropriate for a child. Weren't they usually a white or light gray stone marked by a lamb or some kind of kid-friendly symbol? Spying one with a teddy bear, he stopped the car and hopped out. Walking closer, he saw it was a grave for a six-year-old girl who'd died nearly twenty years ago. Fresh flowers were planted at the foot of the headstone and it was immaculately kept. After twenty years. With a quick glance, he noted all the graves were neat and well-maintained, making it difficult to determine which ones might be more recent.

Lord, show me the way.

He paced up and down the rows. Pausing in his quest long enough to stop and read the occasional headstone, he spied one about three hundred yards away. Made from white marble, it was small and simple with an etched starfish.

Creeping closer, Jackson's heart pounded, and his pulse accelerated. Even before he read the name, he had the suspicion this was the one he sought. He stopped and knelt down in front of it, wincing as he did so. A toy car, a small truck and a set of plastic building blocks sat in front of it. Jackson ran his fingers over the inscription, holding his breath.

Liam Justin Kincaid. Beloved infant son.

The verse on the headstone was well-known and beloved from the Book of Matthew. He spoke the words of scripture aloud, "*But Jesus said, 'Let the children alone, and do not hinder them from coming to Me; for the kingdom of Heaven belongs to such as these.'*"

Jackson bowed his head for a quick prayer, even though he suspected this particular grave was empty.

Next he'd visit the library. What was the name of the librarian Jillian at the Vital Records Office mentioned? Myra? No, whatever the name was, it rhymed with a name in the title of one of the Dr. Seuss books in his office, *Yertle the Turtle*. Myrtle! That was it.

Ten minutes later, he pulled the car to a stop in front of the library, driven by a deeply personal mission to confirm his suspicions. A few people walked the streets, and he waved and exchanged a few words with a couple of people as he headed up the stone stairs and pushed through the front door. He nodded to the librarian behind the counter at the reference desk. When she asked if he needed help, he paused.

"Is Myrtle in, by any chance?"

A broad grin creased her face. "You're looking at her. How can I help you?"

"Jillian in Vital Records gave me your name. I need to look up something in the archives of the *Croisette Shores Daily News*. It's probably on microfilm."

"From what date?" the middle-aged, dark-haired woman asked with a friendly smile.

"Five years ago."

She nodded. "That should be easy enough. Come with me, young man, and I'll get you all set up. Are you new to the area?"

"I'm Jackson Ross."

"Oh, the new psychologist who's working with Doc Rasmussen?"

"The same."

"Nice to meet you." She directed him to a desk, turned on the machine and gave him a quick tutorial. "If you have any trouble, let me know. I need to do some reshelving, but I'll check on you in a bit to see if you need anything."

"Thanks, Myrtle. Much obliged."

"Don't mention it. I hope you find what you're looking for, Dr. Ross."

"Me, too," he mumbled under his breath. Within ten minutes, Jackson had his answers. A birth notice was printed in the paper shortly after Liam's birth, but no death notice was ever recorded. He searched thoroughly under every variation of the name he could think of under both the names *Kincaid* and *McClaren* and cross-referenced everything. He checked three months before and three months following Liam's supposed "death."

Wait a minute. Serenity recognized Dr. Saunders as the name of the doctor who'd signed Liam's death certificate. Was it possible he was somehow in on whatever Elise's scheme had been, if that's what it was? *Think.* When Serenity pulled out Liam's baby things from the box at her house, she had his hat, receiving blanket, birth certificate and the tiny wrist band. He didn't recall seeing a death certificate. What had happened to it? She might keep it in a place where she wouldn't see it often. If she did, he couldn't blame her. Those other items represented Liam's precious and all-too-brief *life*, but a death certificate? It'd bring all the sadness and heartache rushing back, and she wouldn't want the reminder.

With a wave of thanks to the librarian, Jackson departed and took the front steps two at a time on his way back to the car. Why would there be a record of Liam's birth but not his death? While it was entirely possible it got lost in the shuffle, he didn't think so. If the family didn't make sure it was done, wouldn't the coroner or the funeral home send the death notice to the local paper? Even a child who'd died would have an obituary.

As he climbed back in his car, Jackson knew one thing: either Liam's death notice was purposely omitted from being published in the local newspaper.

Or Liam never died.

*S*tanding with a grocery basket over one arm, Jackson eyed the selection of fresh-baked breads at McHenry's Market mid-afternoon.

"You're in love with her, aren't you?"

Jackson turned around slowly, not recognizing the female voice. He tried to keep the shock from his expression. With a bright floral scarf tied over her head and big sunglasses, it was *her*. Carmen.

"Excuse me?"

"Serenity McClaren. You're in love with her."

Not sure how to react, he extended one hand. "Jackson Ross. Before I admit to loving someone, I like to know to whom I'm speaking." He kept his tone light. If he barraged her with all the questions in his mind, she'd run away faster than a jackrabbit. He needed answers, and she'd approached him. Mentally willing his heart to slow down, he swallowed a quick breath. "Carmen?"

Her head dipped down for a moment. "I'm a friend. Leave it at that."

"Then we're in agreement. I'll admit to caring about her very much, too." Hopefully, that would satisfy her. He loved Serenity, yes, but he wasn't about to tell this woman. Who was she, really? Why did she want to know and what was her purpose in following Serenity?

He pretended to study the bread and picked up a loaf of rye. "She's coming for dinner tonight. Want to come?" He glanced over at her. Yet another woman who wouldn't remove her sunglasses.

She blew out a breath. "I'm not sure that would be such a good idea."

"Does David know?"

"Know what?"

"Well," he said, trying to contain his aggravation, "for starters, does he know you follow people around? I didn't know that's what retired flight attendants do, as a general rule."

Her cheeks colored. "How do you know I'm following your girlfriend?"

"Serenity's noticed you a few times."

A slight smile curled her ruby lips. "Don't think I didn't see you two in the library."

"This isn't about me."

"Even so, it's obvious Serenity's not immune to your charms, Dr. Ross."

This conversation was heading nowhere fast. "I repeat, does David know? Because, I have no qualms whatsoever in telling him. I'm sure he'd be interested." If she wanted to play hardball, he'd lob it right back at her full force.

Carmen visibly stiffened and squared her shoulders. "This has nothing to do with David."

"Are you being paid to watch Serenity? Who hired you?"

"Shh," she said, darting her head back and forth. "Keep your voice down. This town's small enough."

"Sure, I'll pipe down if you answer the question. Let me guess, Elise McClaren?"

He could tell that question touched a nerve. Opening her mouth to speak, she quickly closed it.

Jackson touched her forearm, relieved when she turned back toward him instead of bolting. "Serenity's coming to my house for dinner tonight. You're welcome to come. Better yet, bring Elise." He bit his tongue not to add she'd better have a good explanation why he shouldn't go to the police.

I guarantee you've never heard a story like ours. Those were the words used by "Mrs. Johnson." He couldn't wait to hear her story and it was long past due.

"Okay, listen." Carmen beckoned him closer. "Yes, she hired the agency I work for, but my job is only to keep an eye on Serenity. See where she goes, who she sees, that sort of thing."

"Why?"

"She has her reasons."

"And the boy?"

When Carmen didn't answer, Jackson shook his head. "I'd like to know how she can justify what she's put Serenity through the past five years. It's unconscionable."

"Elise is a good woman and she loves her daughter, Dr. Ross. She's taken excellent care of Justin. Surely you, of all people, know that." Her dark eyes bore into him. "Keep an open mind. Once you hear what happened, you might be more forgiving."

"I'd like the opportunity to find out so I can do that very thing, *if* it's warranted." Jackson lowered his basket to the floor. Reaching into his back pocket for his wallet, he looked up and found her gone. No big surprise there. His eyes opened wider as he spied a loaf of bread in his basket. Sourdough. He hadn't picked it up, so Carmen must have added it at some point. Was it random or intentional? Well, it'd complement the rest of the planned meal—and the seal on the wrapper wasn't broken—so why not? Gathering the last of the ingredients he'd need for their dinner, Jackson walked toward the checkout lane, lost in thought. This whole situation was driving him crazy, and he needed to try and find a way to bring it to light. Going about it in a way that didn't compromise his ethics was the tough thing, but he had to do it.

He'd figure out something. For Serenity.

*H*eading out of McHenry's, Jackson spied Carmen on the sidewalk the next block over, talking to a man. A man in a suit. Not many wore suits in Croisette Shores, especially on Saturday. Putting two and two together, this must be the same guy who'd come into Serenity's office and looked at the photo of Elise on the wall. Now he was speaking with Carmen.

After opening the trunk of his car, Jackson lowered the bags of groceries inside. They might spoil, but he needed to follow these two and see where they went next.

Carmen said something to the man and took off as Jackson closed the trunk and walked across the street. The man might have been alerted to his presence by Carmen, and he was smooth. Shoving his hands in his slacks, he strode down the street in the direction of the hardware store, whistling a jazzy tune.

When the man pushed open the door of Harry Maine's Hardware, Jackson followed a few feet behind. Blast that bell on the front door that jingled when he stepped inside, announcing his arrival. Why did shop owners insist on those? His footsteps sounded equally loud on the old wooden floor. A few other customers shopped in the store. Seeing one of the deacons from the church, Jackson skirted around another aisle, hoping to avoid him. Normally, he'd be glad to stop and chat—he'd be the one to initiate the conversation—but not today.

Glancing around the store, he spotted the man in the fishing aisle. Headed that way, Jackson feigned interest in a rack of tackle and assorted supplies, attuned to Mr. Suit's every movement. Darting a glance Jackson's way, the other man moved his arms across his broad chest, feet planted slightly apart, but he didn't budge otherwise.

Feeling bold, Jackson sauntered—the only word for it—and positioned himself next to him. "So, which one do you recommend?"

"Depends on what you're looking to catch." The words were tinged with a touch of humor. That was unexpected but a weird relief at the same time.

"I'm, uh, new at fishing, but I'm hoping to hook a pretty big one."

The man chuckled under his breath. "Yeah? How many pounds?"

"A hundred and ten, give or take. Any suggestions?"

"That's too big a challenge for a beginner without the proper equipment. I'd suggest you start out with something a little less...complicated." When Mr. Suit's gaze fell on him, Jackson held his brown-eyed stare steady. "Something less dangerous. After all, you don't want to get pulled into the water, in over your head, now do you?"

"I'll take my chances. I've known how to swim since I was a baby." Jackson didn't bat a lash although his palms grew moist and his jaws flinched.

"Good. Watch out for shark-infested waters, and you should be okay."

Interesting exchange. It didn't sound like a threat so much as sound, practical advice. *What's going on here?* Jackson committed it to memory, something to puzzle over later. The man shoved his hands in his pockets and walked away, whistling again. It wasn't like he could follow and badger the man with questions. Or could he? His groceries were already wilting in the trunk of the car, necessitating a return trip to McHenry's, so why not?

Starting back toward the front of the store, Jackson pretended he didn't hear his name called. No time. After exiting the store, he rounded the corner, but Mr. Suit was nowhere in sight.

"Stay out of it, buddy." The man's low growl reverberated in his ear as he strong-armed and half-hauled him away from the sidewalk, toward the bushes lining the nearby park.

Wrestling his arm free, Jackson pulled back, prepared to strike. The man caught his forearm mid-air. "I wouldn't advise it. You'd only be hurting yourself." His grip was like a steel trap. Where'd this guy train? He must spend most of his waking hours in the gym.

"Fine," Jackson managed between clenched teeth. "Tell me who you are and what you're doing in Croisette Shores."

"It might help you to know it's about protection, pure and simple. You can trust me that I'm not going to hurt anyone, you included, if you calm down and don't make a scene."

For some reason, Jackson believed him. This guy could have knocked him out cold, sprawled him flat on the sidewalk. Or worse. Tomorrow he'd feel muscles he didn't know he had since his stint in the Army.

"I'm going to release my hold now, and you're going to behave. We'll have ourselves a nice, calm conversation," the man said. "Got it?"

"Got it." At least Mr. Suit seemed willing to talk. When he released his arm, Jackson rubbed the sore spot where the man's nails dug into his flesh. "So, talk already."

"Relax, buddy. Your girlfriend's involved, but she doesn't know it."

"What's that mean? Speak English, *buddy*. Is she in danger? Tell me that much."

The man shook his head. "From what I can tell, no. For her sake, I hope not."

Jackson crossed his arms and stared him down. "And that's supposed to make me feel better? You must suspect she might be in some kind of danger or else you wouldn't be hanging around town, going into her office and staring at a photo on the wall. What does this have to do with Elise McClaren?"

The man narrowed his brown eyes, and the creases surrounding his eyes deepened. "You've used up your quota of questions. Look, I'm not a threat, but a word of advice?" His voice lowered. "Keep her close."

"Until when?"

"You'll know."

Jackson watched Mr. Suit walk away and tried to shake the pervading sense of foreboding. Suddenly, he felt very, very cold.

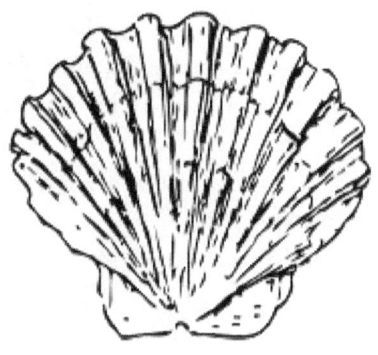

~CHAPTER 39~

*A*fter pulling his car in the driveway at the McClaren home, Jackson cut the engine and bowed his head. *Lord, help me in what I'm about to do. You know my motives are pure and I'm only trying to help the woman I love. If Serenity's in danger, I need to know so I can help her. Use me as Your servant. Let her look to You, too, and draw her close.*

"It's confrontation time," Jackson muttered, climbing out of the car and clicking the key fob to lock the doors.

Clinton answered his knock a minute later. Swinging the door wide, he smiled. "Hey, Doc. Always nice to see you. Come on in." The older man's smile faded as Jackson pushed past him into the house.

"This isn't a social call, Clinton." Jackson's gaze fell on a book on the sofa. A thriller. Stalking toward it, he grabbed it and held it up. "Are you reading this book?"

The older man's face paled. "What's going on? Has something happened? Is Serenity okay?"

Jackson dropped the book on the sofa. "Why do I find that question ironic? Tell me what's happening. The truth."

"About what, exactly?" Clinton licked his lips and avoided his gaze.

Stepping closer, Jackson waited until he had his eye contact. "Start with admitting your wife's alive and right here in Croisette Shores. With a boy who might possibly be Serenity's son. He's the age Liam would be now, and the kicker? Justin's the spitting image of Daniel Kincaid right down to the hair, the eyes and the dimples." Lowering his head, Jackson fought for control. Part of him wanted to tackle Clinton and wrestle him to the floor and demand answers. Considering the man had a recent medical procedure, acting on his impetuous instincts wouldn't be advisable.

"You'd better come into the family room so we can sit and talk about it."

"No, I'm fine right here," Jackson said. "Go ahead and sit down if you need to. Do you need some water or something?"

Clinton shook his head and dropped down on the sofa. "In answer to your first question, I'm not reading this book."

"Is Elise here in the house now?"

"Yes. She is."

Jackson snapped up his gaze to where Elise stood in the doorway. When she lifted her head, her eyes softened as they met his. Serenity's beautiful blue eyes were the mirror image of her mother's. Intense and intelligent. *Breathtaking*. He might have guessed her secret long before if he'd been permitted a glimpse of those eyes. Now he understood why she always wore sunglasses in their sessions.

"Does Serenity know?" Elise walked further into the living room. She appeared fragile and brittle as though she'd snap if he touched her arm. Her voice was every bit as thin.

Jackson shook his head. "Not yet, no. She's aware she's being watched, although she can't imagine why. Or by whom." Jackson swallowed and his throat tightened. "Justin is Serenity's son? Liam?"

Tears welled in her eyes. "Yes."

This was one of the few moments in his life when he didn't know how to react, how to feel. While ecstatic, he was full of questions. "Where's Justin now?"

"With a friend," she said, seating herself beside Clinton and taking his hand.

"Let me guess. Carmen?"

Elise nodded. "All I ask is that you allow me to tell Serenity in my own way and in my own time." She darted a quick glance at Clinton. "My husband knows I've been to see you, so you're not breaching any professional ethics by admitting I've come to you with my grandson in a professional capacity, Dr.

Ross."

Jackson considered his options. "I can't agree to wait much longer," he said, his glance encompassing them both. "You know I can't tell Serenity because of professional ethics, but if you don't tell her, I'll come up with something. Mark my words."

"Now, just wait a doggone minute," Clinton said. "You're not threatening us are you, son?"

Jackson heaved a sigh. "No, of course not. I'm just...frustrated." He met Elise's gaze and held it. "As you know, I have a vested interest."

"Because you love her."

"She's my friend, and yes, I love her. Very much." It was the first time he'd admitted it out loud. But this was Serenity's mother and father. In spite of history, in spite of what Elise might or might not have done, she'd returned to Croisette Shores, and brought Serenity the best gift she'd ever receive. *Two* gifts, really.

"Better start at the beginning, Elise," Clinton said.

Elise inhaled a deep breath. Jackson watched as she scooted closer and Clinton moved his arm around her.

"Danny was a good boy, but he wasn't particularly bright," Elise said. "With a baby on the way, he wanted to give Serenity and his child more stability. He worked at a convenience store in town that's since closed down. I don't know how, but he got himself involved with some guys that were no good and started running drugs. Started out small and, when he proved himself trustworthy, he got more involved in an operation that ran up and down the east coast."

Finally dropping into an armchair across from the sofa, Jackson rubbed his hand over his chin. Serenity suspected her husband's death had been anything but random, and her instincts had proven correct. "Why doesn't Serenity know this?"

Elise glanced at Clinton as though for reassurance. "Because she was pregnant and distraught enough over Danny's murder. I—we—were concerned for her health, and for the baby, and wanted to protect her. To this day, no one in town knows what really happened."

Jackson shook his head. "I mean, how did she not know her husband was traveling? Wasn't he gone overnight?"

"Only a couple of times that we know of," Clinton said. "Danny told her he'd gone fishing with some of his buddies. He mainly drove from Croisette Shores to locations nearby and met up with others."

"Serenity said his murder was unsolved, a random act of violence," Jackson said. "She also said she'd always thought there was more to it."

"Danny got into the big leagues with an organized crime family. When he got greedy and made some stupid demands and double-crossed them, they killed him with one shot to the head at pointblank range. The poor boy didn't even have a chance." A tear slipped down Elise's face and she swiped it away.

Jackson's heart raced with such an unexpected and shocking revelation. The newspaper reports hadn't mentioned Danny was murdered execution-style. Of course, there could be any number of reasons for that—not wanting to alarm the townspeople, incomplete evidence or else someone managed to pay the newspaper handsomely to leave it out. Leaning forward, hands on his thighs, Jackson stared at Elise, his mind swirling with questions. "How do you know all this?"

A deep frown creased Elise's brow. "The night of Liam's birth, I'd been on duty at the hospital and had just changed into my street clothes. Clinton was meeting me there and hadn't arrived yet. The service elevator wasn't working. I used the main elevators, something I rarely did even when I was off-duty. Two men—dressed in suits and out-of-place with their New York accents—were in that elevator. I overheard one of them say Danny's name and mumble something derogatory and then laugh. Since Danny was already dead, I wondered what they were talking about. Maybe I've seen too many crime dramas, but they looked, acted and sounded suspicious, so I followed them into the cafeteria. They talked about tying up loose ends and making the 'hit' like it was nothing." Another tear escaped, and this time Clinton wiped it away for her.

Nerves clenched Jackson's stomach but he had to hear it all. As unbelievable as it seemed, he knew Elise told the truth.

"Apparently, they thought Danny told Serenity everything and couldn't take a chance she'd go to the authorities, but they wanted to wait until the baby was born so they could make it complete and eliminate Danny's immediate family."

"What happened?" Hardly breathing, Jackson sat up straighter, waiting.

Elise heaved a huge sigh. "I got in the cafeteria line behind them. One of the men said something about 'the old man' having emphysema and how his private duty nurse was gone." Her eyes met Jackson's. "I don't even want to think about what *that* meant. Then they made some disgusting joke about grabbing one of the nurses in the hospital and taking her back to Long Island with them. They probably *would* have kidnapped one of them. I didn't have to think about what I did next. I sat down at a nearby table, pulled out my cell phone and engaged in a fake telephone conversation, making sure I spoke loud enough for them to hear. I played my part well with a sob story about not getting the job at the hospital and how I needed something soon or I wouldn't be able to pay my mortgage."

"Thinking they'd take you since they knew you were a nurse, at least from your conversation, I'm assuming?" When she nodded, Jackson frowned. "Wouldn't they check you out, know your relationship to Serenity?"

Elise lowered her head before raising it again. "Long story short, they didn't come after Serenity because I made a deal. Not quite like selling my soul to the devil, but not far from it. In exchange for paying off Danny's debt, and in exchange for keeping my family safe, I offered my nursing expertise for the family patriarch."

"So," Jackson said slowly, "you worked for the crime boss? What about Liam? How'd you convince—" His heart pounded in his chest.

Elise's eyes sparked and her jaw tensed. "I lied out of both sides of my mouth and betrayed everyone I knew and loved most. I risked everything and told them I'd go back to New York with them and take care of the old man. They could have still killed me, Clinton, Serenity and Liam without blinking an eye, but I had to try. I was desperate. I'd have done anything. For whatever reason, they bought my story and agreed to it. I planned an elaborate scheme and told the hospital staff that my grandson died shortly after birth, but I waited long enough so Serenity could hold him and nurse him."

She lowered her head. "I'm not sure that was the wisest decision, but I wanted her to bond with him, even if only for a few moments. I'd worked at the hospital a long time and got away with my plan because they trusted me. I also played the grieving part well and told them I needed to take care of the arrangements for Liam myself. All the lies and knowing I was taking her son away from Serenity broke my heart all over again."

Running a hand over her head, Elise appeared distraught. "I convinced them Serenity was mentally unstable and no threat. Honestly? I'm not sure

Serenity *would* have been in any condition to properly care for Liam."

Slumping back against the chair, Jackson stared at her. "Go on. Please."

Elise raised her chin and squared her shoulders in the same way he'd seen Serenity do many times, making his pulse race faster. "For whatever reason, Mr. Gam—" she stopped—"my patient believed me and seemed to appreciate my honesty, ironic as that sounds considering his position. Faced with the same situation, I'd do it all over again. God can condemn me for it, but I did what I had to do to keep my family safe."

"You lived in Long Island with the old man? In his home?" Jackson could feel his anger slowly ebbing. Elise was right. He'd never heard a story like this outside of some fictional drama. In another way, he could understand it happening in spite of the sadness and tragedy. Carmen was right, too. Now that he'd heard the reasoning behind Elise's actions, he could forgive her for what she'd done. Her motives were pure in order to protect her loved ones.

The corners of Elise's mouth tugged downward in tandem with her slender, almost bony shoulders. "This all sounds crazy, I know. I'm not fabricating some wild story in order to cover my actions, Dr. Ross. It's real because I breathed it, agonized over it, ate it, slept it, *lived* it for nearly five years. Why else would I kidnap my own grandchild and put him at risk? Why would I torture my already grieving daughter?"

Elise wrung her hands. Jumping to her feet, she began to pace. "I didn't know what else to do. The body count in my family was already at one, and I couldn't risk it going any higher. Liam was this beautiful baby boy, so tiny and innocent. He shouldn't have to pay for the sins of his father." Her cheeks wet, Elise brushed the back of her hand over them. "I loved Danny, too, but he couldn't see how he was putting his family at risk. The irony? That poor, misguided boy thought he was doing a good thing for them, making a better life. I'd have given my own life in exchange for Liam or Serenity's, and don't think I didn't offer." Her eyes met his. "Whatever it took. I'd have done anything."

"I'm not judging you, Elise," Jackson said. "It's okay if I call you that?"

The welcome hint of a smile surfaced on Elise's face, relaxing her features. "It's preferable to some other names you might want to call me right now."

"I can see where Serenity gets her strength." He glanced at Clinton. "No offense intended, sir. She also got a lot of great qualities from you."

Clinton grunted. "None taken. Always appreciated your diplomacy, son. I freely admit I'm thankful my girl got more of her mama than me."

Jackson focused on Elise as she sat beside Clinton again. "How'd you get away?"

"The old man died a couple of months ago, and my contract, so to speak, was released. That was our deal. I'd paid off Danny's debt. I have it in writing no harm will come to Liam, Serenity, me or Clinton. Not that a piece of paper means much." She looked away and swallowed. "In five years, I saw a lot of people come and go. I stayed quiet, out of the way and never asked questions. I didn't say much, and I focused on taking care of the old man and keeping Liam safe. The entire time, I kept thinking about the day I'd reunite Serenity with her son, and that's what kept me going. Once she gets over the initial shock, I hope she'll accept what I did, even if she doesn't understand."

"You've done a wonderful job with him. He's a great kid, and probably one of the more well-adjusted patients I've ever seen in my practice." He met Elise's bright gaze. "Especially now that I know the truth."

"I documented every milestone in his life for Serenity—every birthday, his first steps, first words, all of it, some on video and I took tons of pictures. They went through every one of them to make sure I didn't have photographs of anyone in the family. But they let me keep them. I can't give Serenity those years she missed with her son, but it's the best I can do, given the circumstances."

Jackson nodded. "Thank you. Those will be precious for her." He paused a moment. "I had an interesting rendezvous this afternoon with a man in a suit at the hardware store," Jackson said, directing the question to Elise. "He's the same man who showed up at Inner Serenity one afternoon and stared at your photo. Who is he?"

"He's hired by...the family." There was no mistaking her meaning. This whole thing made him feel like he was in another dimension. "He's making sure everything's in place and no one followed me here."

"Who else would follow you?"

"You ask a lot of questions, Dr. Ross."

"Call me a pest. Answer me, please."

Elise's lips upturned. "Does Serenity know you're bossy?"

"Yes, and I like to think she adores me for it. Trust me," Jackson said, allowing a small smile of his own, "she keeps me sharp. Your daughter is incredibly intelligent and intuitive."

"And I'm sure she adores *you*, too," Elise said. Clinton put his arm around her shoulders. Drawing her close, he kissed her cheek.

Jackson waited as Elise appeared to gather her thoughts. "You must understand there's always a rival family watching, ready to pounce. The way I look at it, it's only by the grace of God that I was allowed to keep Liam and come back home again. Respect for their elders is revered and the wishes of the family patriarch is paramount. In his own way, the old man protected me. And his son is doing that for me now. For that, I am—and will always be—eternally grateful."

Jackson rubbed his hand over his face. "He reciprocated your loyalty. So, how long is Mr. Suit going to be hanging around town? I have to say, he makes me nervous." He already knew he'd be icing his arm when he got home.

"He'll be gone in a couple more days. Then we're on our own."

"And Carmen?"

"She works for a private surveillance agency. Even though I had the old man's word no harm would come to us, I had to make sure I wasn't followed and that no one was in danger. Carmen was hired to keep an eye on Serenity, Clinton and...you, too, Jackson."

That was news, but not much could surprise him after what he'd just heard. "Any idea how or when you'll tell Serenity?"

"That's what we're trying to figure out," Elise said. "I first came to see you because you were the new psychologist in town. Then when I saw Arnie on your bookshelf, I knew you were important to Serenity. My daughter wouldn't give Arnie to anyone who expressed an interest in him. That little giraffe is priceless to me and she knew it."

"She's an amazing woman...and so are you," Jackson said. An hour ago, he couldn't have guessed he'd be sitting with her now and saying these things. But it was the truth.

"Thank you." Elise lowered her head. "My poor baby. What she must have gone through."

"You've suffered every bit as much," Clinton said, his voice quiet.

"Yes, you have," Jackson said. Clinton shot him a grateful glance. "It might take her a while to recover from the shock of it all, but in time, I'm sure Serenity will understand. Does Justin know his real first name is Liam?"

Elise shook her head. "No. It's his middle name, and I've called him that to minimize complications. He knows his last name is Kincaid, and he only learned in the last few weeks that my last name *isn't* Johnson."

Jackson moved his gaze to Clinton. "If I may ask, sir, how long have you known?"

"Only a week," Elise answered for her husband. "I got a letter in the mail this week from the son of...my patient, and he's now the new head of the family. He thanked me for services rendered and again assured me I was released from any further obligations to the family. Said I'd meant a lot to the old man and earned his trust. Knowing whom they can trust and family loyalty means everything to them."

A tear escaped from the corner of her eye. "I found great solace in reading a Bible I'd taken with me to New York. I was never much of a 'God' person, but somehow I knew I might need it." Wiping away another tear, Elise managed a small smile. "I was raised in the church, but I'd turned away from it. Funny how those things I'd learned as a child came back to me. In a way, it was like I was in a prison, and I took comfort in reading the letters written by Paul when he was imprisoned. Even tortured and chained, he found joy and peace in the midst of unspeakable pain. There's a verse in Second Corinthians that says, *When I am weak, then I am strong*, and that hit home for me. In my weakness, my faith in the Lord kept me going. He sustains."

When Elise hesitated, Clinton brushed away her tears with the pad of his thumb. Jackson shifted in the chair, feeling like he was an intruder in their private moment.

"I knew God had a plan in what happened," Elise continued. "I even tried to share with my patient one day, but he wouldn't listen. Said he was too far gone in this life. I told him no one was beyond redemption and insisted it was never too late. He listened to what I told him, though, but only God Himself knows a man's soul." Lifting her shoulders, she shot a helpless glance his way.

Rising from his chair, Jackson walked across the room. When he looked at Clinton, he nodded, as if sensing what he was about to do. Pulling Elise to her feet, Jackson kissed her cheek and drew her into a hug. "Thank you for coming home again. Thank you for giving Serenity her life back even though she doesn't know it yet."

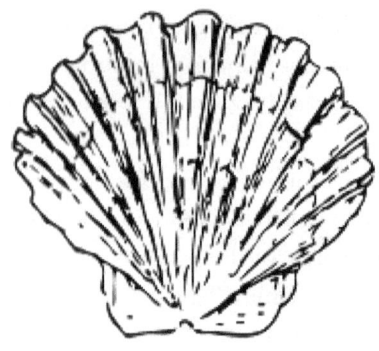

~CHAPTER 40~

*J*ackson smiled as he opened the door to the cottage. "You came."

Serenity's soft laugh enchanted him all over again. Sexy and sweet. Great way to start the evening. On the other hand, he was probably in big trouble.

"No, I'm a figment of your overactive imagination. I enjoyed a nice brisk walk, so I've worked up an appetite."

"Come in."

"Don't mind if I do." She shoved a bottle of something cold in his hands and walked across the threshold. "Put me to work." She seemed happy and more animated than he'd ever seen her. He glanced at the label on the bottle. Sparkling grape juice.

He watched as she marched straight into his kitchen, all that long blonde hair swinging and bouncing with a life all its own. In her blue jeans and simple white top, this woman did things to his heart rate that were unprecedented. Standing rooted to the floor like an idiot, one hand still on the front door, he stared at her. Consciously closing his open mouth, he pushed the front door closed and followed her into the kitchen.

Above all, he needed to try and relax so she wouldn't suspect anything was wrong. Not give anything away to make her suspect her life was about to change in a completely unexpected and shocking way. Now that he knew the truth, he wanted to get it out in the open so they could move past it and get on with their lives. He wanted Serenity beside him as his wife, and the sooner the better.

His mind went back to what Elise said earlier in the afternoon. Although nothing like her circumstances and what she'd endured, he was stuck between the freedom of telling Serenity the truth and the prison of upholding his sworn duty to his patient. Not an enviable position, to be sure. God would have to see it through because he sure didn't know how it'd play out. If he stopped to think about it, he'd groan. On the one hand, the heaviness in his heart had lifted. On the other, a sense of foreboding threatened to overwhelm him.

You haven't even told her you love her yet. He'd need to remedy that soon, too, although she had to know. They'd pretty much said it in every way except with actual words. But he couldn't tell her. Not yet. First, she needed to know about Elise and Liam. Then he needed to give her time to absorb the truth. Then hope and pray she wouldn't harbor feelings of resentment or betrayal against him. If that happened, he'd die a slow death. But he'd wait it out. Serenity was worth fighting for, worth waiting for. No matter how long it took.

Lord, be with us.

Serenity watched as he put the bottle on the table. "That's the next best thing to alcohol. It's fizzy and goes up your nose. Always makes me sneeze." Her smile lit up his house, his world. "But it's really good."

"That it is. Thanks," he said, turning around to go check on the food. "I trust you like linguini." His mind sprinted in a hundred different directions, all fighting for precedence.

"Mmm, I love linguini. Smells wonderful."

Someone was definitely in a flirty, playful mood. When Serenity moved away, she left behind a wonderful scent. Normally he didn't like perfume on a woman, but this was something light, fun and entirely Serenity. It lingered in the air, and he suspected it would linger in his mind a whole lot longer. She could have no idea of the emotions coursing through him like a tidal wave.

"Is there a salad in the fridge? Need me to chop or dice anything?"

For whatever reason, her question struck him as amusing, but he managed to keep a straight face. "Second shelf. There's homemade ranch dressing in the blue container beside it. Croutons are in the pantry." He angled his head toward the side wall.

A minute later, she stood by the counter and tossed the mixed green salad. "Do you have something to put the dressing in? Not that I'm fancy. We can leave it in the container."

"Nothing but the best." Wiping his hands on the dish towel, he walked around the corner to the small hutch and pulled out a crystal pitcher. "Here, this should do the trick." When he handed it to her, their fingers touched, shooting awareness of her through every inch of his body.

Taking it from him, Serenity gave him a curious look. "Thanks. Are you okay? You seem...I don't know, sort of bothered."

This is why he could never earn a dime from acting. He stunk at it.

"I'm hoping you like my cooking." Not a total lie.

She smiled. "I don't think you have to worry about that. It's a very romantic thing to do."

He almost groaned with those words. They'd eat and then he'd take her away from the cottage. Take a walk on the beach with Freud. Drive somewhere.

Perhaps it wasn't the smartest idea to have her in the cottage for dinner, especially after what he'd learned earlier in the day. Not that he'd had any idea when he'd issued the invitation. The better option might have been to change their plans and take her to a public place. The intimacy of being alone with her appealed to him on many levels and spending time with Serenity was top priority. But his common sense should prevail over his need for privacy. Faire Kingdom had been safe enough since it was loud with lots of people around. When he'd sat beside her in her bedroom, he'd almost lost his composure when she talked about Liam and opened that box with his baby things. And that was *before* he knew the story.

She peeked at the bread wrapper on the counter. "Sourdough. How'd you know it's my favorite?"

His pulse increased. "Maybe I had a little help." She'd probably assume from her dad.

"And what sauce have you prepared for us tonight, Chef Ross?"

"Clam with white wine." Good. She didn't seem to pick up on anything amiss. "All the flavor but not enough to get us drunk."

"Right. Drinking might make us lose our inhibitions. We couldn't have that." When she lowered her lids, the look she gave him was nothing short of alluring.

Was she testing him? *Father, I could be so weak with this woman. Help me be strong.* He stilled the spoon in the sauce. What he felt for Serenity was so much more than physical desire, although there was certainly that element to their relationship. He needed to concentrate on anything other than how beautiful she was, how tempting her eyes, her lips, her *everything.*

He cleared his throat. "You don't have to worry about me in that way." The Lord knew it took all his fortitude to say those words.

Her blue eyes widened, drinking him in. "A bottle of cheap wine was all it took when I was younger."

"I'm not Danny."

"Trust me, I know that. I don't expect you to be Danny. I want—"

"Shh," he said, putting two fingers over her lips. Best if he didn't hear the rest of that sentence with his defenses already lowered. He put the spoon on the counter and gathered his thoughts. Taking Serenity by the hand, he led her away from the stove and to the middle of the room. "You are an incredibly beautiful woman, and guys are...well, guys. Most of them are going to try and push the limit, at least a little. I suspect Spencer what's-his-name tried something." Maybe he *was* fishing with that one.

"He did, but I wasn't taking the bait," she said. "Not when I'd already found the best."

He almost staggered. With those words, she'd blessed him. The unasked question flickered in her eyes. It wasn't a challenge, but he sensed her deep need to know his answer.

Jackson's gaze melded into hers. "Being completely honest here? If I hadn't become a Christian, I wouldn't want to end this evening tonight." He couldn't say what he wanted to say without touching her, right or wrong. Closing the distance between them, he slid his hands around her small waist. She came willingly and rested her hands on his arms. The touch of her fingers on his skin was warm.

"It'd carry over into the morning...down the hall," he said, not surprised by the huskiness in his own voice. "If that's what *you* wanted, because sure as anything, guaranteed it's what I'd want." He heard the slight hitch in her breath, saw her lips part. "But," he said, relishing the look in her eyes, "*because* I'm a Christian, and a man of honor and have all the respect in the world for you, sweet Serenity, I won't tempt either one of us." Touching her hair, he smiled. "And you are, without a doubt, the most tempting woman I've ever known."

"Thank you for respecting me enough," she whispered. "You are truly a prince among men."

"It's also about respecting yourself," he said. "You've beaten yourself up over getting pregnant when you were young. You think you're not worthy in some way."

Easing out of his arms, Serenity's cheeks grew flushed and she lowered her gaze. "I never said that."

"You didn't have to." Cupping her cheeks between his hands, he raised her face, caressing her. "You did nothing wrong other than give your heart to a man who squandered that love. Nothing you did caused any of those other things that happened and in no way was it God's punishment."

As he suspected, she withdrew again, leaving him bereft. "I was thinking that very thing last night. The Lord's working on me, but I've got a lot to learn." She crossed her arms over her middle and turned in the opposite direction. "I think you know me as well as I know myself, Jackson. As comforting as that can be, it's also a very scary thing."

Lord, I can't stay away from her now. Moving behind her, Jackson brought his arms around her. "That's what happens when you care about someone, baby. You want to understand them so you can help them resolve or get over whatever makes them sad." He turned her around again, relieved when she didn't fight. "You deserve happiness. You deserve love."

When Serenity finally met his eyes, he saw the tears glistening as one tear coursed its way down her cheek. "I'm not sure I deserve *you*, and I hate to say this, but I think your sauce is burning."

As he walked her to her door, Jackson thought over the events of the evening. She'd been quiet through dinner, but it was a comfortable silence, just as it was now. She'd devoured two pieces of the sourdough bread and a full plate of the linguini, claiming it was the best she'd ever eaten. Even though it was only cooking a meal, he wanted to please her and bring that gorgeous smile to her beautiful face.

More importantly, he'd managed to crack through her armor. She'd been through so much and, as he'd told Elise, accepting the truth might take some time. How long would depend on Serenity. Some people might never get over what had happened to her, but she'd proven she was stronger than most. He suspected she didn't know how strong she was.

He'd seen the power of prayer work in the lives of a number of his patients and their families, and that's what he'd do for Serenity. It was the *best* thing he could do. That, and love her—from the sidelines, if that's what she wanted. He'd cover them all—Serenity, Elise, Justin, Clinton—in a blanket of prayer. *Lord, help me be her friend even if she doesn't want me to be once she finds out the truth.*

She reached for his hand. Raising it to his lips, Jackson planted a soft kiss on her open palm and felt her pulse escalate. That pleased him, too. The slight breeze sifted through her long hair, tousling it. A couple walking down the street with their dog waved and called out greetings.

Serenity's long lashes fluttered on her cheeks, and it started his heart pumping harder. It really didn't take much.

"Surely you can do better than that." With one finger, she traced the side of his face. Oh, the things she did to him without even trying.

Jackson pulled her close, so close he felt the contours of her body. Not the best idea. Stepping back an inch without making it seem like he was rejecting her—far from it—he kissed her. He kept it purposely soft, quick and sweet but couldn't seem to disengage from it. Although he didn't deepen it the way he wanted, it was unlike any kiss he'd ever experienced. For his sanity, he couldn't give into the overwhelming passion he felt for her.

I love you more than you know, Serenity. It was on the tip of his tongue to say the words. He felt pretty sure she'd reciprocate. *Be patient. It's not the time.* Leaning his head on hers, he held her tight before releasing her.

"Save me a spot on your pew for the service tomorrow?" he asked from the walkway.

She nodded with a sweet smile. "I'll be there."

No doubt about it. For the first time in his life, he was completely in love, in every part of him—mind, body and soul.

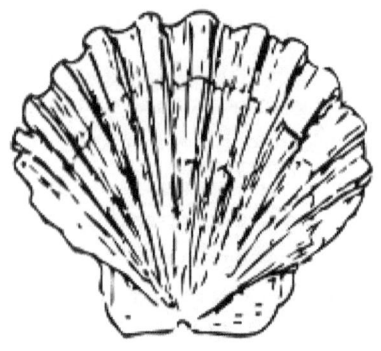

~CHAPTER 41~

When Serenity stepped inside the front foyer of the church the next morning, she barely had time to get her bearings before Maya barreled into her, throwing her arms around her legs and hugging her tight. "Serenity! You came for Sunday school!"

"Don't run the pretty lady over, Maya," Charlie said with a chuckle, pulling her into a warm hug. "Good to have you join us."

"What a nice welcome," Serenity said. "Good morning."

Maya tugged on her hand. "Dr. Ross is teaching my class. You've gotta come!"

Serenity raised a brow and glanced at Charlie. That was a surprise. She wondered why Jackson hadn't said anything. "I thought I'd sit in with the ladies' class, if there is one."

Charlie gave her a curious smile. "I'm a greeter this morning. Do you mind taking Maya downstairs to her classroom?"

"Not at all. It'll be my honor."

Maya slipped her small hand in hers and pointed to the back of the choir loft. "We go through the door up there and then down some steps." The little girl tugged on her hand when they reached the bottom of the stairs and led Serenity past a number of classrooms. Several ladies waved and a couple of the men nodded as they walked down a long hallway.

"Here it is." Maya dropped her hand and skipped inside a bright, colorful classroom.

Following her, Serenity stopped short. Familiar brown eyes met hers and the corners crinkled, prompting her heart to do a silly little flip flop.

"The pretty single ladies meet upstairs, Miss McClaren."

"Thanks. Guess I'll go find it," she said, pivoting on her heel. Jackson moved beside her in an instant, taking her by the shoulders and turning her around to face him.

"Not on your life. I'm thrilled you're here. Stay." Like Maya before him, Jackson took her hand and led her to the back of the room where a woman pulled crayons and papers from a cabinet. "This is Karyn," he said, releasing her hand. "Her twins, Trevor and Traci, are in this class. Karyn, this is my friend, Serenity."

The red-haired woman pushed bangs away from her eyes and gave her a weary smile. "Nice to meet you. That's a really cool name you have."

"Thanks. Can I help you do anything?" Serenity watched as Jackson moved back over to the circle of chairs and greeted more children.

"Everything's under control for now," Karyn said. "If you want, you can help get the snack together after the lesson. For now, sit and listen. Jackson gives a really good lesson and the kids all love him." She stifled a yawn. "I'm sorry. Don't mind me. My youngest is teething and I was up and down with her last night. We're both cranky this morning."

"Okay, it's time to start our lesson," Jackson said, motioning for the kids to join him in the circle.

"I'm going to rest over here at the table." Karen laughed. "If you see me dozing off or if I start to snore, give me a little nudge."

The children scrambled into chairs. "Come sit by me," Maya said, patting the chair next to her with a big smile.

Serenity sat down, praying the kid-size chair would hold her. "I feel like Goldilocks trying to squeeze into Baby Bear's chair."

"Hold on a sec," Jackson said, retrieving a bigger chair and bringing it to her. Murmuring her thanks, she took her seat. Jackson picked up his Bible from a table and sat across the circle from her in another "adult size" chair. Serenity hid her smile when two girls scooted their chairs closer to him and gave him adoring grins. Glancing around the circle, she counted thirteen children.

"We have a very special guest with us today," Jackson said after the kids settled in their chairs and most of the chatter subsided. "This is Serenity McClaren."

"What kind of name is Serenity?" That from one of the girls next to Jackson.

"It's a *be-au-ti-ful* name," Maya said, bobbing her head.

"Serenity means calm and peaceful," Jackson said. "The word 'serene' means the same thing. If you met a queen, you'd bow or curtsy and address her as 'Your serene royal Highness.' It's a title of honor and respect, and that's how Jesus wants us to treat everyone. Why don't we go around the circle and everyone tell Serenity your name? I'll start. I'm Jackson Ross, and I'm your substitute teacher today while Mrs. Cooke is in Virginia helping take care of her new grandbaby. Trevor and Traci's mom, Mrs. Raeborn, is our helper today." Karyn waved from the nearby table. As they went around the circle telling her their names, Serenity hoped she'd remember them all.

"If you have your Bibles, open them to the Book of Exodus," Jackson said, giving them the chapter and verse.

"Here, I'll share with you," a girl named Emilee said, placing her Bible on Serenity's lap.

Glancing down and seeing it opened to the passage, Serenity felt her cheeks burn. Why hadn't she remembered to bring her Bible? Her breath caught when Emilee rested her curly head against her arm, looking up at her with trusting dark eyes.

"Maya, why don't you read for us?" Jackson asked. Serenity suspected most of the children either knew how to read or could at least follow along. Emilee ran her finger across the page as Maya read. Jackson helped out a couple of times when Maya stumbled over a few names, but she did an impressive job.

"Great job reading. Now, what's this story about?" Jackson said.

"Moses!" Erik said.

"It's about Miriam, too," Traci said, seeking out Karyn for her approval.

"You're both right," Jackson said. Serenity watched as he managed to draw all the kids into the discussion. When Maya suggested they act out the story of Miriam placing her baby brother, Moses, in the bulrushes, Jackson agreed. "Great idea."

Maya ran over to the small play area and dug around in the toy box, tugging out a small basket. Pulling out a baby doll, she placed it inside the basket, and accepted the blanket Amber offered.

"Hey, that's a boy baby. No fair, Maya. You can't put a pink blanket on him!" Trevor jumped up, grabbed the blanket and tossed it aside. Snatching the blanket from the floor, Amber glared at him.

Serenity suppressed her grin and Karyn shook her head. Jackson asked the children to proceed with their playacting. A few minutes later, he finished the lesson with some final questions. "Why do you think Miriam did what she did?"

"She wanted to keep Moses safe," Trevor said.

"That's right," Jackson said. "And why do you think she wanted to keep him safe?"

"Because she was his sister and she loved him," another little girl—the one she thought was Nikki—said.

"Exactly." Jackson nodded. "When you love someone, you want them to be happy. My brother caught a baseball once signed by my favorite White Sox player. Chad gave it to me because he knew I'd treasure it more than he ever would. Moms and dads, brothers and sisters, grandmas and grandpas, they all do nice things for us, too."

"Gram took me to the American Girl store in New York," Amber said. "She took Molly to the doll hospital because her eye sort of lost its color."

When Jackson shot her a *Help me!* look, Serenity nodded. "I've heard about that doll hospital." She tried not to show her surprise when even the boys strained forward, listening. "When Molly came back home, was she wearing a hospital gown?"

Amber beamed and nodded with enthusiasm. "She had a balloon, and her eye's all better now. They even fixed her braids since my little brother messed them up."

All the children took that as their cue to speak up at the same time, their voices raised in excitement.

"I helped my mom make cookies even though I hate cooking. It's for silly girls," a boy named Ian said. He scowled when Maya and Amber protested.

"I gave our dog a bath last night. Does that count?" Trevor asked. Traci rolled her eyes and punched his arm. When he yelped like a wounded animal, Karyn moved in to corral the kids, silencing them with a stern look.

Emilee's comment was swallowed by more animated chatter all around the circle.

Jackson raised his hand and the room quieted in seconds. "That's better. Emilee wants to say something and we all need to listen." He nodded at the shy girl. "Your turn. Go ahead."

Emilee twisted her hands in her lap and looked at Maya. It tugged at Serenity's heart when Maya gave Emilee an almost imperceptible nod. "My grandpa doesn't remember so good anymore, and my grandma is always with him. She feeds him, takes him to the doctor, reads to him and works puzzles with him." She shrugged. "Stuff like that."

"Emilee, your grandmother does what Miriam did for Moses, too." Jackson made sure he had their attention before continuing. "Soldiers fight for our country so we can be free." His eyes met hers briefly. "Teachers help us learn. Doctors keep us healthy. Firefighters and policemen keep us safe. And, most importantly, boys and girls, Jesus loved us enough to give His *life* for us. I want you to think of something you've done because you love someone. Now, think of someone who's done something for *you*. It can be anybody, it can be anything. Close your eyes," he said. "Time to thank Jesus for giving that special person to you, and thank Him for loving us enough."

"Thank You, Jesus, for loving us enough," the children said in unison. Jackson must have taught them this before, but their chorus of young voices—so earnest and sweet—was incredibly precious. Serenity glanced around the circle as the youngsters bowed their heads and listened to Jackson's prayer. Such a sweet, trusting faith they shared.

"You okay?" Jackson worked beside her a few minutes later, pouring juice while she measured Goldfish crackers into plastic cups.

"Fine, but incredibly humbled." Continuing her task, she avoided eye contact. "These kids have such an amazing purity of spirit. I wish..."

"What do you wish?" Jackson's voice was gentle as he worked beside her.

"Liam was very close in age to Maya. He'd be in this class." Serenity blinked back tears and met Jackson's gaze. "I like to think I would have brought him here." She sniffled when he brushed a wisp of hair away from her cheek, his fingertips lingering. "How I wish he could be here."

"Me, too," Jackson whispered.

"We need to tell Serenity as soon as possible." After arranging to meet Clinton for Sunday brunch after the church service, Jackson kept his voice low as they talked. Serenity had excused herself and gone to the ladies room. "Should we enlist Charlie or Deidre?" He stopped at the expression on the older man's face. "Do they already know?"

"Charlie doesn't know yet, but I think you're right where he's concerned. Elise called Deidre yesterday and told her everything," Clinton said. "She's having lunch at their house today."

"I'd love to be a fly on the wall during that conversation."

"Me too, son." Clinton chuckled. "Knowing Deidre, she'll go off and do a little ranting, but she'll get over it quickly. Then the ladies will cry and hug, cry and hug some more, and then they'll probably start making plans to get everyone together for a cookout."

Jackson smiled. "I can see that happening. But Serenity's intimated that Deidre can't keep a secret. Are you sure that's wise? All the more reason to tell Serenity now, I should think."

Clinton nodded. "Elise and I are discussing the best way to handle it. For both Justin and Serenity."

"Seems to me you tell Serenity first and then arrange a meeting," Jackson said. "After all, Justin's already met you and understands he's meeting his mother here in Croisette Shores. He's had a little time to prepare mentally and emotionally. Serenity obviously hasn't had that advantage."

Every day, Clinton appeared healthier with better color and improved spirits. Of course, having Elise back must have a whole lot to do with his more optimistic outlook and attitude. Surely Serenity had noticed it, too. All the more reason to stop stalling. If they didn't tell her in the next few days, Jackson had the uneasy feeling she'd find out in another way—how, he hadn't a clue—and the ramifications could devastate her all over again. That was his primary concern.

"Got any suggestions for the best way to tell her?" Clinton asked. "Your professional opinion, Doc."

"I'll try to pave the way as best I can. I taught Maya's Sunday school class this morning and Serenity came to help. We talked about Moses and his sister Miriam."

"I don't follow. Never been much of a man for the Bible."

"An Egyptian Pharaoh ordered all the male babies born to Hebrew women killed. Miriam saved her baby brother, Moses, by putting him in a basket and hiding him on the banks of the Nile. Pharaoh's daughter found him and adopted him but Miriam went to her and arranged for their mother to be her own son's nurse."

"Clever." Clinton grunted and wagged a finger. "I see what you're doing. In a way, that's what Elise did for Liam. Protecting him from the powerful man who ordered him killed."

Jackson sat back in his chair. "Like I said, I'm trying to pave the way in my own subtle method. The kids had a ball acting it out." A grin tipped his lips. "Next time, I told them we'll act out Daniel in the Lion's Den."

Clinton's smile sobered. "Yeah, I know a little something about that Bible story. God didn't protect *our* Daniel now, though, did He?" He drummed his fingers on the top of the table.

"No, unfortunately. I'm very sorry for your loss," Jackson said, briefly taking Clinton's hand and squeezing it. "No one should have to go through something like that. But, for what it's worth, I'm glad he married Serenity and was happy about the baby."

"Yeah, he was. He'd loved Serenity since they were kids, but he was a kid himself and wasn't ready to take on the adult responsibilities of a wife and child."

"Why did Serenity take her maiden name back?" He hadn't thought to ask it before.

"The scandal as much as anything," Clinton said. "After Danny and everything...well, I didn't know what would happen to Serenity. You know I'm not much of a praying man, Jackson, but I think a little of this God stuff might finally be rubbing off on me. I've seen a difference—a real good one—in both the women in my family since they've joined the Almighty's team, so to speak. Not to be irreverent and no offense."

"None taken, sir." Clinton's words brought him more satisfaction that he could know.

"They're strong women, but I guess you could say I never knew how much until the events here in Croisette Shores that sent them both running away from home." Clinton smirked. "When you think about it, a man's death sent Elise away but another man's death brought her back home again. You know, Jackson, I can only thank God for bringing my family back to me." His eyes misted as they focused on him again. "You've done a heap of good for my girl. She loves you and I know you love her. Once we're past all this craziness, I hope you plan on marrying her and giving me and Elise lots more grandkids. Justin wants a brother or sister. He told Elise, and I know Serenity never liked being an only child." Taking a sip of his water, he laughed. "No pressure, of course."

"That's my plan, sir.'"

"You've already got my blessing, son. Elise's, too. That day on the beach when we first shook hands? You said you were honored to meet me." Clinton narrowed his eyes. "By saying that, you honored my daughter and earned my respect all in one swoop." Raising his glass, he grinned. "All right. Enough of this mush. How are the plans coming along for the landscaping and the playground renovation?"

"Thanks to Serenity and Deidre, things are great." Earning Clinton's approval meant more than he could know. "They're planning a gala fundraiser and scheduled it at The Summer Palace for the early fall."

"Don't worry, son," Clinton said. "By then, everything will be more...settled. Mark my words."

"I hope you're right."

"What are you two discussing now?" Serenity dropped into the chair beside him.

"The playground renovation and gala."

Serenity smiled. "Did you warn Dad he'll need to wear a tux?"

"It's bad enough *I'll* need to wear one," Jackson said. When Clinton groaned, they all laughed.

"You'll both look very handsome and that sight alone will be worth all the effort." Serenity leaned her head on Jackson's shoulder and tucked her arm through his. He loved how she felt comfortable enough with him to share gestures of open affection as if they were the most natural thing in the world.

"And it'll be worth the effort to see you in a gorgeous, slinky evening gown," he told her, planting a quick kiss on Serenity's nose.

Clinton laughed and Serenity squeezed his hand. "I'll see what I can do."

At the end of the meal, Jackson picked up the check and Clinton insisted on leaving the tip. As they walked through the waiting area by the front doors, Art Masmer rushed over to them. "Clinton, how are you, buddy? Heard you had an overnight stay in the hospital."

"Hey, Art," Clinton said, taking the other man's hand. "I'm healing up, thanks. Think I'm gonna live. Almost good as new again."

Art winked at Serenity. "It's nice to see you again. And you must be Dr. Ross. I've heard a lot of real good things about you, Doc. Pleased to make your acquaintance. Haven't we met somewhere before?" He gave him a curious look.

"I was waiting to meet Serenity at Martha's when you spied her coming through the door."

"Well, right you are. Sure is nice to meet you officially, then."

"Likewise." Jackson gave him a warm smile and put a hand on the small of Serenity's back as they headed for the door. "If you'll excuse us. We'll meet you outside," he said to Clinton.

"I sure hope I can count on you to play in the Fourth of July band with us in Queen Victoria's Square," Art said to Clinton from behind them.

"Serenity's trying to convince me," Clinton said. "Gotta pull out the horn from storage. It's antique now and rusty beyond recognition."

Art laughed. "Nothing a little valve oil and cleaner can't cure."

Stepping outside into the overcast day, Jackson spied Charlie, leaning against his car. Something about his body language and expression alarmed him. Seeing them, Charlie strolled toward them with purpose. "Afternoon." He opened his arms for Serenity's hug and allowed a small but tight smile. "Is your father with you?"

"Art Masmer waylaid him," Serenity said. "He'll be out in a minute. Everything okay, Charlie?"

"Nothing to worry about, child, just something I need to discuss with Clinton."

"What's on your mind?" Clinton asked, catching up to them.

Charlie nodded to his friend. "A word, if you don't mind."

"Sure thing."

"In private," Charlie said, his voice firm.

Clinton nodded to them. "Thanks for lunch, Doc. Take care of my girl, will you?"

"You know it, sir." Jackson nodded to Charlie, but the man remained stoic.

"Wonder what that's all about," Serenity said as they walked down the street together.

"Oh, I'm sure time will tell."

A block from her house, Serenity stopped, disengaging her hand from Jackson's. "Mama?" Her knees felt like noodles as she wavered on the sidewalk, her breathing labored. The world was spinning.

Beside her, Jackson stopped. Thank goodness, he put his hands on her arms to hold her steady. Otherwise she might have slipped to the ground. "What is it, baby? Are you okay?"

She stood transfixed, staring at the woman, unable to move. Thinner than she'd ever seen her with shrunken shoulders. So gaunt it shocked her. Was she ill? Her hair was colored dark red and cut very short. "Mama," she said, the name escaping over her dry lips.

Elise smiled at the small boy standing beside her. Serenity watched, fascinated, unable to tear her eyes away, as he propelled himself against her, wrapping his arms around her mother's waist. This child trusted her. *Knew* her.

Serenity moved one hand over her mouth. Who *was* this little boy? He couldn't be any older than what, four? Five? Tears escaped from the corners of both eyes and dropped onto her cheeks. Elise turned then and stared straight at her. Her eyes rounded and her face drained of all color.

"No," Serenity whispered, taking a small step backward. "No, no, no, no no!" This scene before her made no sense, but this child obviously held an important place in her mother's life. Shared a place in her heart. Mothers loved their children this way. Was he also Elise's child? That wasn't something she'd ever considered in her wildest imagination. Mama told her she couldn't have more children. Had she adopted him?

Tilting her head, Serenity attempted to glimpse the boy's face, but his head was turned in the opposite direction.

"Serenity." Tears slipped down her mother's face and she didn't bother to wipe them away.

"What's wrong?" she heard the boy ask in a sweet little voice.

"It's okay, honey. Come on, it's time to meet someone very special."

Looking up at her mother, the boy lowered his gaze and then turned toward her. Dark eyes pierced hers. Wavy hair, high cheekbones, full lips set in a firm line. His lips upturned slightly and something akin to recognition flickered in his eyes.

"Is that her? Is it?" He pulled on her mother's hand as they advanced in her direction.

Oh, Lord, what's happening? Deep chills ran through her, and Serenity dropped her purse to the ground. "Danny," she murmured, over and over, putting her hands over her face. Maybe she *was* finally going crazy. This was too surreal, and the ground beneath her was spinning out-of-control.

In the recesses of her mind, Serenity heard Elise calling Jackson's name. *Mama knows Jackson? How is that possible?*

Slumping to the ground, Serenity surrendered to the darkness. It enveloped her and swallowed her whole. Sweet, blessed relief.

It was comfort, it was *peace.*

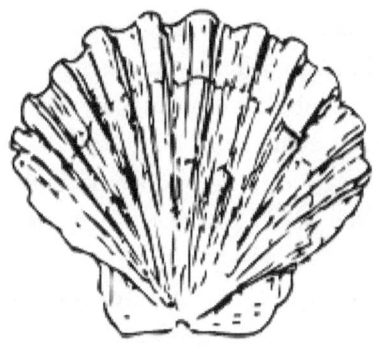

~CHAPTER 42~

*S*erenity's eyes fluttered open. The unmistakable smell of antiseptic flooded her nostrils, making her nauseous. The smell of death. A hospital. The last time she was a patient in this same hospital, she'd lost the most important part of her heart. Her baby boy.

The dark-haired nurse gave her an understanding yet dispassionate smile. They must get a lot of practice dosing out that particular brand of medicine.

"Your mother and boyfriend are outside. I'll tell them you're awake." Serenity glanced at the monitor and then to a thin tube attached to her wrist. Leaning back against the pillow, she opened her mouth to protest, wishing they'd leave her alone. All that came out was a low moan.

She must look like a frightening mess. Nothing made sense right now, but no matter her scattered emotions, she still wanted to look pretty for the man. What a disgruntling thought. How vain could she be?

Her mother came into the room and stood on one side of her hospital bed, Jackson on the other. "How are you feeling, honey?" Elise asked. When she reached her hand toward her as though to brush hair away from her forehead, Serenity shook her head.

"How do you expect me to feel?" she barked. Her gaze fell on Jackson. She could have two heads, an inverted nose and a misshapen mouth and this man would find a way to love her with his eyes. He took her hand in his. She couldn't do this. When she removed her hand, she glimpsed the pain flickering in his eyes. Although she hated it, she couldn't help the anger, the confusion.

"Serenity, do you remember what happened?" Jackson asked.

She moved her gaze to her mother. *Mama.* This was a much thinner version yet with more muscle definition, oddly enough. She took in the short hair dyed a deep red. Why had she done this to her beautiful blonde hair? Nothing made any sense.

"Depends. Are you talking about present day events or five years ago?" Her voice felt detached and she felt like she was floating. Reaching for the tube attached to her wrist, she started to yank it out of her arm. Jackson stopped her. Without saying a word, he kept his hand over hers until she finally relented and dropped her hand to her side.

Nodding to her mother, Jackson quietly took his leave. She watched him walk out the door. Although she wanted to call after him not to leave her, the words were again stuck somewhere inside her.

"You can start by telling me why I'm here. I don't want to be here."

"Jackson insisted on bringing you here for observation." Elise's eyes softened as they lingered on her face. "He was right."

"Ironic isn't it," she snorted. "The last time I was here, my baby died and you disappeared." Tears stung the back of her eyes. "You left me! You're my Mama, and you left me all alone!" The tears began in a steady stream down her cheeks.

"I know, and you have to know it broke my heart, Serenity. Try and hear me out. You have to know I had my reasons. I never would have left you willingly. *Never.*" She grabbed the tissue box from the table beside the hospital bed. Taking one out, she leaned closer and started to dab beneath her left eye.

"I'll do it myself," Serenity said, taking the tissue from her. "Start by telling me about the boy. Who is he? Did you run off with a lover and he's your love child?"

"You're my one and only child, my precious daughter," Elise said, keeping her voice low. "You fainted, honey. There's a reason for that."

"I'm not playing guessing games. Tell me the truth, Mama." Serenity frowned. "I'm not even sure I should call you that anymore. You more or less lost that right when you left us." She took a long, hard look at her mother's face. Like her father, her mother had aged more in the past five years than in the ten years before she'd left. Whatever happened had drained her emotionally and physically.

Her mother didn't speak for a long moment. Smoothing a wrinkle in the lightweight blanket, Elise sat on the end of the bed. "There's a lot you don't know about your husband. Things you *need* to know."

Swallowing the hard lump in her throat, Serenity looked into her mother's blue eyes. "What did Danny do?"

Elise blew out a long, extended breath, but she held her gaze. "He got mixed up with the wrong people. Bad people."

"I knew about his poker friends, Mama. And his drinking buddies. But he always came home at night. Danny was faithful to me. I wasn't sure I could trust him, but not in that way."

"I don't know how he met them, but Danny got mixed up with organized crime, Serenity. He started running drugs up and down the east coast."

Serenity struggled to sit up. Sliding off the bed, Elise moved forward, propping the pillows behind her back. "Danny was involved with the mob? The mafia or whatever?" She slumped back on the pillows. "This is crazy!"

"That's exactly what she's telling you."

Clinton walked into the room.

Serenity gasped. "Danny's dead. Why can't we let a poor dead man rest in peace? He's gone, so what good is there in denigrating his name now? Mama, what did you do?"

The words choked in her throat, and came out in a rasp. But Elise heard as evidenced by the pale mask that sheathed her face and the fear or anger that narrowed her eyes. The lines between her brows deepened and the set of her mouth hardened.

"I don't know why you're so convinced I did something wrong, as if I purposely set out to hurt my only child." Elise clenched her hands at her sides. Straightening her shoulders, she lifted her chin to meet her stare head-on.

"If you'd stuck around when I really needed you, you'd understand."

The hurt surfaced in her light eyes, and a tear coursed down Elise's face. "I had to leave, Serenity. Someday you'll understand. I didn't have a choice."

"That makes no sense!" This time it came out loud and clear. "You keep telling me you had no choice. Then tell me why. You abandoned me. Mothers who love their children don't do that, especially when they need them most.

Why?" She steeled herself against the tears threatening to gush in a geyser of anger and grief. "My husband was dead, my baby died, and then you took off, leaving me with a shell of a father who could barely make it through his own grief much less take care of me."

Raising her arms, Serenity let them fall to her sides, shaking her head.

"Serenity, I'm only going to tell you this once and beg you to believe me. If I meant anything to you in the first twenty years of your life, you need to cling to the fact that I loved you with everything in me."

When she stepped closer, Serenity waved her away. "Don't come near me, please. Just leave! It's what you do best." Crossing her arms over her chest, Serenity closed her lips, determined not to say anything. If she fell asleep again, would she wake up and find this was all a dream? Her mother would still be gone, but she'd be fine on her own. After all, she'd done it before, and she'd gotten pretty good at it. She couldn't—she wouldn't—go through the heartbreak of losing her all over again. Once in a lifetime was enough.

"We'll talk when you're in a better frame of mind. When you're ready to listen. You're still in shock."

Clinton patted her mother's arm. "I'm going to bring Jackson back in here. He'll know how to handle this."

"Handle *what?*" Serenity stared at her father. "I wish you'd stop treating me like a…a patient. Sure, I'm in a hospital bed, but because I fainted." Her eyes opened wider. "I fainted. What happened?" She was vaguely aware Clinton left the room. Good. If he brought Jackson, *he'd* be the voice of reason. He'd tell her the truth or whatever was going on here.

"The boy," Serenity whispered. Seeing Mama on the sidewalk with a young child earlier in the day came rushing back to her with surprising and shocking clarity. "I thought it was my baby." Closing her eyes, she squeezed them tight, as if it would block out the memories of the smooth, soft skin, the beating heart of her newborn son she'd briefly held in her arms in this very hospital five years ago. Yanked away from her arms and taken to places unknown. Her life became a blur at that point and by the time she'd regained any clarity, Liam was already buried in Croisette Shores Cemetery.

"Serenity, your mother left to protect you. And someone else." Jackson's deep voice soothed her. In the current storm of her life, he was her harbor. She opened her eyes to find Jackson standing beside her bed again. This time, she offered her hand to him.

"I don't get it. Will someone please get to the point and tell me what this mystery is all about? Is there some big secret you're all hiding? Would one of you please spit it out, and put us all out of our misery?" She released an exasperated sigh and stared from one to the other.

Mama glanced at her father, who looked at Jackson.

"Someone please tell me *now*." She felt like screaming. "*Please*."

"Honey, your son didn't die." Her mother's voice trembled and she took her hand. "In fact, he's very much alive. And right here in Croisette Shores."

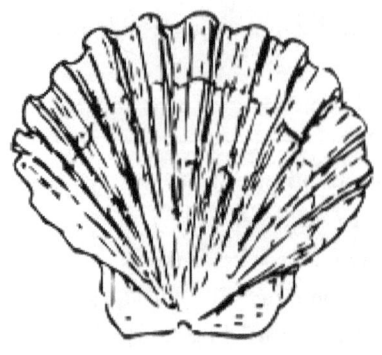

~CHAPTER 43~

"*D*idn't...didn't die...when?" Clamping a hand over her mouth, Serenity's tears spilled over her hand and onto the blanket. "What are you talking about?" Part of her wanted to cover her ears, bury under the warm cocoon and comfort of the covers, never to emerge again. But it wasn't her bed, only an impersonal hospital bed where hundreds of other patients had rested, even died. She released an anguished moan, and Elise started to push the button for the nurse.

Serenity clamped her free hand on Jackson. "I'm okay. Don't call." She forced a calm into her voice but couldn't quiet her thundering heart. "Tell me, Mama. What happened to my child?"

Elise rubbed her hands up and down both arms and darted a nervous glance at Jackson.

"Are you...are you telling me my little boy is *alive*? Liam!" Her voice broke on her sobs. Serenity reached for her mother and clung to Elise as she gathered her close. She rocked her, held her tight and kissed the top of her head. Their tears mingled.

Cradling Serenity's face between her hands, her mother looked into her eyes. "It's Liam, but I've called him by his middle name, Justin. The little boy you saw me with when you fainted. He's your son. He's alive and well, he's intelligent and handsome..."

"Stop!" Serenity pushed away, and saw the hurt in Elise's eyes. "Why are you telling me these lies? Haven't you done enough damage to our family? Why would you hurt me like this? You know," she sobbed, her shoulders heaving, her breath catching in her throat, "you know that child was my lifeline, all I had left of Danny."

Collapsing back against the pillows, sobbing, she buried her head in the pillow. She felt like she was losing the biggest part of herself all over again. She groaned. This was too much.

"She's not telling you lies, Serenity," Clinton said. "Justin is the boy you gave life, he's as much a part of you as Danny. You noticed the strong resemblance to your husband, and it's a fair bet that's why you fainted."

"Serenity."

As it had before, the whisper of her name from Jackson calmed her. "Listen to her. She'll explain."

More tears welled in her eyes and coursed a steady stream down both cheeks. "That's impossible," she gulped, swiping her hands across her face, small sobs escaping. "Liam died."

"Honey, listen to me," Elise said. "Did you ever see your baby again after they told you he died? Did you hold him, tell him goodbye? Touch his skin to know he was truly gone?"

Serenity cringed at her mother's words. "I asked, but they said I couldn't. Then I was out of it for so long. When I was finally coherent again, they told me they'd already...taken care of him." A shudder shook her, jarring her and she widened her eyes. "If what you say is true and my son's alive, who's buried in that little white coffin in Croisette Shores Cemetery?"

"It's empty. There's nothing but trapped air inside," Clinton said.

"Why would all the other nurses lie?" When Elise remained silent, Serenity looked over at her father. "Would one of you please answer me?"

When Elise nodded, Clinton cleared his throat. "Only a couple of them knew, but they felt threatened too. They lied to protect your mom, and you and Liam."

"And after all this time? They've allowed us to continue believing the lies? *Why?*"

"They hoped I'd come back home, but they had no idea of knowing when."

"If what you say is true," Serenity said, "what finally brought you home?" Her words were clipped, her mind a jumble of mixed, warring emotions.

"I paid off Danny's debt. In trying to make a better life for you and Liam, Danny double-crossed them. I was a private duty nurse for the patriarch of the family that killed your husband. Let me back up. The day you were in this hospital giving birth to Liam, I overheard two men talking. And..."—Elise's eyes filled with tears—"I offered my nursing services, but stipulated I'd bring Liam with me to keep watch over him. You weren't in any frame of mind to take care of him on your own. They could have killed any one of us—me, you, Clinton, Liam—at any point and not think twice about it. But I had to try to protect my family."

"So the old man died?" Serenity asked.

"Yes, and I was given permission to leave."

Clutching Jackson's arm, Serenity allowed him to pull her close. She leaned her head against his chest, holding on to him, hoping to derive strength from him. Stroking her hair, he murmured soft endearments, but she couldn't concentrate, couldn't focus. When she gulped, she swallowed air and burst into a coughing fit. Elise filled a cup of water and handed it to Jackson.

Once the coughing subsided, she lifted her head and stared at her mother. "Why did you take my baby, Mama? *Why?*" She shook her head when Jackson offered the water to her.

"Because the same people who killed Danny also threatened you and Liam." Her voice sounded stronger now.

"Why on earth would they threaten a newborn baby? That's inhumane. What kind of monsters..."

"They wanted to make sure all the loose ends—as they termed it—were covered. In their minds, people are disposable. They're nothing. These men have no feelings, no spines where most people are concerned. They don't have *souls.* They're paid to kill and then go get a steak dinner like they didn't just destroy someone's world."

Shaking her head, Serenity pushed away from Jackson and raked her hands through her hair, tangling it. "Let me get this straight. You ran away and took my baby because some organized crime goons killed Danny and you heard them make threats against me and Liam? And you lived in a house with the man who ordered my husband killed and took care of him? How could you *do* that? How?"

"Because I'm a nurse and that's what I'm trained to do. Tell me you wouldn't look in the eyes of a dying man and try to help him. He could have died in two weeks. I never knew he'd hang on for almost five years."

Serenity stared, her head pounding. "I'm supposed to believe this crazy story?"

Elise blew out a sigh. "If I hadn't run away, and taken Liam with me, most likely you *would* have lost your child. The saving grace is they didn't order you killed before you had your baby. Only the Lord knows why, but I thank Him every day for that mercy."

"She's right, Serenity," Jackson said. "Your mom saved his life. And, more likely than not, she saved *your* life, too."

"Where have you been all this time, Mama?"

"Long Island, New York." Elise's jaws flinched. "I did the only thing I knew to do, Serenity. At the time, I didn't think I had a choice. I still don't. Given the same circumstances, I'd do it all over again." She turned away, brushing her hands over her face. Her shoulders began to shake and, even though no sound came from her, Serenity could tell she was weeping. After a few moments of tortured silence, Elise raised her head. Turning toward her again, she threw back her narrow shoulders and dragged in a deep breath. Unable to speak, Serenity watched. Jackson still held her hand, and she continued to hold on tight, needing the anchor for her frazzled, confused emotions.

"Let me tell you something about your son, Serenity. He kept me *sane*. He got Danny's sense of daring and his dark hair, deep brown eyes and those adorable dimples. But Justin got his sensitivity, his intelligence and strength from his mother." Her shoulders slumped and she walked to the window and retrieved her purse, clutching it against her chest with both hands. "He's an incredible child, and he's capable of so much."

Serenity's heart pumped overtime, and she brushed away more tears. "Does he ask about me? Where does he think I've been? Did you tell him I'm…" She couldn't even say the words.

"I showed him your picture so he could see how pretty you are, and I told him I'd take him to meet you, but I didn't know when." Elise smiled through her tears. They ran down her cheeks, but she let them go. "He knows that's why we're in Croisette Shores now. He knows the old man died and that I no longer work for him. Justin actually calls you Princess Serenity sometimes, like your dad used to on the beach. I think there's a part of Justin that believes you really do live in a castle by the sea in some far-off, magical kingdom. I didn't have the heart to tell him otherwise. I promise you this. I kept your son as far away from everyone as possible. I homeschooled him and kept him practically attached to my hip. He even slept in a twin bed in the corner of my room. There wasn't one minute when he was out of my watch care."

Jackson kissed the top of her head and his arm moved around her shoulders, pulling her to him. Serenity placed one hand against his chest, feeling his strong, reassuring heartbeat pulsating against her palm. His hold on her tightened.

Elise wrapped her arms over her middle. "What I've told you goes no further than this room." She glanced at all of them in turn. "I don't care what anyone in this town thinks, but no one can know other than those of us in this room, Deidre and Charlie. Let them think the worst of me. I don't care."

"Those monsters held you captive for almost five years and we can't go to the authorities?" Serenity shook her head.

"Honey, you have your son back. For what it's worth, I have my daughter back," Elise said, her voice low, defeated. "At least, in time, I hope I will. Bitterness can tear us apart, or we can let grace flow over us. Let the God of everyday miracles help us to be a family again. Because," Elise said, stepping close and taking her hand, "that's my greatest prayer." Kissing her hand, she lowered it to the sheet.

Serenity raised her eyes to her mother's and knew it was true. "Jesus found *me* when I was in Atlanta." Her mother's expression was one of shared understanding. "You wrote the note, didn't you?"

Elise's eyes softened. "It came from me, yes, but I had someone else write it. I knew you'd been living in Atlanta most of the last five years. I was so proud of you for getting your degree."

"Degrees," Jackson said, the slightest hint of a smile curving his lips.

"I need to meet my son," Serenity said. If this story was true, she needed to see him, touch him, smell him, hold him, kiss him. Know he was real. Reconnect. If Justin knew about her and had been prepared to meet her, the sooner the better. That had to be her focus now and nothing else. *My son.*

She caught the looks between her mother and father before both turned to Jackson.

"Is it all right if I come along?" Jackson said. "We can arrange something for whenever you say. Your call."

"Tomorrow morning. Ten o'clock at the beach." She looked up at Jackson. "I'll show up this time. Promise, Doc Jack."

*U*nable to sleep, Serenity tossed and turned all night. Finally, she went into the living room, curled up on the sofa, read her Bible and prayed. Deidre had left her a lengthy message on her voice mail and she listened to it a couple of times. Hearing her best friend's voice made her smile. "Your mom came to see me and told me everything, but she swore me to secrecy. You know I'm rarely at a loss for words, but…wow. When you think about it, this is the best thing that could ever happen! I mean, your mom's alive and she's been taking care of Liam this entire time? That's nothing short of amazing, shocking, you name it. Can't think of enough adjectives to cover this one. And how everything played out, it's like a movie, only better. Look, if you need me, I'm there for you. Say the word. I'll bring over some movies. Reunion movies. Finding lost loved ones movies. Oh, wait, is that insensitive? You can tell I've never helped anyone through this kind of thing before. Know this, Serenity." Deidre paused and she heard her sniffling. "I love you and can't wait to meet your little guy. Call me if you need me, any time of the day or night, and I'll be on my way over."

About four in the morning, Serenity finally dozed on the sofa until the alarm on her cell phone sounded at seven. Taking her time to get ready, she stood under the shower, praying some more as the warm water flowed over her. She wanted to look pretty for her son, wanted to be worthy of him. Shortly after nine o'clock, she grabbed her small tote bag and the pink plastic sand pail Jackson had given her. It was a gorgeous morning, a morning meant for walking, not too hot or humid.

Serenity arrived at the meeting spot on the beach almost thirty minutes ahead of their prearranged time. The low tide lapped on the beach. As it always did, the sound of the rolling waves brought its own brand of comfort. Dropping her tote bag on the sand, she pulled out an oversized blanket. She shook it out and then smoothed the edges, sitting down in the middle, drawing her knees to her chest.

She never would have dreamed this day possible. *My baby boy is alive.* Even Deidre with her fanciful imagination couldn't dream up a scenario as far-fetched as the true events of her life. *Only You could make everything come together like this, Lord.* The best way to thank the Lord was by forgiving her mother and honoring her sacrifice in raising Justin and keeping him safe. Her heart turned over at the very thought of him.

My son. She'd never get over how great it was to think it, say it, know it, breathe it, *live* it.

Her heart pounded loud in her chest and she fought to control her breathing. Even though she drew great comfort from her prayers, she was too antsy to concentrate on anything but talking to him, holding him, kissing him. She'd need to restrain herself and not overwhelm Justin with everything all at once. How would he react? Would he shy away from her and run to her mother? If he did, she'd have to be mature and understand it would take time. From what her mother said, he probably hadn't played with other children or gone to school. If so, was he emotionally or educationally stunted?

"Serenity!"

Hearing her name called, Serenity opened her eyes. Squinting in the sunlight, she spied Jackson walking in her direction. His hand was wrapped around Justin's. A random observer would think they were father and son with their dark hair, eyes and even the dimples. Watching them, Serenity blinked back her tears. *Help me be strong for Justin.*

Her heart swelled so fast she thought it'd burst with joy. Justin kicked a spray of sand into the air and laughed. Such a wonderful sound. *My son is happy.* No matter what had happened the last five years, he radiated the uninhibited joy of a child who'd been loved.

She dragged air into her lungs as the two approached. Jackson's eyes and gentle smile filled the remaining spaces in her heart.

Lord, please be with us.

In her soul, she knew He was. He'd been beside her every single step of the way. A long journey, but one that led to this beautiful moment she wanted to always remember.

Lowering her head for a few seconds, Serenity whispered words of thanks. *Thank You, Lord, from Whom all blessings flow.*

"Mommy?"

Serenity looked up into the sweet, expectant face of her son.

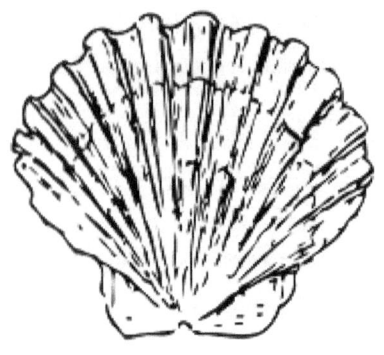

~CHAPTER 44~

Jackson stretched out his hand to her. Grabbing hold of him, Serenity quickly rose to her feet. She hoped she'd absorb some of his strength as he stood next to her. A sudden, unexpected awkwardness overcame her and she stared wide-eyed at Jackson, not knowing what to do. Her parents stood on the beach a hundred yards away, looking on and holding hands. She felt dizzy again and swayed, putting her hand over her forehead.

"It's okay," Jackson said, his voice low as he moved beside her, one hand supporting her arm. "You're fine."

"Are you sick?"

Justin's question shook her into reality and Serenity dropped to her knees. "I'm fine. Hi, Justin. I'm Serenity."

"You're my mommy."

"Yes," she said, swallowing hard, "I am. And you're my son. We have a lot of catching up to do." She restrained the urge to gather him close and never—ever—let him go. She forced a smile. "I can't tell you how happy I am to meet you."

Her son's dark eyes, so like his father's, roamed over her face, drinking her in, memorizing her. "You're beautiful pretty, like Doc Jack said." He fingered her hair. "I like your hair."

"Thank you." A sob caught in her throat, and Serenity moved one hand over her mouth so she wouldn't cry out loud. Was there any protocol for a situation like this?

"Don't cry," Justin said, putting one small hand on the side of her face. Touched by his tender gesture, she summoned every last ounce of strength not to burst from pure happiness. Her son had inherited such a tender heart. Or was such a thing innate or a learned behavior?

I'm so blessed he's mine, Lord.

"She's not crying because she's sad, Justin," Jackson said, his voice as gentle as she'd ever heard it.

Serenity nodded and swallowed her tears. "The happiest I've ever been."

Justin took a step closer and wrapped his arms around her neck, laying his head against her shoulder, his dark, beautiful curls splayed over her cotton top.

She ran her fingers through his hair. Not wanting to be maudlin, she inhaled a deep breath. "I've brought my sand pail that Doc Jack gave me. Would you like to help me build a sand castle?"

"Yeah!"

"It's pink," she said, pulling it from her tote bag. "I hope you don't mind."

Justin scrunched his face. "Pink is for girls, but you're a girl, so I guess it's okay. Thanks!" Grabbing the pail, he took off running toward the shore.

"I like his reasoning," Jackson said with a light chuckle.

"Can I cry now?" Serenity asked, choking on more tears. "I'm trying really hard here, Jackson, but he's the most beautiful child I've ever seen."

Without speaking, Jackson lifted the corner of his shirt and offered it to her. She half-laughed, half-cried as she mopped her wet cheeks with the back of her hand. They watched as Elise and Clinton joined Justin and found a spot a few feet away from the waves. Mama helped Dad lower to his knees in the sand. Laughing. Smiling. A *family*.

"They're making a sand castle," she murmured.

"Sit with me a few minutes and then we'll go join them," Jackson said.

When she dropped down to the blanket, he settled beside her.

"Your son's incredibly smart and well-adjusted considering his unusual environment the last five years. I'm not sure how much he knows, but in time, he'll be told. When he's mature enough to accept it or when he starts asking questions." Jackson traced a cross-hatch in the sand and, using one finger, drew an "x."

A sudden breath of air whipped strands of her hair across her cheeks. Pushing them aside, Jackson planted a sweet kiss in their wake.

With her finger, Serenity circled an "o" in the sand. "Mama probably did a better job raising him than I would have done."

"You can't know that." He added another "x."

She felt his brown-eyed gaze on her. "Oh, I think I do." She drew another "o."

"We're going to take you to dinner at Chez Ross tonight," he said, etching the final "x" in the sand and then drew a long, slow line through the three. In her distracted state, she hadn't paid attention and he'd won easily. "Justin has something very special to give you."

"I've had enough surprises to last a while. Tell me now, so I can be prepared."

"Sure about that? It's a great surprise."

How she loved Jackson's lazy grins. "Yes, I *really* want to know," she said.

"Okay, then. Since you insist. Elise made a huge memory album with photos detailing every week of Justin's life, and she kept a journal. She took meticulous notes, detailing every milestone in his life, large and small. There's a DVD, too. From what your mom told me, she recorded him turning over, crawling, learning to pull himself up, his first steps, everything."

She nodded slowly, her mind churning with thoughts and questions. Accusations she didn't welcome took precedence in her cluttered mind. "Have you seen these things?"

"No, but she's mentioned it several times."

A sudden surge of emotion struck her with such force it could have blown her down. Taking a gasping gulp of air, her heart sputtered and she lifted her eyes to his. "Jackson, how do you know all these things?"

*H*is mouth went dry and Jackson slicked his tongue over his lips. *This* was the defining moment. The moment he'd dreaded but knew would arrive sooner or later. The moment they needed to overcome in order to move forward with their relationship.

"I can't say," he said.

"What do you mean?" Although her voice remained calm, she'd raised it a notch.

"I mean"—he turned to meet her gaze head-on—"I *really* can't say."

She frowned. "Not a good time to clam up on me now."

"Exactly what I said. I. Can't. Say. Trust me when I tell you I have my reasons." He could tell she was more confused than ever. When the clouds cleared, she'd figure it out, but until then, anything was possible. He'd never seen Serenity truly angry with anyone or anything. Early on, she'd been aggravated with her dad, but that was understandable. Even in her hospital room, she'd been remarkably controlled with her mother. Sure, she'd lashed out at her, but that was realistic. But she'd maintained her calm and managed quite well, considering. He'd been very proud of her, not sure he had the right.

"You'd met Mama before we saw her on the street with Justin yesterday afternoon?"

He remained silent, avoiding her eye contact. Hating every second. Love should trump professional ethics, but neither should it be a choice. That niggling little voice inside his head urged him to go ahead and tell her. He loved this woman. How could it be wrong? If she figured it out all on her own, who was he to refute it?

She'll resent you at the least, despise you at most.

Jackson's shoulders sagged, and his jaw tightened to the point where he thought it might snap. Oaths before the board meant something. They were important for his professional honor. *What about your promise to the Lord you serve? The Lord you love more than life itself?* As strong as his love was for Serenity—a love which grew deeper, richer and more intense each day—he would not violate his word to man and especially not his God. If he did that, he wouldn't be able to stand with any semblance of loyalty, honor and dignity. In that case, he might as well have died in Afghanistan.

"I think it's time to go and join them," Serenity said, pushing to her feet. Her words were clipped, alerting him to the tempest raging inside her. Starting to walk away, she paused and turned. He couldn't begin to decipher her expression. Confusion. Bewilderment. Betrayal wasn't there….but Jackson knew it might very well hover just around the bend. In the corners of her mind, the dark place she wouldn't want to go. A place where he didn't *want* her to go and prayed she didn't. A place she'd reach and it was there she'd face the decision that could change the course of *his* life.

Lord, help her to see I can't tell her. Help her to know why.

"I think it's best if I meet with Justin at Mama and Dad's house tonight."

"Fine," he said. "Not a problem."

"*Alone*, Jackson. It's best if you don't come."

His mouth gaped as she turned her back and walked away.

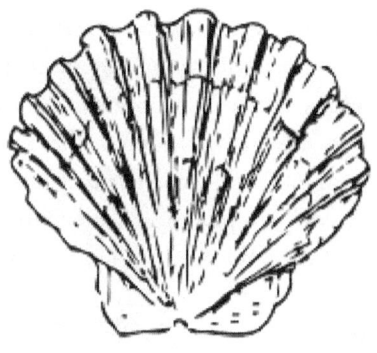

~CHAPTER 45~

*S*erenity's steps felt heavy, weighted down. She had that odd sensation again, as though she was moving in slow motion. Observing from a distance. While she wanted to be an active participant, something held her back. Fear? Shock? Justin needed his mother, not a shell-shocked woman incapable of taking care of either one of them.

"Everything okay?" Elise asked.

"That's the question of the day, the week, the month..." Serenity shook her head as she took her place beside her mother. "I'm sure you get the picture." She glanced at Justin. Giggling, he talked with Clinton like they were long-lost buddies as they worked on the sand castle. "What a beautiful sight. One I never would have imagined. Until now." She moved her gaze back to her mother, uncertain whether she should thank her. For so long, she'd been riddled with doubts, guilt, accusations. Acceptance and forgiveness could be a tricky proposition. Were there any road maps or guidebooks for dealing with conflicting emotions in a situation like hers?

Read my Word, child. There you'll find your answers. A chill ran through her. Was that the Lord whispering in her heart or was she truly going crazy?

Elise nodded. "The best sight in the world, other than seeing *you* with Justin." She handed her the sand scooper. "Justin assigned me the task of digging the moat. You're supposed to build a tower."

"A tower?" Serenity asked, trying to ground her thoughts in the reality on the beach, surrounding her. Taking the scoop, she speared it into the damp sand, ripe for digging and molding. "Why? To imprison someone?" Dumb question. She was thankful Justin wasn't paying attention to them and hadn't heard.

"No," Elise said, her voice low. "More like to set someone free."

"That makes no sense." Curling her hands around the sand, Serenity fashioned the beginnings of a round tower. "Then again, a lot of things don't make sense right now."

"I'll tell you a little story that might help put it in perspective." Elise continued digging in the sand, and a narrow, shallow trench was taking form. A perfect moat. "Justin has a great imagination. He's been reading above age level since he turned four. We had a lot of fun making up bedtime stories, too. One of his favorites is about a young prince who lives in a tower bedroom in a castle far, far away."

"In a kingdom called Croisette Shores?"

"We never named it, actually." They shared a smile. "He called it the tower of his imagination. You see, when he was in that tower, he could do anything, be anything, go anywhere, be anyone. One night he'd pretend he had the ability to fly. Another night, he'd possess the power to scale tower walls. He loved riding the flying, fire-breathing dragons. Each time he told the story of the prince in the tower, he'd add something new. Sometimes it was more mundane. He'd speak in a foreign language, meet a new playmate, ride a bike...you name it."

"So, you're saying the tower was his escape, his gateway to a different world where anything was possible?"

"That's exactly what I'm saying." As they worked together, side-by-side, Elise nudged her shoulder. "I'll tell you something else. Justin's favorite story? It was about a beautiful princess with long blonde hair named Serenity."

Serenity laughed under her breath. "I'm afraid I'll be a big disappointment to him if he thinks I'm goodness and light all the time."

"Trust me, he knows that. I kept him as sheltered as I could, but I also made sure I grounded him in reality. But he's still only a very young boy. Let's try to keep him that way as long as we can. I took him places, like your dad and I used to do with you. I've tried to cultivate a love of history, of the wonders of architecture, the marvel of what God's made. Justin's been to New York countless times. I've tried to encourage a love of the finer things in life."

"How'd you manage that?" Serenity asked. "I mean, knowing your circumstances."

"We always had a chaperone, but they kept their distance. We were never allowed to be alone, just the two of us. So, in a way, we were imprisoned, too. But, above all, I wanted Justin to feel safe. I never wanted that child to feel as though we were in any kind of danger."

"Were you afraid?"

Elise flinched. "There were times, yes. But I clung to God's promises, Serenity. Before I left Croisette Shores with Liam, I saw my Bible, forgotten in a drawer. Something—most likely the Holy Spirit—cried out to me to take it. And I mean cried out because it was no soft whisper. It was more like a command. For once in my life, I obeyed. Reading the scriptures comforted me."

Serenity nodded. "I've been reading my Bible. I never realized how things that took place so long ago could have such relevance for today's world. I can see the strong parallels, and it reinforces how timeless God's Word is."

"Exactly. He's the God of all things, the Ruler of all time." When she glanced at her, Elise's eyes were bright with emotion. "It fills my soul with joy to know you've embraced your faith and we can share that bond. Did you say this is when you lived in Atlanta?"

"A friend invited me to church. Trust me," Serenity said with a small laugh, "I've got so much to learn."

"We never stop learning. We're not meant to know everything in this world, but if we pray and try to live according to His Word, we'll have a good life. At least the life He wants us to enjoy here on earth. Each person, each moment is a blessing. Sometimes I'd find myself questioning Him and His purpose in being so far from home with your son, but I loved the verse in the Book of Job that says, '*And to man He said, behold the fear of the Lord, that is wisdom; And to depart from evil is understanding.*' There are a number of verses in Job that talk about evildoers. There's a verse that says, '*The murderer arises at dawn; He kills the poor and the needy, And at night he is as a thief.*'" Elise shook her head. "I tried not to think about the things that went on outside the walls of that house, things that were being ordered, evil being carried out on the orders of an old man I was keeping alive, on borrowed time." Her mother visibly shuddered.

"What a terrible position to have been in," Serenity said.

"I prayed for him to die plenty of times. I always thought I'd wake up one morning and he'd have passed in his sleep. The more I think about it, the more I realized—as difficult as it was—God had everything in His control the entire time. Just as He always has, and always will. I cried out to Him, and He answered my prayer. In *His* perfect time." Elise placed her scooper on the ground and sat beside her. "May I?"

Not sure what she meant, Serenity nodded. When Elise moved her arm around her shoulders, she rested her head on her shoulder. "I've missed you, Mama. More than you know. There were times when I didn't want to feel that way, though."

"I know, honey. You must have hated me."

"No," Serenity said, determined not to cry although she sniffled. Then she took a deep breath before continuing. "I couldn't hate you. I hated what I thought you'd done. More than anything, I hated what you'd done to Dad."

"I'll spend the rest of my life making it up to him."

"I don't think Dad expects that. Did you visit him in the hospital?"

She lowered her gaze. "I didn't go to his room, but I brought flowers and left them at the front desk."

"Didn't anyone recognize you?"

A slight smile lifted the corners of her mouth. "Surely you've noticed I've changed my appearance somewhat. Besides that, most people in this town either believe I'm dead or thought I'd never return to Croisette Shores. There will be speculation, but I'll never say a word. We'll be known around town as the Mysterious McClarens. Kind of has a ring to it, don't you think?"

Serenity's gaze collided with her mother's. "Why not? I've heard the whole French royal family speculation my entire life." She smoothed her hand over Elise's head. "I miss your blonde hair. Are you going to let it grow again, dye it?"

"Yes. Your father hates the red hair. Well, it's more that it's short, not so much the color. And he's trying to fatten me up. Don't worry," she said, with a sidelong glance. "He's doing it the healthy way. You've been good for him since you've come home again. In so many ways. Thank you for that."

Wrapping her arms around her mother's slender frame, Serenity held on tight, clinging to her. "I'm sorry I ever doubted you. Not only did you give me life, but you gave me my life back. Thank you, Mama." Leaning back, she placed her hands on either side of her mother's cheeks, looking into the face she'd always remembered. *Lovely.* A few lines were more deeply etched, but she was beautiful for a woman who'd been through so much. More than she even knew, most likely. Pulling away, she murmured, "*Thank* you. You suffered so much for my sake, and for Justin."

Elise's blue eyes, so like hers, softened. "That's what you do for those you love more than life itself, Serenity. You sacrifice. It's part of life. Although, in our case, we all gave more than our share, I'd say. I understand it works both ways. You and your Dad sacrificed a lot, too. My actions impacted you as much, if not more, than me. I hope you can find it in your heart to forgive me."

Serenity kissed her forehead. "You don't need to ask."

Another tear slipped down Elise's face. "I do, but thank you."

"I don't understand everything about what it means to be a Christian—a *good* one—anyway," Serenity said. "But I know He forgave me for all the things I've done wrong in my life." Pulling out of the hug, she shaped the tower as she cupped more sand in her hands. "I just wish there was some way you could have let Dad know somehow, but what's done is done. We can't change the past, but we're together again...this side of Heaven."

"Justin knows the Lord, too. He understands about sacrifice and what Jesus did for us on the cross. I think, in time as he grows and matures, we'll explain more to him about what happened. But let's wait until he's older and able to grasp the enormity of it all."

Serenity nodded and brushed away a tear from her mother's cheek. "How'd you explain to Justin about...me and Dad?"

Elise's shoulders sagged and she sat back on her heels. "That was the toughest challenge and I had to twist the truth a little. It's difficult to be honest with a child as smart as Justin and yet shield him from the harshest realities. Justin has only known about you and your father for the past year. I waited until he came to me, asking questions. All his book reading clued him in that families were often more than just a grandmother. I simply told him that we had to leave our home. I asked him to believe me when I said we'd go back one day."

"And he didn't press for more details? He accepted it at face value?"

"Yes, he did," Elise said. "Because I'd never lied to him before."

"It's all about trust, isn't it? Trust in the ones you love, and trust in God to work it all out in His perfect timing. I mean, what's five years to the Almighty?" Her lips curved. "Probably a tiny blip on the radar that barely registers." Her smile sobered. "Justin knows Jackson, too, doesn't he? I don't mean in a 'just met' way, either. They're familiar with one another."

"You're getting it. Keep thinking along those lines," Elise said, digging in the sand.

"Justin called him Doc Jack." Putting her hand on her mother's forearm, she stilled her actions. "You've taken him to see Jackson? In a professional capacity?"

Elise met her gaze and held it steady, but she neither confirmed nor denied the truth.

Serenity tossed the sand scooper to the ground. "He *knew*?" Struggling to gain control of her emotions, she felt as though her head might explode. "How long, Mama?"

"I don't know. I think he began to suspect the truth early on when we moved here. You have to understand I needed to ease Justin into coming here and meeting you and your dad. I needed advice from someone better equipped than me to deal with the fragile emotions of a child. Justin's so bright that sometimes I forget he's only a little boy."

Serenity sat back on the sand, cross-legged, shaking her head. "He knew. All the times we were together, he never hinted. Never said a word." She could tell something bothered him on occasion and weighed on his mind, but she assumed it was patient-related. Little did she know.

"Oh, honey, that man was hurting inside. Jackson loves you and I'm sure he wanted to tell you the truth from the moment he first suspected. He put everything on the line in loving you, but he wanted you to see for yourself or he risked you thinking he'd betrayed you."

Confusion reigned once more in her mind. "Isn't that what he did by not telling me?"

"If you believe nothing else, you must listen to me on this one," Elise said, her voice firmer.

"What's that?"

"Jackson never betrayed you. He loved you by helping your son come to grips with meeting you and your father. He stayed by your side, helped you talk through everything. He was your friend. From what I hear, he even got you to eat a hot dog, something I never thought I'd see in my lifetime."

Serenity opened her mouth to speak, then closed it. Carmen must have reported back to her about the hot dog.

"He knows you need time to absorb everything. More than that, you need time with Justin. Time to get to know your son. Jackson's willing to give you that time. That, in itself, speaks volumes about his character and values. He's a good man. He can't take Danny's place in your heart, but he wants the best for you in life and can give you so much. Don't you see? He put everything on the line and risked your love because he couldn't tell you what he suspected. A man like that isn't going to walk away from you now. Unless you push him away. I'd hate to see that happen. The Lord brought him to our little town for several reasons, and I'm looking at one right now." Her gaze moved to Justin. He and Clinton had made measurable progress in building their sand castle. No doubt, her father would tease them about lagging behind. Based on his glances in their direction, he appeared thankful they were talking things out between them.

"I wonder if Jackson ever felt like he was in a tower?" Serenity whispered.

"I'm sure he did," Elise said, patting her hand. "We'd better get back to our assignments or the little prince over there will think we're not worthy subjects. As far as Jackson, my advice—take it or leave it—is to pray about it. We all understand it's a process and it can't happen overnight. But it's my prayer you'll eventually open the gate guarding your heart, Serenity. And then go to Jackson. For in doing so, you'll set *him* free."

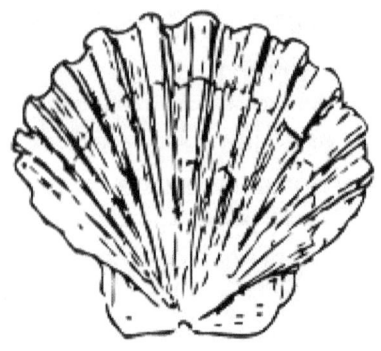

~CHAPTER 46~

"*L*adies and gentleman, on this glorious Fourth of July, we celebrate the birth of our great nation. Today we'd like to pay special honor to our heroes who have served our country well—both here and abroad, in several wars and conflicts, and representing all branches of the military."

The mayor's deep, resonant voice rang out loud and clear across the hush of the crowded Queen Victoria's Square. "Their selfless service and bravery in the face of adversity, and their willingness to sacrifice their lives to uphold the ideals of our Founding Fathers demonstrates the best of the American spirit. It's with great pride, humble admiration and the greatest respect that I read the names of these men and women."

He paused, canvassing the crowd. "They can be the man or woman sitting beside you. Quiet heroes, willing to give the ultimate sacrifice to secure your freedom. Some on the list are here with us today, and I'd ask that they come forward as I read their names. Please save your applause until all the names have been called. Others of our heroes have passed on, but their legacy will always remain."

Serenity dabbed beneath her eyes with the tissue she'd tucked into the pocket of her cotton skirt. Poignant ceremonies like this always made her emotional, and a swell of patriotism mixed with admiration and humility almost overwhelmed her. Although her dad was never called to serve in a war, several of her classmates had served, and two had fallen. War left no family untouched, even in their small community. As the names were read, the crowd was reverent with only a baby's whimper or a cough here and there to punctuate the quiet.

"Jackson Ross, First Lieutenant, United States Army, awarded the Purple Heart for service above and beyond the call of duty."

A clarinet hit a soaring, gloriously wrong note that blasted like a bullhorn in the middle of a funeral. Cheeks on fire, Deidre slumped in her seat, ignoring the snickers and curious looks from her fellow band members. *Whoops.* She hadn't filled Deidre in on that little tidbit from Jackson's history. Based on the hum of conversation across the park, a number of the town's citizens were equally surprised to learn of Jackson's military achievement. He was indeed a hero, in so many ways. Ways to reach and hold her heart forever.

"Look, Mommy, it's Dr. Ross!" Clambering to his feet on top of his chair, Justin's voice carried across the crowd. "Hey, Doc Jack! It's me, Justin. Over here!" He gave his all to waving his arms and Serenity feared he'd topple over.

As she helped him settle in his seat again, Serenity caught Jackson's smile. Like always, her heart spun nearly out-of-control. With his broad shoulders straight—tall, handsome and swoon-worthy—he approached the podium in his full, dark blue dress uniform, complete with hat and gloves. After saluting the crowd, he took his place in the line of other military members to one side of the podium. When he turned to them, Serenity glimpsed the medallion around his neck. A swell of emotion bubbled up inside, and she clamped a hand over her mouth. Jackson the military man made her heart riot.

How I've missed him, Lord.

She glimpsed her father lean forward from his seat directly behind Deidre. He whispered a few words and then squeezed her shoulder before settling in his seat beside Art Masmer.

Thanks, Dad.

Standing at the podium as he finished calling the names, Mayor Anderson raised a hand and waved it in the direction of the men and women on the podium. "Our brave, strong heroes, we salute you, and we, the citizens of this great community of Croisette Shores, are indeed blessed to call you our own. Thank you for your service."

Serenity searched the crowd as the ceremony ended a short time later. Jackson was easy to find from where he stood talking with a group of veterans. He stood head-and-shoulders above the rest. As if sensing her eyes on him, Jackson turned toward her, nodded and tipped his cap. A slow flush crawled up Serenity's neck, and her heart fluttered.

Her dad chatted with some of the band members, and it was great to see him socializing again. Even self-proclaimed hermits can change well-ingrained habits.

A few minutes later, Jackson crossed Queen Victoria's Square to where she'd finished her conversation with a former classmate. Removing his cap, he bowed low, "First Lieutenant Jackson Ross, at your service, Miss McClaren." When he clicked the heels of his shiny shoes and saluted her, Serenity almost lost it. Biting her bottom lip hard, she turned away, not trusting her emotions.

"Whoa! I didn't expect that reaction." With his white-gloved fingers on her arm, Jackson guided her to a quiet area. The lights in the square twinkled overhead against the backdrop of a glorious sunset. Combined with the moderate temperature and slight ocean breeze, it was the perfect evening for the fireworks display over the waterfront.

She could tell she surprised him when she fell against his broad, solid chest and threw her arms around him. Through his uniform, she felt his chuckle as his arms encircled her. Dragging air into her lungs and making a concerted effort to compose herself, Serenity stood back and gave him a shaky smile. Removing his gloves, he draped them over the inside of his hat and lowered them to the ground. He tipped her chin, his expression full of concern. "Okay?"

"There's something so completely noble and attractive about a man in uniform," she said, sniffling. "You look unbelievable, but I'm crying because I'm so incredibly proud of you even though I know I have no right to be, and you're so handsome, strong"—she patted his chest, thinking how warm he must be in the uniform—"brave, kind and..."

His smile devastated her. In the best way possible. "If I'd known wearing this getup would get this kind of reaction, I'd have worn it a long time ago. Your dad invited me to watch the fireworks with your family. Hope that's okay. Are you ready to spend some time with me again?"

She smiled and ran her finger over the colorful pins and patches on the front and sleeves of his uniform. Such a brave man. Raising the Purple Heart by its ribbon, she looked up at the man she loved. "I think that's a good idea. A very wise idea for my heart. For all of me, actually."

"I couldn't tell you, Serenity." Jackson's eyes were so beautiful, incredibly earnest as they bore into hers. "I prayed you'd understand and not hate me."

She shook her head and dropped her hand. "I could never hate you. You took an oath, the same as you took an oath to serve in the Army. That's a sacred trust. I had to figure it all out in my head, Jackson, but if you had broken my mom's trust by telling me Justin was your patient, that would have been worse." She glanced up at him again. "You are a man of honor. That means more than anything."

"Does that mean you've missed me as much as I've missed you?" he whispered. "These last few weeks, I've been miserable. A sad sack. Mean. Listless. Grumpy, you name it. Even Freud doesn't want me around anymore." They'd run into each other in town a few times and he'd sent her a few emails and texts, just to say hello and encourage her to call on him if she needed anything. Although not much was said, she understood her mother continued to take Justin to see Jackson.

"I've missed you something fierce. You somehow managed to work your way into my heart. When you weren't around, it wasn't the same. Like part of me was missing. I needed time with Justin, and I thank you for giving me that time with my son. So," she said, breathing out a long sigh and smiling into his eyes, "in answer to your question, yes, I'm ready to spend time with you again. Should I salute you...or something?" Her silly giggle escaped, and Jackson moved closer, seemingly charmed by her lapse into girlishness.

"Oh, I'm sure we can think of something infinitely better, Miss McClaren."

"Okay, but please keep the public displays of affection brief. My impressionable son is nearby, and he's probably watching his real-life hero. Don't want to give him any ideas."

"He'll have those ideas all on his own in a few years, you know."

She gave him a playful swat. "It might be against protocol or whatever to hit a military hero, but don't remind me. I want to enjoy every moment with Justin for now. He'll grow up all too soon."

"In that case, let's give Justin and everyone else a real good show." Sweeping her into his arms, leaning her back, Jackson lowered his lips to hers.

I'm actually swooning. When he finally pulled her upright and released her, Serenity was so dizzy she could barely stand. Jackson put a steadying hand on her. "Thanks for catching me when I was about to fall. Again," she said. "I've never been kissed by a man in uniform before." What a silly thing to say, but her mind was mush. The taste of his lips was still on hers. Each kiss from Jackson was impassioned and conveyed the depth of his admiration and love for her.

"And I trust you never will again, by anyone other than me."

"Keep that up and you won't have anything to worry about." Embarrassed and flushed, she ignored the knowing smiles of her parents and everyone else in the vicinity who'd witnessed that display. Had a few people even clapped?

Ah, flirting with Jackson again. She'd missed that, too. More than she'd known. "I didn't realize the Army dress uniform was blue. I'd have thought it'd be that olive green color."

"It's the Army Service Uniform and replaces the Army Greens and the Olive Drab uniforms. This is called 'Army Blue' and goes back to the 'Virginia Blues' of George Washington's first command in Colonial Virginia. This color was phased in a few years ago. Listen, I brought a small bag with a change of clothes. I'm going to find the nearest place to do the switcheroo, run the uniform to my car, and then I'll meet you back here in a few minutes. Do you want to stay here for the fireworks or try and get closer to the waterfront?"

She shot him a sheepish grin. "Do you really need to change?"

He laughed. "The uniform's hot"—he caught her look—"as in the *fabric* is hot. I've got my shorts and T-shirt. Tell you what. I'll lay out the uniform on the blanket next to us if that floats your boat."

That comment made her laugh. "Why don't we stay in Queen Victoria's Square for the fireworks," she said once she'd recovered her senses. "You can see the fireworks just as well from here, but it's quieter since most of the spectators gather close by the waterfront. I brought a blanket, and I'm willing to share a corner." She gave him a coy grin.

Jackson laughed. He tugged his hat down over her head and angled it. "You look a lot better in it than I do. Wanna wear it tonight, beautiful pretty?"

When she nodded, he saluted and clicked his heels together again. "I'll be back in a few."

"My, my." Deidre came to stand beside her, shaking her head. "A man like that is why the word dashing was invented. Seems Dr. Ross is full of secrets. A Purple Heart, no less. A true hero, and that might also explain the limp. Seems you've been holding out on me." She slanted a grin at Serenity. "Nice hat."

"Where's the rest of your gang?" Serenity said. "Want to join us for the fireworks?"

"They're around somewhere. With their friends. We were over at Wes's brother's for a family picnic most of the day. Wes stayed to help break down the grill while I played taxi mom for the kids. I'm meeting him back at the house. We can see the fireworks from the deck and thought we'd enjoy some private time." She blew out a breath. "Part of me will be happy when the kids can drive themselves, but another part never wants them to give up needing me."

Serenity reached an arm around Deidre's shoulders and pulled her close. "If it makes you feel any better, I'll always need you. And even when they're grown, your kids will always need their mom."

Deidre leaned her head against Serenity's. "It does my heart good to see you with your mom and Justin, sweetie. A few months ago, I wouldn't have thought that would be possible. Now, just look at you." Her eyes were bright in the moonlight. "God *does* work miracles. Your family is a living, breathing, walking example of that." A tear slid down Deidre's cheek. "Even that ornery father of yours," she said, laughing as another tear escaped.

"No more tears," Serenity said. "I've shed enough for the both of us to last a lifetime."

"Okay, then, I suppose I'd better not ask about—"

"He's giving me time, Deidre. Which is exactly what I need."

She tilted her head. "Are you sure about that? Sure, you need time with Justin, but you need 'me' time, too. Serenity time. He's a good man and he loves you."

"I know." She lowered her gaze and swallowed. "I love him, too."

"I'll pop in and see you one day this week and we'll have lunch, okay?"

Giving Deidre a quick, fierce hug, Serenity whispered. "Count on it."

Watching her walk away, she thought of everything that had transpired in the last few weeks. From what Deidre told her, the current thread of gossip leaned toward her mother needing a break from her marriage for whatever reason. Clinton had bristled at that gossip, but he'd kept his mouth closed. No one had figured out the mystery of Justin yet. Anyone who'd known Danny might suspect Justin was his child since he was the spitting image of his father. Deidre pointed out the physical similarities between Justin and Jackson. Some believed Jackson had been her "friend" in Atlanta and was the father of this child. Or some suspected that Elise had mothered another child, or else she'd adopted Justin. Conveniently, no one seemed to recall Liam's middle name was Justin. They'd barely had enough time to tell anyone his full name since her son supposedly lived such a short life. Even if they asked, Justin was a common enough name not to raise eyebrows.

"Of course, Old Persimmonhead is the lone voice in the wilderness who believes your mother's disappearance has everything to do with Danny's death," Deidre also said. "She's trying to ply me with bribes to get me to talk, but you know I'm loyal to the death."

"Hope it won't go that far, but thanks for your loyalty, kind subject," Serenity said. "Persimmonhead is also well-known for watching crime dramas on TV. Little does she know she's closer to the truth than most of the others in town."

As far as Serenity was concerned, no one else would ever know the entire truth. What was done was done. It was their business to reconcile with God, and theirs alone. She'd never subscribed to the "inherent right to know" theory, anyway.

In an interesting development, the crime "family" in Long Island had collapsed with the arrest, imprisonment and impending trial of the son of Elise's patient. It'd been all over the news, both in the newspaper and on the television. "God's cleaning house," was her father's observation of the situation.

That knowledge also seemed to free her mother. Overnight, she appeared much younger, much more like she'd been before her sudden disappearance. She'd returned to her natural blonde and was starting to grow out her hair. "Maybe we can eventually release little tidbits about what really happened," her mother said. "If anyone's still interested. But not until Justin knows." Her mother was adamant on that point, and she was right.

Someday, when he was old enough, Serenity would tell her son the truth. One day he'd come to her, like he had to her mother, and ask about his early years. And she'd tell him the truth because Justin, more than anyone else, had the inherent right to know. She'd tell him how his grandmother had protected him like Miriam did for her little brother, Moses. How she'd protected him with her own life and how she'd sacrificed out of love for him. Then brought him back safely home.

"What about that gravestone out in the cemetery with Liam's name on it?" Clinton asked at dinner one night when Charlie had Justin over for a play date with Maya. "What do we do about that?"

"Can't they fill in or smooth over the date of his supposed death?" Elise asked.

"I don't want to keep it." Serenity had shuddered, a violent force shaking her entire body. "It's morbid. What if Justin sees it or someone tells him about it?"

"I'll make a call and have it removed," Clinton said. "I'll figure out something. There's a new caretaker. I'll pay him well, take a truck out there and tell him we've decided to move it somewhere else." Her mother had run from the kitchen, crying. Clinton had followed her. What a tangled web indeed. Sometimes life held no easy answers. The Lord had become her best friend, and prayer her constant companion.

Serenity had tracked down Danny's parents in Raleigh, and arranged a visit with them in August. A week before the planned trip, she'd call John and Paula Kincaid and tell them the entire story. The element of surprise wouldn't be good, either for them or her five-year-old son. She'd need to first pave the way, lay the groundwork. First, she'd tell Justin about his father and what a good man he was. Danny *had* been good or she wouldn't have fallen in love with him. But, somewhere along the way, he'd lost himself. In her heart, she'd always known Danny was only trying to make a better life for them but got himself killed by making some bad decisions.

The Kincaids would certainly be shocked, but she had full confidence they'd also be overjoyed to meet their grandson. She prayed their happiness would trump any ill will directed toward her mother for her actions. Without a doubt, they'd love Justin and dote on him. Danny had been their only child, and getting to know his son—one they'd thought had been lost to them forever—

would be a precious *gift*. They had every right to know Justin and spend time with them, and she couldn't deny them the privilege. How marvelous to see the ways in which the Lord closed holes in their hearts and souls, drawing them close and giving them comfort in the way only He could.

*W*aiting for the fireworks to begin, Serenity sat back on the blanket and relaxed, enjoying the camaraderie between Jackson and her dad. They sparred back and forth like old pals, and she hummed along to the canned music, one ear tuned into their light banter. Justin's attempts to imitate Jackson's every move amused her. When the light show began, Justin scooted closer and leaned against her.

"Come sit closer to Mommy," Justin said, beckoning with one hand to Jackson.

"Only if it's okay with Mommy."

Serenity patted the spot on the blanket next to her and he complied.

Her mother had invited Mrs. Marciano to sit with them. The two ladies sat and talked quietly in lawn chairs. From the frequent glances directed their way, she knew she and Jackson must be the primary topic of discussion.

Charlie and Maya sat nearby on another blanket. He waved. "Love you," Charlie mouthed to her and she moved her curled fist over her heart and returned his smile.

"Wow, look at that one!" Justin said, clapping at an especially bright display high in the sky. Long streams slowly trailed a sparkling path down toward the earth.

"Those are my favorite." Serenity smoothed Justin's hair away from his eyes. He needed a haircut soon. Those small, mundane things of life—haircuts, making sandwiches, making plans for school and play dates with other kids— those were the most important aspects of her life now. Things she never imagined she might be doing with her son. "Which one's your favorite?"

"The red ones that look like a big starfish with lots of legs," Justin said, smiling as blue and green fireworks spontaneously burst into full, brilliant color.

"I've never looked at it that way," Jackson said. "Interesting perspective."

"Does God make the fireworks?" Justin shifted to look up at her.

Serenity glanced at Jackson, but he nodded for her to answer. "I think God makes His own fireworks," she said. "And they're even more spectacular than what we're watching in the sky now. We might not be able to actually *see* them, but they're every bit as bright and colorful."

Justin's eyes were bright and curious. Such beautiful eyes, such a handsome face. "If they're not in the sky, then where are they?"

Again, Serenity shot Jackson a glance.

"You're doing fine," he whispered, his voice low, encouraging her to continue. He covered her hand planted on the ground between them, squeezing it.

"I like to think they're in the everyday miracles of life," she said.

"What's a miracle?" Oh, he asked the hard questions sometimes. But she wouldn't have it any other way.

"Having you right here with me, for one," she said, smoothing his hair aside again when the light breeze blew it into his eyes. "Being able to do things like take you to get this way-too-long hair of yours cut." When she tugged on a lock of hair, Justin giggled then exclaimed over another bright display of fireworks. As he settled down again, Serenity nestled him closer, moving both arms around him and rocking him.

They watched the fireworks, clapping, laughing and talking quietly together. Like the family she hoped they'd be one day. Raising her face to the sky, Serenity wished upon a star.

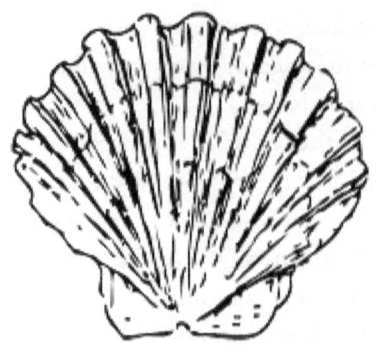

~CHAPTER 47~

*S*erenity marked an "x" in the sand. She sat next to Jackson a few weeks later on the beach. They'd taken to meeting there almost every night, often with Justin playing nearby. Since he would be starting school soon, she'd started a new going-to-bed earlier campaign. Not that it always worked, but tonight Mrs. Marciano was at her house, keeping watch over Justin and helping him climb into bed. He'd probably regale her with his stories of the tower or of Princess Serenity. Or Prince Jackson, his most recent favorite story.

Justin had started asking if Jackson could come live with them and be a "real" family. Cherishing his questions, she'd hidden them in the secret places of her heart, treasuring them. "All in due time," she'd said in answer to his questions. Still, she couldn't help but wonder if Justin asked Jackson similar questions. They'd spent a lot of time together—outside of his office—and that thrilled her as much as anything could. Justin loved it when Jackson taught the Sunday School class, even more when she helped, too. They'd spent time together, the three of them, and with her mother and father, doing all those things that formed tight bonds—talking, being silly, enjoying quiet time, playing games, walking along the beach, playing with Freud, throwing starfish back into the ocean, imprinting the other on their hearts. The times spent in the church, worshipping, were precious. Clinton was slowly coming around and Serenity felt it was only a matter of time. Yes, sometimes these things took time.

"'*The Lord is my strength and my shield,*'" Serenity said. "'*My heart trusts in Him, and I am helped. Therefore, my heart exults, and with my song I shall thank Him.*'" Catching Jackson's grin, she smiled. "I've been reading my Bible. It's quite a fascinating book."

Jackson marked an "o" and raised a brow. "God also blessed you with someone who made you strong, equipped you with the tools you needed to get through the last few years."

Serenity looked over at him, confused, and raised a brow. "Mama." She crossed another "x" in their pattern in the sand.

"Yes. Elise taught you the value of living, the joy in laughing, and the way to forge ahead in the face of adversity. Have you forgiven her, Serenity?" He glanced her way. "I mean *completely* forgiven her?"

"I know Mama only did what she did out of love." She looked over at him. "Like Miriam with Moses, right?" The corners of his mouth tipped upward, but he remained silent as he drew another "o" in the sand.

She drew in a deep breath. "Dad understands that, too. After the initial shock of it all, and thinking through everything and getting my head on straight again, I came to the realization I would have done the exact same thing if I were in her shoes. She didn't have a choice, and Justin has only known love. Knowing I have both my parents nearby is a comfort. The Lord knew all these things, and even though I could never have guessed the way in which the events of the last few years have played out, it's all good."

"And you've forgiven yourself?"

Oh yes, this man knew her so well. Now, she embraced the idea and even welcomed it.

"I'm learning to, yes. A certain smart psychologist keeps telling me I have no reason to blame myself for anything that happened." Leaning her chin on her knees, she smiled. "I'm finally beginning to see the truth in that. Now, I'm looking to the future, not to the past." Marking a final "x" in the sand, she drew the line through it.

"Is Justin registered for school?"

Not what she meant, but she loved talking about her son with Jackson. Loved talking about anything with him. "Sure is. He's so excited. We went shopping the other day and bought his backpack and supplies." She shot him a grin. "He told me all about your fishing trip. Justin loves spending time with you. So do I."

"Speaking of which, we have the gala fundraiser coming up in September, thanks to all the hard work from you, Deidre, Charlie and all the others on the committee. We're going to have an orchestra serenading us at a catered dinner followed by dancing to a jazz quartet. See," he said, nudging her arm, "I knew you'd be a huge help."

"Thank you, kind sir. It's been a lot of fun." Why was it she was the one asking leading questions and he kept changing the subject? She'd thought he'd be thrilled, but he uncharacteristically seemed to be avoiding them. Knowing Jackson as well as she did now, she knew he must have his reasons.

"Jackson," she said, stretching out her legs and stretching out on the sand, wiggling her toes, "did you ever find out who the mysterious benefactor is for the playground?"

When he didn't immediately answer, Serenity glanced at his strong, almost aristocratic profile. He *could* be descended from French royalty with his oh-so-handsome features. The fantasy was nice, anyway, even if his last name wasn't French. Some of his dark hair whipped over his forehead and she pushed it aside with gentle fingers when he stretched out beside her. "It was Charlie, wasn't it?"

"Yes. How'd you know?" He reached for her hand. What a sight they must be, flat on their backs, on the sand, side-by-side.

She shrugged. "A hunch, I guess. For one thing, Charlie wants to make sure Justin has a lasting reminder of his father. He'll think of him every time he goes down the slide or on the swings at the playground."

"But Charlie didn't know Justin was alive when we first made plans for the playground," Jackson said.

Turning her head, she smiled. "I'm beginning to wonder about that now, too. Only God knows for sure. I'm not asking questions."

"I love you, Serenity." Jackson's head rushed with emotion. He'd waited so long to say the words. Desperately hoped she'd say them back.

"I love you, too."

Tears stung his eyes. What a romantic fool he was, but he didn't care. "We'd better get up," he said, his voice husky as he pulled her to her feet.

"You might think you love me," she said, surprising him. "But maybe it's pity you feel. I'm a case study in grief, and you're only fascinated with the inner workings of my brain in processing grief." She gestured with her hands and the look in her eyes was a little wild. "Or something like that."

Jackson ran fingers through his hair, shaking his head and gave her his best *Are you out of your mind?* expression. "That's got to be one of the most ill-founded and absolutely ridiculous things I've ever heard you say." It was another reason he loved her. He never knew what would come shooting from her mind and out of her mouth. That luscious, all-too-kissable mouth. He shook his head again, trying to focus and regain his perspective.

"Which only goes to prove you haven't known me long enough to love me."

Jackson faced her, arms folded across his chest. "We've known each other since early May. Okay, how long do you think it takes to love someone? From what you told me, your parents pretty much knew it the first day they shared a blanket at the Newport Jazz Festival. Charlie knew it the first moment he laid eyes on his wife."

"True," Serenity said, "and Wes told Deidre he'd known after a month of dating her."

"I'll tell you the moment I fell in love with you, if you'd care to hear it." Jackson waited until her gaze traveled upward to meet his, locking them in. While she didn't appear nervous, Serenity looked as vulnerable as he'd ever seen her. "When your swing broke and you sat in the dirt, all dazed and dusty, and you started laughing. You had me then. Especially when you got all flustered and pulled at your skirt and tried to avoid looking at me because you were too embarrassed." He stepped closer, one hand over his heart like a smitten schoolboy, but it went oh-so-much-deeper. "I'd known you less than an hour, but I knew in that moment you would become a very meaningful person in my life. Someone I could love very easily, even though I didn't want to."

Her eyes widened, and that little spark of fire ignited in them, making them luminescent in their beauty. "Why...why," she stammered, "didn't you want to love me?" Jackson took more satisfaction in that question than she could ever know.

"Because I didn't want to love anyone. My parents have never enjoyed the kind of marriage your parents have, or what Charlie and Marcela had together," he said. "My mom and dad could barely tolerate each other, both involved with their pet projects and charities. In all my years growing up under the same roof, I can count on one hand the number of times I saw them kiss, hug or anything more than a polite peck on the cheek."

He uncrossed his arms and moved to sit down again, motioning for her to join him. "I don't want that kind of marriage. If I'm going to marry, it's going to be a full-on, can't-stop-thinking-about-her, wanting-to-be-with-her-as-much-as-possible kind of love." Jackson reached for her hand again, lacing his fingers through hers, holding on tight. He never wanted to let her go. "I want to hear about her day, share her problems and her heartache, soothe her feelings when they're wounded by the world or some jerk who cut in front of her on the road."

Releasing her hand, he rested his elbows on his knees, staring at the ground. "I want to do all the normal stuff like grocery shopping, going to the pound and picking out a dog...or an iguana," he said with a slight grin. "Cook in the kitchen and make a mess, finding out together what recipes we love and which ones we'd rather toss back in the ocean for the fish. Listen to music and curl up on the couch and cuddle together. Find out where she's ticklish and what gets her all hot and bothered." He met her eyes. "Miss her like crazy when she's not there, and send her corny cards and flirty emails. Love her so much there'll be absolutely no doubt in her mind what a precious treasure she is."

Silence reigned for a long moment. Clasping his hands together on his propped knees, Jackson waited, determined not to speak again until she spoke. As it was, he'd probably said way more than he should. He stole a glance her way, but Serenity was apparently stunned speechless. When another minute passed and she still hadn't spoken, he couldn't take it. "In case you're wondering, that speech was about you, by the way."

"Jackson?"

He turned to face her, and a huge lump lodged in his throat. He'd never been so nervous with a woman, but with his heart pretty much on the line, he figured whatever Serenity said next could make or break whatever future they might have together. "Yes?" Somehow, it didn't come out as masculine and deep as he'd hoped, but at least it was intelligible and something more than an adolescent boy's squeak.

"The plastic sand pail and shovel."

He shook his head. He'd put his heart out there for her to stomp on, and she wanted to discuss a plastic beach toy? Serenity smiled and ran a finger down the side of his jaw, moving her thumb to caress his chin before running it across his lower lip. She obviously had no idea what that did to him. The woman was driving him crazy. Still, he'd wait all night for her explanation of that puzzling sand pail comment, if necessary. Hopefully, that wouldn't happen since she needed to get back home to Justin.

She giggled then, giving him immense relief. He was already pretty pumped, and the effect was nothing short of dizzying. If she was relaxed and playful enough to giggle, it meant she wasn't going to slap his face and stalk away, leaving his heart in a puddle on the beach.

"When you sent the sand pail to my office in that elaborate wrapping like it was the most expensive and precious gift in the world. That's when I knew."

He shook his head, puzzled. "How...?" Sure, he'd meant it to be special and thoughtful, but who could have known she'd love it so much? It was true the little gestures sometimes meant the most.

Her eyes softened. "That pail represents so much. You should know I'm actually thinking of having it bronzed." She caught his look and nudged his shoulder. "It helps me remember to experience the joy and freedom in Christ, and to embrace the Lord's blessings in my life. And you know how the sifter part of the pail filters out the not-so-good, leaving only the good? I need to remember to do that in my life. But now," she said, scooting closer, "I'm tired and I'm heady with love. Please kiss me, Jackson."

"My pleasure, your highness," he whispered against her lips. "Happy to oblige, but first, say it again, please."

"I love you," she said, moving her lips on his in a most tantalizing way.

"And I you." He poured such energy into his kisses, she might very well think of knighting him. But he had a much better idea. One he planned on putting into place the night of the gala.

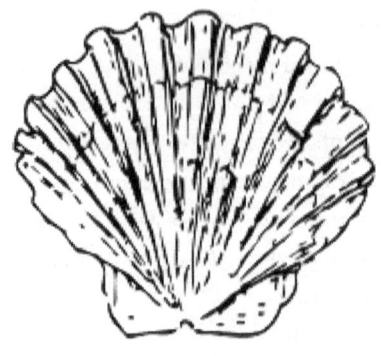

~CHAPTER 48~

*T*he servers worked quietly, clearing the last of the dessert dishes from the tables as Serenity walked back inside the Great Hall after saying goodnight to some of the guests from the gala. What a wonderful evening. They'd raised more money than they could have hoped, enough to start plans for yet another playground renovation. The charity auction had been exceedingly successful, the dinner delicious and the socializing and dancing afterwards had proved the highlight of the evening.

Hayley Foster had been in attendance with none other than Spencer Walton. Serenity had to admit they made a striking pair, he in his tuxedo and Hayley in a form-fitting but modest, pink sparkly, floor-length confection. Spencer acted apologetic over his previous behavior and told her as much. In-between moments of acting like a little boy, he could be remarkably mature. He'd kissed her cheek and told her he was happy she was with Jackson. He truly seemed pleased for her.

In one of those moments she knew she'd never forget, Serenity relished the sight of her handsome father in his tuxedo and dancing with her mother, beautiful in her classic, black and white tea-length gown. Serenity danced once with her father—fully recovered and looking much improved—while Jackson danced with Mama. How it thrilled her heart to see how well her parents interacted with Jackson. They treated him like family. He *was* family.

Charlie, looking tall, debonair and distinguished, danced with several of the single women, including Karen Gorham. Serenity watched as he whirled a number of them on the dance floor. Who knew her old friend could move so well on a dance floor? She laughed when she saw Kelsie tap Charlie on the shoulder and invite him to dance. Whisking her onto the floor, he happily obliged.

Danny's parents had also come for the evening, especially since the playground was being renovated and renamed in honor of their fallen son. "Thank you, Dr. Ross," Danny's father said to Jackson, shaking his hand when they sat at their table and chatted with them during dinner. "Danny would have liked you very much, son. Serenity and Justin are blessed to have you in their lives."

"And I feel the same way about them, too. Coming from you, that means a lot, sir. Thank you," Jackson said, pulling him into a quick hug. They did that thing men do and patted the other's back while Serenity fought more tears. Might as well name a water tower in her honor after the events of the last few months.

Deidre was beyond gorgeous in a deep red gown that set off her coloring and dark, curly hair to perfection. The epitome of the high society matron, her best friend had flitted around the Great Hall all evening welcoming everyone and starting conversations while Serenity worked behind the scenes making sure the caterers circulated the hors d'oeuvres and appetizers before ushering their guests into dinner. Serenity enjoyed the expression on Wes's face as he watched Deidre move around the room. This love business was pretty sweet, and everyone she loved was in this place tonight.

Carmen was also there with David Marsh. "I'm sorry if I caused you any worry," Carmen confided to her when they found themselves in the ladies room at the same time.

"You didn't," Serenity said. "Now that everything's past us, Carmen, I'd really like us to be friends."

Carmen's smile was lovely as was her off-the-shoulder, blue-green chiffon gown. "I'd like that, too. David's asked me to marry him." She held out her left hand and showed her the brilliant, marquise cut diamond.

"Oh, that's wonderful! I'm so happy for you," Serenity said, gathering the other woman in a hug, feeling the slightest pinch of jealousy. More than ever, she hoped Jackson would ask her that same question. For so long, she'd never thought she'd find love again, but then along came Jackson. She'd say yes in a heartbeat if he asked. Besides, if he didn't, Justin would probably blurt it out and be the one to ask. That made her smile.

She'd caught Jackson's eyes on her many times and found it difficult to keep her focus when she spied him in his dark tuxedo. James Bond had nothing on this guy. Although she'd loved his Army Service Uniform, and thought nothing could top it, the tuxedo came close. If she wasn't already in love with the man, she would be after this special evening.

Jackson's knee was bothering him again, and he'd scheduled knee surgery for mid-October. Finally. In the back of her mind, Serenity understood he'd wanted to wait until after the gala. He'd told her he wanted to dance with her without crutches. And, oh how they'd danced. He'd held her as close as possible. Neither one of them had said anything as he'd twirled her around the dance floor. She'd never been a good dancer, but it didn't matter. Serenity felt as though she floated on air as she'd surrendered fully to Jackson's lead. He did it so well and she'd follow him anywhere. Words weren't needed as she curled into his chest and he pulled her close, the connection—emotional, physical and in every other way imaginable—between them as strong as ever.

Hearing sounds from the grand piano in the corner of the room, she stopped. Jackson sat on the bench, running his fingers over the keys, as though warming up his fingers. She'd never heard him play although she recalled him saying something about it the day they met. "Spectacularly terrible," he'd said. Well, the man *was* the king of understatement. She had the suspicion she was going to learn another lesson in humility.

Jackson's tuxedo jacket was draped over the bench beside him and he'd removed his bow tie and unbuttoned his shirt a few buttons. For a long moment, Jackson stared at the keys, not moving. What was he doing? Serenity stood immobile, frozen to the hardwood floor, waiting and listening. Then he began to play. Spectacular was the word for it, all right, but it wasn't terrible in the least. If anything, it was the exact opposite. *Incredible.*

Mozart Symphony Number Five in G Minor.

Jackson must have memorized it, practiced countless hours to play it as well as he did now. More precious was that he didn't know she was there and believed he played only for a small audience of servers clearing tables. Closing her eyes, Serenity drank in the sounds of the beloved symphony. She swayed and brought a hand over her heart, allowing the music to soothe her soul as it always did. How many times she'd listened to this same piece when she'd felt as though her heart was broken. Hearing it played by *this* man, the chords of her favorite symphony infiltrated her heart, swelling it with an intensity of love and exquisite passion she'd never before experienced.

Walking slowly across the room as Jackson neared the end of the piece, Serenity kept her steps light, not wanting to disturb his concentration. Not wanting him to see her. Not yet.

When finally he finished, he bowed his head. Serenity took his jacket and draped it over a nearby chair. Sitting down on the piano bench beside him, she smiled when he raised his head. Surprise flickered in those mesmerizing eyes.

"Hey," she said.

"I didn't know I had an audience."

"I didn't know you were so accomplished."

He glanced at the piano keys. "I'm not," he said. "Not at all."

"I beg to differ."

"Only with this piece."

Taking his face between her hands, Serenity drew him close and touched her lips to his. "I love you, Jackson. You are *my* symphony, my world, my everything."

The love in his eyes found its way to the very depths of her soul.

"Marry me, Serenity Grace. Tonight, tomorrow or whenever you say. I'm yours. Let me build you a sand castle." Jackson's words were barely more than a whisper. She absorbed his masculine scent, and the slight roughness of his beard grazed her skin. "We'll make lots of babies to fill that castle," he said, his voice low and husky, his skin warming hers. He raised his head, his lids lowered. "I love you and want you beside me the rest of our natural-born lives. I'd get down on one knee, but that wouldn't work so well right now. I have something to give you."

Getting up from the bench, he retrieved his jacket and reached into the inside pocket. Serenity stared, wide-eyed, at the deep green velvet box he held in the palm of one hand as he sat back down beside her. "Open it," he said, handing it to her.

Taking it with shaking hands, she opened the lid and gasped at the

beautiful diamond solitaire nestled in its bed of green satin. Her breath caught at
the size and the cut of the stone.

Pear-shaped. Of course.

Overcome, Serenity put one hand over her heart, her eyes moist. She pulled
him to his feet, moving quickly into his embrace when Jackson opened his arms.

"I take it that's a yes?" Pulling back, he gently swiped his thumb beneath
one eye and then the other as she nodded, still unable to find her voice. "I've
already asked your dad for your hand, but there's one other very important
young man I need to ask."

"That man goes to bed early. We'll have to ask him tomorrow." She traced
her fingers along the side of Jackson's face and let them linger, cradling his cheek
in her palm, running her thumb along his full, generous lower lip. "Somehow, I
don't think he'll have any objections." She rested her head against Jackson's
chest, wrapping her arms around his waist, loving the sound of his strong, steady
heartbeat. She'd never tire of hearing it. Her anchor. Her *love*.

"I'd like to start adoption proceedings whenever you think it's best, but
we'll give Justin some time to get used to the idea. He's had a lot thrust on him
in a very short time."

"You've already been a father to my son, and the Lord couldn't have given
him anyone better. You might need to hold me for a very long time," she
murmured.

His hold on her tightened. "I'm here as long as you need me. The rest of
our lives," he whispered, kissing the top of her head. How long he held her, she
couldn't know, but she snuggled into him, loving his strength, his goodness, how
he'd protected her and found the answers to unlocking the puzzles of her life.

"Thank you for giving me my life back," she whispered.

"Thank you for giving me life," he whispered back. "My beautiful pretty,
Serenity," he said, his voice low. "Forever." He dipped his head and his eyes
searched hers. Seeing her shiver, he brought her wrap closer around her
shoulders.

"I didn't shiver because I'm cold, Jackson."

"I'll try my best to be a great husband, a great father..." He punctuated
each statement with more kisses, each one longer and more impassioned. "A
great friend, a great listener, a great provider, and a great..." The last one he
whispered in her ear.

"I don't think you'll have a bit of trouble in that department," she said when she found her voice again. Goodness, this man stole her every breath in countless ways.

"Come dance with me, please. Outside." Taking her by the hand, Jackson led her to the French doors leading to the back of The Summer Palace. "You'll never guess what's out here," he said with a wry smile.

"I have no idea." Following him as he opened the doors wide, she laughed when she spied a sandbox. Quite elaborate, but a sandbox all the same. She watched as Jackson perched on the edge—quite precariously—and removed his shoes and socks before rolling the pant legs of his tuxedo. Glancing up at her, he lifted her left foot as though it was a cherished treasure. With gentle hands and exquisite care, he removed first one sandal and slipped it from her foot. Then he repeated it on the other side. How could Jackson turn the simplest action into a sensual, loving gesture? Rising to his feet, his eyes never left hers as Jackson took her hand and assisted her over the edge of the sandbox. "Dance, Princess Serenity, dance..."

"And all of God's riches shall be added unto you," she said, her hand clasping hold of his as he twirled her in a slow circle beneath his arm. Stepping into the sandbox beside her, Jackson put one hand on the small of her back and clasped her other hand tight in his grasp, lacing his fingers through hers. Their bodies moved in sync to the timeless, silent dance. Serenity felt heady with desire, flushed with a love she knew would only grow deeper through the years.

His tender kisses trailed across her skin in a featherlight path, warming her temple, her cheeks, her mouth. "Put me out of my misery and marry me tomorrow."

"How about in a month?" she managed to murmur.

He sighed and nuzzled below her right ear lobe. "Two weeks."

"What are you *doing* to me?" Her heart pounded, her mind spun, her pulse was erratic.

"Hopefully driving you wild so you won't want to wait any longer than tomorrow." Jackson continued what he was doing, making it impossible to think.

"You're doing an extremely good job of it. How about a compromise?"

"I like the sound of that." Jackson stopped, giving her a heavy-lidded, irresistible grin. "You look incredible in your gorgeous blue gown tonight, Miss

McClaren. A vision. I couldn't keep my eyes off you. And now, I'm having a very hard time keeping my lips from yours." To reinforce his point, he kissed her again, this one deep and slow.

"One week from today, at the same place on the beach where we first built the sand castle with Justin, provided we can get Pastor Tom booked," she said, coming up for air. "If it rains, we'll move to the house. But, what about your family? I've never even met them."

"Sweetheart, I'll make sure Pastor Tom's there if I have to kidnap him myself, and somehow I think the Lord will shower us with the blessing of sunshine." His smile reached his eyes. "As far as my family, I'll invite them. If they're not here in a week, I'll take you to Chicago in a month for a long weekend. Take Justin to see the Willis Tower. I hear he likes it. Mom will want to plan a big reception. She'll need longer than a week to plan it, guaranteed, but nothing's stopping this wedding now that you've agreed. It's a date."

He kissed her again. "You've made me the happiest man on earth and I'm not just talking about tonight." He murmured against her lips, "I promise you the world as best as I can give it to you, my love. Sand castles, Justin, all of me—and anything else your heart desires—included."

"Deidre and my mom will be my attendants. Maya the flower girl."

"Your dad and Charlie will stand up with me and I insist on Justin standing up with us."

"I agree, but be forewarned that he might get antsy. Sometimes I forget he's only five."

Jackson laughed and kissed her again. "He won't be the only one. We'll have a quick dinner at a fancy restaurant and then I'm whisking you away to some exotic island. I'm sure your parents will agree to watch Justin. And then we can start the process of getting to know one another better."

"Oh, Dr. Ross, the things you say," she said, smiling. "Where shall we live? Is Doc Rasmussen ever coming home again?"

"Yes, but there's another luxury cottage further down the beach, rather secluded. I kind of have an 'in' with the realtor if you're interested."

"In decorating it or—"

"Sure, you can decorate it, as long as you and Justin move in there with me. We'll be a family. I realized I missed your birthday somewhere along the way. I need to give you an extra special gift, a really great one since it's belated."

"Not important," she said. "I barely acknowledged it myself. I was so busy with getting the business started, anyway."

"For one thing," he whispered, dropping light kisses here, there, everywhere, "I'd love to give you a little princess at some point."

"So you can spoil her rotten, I'm sure. What do you suggest we name her?" Serenity asked, feeling as though she'd burst from joy.

Jackson nuzzled her neck and pulled her close. "I don't know...haven't thought that far ahead yet." He laughed then, rich and hearty. "How do you feel about Prudence?"

Serenity laughed with Jackson until her husband-to-be silenced her in the best way imaginable.

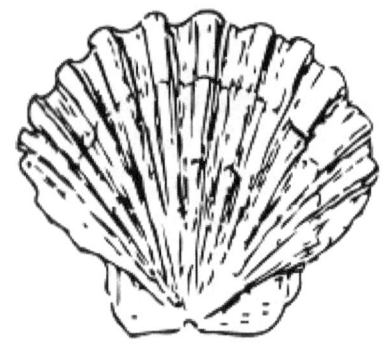

~CHAPTER 49~

*S*erenity smiled into the gorgeous eyes of the strong, loyal man of faith she would soon call her husband. Holding onto her father's arm, she began her short walk on the white runner leading to where the ceremony would take place. How blessed she was to love and be loved by this man who promised her a future of great love, faith and family. Tall and unbelievably handsome in his Army Service Uniform, Jackson loved her with his eyes as she slowly made her way toward him. His gaze traveled from the simple garland of Vi's Violet roses in her hair to the matching bouquet she held before moving to the elegant off-the-shoulder gown made from Chantilly lace and ivory silk and finally to her exquisitely beaded, low-heeled ivory shoes. She'd never felt so cherished and beautiful. *Treasured.*

Clinton patted her arm and Serenity squeezed his hand. She murmured a quick prayer of thanks, especially when she noticed two handsome men—the younger of whom strongly resembled Jackson—and the other one escorting a woman and two young girls. An older couple—a distinguished gentleman accompanied by a lovely woman—slipped into white wooden chairs at the front. *Jackson's family. Thank you, Lord.* She noted Jackson's upright posture and the muscles clenching in his jaw. He fought the deep emotion, just as she did, but what happiness swelled her heart. Reaching for his hand, she held on tight.

She wished she could have met them prior to the ceremony, but they were here, and that's what was most important. They'd have plenty of time to get acquainted later. If she'd learned nothing else, it was that sometimes things don't always work out the way anyone planned. Roundabouts and detours in life were often blessings in disguise.

Diedre held a tissue in one hand and dabbed at her eyes as Pastor Tom welcomed them, his open Bible balanced in his hands. Elise stepped into place beside her and Serenity handed her the bouquet as her dad kissed her cheek and took his position next to Jackson. Justin stood in front of both men, and they each put a hand on her son's shoulders—all three of the men in her life gathered together in this joyous celebration she wouldn't have thought possible even a few months ago.

Further into the ceremony, as they'd planned, they recited short vows, exchanged rings and then held hands and turned to face their guests. "'*Love is patient, love is kind and is not jealous,*'" Serenity said.

"'*Love does not brag and is not arrogant,* '" Jackson said. "'*Does not act unbecomingly; it does not seek its own.* '"

"'*Is not provoked, does not take into account a wrong suffered, does not rejoice in unrighteousness, but rejoices with the truth,* '" Serenity said.

Together in unison, they said, "'*Bears all things, believes all things, hopes all things, endures all things.* '"

"And now, by the power invested in me by God and the great State of South Carolina, I now pronounce you husband and wife, Jackson David Ross and Serenity Grace Ross," Pastor Tom said, closing his Bible. "Jackson, you may now and forever kiss your lovely bride."

Cheers sprang up all around them as Jackson gathered her in his arms and lowered his head. "Hello to the rest of our lives, Mrs. Ross."

"I look forward to every day the Lord grants us together, Mr. Ross."

As they shared their first kiss as a married couple, Serenity smiled when she heard claps and cheers all around them. "I love you," Jackson said against her lips before tantalizing her with promises whispered in her ear. "We'll continue this...and much more...on the island later tonight," he said with an irresistible grin.

"Yes, we will," she said, brushing her lips against his one more time before they parted. "I look forward to it." Easing out of the kiss, loving the sound of his deep chuckle, Serenity spied Justin standing a few feet away. He smiled, opened his arms wide and ran into their embrace.

Serenity swallowed her tears at the handsome picture Justin made, especially dressed in his Sunday best. Like a miniature version of Danny, and a glimpse into the future.

Her groom—so regal in his military uniform—filled her with anticipation of everything to come. She'd asked him to wear the Purple Heart. He'd resisted, and they'd compromised: he wore it beneath his uniform.

This man represented hopes, dreams and the sweetest of promises for a lifetime. Along with them would come disappointment, aches and the inevitable heartache. But hopefully the good would far outweigh the bad.

Her gaze strayed to Mama and Dad, reunited, happy and more in love than ever. Her eyes softened when she looked at Maya and Charlie, Deidre and Wes and their children. And now one more on the way, a happy and welcome surprise. Such dear friends—all with different needs, wants and fears. But they had each other and shared this wonderful community of Croisette Shores. It was more than beaches, palm trees and sand castles. It was *home*. Who knew what the future would bring?

I do.

"Yes, You do, Lord," she said, winking at Jackson when he gave her a curious look.

Rest in Me, child.

I will, Lord. I'm so thankful. Blessed. Eternally grateful.

Lifting Justin in his arms, Jackson tousled his hair and planted a kiss on his cheek. "Did you want to say something, little man?"

"Yup," Justin said, not in the least embarrassed that the eyes of all their wedding guests were on him.

Watching Jackson with her little boy made her so happy, Serenity thought she'd burst. He'd always be Danny's son by birth, and she'd make sure he knew what a good man his father was. But, in his heart, Justin would belong to Jackson.

Her eyes misted. *You'd like Jackson, Danny. He'll be a wonderful husband and a great father to your son. He'll take care of us, shelter us, protect us. Keep us safe. And our gracious and merciful God will watch over us all.*

"Mommy? Are you okay?"

Serenity returned his precious smile. "Yes. I'm just thanking God. What do you want to say, honey?"

"Okay, everybody," Justin said, squirming out of Jackson's arms and planting both feet on the sand. Marching in front of the gathered group, he clapped his hands although he already had their attention. "Let's do it just like we practiced." Her mother gave her a wink and her father beamed from ear-to-ear.

Jackson shot her a grin and raised a brow. "Know anything about this?"

"Haven't a clue." When he slid his arm around her waist, she leaned against his shoulder. He kissed the top of her head, and she breathed a sigh of pure contentment.

Justin raised his arms, holding them like a maestro preparing to cue his orchestra. "Watch me, now. Here we go. One, two, three…"

The voices of their loved ones surrounded them in unison, settling in Serenity's soul and filling her heart with more love than she'd ever imagined as they joined hands and sang a few choruses of "Amazing Grace."

When they finished, Justin planted a warm kiss on her cheek. "And they lived happily ever after."

~The End~

www.ingramcontent.com/pod-product-compliance
Lightning Source LLC
Chambersburg PA
CBHW030359180626
46812CB00005B/1844